By CHRISTOPHER KOEHLER

NOVELS
First Impressions

THE CALPAC CREW
Rocking the Boat
Tipping the Balance
Burning It Down
Settling the Score

Published by DREAMSPINNER PRESS
http://www.dreamspinnerpress.com

Settling the
SCORE

Christopher Koehler

Dreamspinner Press

Published by
Dreamspinner Press
5032 Capital Circle SW
Suite 2, PMB# 279
Tallahassee, FL 32305-7886
USA
http://www.dreamspinnerpress.com/

This is a work of fiction. Names, characters, places, and incidents either are the product of author imagination or are used fictitiously, and any resemblance to actual persons, living or dead, business establishments, events, or locales is entirely coincidental.

Settling the Score
© 2013 Christopher Koehler.

Cover Art
© 2013 Paul Richmond.
http://www.paulrichmondstudio.com
Cover content is for illustrative purposes only and any person depicted on the cover is a model.

ISBN: 978-1-62380-443-5
Digital ISBN: 978-1-61581-652-1

Printed in the United States of America
First Edition
December 2013

This book is dedicated to you, my readers, and to Elizabeth North, my publisher. Thanks for giving me a shot.

Acknowledgments

I depended on the advice of certain experts to get various details right, and if I didn't, then the fault is mine, not theirs. In no particular order I'd like to thank: Amanda Mull of PurseBlog, who keeps her finger on the pulse of fashion; Ruth LeBlanc, for answering questions about the training physical therapists undergo; Tricia Blocher, for answering questions about recruitment for the National Team and for pestering me to get back in a boat—it's great to be missed and wonderful to be asked.

I continue to rely on my beta readers, who made sure the manuscript was fit to be submitted. Even after Burch Bryant Jr., Dahlia Adler Fisch, and Stacia Hess went through it, I still had to submit a revised manuscript to Dreamspinner.

Tracy Faul knows my writing better than I do, and through the course of writing *Settling the Score*, it became quite apparent that if I had a continuity question, it was better to ask her than look through the manuscripts of previous books. Lauralyn Thompson keeps me from wallowing in angst, or at least tries. She's a tough cookie, but she's not a miracle worker. Same with Ellis Carrington. Who loves you, Ellis?

Then there are all the writers with whom I talk shop and enjoy a good cackle every now and then, and yes, it's about like you think it is. We really do all know each other, or many of us are at least acquainted, and yeah, social media is great for linking us together. We're a merry bunch of misfit toys, and you know what? We love hearing from our readers. So friend/follow etc. us. We don't bite. Very often.

I may have written the book, but it did not make it into your hands, dear reader, without the help of many, many people, including

Elizabeth North, the publisher of Dreamspinner Press; Lynn West and the other stalwart women of the editorial department; as well as the no-longer blind editors who worked on my manuscript: Erika, Ian, and Sheri. I don't think they get combat pay, but maybe they should. And of course Paul Richmond, who made my guys come alive for the cover.

Prologue

Concurrent with the end of Tipping the Balance

RANDALL SUNDSTROM'S trial proved to be every bit as grotesque as Philip thought it would be when he'd set his plan in motion. Not that Philip intended to let the Grand Guignol that was Randall in high dudgeon stop him.

Randall had tried to make a mockery of the justice system, ensuring he'd be enjoying the dubious hospitality of the California Department of Corrections for a long, long time. Philip supposed he was lucky that they had room for him at Folsom, because otherwise he'd be driving up to Susanville, or worse, down to Corcoran. Randall was an asshole, but not actually the kind of hardened criminal who ended up on death row, which ruled out San Quentin or Pelican Bay. Through his long-suffering lawyers—his third legal team, since he'd fired the first and the second had quit in frustration—Randall had fought every bit of evidence presented against him, even when it overwhelmingly pointed to him.

Even when Alex Beltran, the man Brad referred to as their father's evil henchman—and really, were there ever good henchmen?—took the stand and laid it all out in sickening detail, Randall blustered and argued and protested. Even when Beltran confessed to ordering several of his less seemly builders to maul Drew St. Charles in an attempt to permanently shutter his efforts to renovate the Bayard House. Philip's jaw clenched at that. They'd almost succeeded in shuttering Drew permanently, all to get Brad to toe the family line and come to work the job with the family firm that was killing him.

For Philip that was the last straw, the absolute last fucking straw. Randall was a monster and a loose cannon, and this sort of thing could destroy Sundstrom Homes, if only because Randall was the sort to take SunHo down with him, and that Philip would never allow. He had endured far too much at Randall's hands to let Randall destroy his inheritance, and if Philip had to remove his father from the company Randall had created out of nothing, then Philip would do exactly that.

He had another, purer motive, too.

The thought of Brad's boyfriend dying in a pool of his own blood because their own father, like some third-rate mafioso, ordered him beaten to a pulp, filled Philip with quiet rage. Age separated the two brothers, along with the lack of a real sibling relationship, but this much Philip could do for his little brother and the man Brad was making his life with. He could make sure Randall paid for his homophobic arrogance.

What Randall didn't know, what Alex Beltran didn't know, was that he, Philip, Randall's quiet, dutiful eldest son, ever the loyal lieutenant, groomed to take over Sundstrom Homes, had set this all in motion.

He had located Beltran's daughter, a lesbian, and told her what their fathers had done. He had struck a bargain with her, too. If she made sure her father turned state's evidence and testified against his, he'd pay Beltran's legal costs and do everything possible to keep him out of prison. Packaged right, it would look like Beltran, stricken by a crisis of conscience, had come forward on his own.

When Serena Beltran asked him why he was doing this to his own father, all Philip had to say was his brother was gay and the man attacked was his brother's boyfriend.

"Damn, that's messed up," she'd said.

But that was all it took.

Philip funneled money to Serena from his personal account, and she in turn made sure Alex sang like a canary. That was enough to crack the case against Randall wide open, because his hands were far from clean, from shady land deals to labor abuses to bribery and fraud with building departments all around the state. There was more, far more, but Philip had limited the evidence the investigators found to SunHo's operations inside California and Randall knew it. No one suspected the straight-laced, by the book, boring heir to the SunHo fortune of chicanery.

The District Attorney had informed her counterparts in those states where SunHo operated. Philip knew Randall kept a double set of files. He suspected Randall kept more files beyond those, even if he couldn't find them. Investigations were ongoing, and Philip cooperated fully.

Or appeared to, and Randall knew that, too.

Philip visited Randall in prison every week where he rotted between phases of his trial. Randall somehow thought he would be vindicated. Philip knew better.

Every week, Philip brought a stack of routine but seemingly necessary documents, and acted as if he thought they were vital for the continued operation of Sundstrom Homes. In truth, they were nothing but tiresome busywork.

"Why're you bothering me with this crap?"

"Because you're still the president and CEO of SunHo," Philip replied calmly. He was always calm. It was part of why he was effective. He also knew it bugged the snot out of his father, the main reason he cultivated the trait. "You may have turned over daily operations to me, but the way you've structured it, I might—might—be able to choose which brand of tissue I use to blow my nose. Which is fine, but it means you have to check the grocery lists and read over my homework."

Randall jerked the stack of papers out of his hand. "Don't fucking call it SunHo. You make the company I built from the ground up sound like a sunburned whore. Pen?"

Philip handed over a cheap ballpoint pen. He certainly wasn't bringing his favorite Montblanc pen into the poky.

Randall looked at it as if his son had handed him a dildo. But he set to signing. "So. How's your useless brother? Would it kill him to visit me once in a while?"

"He seems to be doing very well now that his boyfriend's healed and out of the hospital," Philip said. He added the slightest emphasis to the word "boyfriend." "They've moved in together, you know." He paused. "He's using his trust fund to buy into St. Charles Renovations."

Randall rolled his eyes, but didn't say anything. "Damn, there's a lot of this shit."

"It does tend to pile up," Philip said dryly.

"Why can't you deal with it? It's time for you to stand on your own two feet since I'm apparently going to be sitting around on my ass, thanks to my useless lawyers," Randall snarled.

"Speaking of which, there's an authorization for paying them in there somewhere."

"Goddammit, we just paid them, didn't we?"

"Apparently they want to be paid again," Philip replied, "and you didn't teach me to stand on my own two feet, you taught me to obey."

Philip noted that Randall pressed harder and harder as he signed document after document, the most trivial things Philip and Jyoti, his assistant, could devise. With two notable exceptions: one the entire reason for Philip's visit and the other to cover his tracks when he was done.

"What's this?" Randy asked, frowning at the next document, printed on thicker linen paper than the preceding documents.

"More documents, Randall. This one's about selling off furniture from model homes in South Florida subdivisions, which, by the way, are tanking left and right due to the mortgage crisis. Whose idiotic idea was it to expand so rapidly in a single market?" Philip said. He knew, actually. The culprit sat right in front of him.

Randall shot him a look of pure malice and quickly scribbled his name on every line indicated by a yellow "sign here" arrow.

Philip couldn't have cared less about any of the subsequent documents. Or any of the preceding documents, for that matter. They were nothing but smoke and mirrors. "The next is a letter of congratulations to Brad and Drew St. Charles on the successful renovation of the Bayard House. I knew you'd want to bury the hatchet."

"Goddamn you, Philip!" Randall roared. Other prisoners stared as he swept the stack of documents from the table, his chest heaving.

Philip signaled to the guards, who were already on their way, as he gathered the documents. So long as that one document was relatively intact, the others were irrelevant and he would send the note of congratulations to Brad and Drew himself, handwritten on his favorite handmade stationary.

Once Philip had the documents in order, he walked out the way he'd come in, allowing the guards to search him and the papers once again. Then he retrieved his cellphone and wallet along with his other personal effects. All he allowed himself on the way to his car was a slight smile.

He waited until he had cleared the final search of his car and was outside the prison walls before he cranked up the sound system on his Mercedes coupe, a thudding alt rock beat, and slipped on his mirrored sunglasses. Dropping the pedal, he went from zero to ticket bait in seconds as he sped to the attorney he used for this latest ploy. He was still new enough in the corporate suite that he didn't trust SunHo's lawyers, so he hired outside counsel for his games, a young lawyer every bit as hungry as he was.

Philip laughed long and hard, for he had lied to Randall. His father hadn't taught him to obey, although not for lack of trying. Instead, Philip had learned to play the long game.

"Congratulations, old man. You just fell for the oldest trick in the book."

CHAPTER
One

One year later

THE WAITER held Philip's eye a moment too long. Philip knew what that meant and flushed from the starched collar of his shirt all the way up to the gelled magnificence of his golden bangs. Left to its own devices, his hair flopped down to cover his eyes, and right then, Philip kind of wished it could. Instead, he'd styled his hair like he always did, parting it on the left and then the bulk of the bangs were *up up and away!* in a truly stupendous flight of fancy that was probably on the wrong side of metrosexual for a corporate CEO. When he was by himself, he played the game, but c'mon, dude. He was here with his girlfriend. What kind of trash did he think Philip was? It meant he had to cut the waiter. The cut direct wasn't his style, but Philip felt like he didn't have a choice. Angie was his priority.

"The waiter's certainly attentive this evening," Angie commented.

Philip cocked one eyebrow. "Sweetheart, did you get a good look at yourself? You're stunning."

"You think so?" she said, smiling sweetly. "Thank you, Philip. It's always nice to be noticed."

"I always notice you," he said, smiling back. He raised his wine glass in a salute. "Notice and appreciate."

Angie touched her glass to his in an almost-silent toast. "Charmer. Half the time I feel upstaged by you. Is that a new suit? You look amazing." Then she glanced at the waiter. "I get the feeling I'm not the only one who thinks your tailor is a god among men."

"Boy, you buy one new sport suit—"

"A week," Angie interrupted, her eyes merry. She was enjoying herself.

"—one new suit, and people accuse you of being a dandy." Philip sighed theatrically. "Memo to self: return the ascot and waistcoat ASAP," he said in a stage whisper.

They shared a quiet laugh. Philip reached across the table to caress her cheek, and Angie leaned into his touch. Her beauty struck him once again, and that evening, she'd gone all out, every bit his match in an ivory satin gown with the back down to *here* and her auburn hair done with seed pearls as it cascaded down her back. She even wore a simple cameo around her neck, an antique Wedgwood piece that he'd given her for Valentine's Day the year before. Then he noticed that she'd mounted it on a mauve ribbon that clashed horribly with her auburn hair. What on earth had she been thinking? He'd given it to her on a cream ribbon for a reason—

Dinner arrived and Philip dropped his hand.

He tried to ignore the argument going in his mind about the colors, but it was hard. He'd always had an overdeveloped sense of aesthetics, and at times growing up with Brad and Randall had been nothing but torment. Builders' houses were always one of two types: ramshackle and about to fall over, or palatial monuments to every architectural innovation, and new concept to show up in the design rags. The Sundstrom home was one of the latter type, if poorly decorated, and no sooner had he shoved Randall off stage and into the hands of the police than he called in the cavalry to remove the worst of his father's excesses and atrocities. Gone were the putti pissing into fountains and faux-antique tapestries and superfluous televisions, and there were no more—Philip jerked his thoughts back to the here and now. He sat across the table from a beautiful woman at a posh restaurant. His aesthetic hang-ups could wait.

Philip genuinely enjoyed Angie's company. They might not live together—yet—but they certainly spent a lot of time in each other's company, mostly at her condo. She found his house "creepy, like a funeral home," even with Randall out of there and every room but his mother's old sitting room and her library redone. Not that he blamed her, it was large and foreboding, and maybe it was time to sell it. When he'd called to invite her out to dinner earlier in the week, she'd been overjoyed, even more so than usual. It made him wonder if he weren't missing something, but a thorough search of his day planner by both himself and Jyoti revealed nothing.

After gnawing his guts out for a while, he'd finally given up, and when it came time to pick her up, he gave in and let himself enjoy the evening. "Are you ready to go home?"

"Yes, I think so," Angie said. Was that a tightening around her eyes?

Philip signaled the waiter, who promptly brought him the check. When Philip put a black Amex card down, the man's eyes widened. Philip would've found it comical, but he found it hard to believe no one at this restaurant had ever seen American Express's Centurion Card before.

"Here you are, Mr. Sundstrom," the waiter said when he returned, placing the receipt before Philip and then departing. Philip signed it, including a generous tip.

Philip held Angie's chair for her and then waited patiently while she wrapped her shawl around her shoulders. As they walked out of the restaurant, Philip smiled at their waiter. "Thank you. We had a lovely evening."

But it was only as they waited for his car to be brought around that he noticed that the waiter had written a number—presumably his—on the back of the credit card slip, but lightly and in pencil so it didn't show from the front. Classy. Philip crumpled it up and threw it in the trash.

"They're staring at you out here, too," Angie whispered.

Philip blushed. "I think you mean they're looking at you."

"Some of them, maybe," she laughed. "A few, the straight ones."

But they weren't all straight, he could tell that right off the bat. Sorry, boys. He played, but never when he was in a committed relationship.

"Remind me not to come back here. This is very embarrassing."

She hooked her arm on his. "I think it's hilarious, and you blush very prettily."

"Great." He rolled his eyes.

It made him uncomfortable, that regard, even if he understood it. Thanks to the last year at SunHo, he knew how to project an air of authority, and a lot of people found that attractive. It wasn't quite a matter of "do the opposite of Randall;" after all, his father had run SunHo with an air of power, but in Philip's estimation, that power was based on fear. Employees in SunHo's corporate offices had feared for their jobs, at least when Randall stomped and blustered. But authority? That was something different. Philip knew that when he spoke, he would be listened to. He might be young for a CEO, but by and large, he was respected. He wasn't sure Randall could've said that, or even appreciated the difference.

In his early thirties, Philip was young, fit, and, based on the evidence at dinner, handsome; he was very well situated financially, and the waiter and valets could tell that from the credit card and his car. He loved his Merc, a sleek sports car, the six-figure kind with the spoiler to prevent it from taking flight. At least he assumed that's why they stared. Or maybe he had spinach stuck between his teeth, he thought ruefully, the perils of being a vegetarian there to keep him humble.

They drove back to Angie's condo in silence, insulated from the sounds of the city by the Merc, but what, Philip wondered, isolated them from each other? He bore responsibility for that, the lion's share, at least. He felt bad for neglecting Angie in favor of SunHo. It's not that he preferred SunHo per se, but it seemed so much more immediate to him. More… real, he realized guiltily, but that's not how he wanted his life to be. Angie always understood, or acted as if she did. She got that he'd taken over the family business, even if she didn't know the particulars of how that had come about. As far as he was concerned, she didn't need to, either.

But simply because Philip had chosen this life, it didn't stand to reason that Angie was happy with it. He knew she'd prefer to be living the high life, preferably in San Francisco. Angie cared for him, so no gold digger, she, but he didn't fool himself on that score, either. She enjoyed the life his money afforded them. Buying Brad out a few years ago might've set him back, but SunHo grew and expanded, despite the recession and building slow-down. Philip was loaded, and Angie knew it.

He glanced over at Angie as he drove, her face turned away from him, inscrutable in the passing lights. He knew what he wanted from the next step in life, but was it what Angie wanted?

Unable to decipher his uncharacteristically enigmatic girlfriend, Philip retreated into his thoughts, pretending he was in the cockpit of a spaceship instead of a luxury car, because damn, the onboard computer was almost that complicated. He liked Mercedes for the same reason he liked Macs. They both embodied high performance and elegant design and didn't bother him with a lot of irritating details. Sure, BMW made amazing cars, but they always seemed to want his input on some matter or other, and he got enough of that at work. As for PCs, Philip was sure there was an elegant and highly functional one somewhere, he'd just never heard of it. But really, they'd gone from a charming dinner together full of conversation and laughter to him retreating into his imagination. Again. He'd been doing that more and more lately.

If he were to be honest with himself, it couldn't be a good sign, but they looked good together, and she was someone to hold on cold, dark nights. Angie was someone to cling to when he'd spent too much time reading the Existentialists and felt too alone in an uncaring universe. But was that really a reason to stay in a relationship with someone? On the whole, Philip reasoned, there were worse ones, but it would only be fair if she felt the same way, and he knew for a fact she had no patience for what she called his "navel gazing." This raised the question of why on Earth he was with someone who so easily dismissed his interests and the things he valued. On the other hand, he didn't remember his parents sharing that many interests. So many puzzles.

The keypad at the entrance to the parking lot under Angie's condo tower saved Philip from further omphaloskepsis. After he parked in her designated guest space and opened the door for her, Angie again laughed and flirted in the elevator.

"Dinner was great, but tomorrow night I want to go clubbing in the city," Angie said, moving in close, breathing in his ear, hand roaming south of his belt.

"What're you doing?" Philip said, gasping at the sudden assault.

"What does it feel like I'm doing?" Angie said.

He looked down at her, amazed at her audacity. "Groping me. What if someone comes in?"

"Then I stop."

He leaned back against the elevator's wall. "Damn, you're good. Yeah, you stop and leave me hot and bothered with a bulge in these tight pants."

"That'd sure be a problem, all right," Angie said, leaning into his neck, nibbling along his jaw until she reached the spot where his neck and his ear met, the one that made him shiver.

They were almost to her floor, but he caressed her anyway; he couldn't not touch her, running one hand under her shawl to touch her smooth shoulder, trailing his fingers down, working them under her bodice to touch her breast.

When the elevator doors opened, they stumbled to her door. He pinned her against it, holding her there, kissing her hard, repaying her for her handiwork in the elevator.

"Inside?" she said at last.

He nodded. "Inside."

They ran for her bedroom, shedding clothing as fast as they could.

Clad only in his underwear, Philip stopped to admire Angie as she unwound the surprisingly long strand of seed pearls from her hair. "You really are beautiful."

"Thank you," she said softly, as if somehow those four words made her more self-conscious than making out like horny teenagers in the hallway had.

He stood behind her and unhooked her bra. Then he lifted her hair, kissing her neck as she craned it to give him better access.

"Bed?" he suggested.

She nodded. "Bed."

Philip pulled the covers back for her and then climbed in after. They held each other for long moments, taking pleasure in the physical closeness. But then he decided to move things along. He let go of Angie, resting on his side, her body before him, playground, smorgasbord, an oft-explored undiscovered country, its mysteries a continual surprise.

He gave himself free rein, exploring and playing, making sure her needs were met, and through that, his own. By the time Angie had her first orgasm, his cock was hard and leaking, leaving spots on her sheets.

Philip suited up and slowly pushed his way in, loving the way sensation flooded his body, starting with the top of his cock and radiating up and out in waves. Wave upon wave, growing in strength, faster and faster.

He was well on his way, when his kid brother's description of pussy came inexplicably to mind.

It's like fucking a bowl of pudding....

That thought really didn't do anything for the current effort, and he felt his buzz waning. Maybe it just wasn't happening tonight.

Dammit!

Ass. That always did it. Hot ass. Oh yeah. Ass like… some of those carhops at the restaurant, those valets he hadn't let himself notice.

Only he had. There'd been one guy who'd paid him no attention at all. Jeez, he'd been fine. Black hair, diamond studs in his ear, maybe Latino, and the way his black pants encased his ass should've been illegal.

And he was back in business. Fucking Angie, fucking that ass, riding higher and higher.

"Philip!" Angie moaned.

A few more pumps, and he was right there with her. "Damn!"

Still breathing heavily, he rode the high for a few more moments before pulling out. He removed the condom and knotted it off, then wrapped it in a tissue from the nightstand before lobbing it into the trash. He rolled over and scooped Angie into his arms, cozying up to her.

He drifted, not asleep, but definitely enjoying that after-sex lethargy. Then he felt Angie tense up. "Philip?"

"Yeah?"

"What're you thinking about?"

"Right now? Not a whole lot, why?"

Angie paused. "You seemed distracted while we were making love."

That was just what he needed. She knew he was bi, she even joked about it sometimes, but he didn't think she needed to know it took the thought of nailing a guy's ass, something he'd never actually done for a variety of reasons, to seal the deal. He sighed. "There's a lot going on at SunHo right now. This is going to sound paranoid, but I'm pretty sure at least one of the people at the C-level are trying to get rid of me."

"But it's your company!"

"Doesn't mean they can't force me out as CEO. I'd still own it, but I wouldn't have any control over day-to-day operations. There are things I could do in response, like liquefy it so they'd have no company left to control, but that'd be a Pyrrhic victory at best," Philip said. He didn't want to think about it, not right then. He might hate Randall with the fiery heat of a thousand suns, but the company still had his last name on it, and that meant something to him.

Philip lay on his back, staring at the ceiling. "You ever think about more?"

"I thought guys had to rest before they could go again," Angie said.

"Not that. I meant more between us." He turned on his side to look at her.

Angie ran her hand along his sparsely haired chest. "What're you getting at, Philip?"

Philip sighed. Now that he'd brought it up, the idea scared the crap out of him. But he and Angie? Something needed to change. "I thought… it's time to move forward, don't you think? It's been three years. I'm not ready to get married, but I'm ready for more."

Angie sat up, clutching the sheet to her chest. "Philip, what're you saying?"

"Do you want to move in? With me, I mean."

"Wow." Angie sat back against the headboard. She exhaled noisily.

Philip felt like he'd been kicked in the guts. Not the answer he'd expected.

"I care about you a lot, Philip, but that's not where I am. I mean, we're not even exclusive and you're talking about moving in together?" Angie shook her head. She looked everywhere, he noticed, but at him.

Philip stared at her. This couldn't be happening. "I thought we were." Without being aware of it, he sat up and swung his legs off the bed. "Hell, if I'd known that, I'd have kept the waiter's phone number. Maybe I should go back to the restaurant and bone the parking valets.

As you so helpfully pointed out, some of them were interested. You know, since we're not exclusive."

Angie flinched like he'd hit her, but his only weapons were his words and feelings. "I'm sorry! I thought—"

"Three years, Angie!" Philip thundered, searching for his underwear. "We've spent every moment, every holiday, you name it, together for three goddamn years, and that's not exclusive?"

"No, not every moment, and you know it," Angie spat back. "You've spent plenty of time during those three years at work. Did you hear yourself a few minutes ago? You say that a lot, Philip. You work all the time. You're ready for more? What a laugh. You're already committed to something. Hell, you're already married, you know. You're married to your job."

"That's not fair! I want more out of life. I'm looking for—"

Angie laughed, whether at him or the situation, Philip was never sure. "Why would I want to move in with you, let alone marry you? I love being with you, don't get me wrong, but this way I see you and still have my own life."

Philip snorted. "Apparently so. I had no idea that included a love life, however."

"That's not love, Philip, that's sex," Angie said.

Philip yanked his pants up. "Just like us? Or were we only about the money?"

"That's beneath you," she said.

He bit his tongue to hold back the vicious responses that sprang to mind. Instead he said, "But the money didn't hurt, did it? If I'm so wedded to work, something tells me you'd have dumped me a long time ago without the money."

Philip collected the rest of his clothing as he stormed through Angie's condo, retracing his steps from earlier in the evening. He stopped in the living room to button his shirt and jam his shoes on. He glanced at his watch. It was a bit early for a truly stellar walk of shame, but it would do.

He looked up and Angie stood at the other end of the room, dressed, he noted with grim amusement, in a velvet robe he'd given her for some reason or other. "So is this it?" she said.

"Ya think?"

"I can't believe you're throwing away three years over a miscommunication," Angie said, crossing her arms.

"Good-bye." Philip placed his keys to her place on the mail table and closed the door behind him.

A miscommunication. He snorted as the elevator descended to the parking garage. A steak house when he had his heart set on Chinese, that was a miscommunication. Seeing other people behind his back? That's what it was, too, because she'd certainly never mentioned it, and that was a big red flag if ever there were one. He also knew damn well what she'd have said if he'd tried to see other women. Or men.

Clearly, Philip thought as he drove home through a light spring rain, his question had not lived up to Angie's excitement about dinner when he'd invited her. He wondered what she'd expected. Given her extracurricular activities, he doubted it had been a marriage proposal. He sighed. He wanted more from life than what he had. Was that asking too much? Apparently it was.

None of this changed the fact he was lonely.

CHAPTER
Two

STUART COCHRANE raised his head from his boyfriend's chest, brushing his hair away from his eyes. For long moments all he did was stare at Jonathan as he dozed in post-coital bliss. They made quite a pair, the taller Jonathan with his café-au-lait skin and moss-colored eyes, he with his pale skin and fiery hair and jade-green eyes, tall and short, dark and light. Lately Stuart thought the only part of them that matched was their eyes, and sometimes not even that.

He was grateful Jonathan was the "pass out after ejaculating" sort. It gave Stuart time to think. He thought a lot, maybe too much. Jonathan always said so. Stuart never understood how that was a bad thing. Morgan Estrada, his former roommate and definitely still close friend, had never said it was a bad thing, but he and Morgan weren't dating, had never dated, never would date, regardless of how Stuart had once felt. Morgan was taken… really taken. So there he was with Jonathan.

They were in Jonathan's room. It had once been Morgan's old room. Stuart was only grateful it no longer bore any resemblance to where Morgan used to sleep, or he'd be totally weirded out. He sighed. They were always in Jonathan's room, in his queen-size bed. The inevitable joke had been old and stale before they'd been living together a week. Stuart had to admit it was more comfortable for Jonathan, particularly when they had finished, but his own twin bed suited him just fine. It was all he could afford when he'd started at California Pacific College five years ago, and it still sufficed, although not for the tall rower who'd fallen for him from the time they'd first met.

But then, nothing about the apartment seemed adequate to the Poisonwood family, and Stuart knew Jonathan's parents had judged it and him from the get-go. Jonathan's mother, for instance, had taken one look at the apartment, or flat as she'd called it in her BBC accent, and blanched. "Oh, this will never do."

Stuart had looked up from his studying, glancing around the apartment. He didn't see the problem. Sure, it wasn't fancy, but it served him and Morgan well enough. He and Morgan both knew their digs were temporary and not worth getting invested in. Long term, perhaps, but temporary.

Jonathan's father had simply shaken his head. "There's no use protesting once Lady Melroy gets the bit between her teeth."

Lady Melroy? Stuart's eyebrows raced up his forehead. That explained Jonathan's accent. Since Stuart didn't know how to deal with an actual aristocrat, he chose not to, just as he ignored the decorators when they showed up. Instead, he retreated to his room or to the library, grateful he'd insisted Jonathan's name be on the lease. But really, hadn't they fought a war against imperious aristocrats? Apparently Jonathan's mother never received that memo.

And that was before she'd presented Stuart with "his" half of the bill.

"I never agreed to this… this." He waved his hand at his now radically different domicile. The once white walls had been painted a crisp blue. The generic and admittedly tiresome vertical blinds had been replaced with curtains. The inner layers were a sheer material that diffused the light while the outer layers were made of a creamy damask that wasn't even remotely masculine. "You didn't consult me and I can't afford it, and that's before we discuss how it violates the terms of the lease."

Lady Melroy stood there, her mouth working soundlessly, while Mr. Poisonwood chuckled softly to himself. "I'll deal with this," he assured her, as she swooned on one of the new sofas—chesterfields, she called them.

As Stuart stood there with his arms crossed, Mr. Poisonwood simply rolled his eyes and shook his head slightly. "Don't give it a second thought," he whispered to Stuart.

Throughout it all, Stuart noticed, Jonathan hadn't said a thing or tried to rein his mother in at all. Interesting, and in some way, Stuart now realized, it should've given him a clue to their entire relationship—toffs, as the British called them, heedlessly spending huge sums of money without realizing not everyone was as rich as they were. Also, Jonathan was a total mama's boy.

But Stuart was used to standing on his own legs, and when Mrs. Poisonwood struck again a month later—he refused to call her lady *anything* on these republican shores—he was ready, or at least unsurprised, when two enormous boxes from Harrods arrived on their doorstep.

"Jonathan! Your mother's at it again. Boxes for you," Stuart had called before he went back to his books.

Jonathan had dragged himself away from the television in his room. "Uh… Stuart? Did you look at the tags? These are addressed to you."

"Shit."

Jonathan had helped him lug the boxes in, because they really had been bigger than Stuart could get his arms around easily. Not that that meant much. He was the crew's cox'n, after all, selected because he was short and didn't weigh much, one hundred and five pounds soaking wet.

With the boxes inside, Stuart and Jonathan carefully opened them. Each box contained several neatly wrapped bundles of new clothing, each marked with a season, as well as boxes of shoes and packages of socks and underwear. On top of one of the boxes was a letter addressed to Stuart.

> *Dear Mr. Cochrane,*
>
> *Enclosed you will find garments more appropriate to your new station in life. Please wear as indicated by season. You may wish to give your old clothes to the local charity shop if they'll have them.*
>
> *With regards,*
>
> *Lady Melroy*

"What a bitch," Stuart muttered.

"Have a care! That's my mother you're talking about," Jonathan said hotly.

Stuart looked at Jonathan to see if possibly his boyfriend had misheard him, because that note was not only offensive but quite clear—he simply didn't measure up. He pointed to the handwritten note with the Melroy crest on it. "See? There's a wolf on her coat of arms or whatever it's called. I'm only being accurate."

"Ha ha ha," Jonathan said.

"Seriously, this shit needs to stop," Stuart said flatly, "so man up and talk to her."

Jonathan sighed. "It's not that easy. She knows we're close—"

"If you want to stay close, you'll talk to her. Or talk to your dad. He seems sane."

He could tell Jonathan had struggled with his demands, but he didn't care. He knew how to deal with overbearing parents, and at the slightest display of weakness, they'd set up camp on the doorstep. Stuart had felt like he'd let the Poisonwoods get carried away as it was.

As for the clothing, except for a few things he especially liked the looks of, it went to the so-called charity shops. Jonathan didn't speak to him for a week. Stuart took the high road and refrained from exacting revenge at practice.

But those experiences and countless others had only cemented his opinions about wealth and the wealthy. They were different from ordinary people, and Stuart had grown up with practically nothing, fighting for everything he had. His parents were the kind who counted on pennies in heaven, because as near as he could tell, they were so focused on their evangelical caterwauling they didn't have time to accumulate real pennies down here on earth. They didn't have a lot to say to him, not since he'd come out and definitely not since he'd moved out west to attend that "heathen" school, not realizing they'd already imparted the most important lesson to him—he could only depend on himself.

Stuart shifted closer to Jonathan. The larger bed certainly fitted Jonathan, but Stuart always felt small and alone in it, like a castaway at sea, with Jonathan the only driftwood to latch onto. Such a flattering metaphor for the man everyone expected him to love.

Stuart sighed. He really didn't want to go there, even as he feared Jonathan was stumbling toward it. On paper, as it were, they should've been a perfect match, but in real life, the only place where the calculus of attraction mattered, things didn't add up. He knew what to do on paper, but when it came to living, breathing people? He solved other people's problems fine. His own he found quite baffling.

Jonathan opened his eyes and smiled. "Hey, beautiful," he said, pulling Stuart close for a kiss.

Stuart had to smile as their lips touched. Jonathan was never stingy with his affection, even if he didn't always—or often—think things through, like the differences in their backgrounds. "Hey."

Jonathan kissed him for a while, and Stuart allowed the gentle pleasure to carry him away. They worked well in bed. The only problem afflicting them was that sooner or later, they had to leave it.

"Congratulations, Mr. CalPac Graduate," Jonathan proclaimed grandly when they stopped kissing long enough to breathe. "So tell me, what're your summer plans? It's only mid-May, so you've got lots of time to play."

"Work," Stuart said, again resting his head on Jonathan's muscular chest. He might wish otherwise, but with no help forthcoming from his family, there really wasn't an option.

"I've got a much better idea."

"Oh?" Stuart said, freighting the one word with a load of meaning.

Jonathan turned to look at him. "Yes. Come back to the UK with me. I've got one year of school left, so this is my last summer to drink, play, be utterly irresponsible, and drink." When Stuart stared at him, he added, "My parents would love to see you."

"We both know that's not true," Stuart said with a laugh.

"All right, my *dad* would love to see you," Jonathan admitted. "Anyway, come back with me. I'll graduate next year, then it'll be my gap year and I'll probably have to do something horribly ennobling like bathe lepers when what I really want to do is sleep for a month and then spend the rest of the time drunk."

"Charming," Stuart said. He'd never really understood or approved of the tendency of some rowers to drink like fish when they got the chance. Sure, they worked hard and deserved to let off steam, but why not do something good for the body? Because the very next practice, Stuart and the coach were going to do something god-awful to them, so nutrition and rest might've made sense, no?

"You know I need to work," Stuart said.

Jonathan groaned and flopped back on his pillow. "*You.* Work, work, work. You know, all work and no play makes Stuart a very dull boyfriend."

"Sorry." Stuart said, and they both knew he was anything but. "I need everything I can earn before I start med school this fall."

"You know," Jonathan said, sitting up, "it really doesn't matter how much you earn at that grocery store, because it's going to be a drop in the bucket compared to what medical school costs, even a public one and even with your scholarships. You're going to end up taking out loans sooner or later, so you might as well come with me this summer and make it sooner. No one ever said as he lay on his deathbed, 'Gee, I wish I'd worked longer'."

Stuart's mouth hung open. That fucking hurt, and he'd really thought Jonathan—of all people—understood why it mattered to him that he pay his way as much as he could, as long as he could.

"What?" Jonathan protested. "You know I'm right. So what'd you say? Give 'em your two weeks' notice while I book our tickets. Then I'll call my dad to tell my mom to take a damn chill pill."

Stuart felt icy all over. The offhand way in which his so-called boyfriend dismissed his ideals and fucked over his future blew him away. Was everything that mattered to him nothing more than a joke to Jonathan? Stuart had always believed that the harder you worked for something, the more you valued it. The corollary to that sat right in front of him. If you had piles of money and never had to work for anything, then that's how much you valued what you had. When what was given to you mattered little, then what wore out would be thrown away, not repaired. So Jonathan apparently cared little for Stuart's work ethic because he had none of his own.

Jonathan waited for an answer. "So what'd you say?"

Stuart inhaled to rip Jonathan to ribbons but then realized it didn't matter. It was the culmination of too many things to count, too many assumptions and attitudes that marked Jonathan as nothing more than a rich jackass who ignored the realities of his boyfriend's circumstances in life. Stuart couldn't imagine how he'd missed it all. He glanced at

Jonathan where the sheet had fallen away from him. Oh yeah. Dickmatized.

"Look, if it's about the money, I can pay for your ticket—"

"It's not about the money," Stuart said. He got out of bed and got dressed. Suddenly he was reminded of an old Monty Python sketch, "The Upper Class Twit of the Year." He'd been dating him.

Jonathan brushed absently at the dried cum on his chest. "It's going pear-shaped, isn't it? Right at this very moment. I can see it in your eyes."

"I have no idea what that means." Stuart sighed. "I have to leave for work soon."

He turned as he left Jonathan's room. "I hope we can be civil about this."

"It doesn't really matter. I'll be leaving for home soon," Jonathan said. "We can sort out the rest this fall, but I think a change in roommates by one of us is in order."

CHAPTER
Three

OVER THE succeeding weeks, Philip discovered that *his* friends had, for the most part, been *their* friends. Not that he had that much discretionary time to burn, but he'd grown accustomed to grabbing a beer with the guys once in a while. As it turned out, those guys dated women who were friends with Angie, and so Philip had spent that first weekend alone, working, which wasn't objectionable but certainly surprised him. So much for his hunger for more, but he did what he always did and threw himself into SunHo.

As the weeks wore on into a month and then two, Philip realized that he had friends Angie couldn't alienate, and he decided the upcoming weekend would be a great time to invite Brad and his partner Drew over to dinner. If they were available. They seemed to have a large social circle and either entertained or went out quite often. If Philip were honest, he was a bit envious. As far back as he could remember, Brad had made friends easily. It was a good skill to possess. Or was it a trait? Either way, it wasn't just good, it was wonderful, verging on being a superpower, or so it seemed to Philip, who ended up faking it most of the time. He'd been a painfully shy kid, which is how he'd ended up under Randall's thumb in the first place. It made it very easy to be the studious, silent sort who missed nothing, and that certainly had served him well. But still, a little company might be nice.

Philip spun around in his desk chair, bored and restless at work. He shouldn't be. He had enough to do. It was probably a character flaw, one of many. Lord knew, Randall had liked to point them out often enough.

He flipped through the contacts in his iPhone to call Drew, since it was the middle of the afternoon and Brad was no doubt busy with the renovation end of their joint endeavors. They really had a good thing going, and Philip was happy for them. He felt that Brad, in particular, deserved to be happy. Drew too, of course, but Philip didn't know much about him besides the fact that Randall had tried to destroy him, which still infuriated Philip. But Brad? Philip knew what his little brother had grown up with, and where their father's abuse made Philip retreat into his shell, every word and occasional blow killed Brad's spirit a little more each time. That was why, when Brad had finally reared up on his hind legs and confronted their father, he, Philip, had fronted him the money for a deposit on an apartment, the inevitable first and last month's rent. Then Philip had an idea. He pulled a browser window and opened Drew's page at his real estate agency. Not that he spied on his brother-in-law or anything. Because that would be wrong. And creepy. But as it happened, Mr. Drew St. Charles had an open house this afternoon, right this very minute, in fact, and continuing for the next hour and a half. Well, now. He hadn't seen Drew for some time and he was suddenly bored to tears. Next week? Different story when the audits came in, but for now, he was counting the nails in the wood paneling in his office. It was reclaimed from old barns, very interesting stuff. Oh who was he kidding? He was bored, and since the housing bubble burst in the Sacramento Valley, he was willing to bet that Drew had some time on his hands, too.

Philip jotted down the address and then stuffed his laptop into his messenger bag. "Hey, Jyoti!" he called.

"Yes, boss?" Jyoti said, coming into the executive suite.

"Anything on the schedule we need to worry about for the rest of the day?" Philip asked.

Jyoti shook his head. "Not a thing, Philip. It's blessedly clear."

"Then let's get the hell out of here before someone comes along and dumps something on us," Philip said.

"Will we be taking the back lift to the car park?" Jyoti said.

Philip looked at his assistant as if he were simple. "Do you want people to find things for us to do?"

Jyoti shuddered. "Not especially. I'll be right back. I need to let Amrit know I'll be picking the children up from daycare early."

As soon as Jyoti got back, Philip locked the doors to the executive suite and then he and his assistant ducked down the special elevator that Randall had had installed so he could make his escape without anyone noticing. Philip tried to be more accessible to his people, but every once in a while he and his personal assistant ran like frightened rabbits.

They waved good-bye in the parking lot, but both of them had other places to be. Philip tossed his briefcase and blazer into the back of the Merc, and after he'd strapped himself in, fed the address of Drew's open house into the navigation system, and drove out of the underground garage beneath SunHo's corporate headquarters. Some days he couldn't show that place his backside soon enough, even if he did own it.

The navigator directed him to a good part of Sacramento, Land Park. Maybe Drew had a chance of unloading this property, after all.

Then Philip turned onto the street with the open house and he re-assessed his optimism. The only car he saw was Drew's BMW X5. There weren't even cars parked in front of other houses farther down the street. This didn't look good for Drew, even if it meant Philip wouldn't be interrupting him.

Philip pulled up in front of the open house and parked right behind Drew. He wouldn't be there long and it wasn't as if Drew would be leaving before he did. He felt funny walking in unannounced, but that's what you were supposed to do at open houses.

He also figured he moved too silently, because he was able to come within twenty feet of Drew without him noticing, since he was face down over his smartphone, playing some sort of video game, based on all the beeping.

Philip leaned against a wall with a pleasant but vague smile on his face, watching. He wanted to see how long it would take for Drew to look up. He surreptitiously checked his watch. The first few minutes weren't bad, but as it turned out, standing still and watching someone play "Angry Birds" or whatever it was bored Philip to tears, even if that someone was his kid brother's husband.

Philip coughed. Drew looked up, panicked, sliding his phone under some papers. "Philip! Damn, don't sneak up on people."

"Hi, Drew." He pushed off the wall and walked the rest of the way into the room. "I'm sorry. You were so engrossed in that video game, I wanted to see how long it would take for you to notice me."

"So," Drew said, leaning back in his chair, "how long?"

Philip shrugged. "I got bored after five minutes."

"Have a seat. I'm getting a cramp in my neck staring up at you," Drew said, kicking a chair out.

"So they're really beating a path to your door today." Philip took the indicated seat.

Drew groaned. "This is horrible, but we're desperate. The house has been on the market too long and it's starting to stink."

"Really?" Philip sniffed the air. "I don't smell—"

"It's an expression, Philip."

"Oh." Philip blushed.

Drew rolled his eyes. "So what brings you out here? I doubt you're in the market for a house in Land Park."

"Not really, no," Philip said, shaking his head. "I mean, it's nice enough and all, but it'd fit in my swimming pool."

"It would not," Drew said, pausing. "Would it?"

Philip shrugged. "Close enough. Anyway, I'm here because I guessed—correctly—that with the state of the market you wouldn't be busy—"

"Thanks!"

"—and Brad probably wouldn't hear his cell phone," Philip said.

"You could've called," Drew pointed out.

"And interrupt your video game?" Philip said. "Anyway, I wanted out of my office."

Philip could almost feel the waves of frustration rolling off Drew. This was kind of fun. Sure, he'd enjoyed doing it to Randall, but he'd never dreamed it'd be this amusing to do to friends.

"The point, Philip?" Drew said through clenched teeth.

"Hmmm?"

"Why. Are. You. Here?"

"Oh. Yes. I told you I was a bit bored," Philip said.

Drew shook his head slowly. "It must be nice to own your own company. Be able to knock off whenever you want, to be beholden to no one."

"No less than you, I'd imagine," Philip said. "If memory serves me, you and Brad own Renochuck jointly, yes? You own your own real estate brokerage now. I saw that much on the way in. Might've been nice if one of you had told me, but congratulations nonetheless."

Drew peered at him. "You're serious."

"Of course I am! You're my brother-in-law. You're domestically partnered to my younger brother, so yeah, I'd like to know when good things happen to you," Philip said. "Bad things, too. Isn't that what normal families do? Not that I'd know personally, but I've read about them."

Drew snickered. "I guess they do, Philip, and I'm sorry we didn't tell you. Brad and I... we thought you'd be too busy to... well, to tell you the truth, we thought you'd be too busy to care about something as minor as me striking out on my own."

"Ouch," Philip said, holding his hand over his heart.

"I... we're sorry," Drew said.

"Better check with Brad before you say that." Philip sighed. "It seems like two steps forward, one step backward with him. But I'm trying, I really am. I can never recapture the past, but I hope he knows how much I want to change how we go forward."

"He does," Drew said quietly. "We both do." He coughed. "So... uh, what brought you out here this afternoon?"

"Like I said, I needed out of the office, and I—"

Drew shook his head. "Oh no you don't, if you start over again I'll never get your real purpose out of you."

Philip smiled faintly. He'd been found out already, had he? "I came to see if you and Brad might like to come over to dinner on Saturday."

"What did Angie say?" Drew asked. "She always seemed kind of lukewarm on us, Brad in particular, if we're being honest."

"Angie isn't a factor anymore," Philip said quietly, "and if I'd picked up on that sooner, or if you'd mentioned it.... Oh well, what's done is done."

"Can I ask what happened?" Drew said.

Philip laughed, even if he didn't find the whole situation very humorous. "I asked her to move in, only to find out that we weren't exclusive." At this, Drew snorted. "Right? After three years? But it's over. The Desertion by Mutual Friends is complete, so you know it's official."

"I'm sorry," Drew said.

"Me, too. We had some good times together, but if she didn't like Brad, then she had to go, didn't she? I doubt it was a gay thing, so maybe it was a Brad thing or the fact that he can be rather boisterous...." Philip shrugged. Then he glared at Drew. "I just wish I'd known sooner."

"Boisterous. That's cute. He can be a disaster looking for a place to happen," Drew said, looking anywhere but at Philip. "We didn't tell you because we weren't sure how you'd take it."

They were silent for a moment. Then Drew said, "Anyway, Saturday should work. They're usually pretty low-key for us. Brad's busy with rowing and I'm busy—hopefully—with open houses, but I'll make sure we take our disco naps."

"Great," Philip said. "See you about six?"

Drew fiddled with his iPhone. "There. It's on the family calendar, so it's official. Six o'clock it is. Can we bring anything?"

Philip shook his head. "It's all under control."

"Brad said you were a control freak," Drew said with a laugh.

"You really have no idea." Philip got up and headed for the door. But right before he reached it, he turned. "Oh, and Drew? You're wrong. I'm beholden at work, all right. I've got a bunch of board members left over from Randall's tenure who're convinced they know better than I do, several of whom I'm convinced are trying to oust me from my own corporation. Your real estate company may be small, at least for now, but no one's trying to stick a metaphorical knife in your back to take it away from you."

STUART NEEDED to get ready for work. Instead, he checked his e-mail . He couldn't help it. He needed human contact, or at least contact from people he knew and liked. Meatheads from the crew didn't count, but Morgan didn't count as a meathead. Unfortunately he didn't see Morgan's name in his inbox. Nick's, either. There was something from US Rowing, but whatever it was, he didn't want to know. He'd read it later. And—Valerie!

He loved hearing from his younger sister. Valerie was seventeen now, but at eleven she'd been fairly young when he'd left home. At some point during his absence, however, she'd wised up to the fundamentalist bullshit their parents tried to cram down their throats and started thinking for herself. She'd sought him out two years ago when she turned fifteen, probably through CalPac's online white pages. The hope of something like that was the major reason he allowed his information to be listed. Over the last two years they'd established a regular correspondence that had grown to include Skype when Valerie could get away with it. And when she'd come out? He'd never been prouder.

Valerie contacting him was also the only way he'd gotten to know his youngest brother, Frederick, who hadn't existed at all when Stuart, sick of the Jeebus-wheezing homophobia, packed up everything he could and struck out west to California Pacific College, where his small size and intense personality made him an asset to the men's crew, instead of an object of ridicule at the suburban Philadelphia high school he'd attended. He only wished he knew a way to liberate Valerie, but that took money he didn't have. At least their parents treated her better, if only because they didn't know what lesbians were. Gay? They knew too well what that was, and he still had scars to prove it.

He clicked on Valerie's e-mail and started reading.

Hey there, Big Brother,

Congratulations on graduating! I got the announcement a few weeks ago. Thanks for sending it to my friend Cynthia's house. She's prez of our school's GSA. You and I both know Mom and Dad would stroke out if anything showed up from you. They freak out any time anything shows up from Cali as it is. Stupid.

Anyway, that's way cool! I'm really proud of you. I can't wait to get out of here and follow in your footsteps. So far the scholarships aren't looking that good, but I'm still hoping the Point Foundation comes through. I've got some money saved, though, so I'll jam out of here and work and go to a junior college. You'll let me flop out on your sofa, right? I'm kidding, but not really.

Oh, and get this. Since our lame ass parents can't afford groceries… I mean reparative therapy, guess what we're doing for Christmas? Yep, another fucking tent revival. "Giving the gift of eternal life." [insert gagging noises here] Jeez I hate those things.

Anyway, write when you can. Sometimes your
letters are the only things that keep me from shivving
those losers in their sleep.

xoxo,

Valerie

Stuart read it twice. Damn. He wished he had the cash to get her out of there, maybe help her through the emancipation process. If ever there were a candidate for it, it was Valerie Cochrane. The courts in Sacramento would definitely be sympathetic as soon as she mentioned reparative therapy, and who knows, the Philly courts might be, too.

He had to clock in at Food Faire in less than an hour, but Valerie needed to hear from him.

Hey Little Sister,

Sorry this is short (if you say "like me," prepare to
lose an organ and not a few square inches of skin, one of
the important ones), since I have to be at work soon.

Get your ass out here. I need a new roommate. I'll
have to make do until you graduate, but after that? Mi
casa es su casa, as they say.

Just occurred to me, but is there any chance you
could get declared an emancipated minor? You're not so
far out into Pennsyltucky that you won't get a
sympathetic hearing. Oh, and California recently
outlawed reparative therapy :-) Seriously, get out here.
You can finish high school in Sacramento.

Ugh, tent revivals. They'll hoot and holler with the
other social rejects while you try and hide. Stay away
from the snakes and you'll be fine.

xoxo

Stuart

CHAPTER
Four

STUART LIKED working at Food Faire. It was a great place to work, since the management bent over backward to accommodate students' class schedules. In his case, his crew schedule, since his undergraduate education was in the rearview mirror. It meant he had to work a lot of afternoon and evening shifts. That accommodation and the fact that he was consistently happier at work than the people who worked at the big chain stores in town were the only reasons he overlooked the fact that it was a non-union shop. Political commitments were one thing, but he had to live in the world. Besides, political commitments ranked higher up the need hierarchy than his income allowed him to shop.

Friday evening was well along when he noticed a pack of college students wandering throughout the store, probably UC Davis since the store was in Davis, but it hardly mattered. They didn't look like they were all that serious about shopping. Stuart didn't see a cart, at any rate. He caught the eye of one of the PICs—people in charge—who nodded, and Stuart followed them at a discrete distance. That late on a Friday he found plenty to do straightening out the shelves in the wake of the after-work locusts. He always looked busy whenever one of the pack looked back, but this way an employee was on hand to curtail the damage if—when—they got out of hand. Experience and all that. Stuart had seen it before. He still shuddered when he thought of the "soap-skating incident," and each year's Thanksgiving always brought with it a few frames of frozen turkey bowling.

Then the pack moved on to the next aisle, and Stuart quit pretending to be fascinated by re-stacking cans of dog food. They were going to do something stupid. He could feel it. He really hated people his age sometimes.

By the time Stuart slid around the corner after them, they were taking long, running jumps to try to hit one of the hanging signs that indicated what the aisle contained. No way that wouldn't end in tears, he snorted, no way at all, and of course it was the one on the other end of the aisle. Not far from the pack, he saw a man examining items on the shelf, but he didn't have time to note much more than that his blond hair was sticking up at a fantastic angle and that he was annoyed.

Stuart looked about, but saw no other Food Faire employees, no one to run for a PIC or the manager. He was about to do it himself when the inevitable occurred. One of them overshot his mark and landed in the middle of an endcap display.

"Crap." Stuart took off, but by the time he arrived at the disaster, the man with the trippy hair was doing something that he as an employee never could.

"So what was that all about?" Stuart noticed the man with the hair didn't raise his voice, but somehow the pack of college boys looked like whipped dogs.

"We were only having some fun," one of them, maybe the leader, said.

Trippy Hair folded his arms across his chest. "Fun. You were having fun. What you call fun, this man here in the Food Faire shirt and apron calls the next hour of his evening as he restacks all those cereal boxes. Good going, you selfish assholes."

"We didn't mean to," another one of them muttered.

Trippy Hair was taller than Stuart, but then, a lot of guys were. He was used to it. Trippy Hair wasn't all that muscular, but he was lean enough that Stuart could tell he'd made the most of what he had. Indeed, his parts went together well. Very well, truth be told. Trippy Hair wore clothing that looked like it cost a fortune and, based on the way it fitted him, was worth every penny. Stuart found himself wishing they were anywhere else, but in his experience, people working at Food Faire were next to invisible to the people who shopped there.

"Who cares if you didn't mean to, you did it. Next time you have the urge to commit vandalism, do everyone a favor and be honest about it. Go break windows at your school's administration building or knock mailboxes off their foundations with a baseball bat. Just don't key cars. I drive a BMW and touching up the paint's expensive."

"That's illegal!"

"This should be," Trippy Hair shot back. "Now get out of here so this can be cleaned up."

"Why the hell are we listening to you?" one of the pups demanded.

"Because he's right," the leader sighed. "Sorry, guys."

And just like that, like people who've made fools of themselves in public, they made themselves scarce in surprisingly short order. Stuart sighed and started restacking cereal boxes, letting his mind wander a bit, wander back to that handsome stranger.

"Such jackasses. I'm sorry you have to put up with that. Does it happen often?"

Stuart started from his reverie. He looked up into warm brown eyes. "N-no. It's not so bad. They were just trying to have a good time."

Fun. Hadn't he been saying he hated people his age?

"But at your expense. Maybe someday they'll grow up and figure out how to enjoy themselves without making messes for other people."

With Trippy Hair helping him, the restacking passed quickly, and by the time he heard "Cleanup on aisle…." the job was almost done.

There were only a few boxes left when their hands touched. "I guess that's my cue to get back to my shopping."

And then Stuart realized that the man with the tricked-out bangs was about to walk out of his life as quickly as he'd walked into it. Why was he disappointed? "Hey… what's your name?"

"I'm Philip," he said. He stuck out his hand. "Yours?"

Stuart took his hand and shook it. "Stuart."

"Pleased to meet you, Stuart."

Stuart stared, transfixed, as the older man, who after all wasn't that much older than he was, returned to his shopping. He was still staring when Philip stopped not ten feet away and looked back over his shoulder to see Stuart looking at him. Philip grinned and winked.

Stuart turned as red as one of the tomatoes in produce and got back to work, even if a part of him continued to hum for the rest of his shift.

PHILIP WAS glad he'd decided to go to Food Faire that Friday after work. Besides, what else would he have done? That it was in Davis didn't bother him. What was silly was that he'd be back in Davis the next morning for the farmer's market. In his defense, it was a very good farmer's market, written up in travel magazines and guides to such markets and everything. He could've combined the trips, but then what would he have done with his Friday evening? Internet porn got boring after a while. Besides, if he hadn't, he might not have met that hot little ginger. He forced himself not to grin like an idiot.

Philip had to adjust himself, damning his tight flat-front pants. They looked great, but they hid nothing, like the boner he'd thrown merely by thinking about Stuart. Wow. Who knew you could go to the store to make dinner for your brother and his partner and come away with wood? He'd have to shop here more often. The silly grin fell away from his face when he realized he was going to do exactly that. Sure, he could deny it all he wanted, but he knew himself well and recognized all the signs. He might as well clear his calendar now.

As he continued up and down the aisles, Philip continued to think. Sure, he'd had a few boyfriends in college, but none since moving home to work at SunHo. The climate at home certainly had never been conducive to regular boyfriends. He thought of how Randall had treated Brad during that awful time when Brad had thought Drew had broken up with him, and Drew had been in the hospital thinking Brad had done the same thing to him. Of course, that brought his mind back to his little brother telling him how hot it was to fuck a guy's ass, and suddenly his pants were way too tight again, because all Philip could think of was Stuart's ass.

But he was bi. He'd long known that. No guilt, no shame, but no real relationships with men, either, only curiosities satisfied and itches scratched. Based on the unabashed staring, he was reasonably sure Stuart was gay, or at least bi like him. Maybe he could be okay with a relationship that didn't end at the altar, or at least Crate and Barrel.

Philip was single, not by his own choice, and that sucked, especially since he'd wanted more. He wondered if Stuart were seeing anyone.

Philip finished with his shopping and found a checkout line without too many other people in it. He paid little attention to his surroundings, preferring instead to read on his iPhone. He had an entire library on it, so why should he pay attention to the gossip rags by the cash register? He prided himself on not recognizing any of the people on the covers unless they were members of Britain's royal family, and even then he didn't much care. Pop culture was one thing, but he had a thing against making stupid people famous.

Philip looked up in time to see Stuart pushing a grocery cart out of the store, helping someone with her bags of groceries. He knew it was Stuart by the hair. Gingers? Sure, a dime a dozen, but that blazing red color couldn't be that common, could it? So Philip stared. He couldn't help it. That ass. That tiny, perfect ass. Damn, that man must work out. He couldn't yank his eyes off it with a tractor.

"Good evening, sir. Did you find everything you needed?"

Only then did Philip jerk his eyes and attention back to the moment. "Yes, I did, thanks." And then some.

Then Philip did some figuring. If Stuart was out there right now, there'd be no way he'd be available to help him. He sighed. Next time, dammit, and there *would* be a next time. He knew that already. He was there to perv on Food Faire's hottest employee. Jeez, he was pathetic.

"Can I get these for you, sir?" the courtesy clerk said.

"No, thanks. I got it," Philip said, pushing his cart into motion, and truth be told, he'd only shopped for one meal plus a few sundries. It's not like the cart required the labor of two in order to reach his car.

Philip amused himself with that flight of fancy, picturing himself and Stuart in pith helmets with canteens of water to make it across a desert parking lot strewn with perils. He added lions and then vultures lurking on the lights.

So engrossed was he in the playthings of his imagination that Philip didn't see Stuart standing directly in his path until he caught the front of Philip's cart to keep it from hitting him.

"Can I help you with that, sir?"

Philip blinked, all thoughts of a parking lot full of sand and lions vanishing. "Oh! Sorry, I was only… never mind. Um… sure!"

Was that a gleam in Stuart's eye? Philip couldn't tell, but he sure hoped so.

"So which car is yours, Philip?"

Philip pushed a button on the chunky Mercedes key and the trunk of his car slowly went up. "It's the one that's waving at us."

"That looks handy," Stuart said.

Philip snorted. "It's helped me find my car on more than one occasion, yes."

Stuart laughed. "You lose your car?"

"Do I have to answer that?" Philip said plaintively.

"In a way you already have," Stuart said. He looked at Philip out of the corner of his eye and smiled.

As Stuart started loading bags into the trunk of Philip's car, Philip hastened to help. Maybe their hands would brush against each other's again….

"You really don't have to do that, you know," Stuart said.

Philip looked confused. "My groceries, my car. Why not?"

"Uh… because it's my job?" Stuart said, a little uncertainly. Then he looked down at the car. "Wait… you told those brats you drove a BMW!"

"I'm not a complete idiot," Philip said with a little smirk. "Only you and I will know the truth."

They stood behind Philip's car looking at each other for a few moments as the trunk slowly closed itself. There was something about the other man that set all of Philip's energies to buzzing, and he never wanted it to end. As near as he could tell, Stuart appeared just as enchanted.

Then another courtesy clerk trundled by with a cart full of groceries and the moment ended.

"I should be getting back in there," Stuart said. Was it Philip's imagination, or did he sound regretful?

"I'm sorry, I shouldn't have kept you," Philip said. Then it occurred to him that Stuart might only have been waiting for a tip, but before he could do more than reach for his wallet, Stuart stopped him.

"We don't take tips… sir. Store policy."

Philip caught the change in demeanor. Ouch. Good going, Sundstrom. "I'm sorry, I didn't mean—"

"No, I'm sorry, I shouldn't have snapped. It was a logical assumption," Stuart said, his voice soft once again.

"I didn't mean to offend you," Philip said.

Stuart smiled. "You didn't."

Philip laughed. "If I don't get in my car *right now*, I will keep you here all night."

"Yeah, I… work," Stuart said, sighing. He took Philip's cart plus a few others from the cart return back to the store.

Philip watched him in the rearview mirror. He saw Stuart standing on the curb watching him right back, and it took all his willpower not to turn the Merc in a tight circle and lay rubber back to where Stuart stood. Then he'd give the shorter man his phone number…. No, he'd kiss him until one of them had to come up for air and—no. Just no.

It was a long drive home.

CHAPTER
Five

WITH THE approach of the June close of the fiscal year at Sundstrom Homes came the semiannual audits of every division, whether it involved building houses or back-end support services. Philip read them all closely, and not only the bullet points. He'd caught more than one manager or vice-president attempting to hide something Philip needed to know. The weeks after the audits came in might be consumed with reading the sometimes-labored writing of various levels of management, but short of surprise drop-ins at regional headquarters or even specific developments, Philip didn't know of any other way of keeping track of the company's far-flung interests. In fact, Philip actually made such unannounced visits and had seen some beautiful parts of the country as a result. His itinerary would be determined by the piles taking up a large part of the conference table in his executive suite. The audits had been Randall's idea and Philip thought them a good one, or at least he hadn't been able to come up with a better way to keep tabs on all the many parts of Sundstrom Homes.

Philip picked up the first one, a report from one of the regional offices in Florida. Not much change from last year. The upscale subdivisions hadn't recovered from the implosion of the housing bubble. Philip knew they never would. Economists could vapor on all they wanted about recoveries, but until or unless those academic and abstract definitions matched the real experiences of Americans in their daily lives, those homes and lots were very expensive albatrosses around SunHo's neck. Maybe it was time to sell the empty lots to whatever developer wanted them. He jotted some notes on a steno pad and clipped them to the cover before setting the report in what was now the "further action" stack.

Philip found the next half dozen reports remarkable only for their unique approach to English grammar and orthography. He guessed it was time for another company-wide memo about letting interns write official communications. He hoped interns were responsible for this malarkey, because paying another consultant to teach senior management how to write would be embarrassing.

Then he found a report from one of his senior vice-presidents, Winchester Chapman. He knew he could count on Winch to string coherent sentences together. Winch was in a unique position. He was responsible for the operation and success of all of SunHo's subdivisions across the country, and that included the tract homes in the Sacramento region. The worst subdivision in the country? Suburban Symphony. Again. That tickled his memory. He'd have to check with Brad, but he was reasonably sure that had been the subdivision Randall had ordered Brad to turn around. Such an ass.

Miranda Valparaiso, his assistant manager in charge of that travesty, reported directly to Winch. Winch should have either dealt with it himself or outlined the steps necessary to remedy the situation before it ever reached Philip's desk, and Philip wanted to know why. He pushed the intercom button. "I want Winchester Chapman in here ASAP."

"Will do," Jyoti replied.

At least his PA was competent, Philip thought.

Within a few minutes, Winch knocked on the door to the conference room. Sometimes, Philip reflected, it was good to be king. "Winch, come on in."

Winchester Chapman was a handsome man, one of the so-called "silver foxes"—silver hair and beard, blue eyes with squint lines radiating away from them. He kept himself fit, and Philip didn't doubt he had his pick of partners. To Philip's eyes, there was something that screamed alpha male. "You wanted to see me?"

Philip looked up. "Yes, have a seat. I want to talk about this audit for the Sacramento region."

"Can I see it again?" Winch said. Philip slid it to him, and Winch put his reading glasses on and quickly perused it. "Ah, yes. Miranda's report. It looks fine. What's your beef with it?"

"What's my beef with it?" Philip repeated. Was this man for real? "My 'beef' with it is that the worst, the absolute worst, subdivision in terms of sales, visitors, residents' complaints, repairs, etc. is right here in Sacramento, and you and Miranda haven't even bothered to try to remedy the situation. Again."

Winch leaned forward, his elbows on the table. "Let me tell you about Suburban Symphony. It wasn't originally one of our properties. We acquired it when we bought Sunset Homes, and it's never performed well and it never will."

Philip leaned across the table, too. He knew Winch wanted to intimidate him. "Not with that attitude. So why don't you tell me what you've done to try to turn it around?"

"Done? I haven't done anything, I'm not directly in charge of it," Winch said, a flicker of annoyance showing.

"All right, I'll rephrase it. What steps have you instructed your underling to take to turn that place around?" Philip said.

Winch rolled his eyes. "There is nothing that's going to save the subdivision right now, because the economy is in the crapper. Look around Sacramento—the city can't even get its act together to develop the old rail yard, probably the biggest development bonanza in a generation, because no business can afford to move in. The K Street Mall, the anchor of downtown commerce, is as lively as a necropolis because it's where retail goes to die. The only major sports team this city can lure in will bail just as soon as another city makes the idiot owners an offer that allows them to pay off their debts. People here can't afford to move out to that disaster."

"That's bullshit and you know it. Everything you've rattled off is public money, but we're talking about individual residences, Winch," Philip said softly. He refused to raise his voice, although in the back of his mind he was already composing the letter he planned to put in Winch's executive file. "Start thinking of ways to help your report turn this around, because if I go around you to deal with her directly, it will result in her termination and your demotion. You have a month."

Philip added the Sacramento region's report to his "further action" stack, right on top where Winch could see it. When Winch didn't get up right away, Philip looked his senior vice-president right in his hate-filled eyes. "Was there something else?"

"No," Winch grunted, getting up. He paused at the doorway. "You know, your father would never have treated his senior people like this."

Philip leaned back in his chair. "And what way is that, Winch? Expecting them to do their jobs? Maybe that was part of Randall's problem with running this company. When I took over, we had another year, maybe two before it caught up with us. As for you, I'm told the economy's horrible, simply horrible. Must be a rough time to look for work."

Philip didn't let the smile show until after Winch shut the door so hard the frosted glass rattled. Only after Winch was gone did he lean back in chair, thinking. This disaster of a subdivision was something he needed to see for himself.

He activated the intercom again. "Jyoti, I'm going to be out of the office this afternoon. You can reach me on my iPhone. I'm going to check out an underperforming subdivision."

"Suburban Symphony?"

"You've heard of it?"

"I read the spreadsheets in my spare time," Jyoti said dryly.

"It beats playing Minesweeper, I guess," Philip said, then cut the intercom.

Philip grabbed a stack of audits and put them in his briefcase. Maybe he'd read them this evening, but probably not. He could swear he was out of something that necessitated a trip to the grocery store.

PHILIP CURSED the navigator in his Merc. He was lost. Again. He'd been driving around out past the backside of beyond in unincorporated Sacramento County for what felt like forever, but was probably more like two hours. But how hard could a subdivision be to find?

He looked at his fuel gauge. "Oh, that's just jolly."

He pulled over and reset the navigation system to find the nearest gas station. The route mapped out, he took off. He loved his car, and even petted the dashboard on occasion, but it did require frequent feeding. He certainly hadn't bought it for its fuel economy.

Fortunately the gas station wasn't that far, and after he'd taken care of his car, he went inside to ask for directions and buy a soda. He emerged a few minutes later feeling like an idiot, because the road that led to the gas station also led to Suburban Symphony. But one road into a development? Not a good sign.

Philip drove for another ten minutes until he reached Suburban Symphony. He pulled over and looked at the development from the outside, the "curb appeal" of the entire place. Apparently Sunset Homes had been aptly named, because if this place had in any way been indicative of what they had on offer, he understood why the sun had set on the builder. Tacky signage and why the hell hadn't anyone upgraded the landscaping? Then Philip had an unnerving thought—what if someone had? He took some notes, because both the sign and those ridiculous weeds would never do.

He skipped the sales office. Even if the salesperson failed to recognize him, he didn't want his visit to bump the stats on the number of visitors drawn out to this dustbowl. Instead he drove around looking at the already-occupied homes. He found that the development wasn't even close to a quarter built out, which was less than he expected and nowhere near what it should've been, given how long it had been part of the Sundstrom Homes family and how many lots were available. All in all, he was looking at perhaps a tenth in total.

SunHo couldn't be blamed for the poor choices or neglected yards of owners, but the rest of the place looked like hell, and that needed to be addressed, along with one other issue. The houses were just ugly. He couldn't imagine what the interiors looked like. He needed to know for sure. He'd have to give it some thought, but he was sure he had some friends he could put up to going in there to get a set of floor plans and front elevations. Or he could send Jyoti into the archives for them. That would work, too, but wouldn't be nearly as much fun. But this whole place needed a refit from top to bottom, and he had no idea why Randall had let this place slide or how he'd expected Brad to turn it around single-handedly.

Before he headed out, he e-mailed Jyoti. His PA had left for the day, but at least this way Jyoti would get on it first thing in the morning. Something about his conversation with Winch didn't sit right. Winch was one of the more ornery of the leftovers from Randall's time in the CEO's suite, one who had been outraged rather than surprised or shocked when Philip took over. Sure, he'd covered it quickly, but not quickly enough. There were a few of those, and Winch seemed to be the ringleader. He bore watching.

Then he texted Brad. Dinner with Brad and Drew had gone so well he felt comfortable texting Brad.

P: I'm out at Suburban Symphony. Isn't this where Randall made you work?

Brad must've been done for the day, because he replied right away.

B: WTF are you doing out there? That's way below your pay grade.

P: Nothing's below my pay grade, especially when this shitshow is dragging down SunHo's Sac region tract home numbers.

B: LOL! I called it Suburban Graveyard, U know.

P: And that's why I'm hoping to talk to you about this place. Too complicated to fat finger on my iPhone. If I feed you&Drew again, will you tell all?

B: Lemme check w/Drew, but shouldn't be a prob. I'll call you.

P: Thx, Brad. I'll wait to hear.

Philip wondered if it was too soon for a smiley. Not for the first time, he cursed his father for making his younger brother a stranger to him.

AS HAD become his custom, Stuart checked his e-mail before leaving for work. He fretted about clocking in on time, but with the time difference between Sacramento and suburban Philadelphia where his family lived, it worked out best. Scratch that. Valerie was his family, the adults she lived with had only whelped them. In no sense of the word were they his family, and he knew Valerie felt the same way because they'd discussed it during one of their rare Skype sessions.

Tons of e-mail awaited Stuart, most of it related to crew in some way, but the only one that mattered to him right then was Valerie's.

Guess what, Big Brother!

I hate our parents even more than I already did. Wanna know why? Go on, guess!

Yep, they found my webcam and flipped the fuck out. Mom was snooping in my room. I guess she was looking for birth control or something, which is stupid. I don't usually keep that at home. Sure, Mom said she was looking for a shirt she thought I'd borrowed. As if. I guess she thought I'd borrow her clothes and then hide them under my bed up inside the box springs in the far corner.

So now she and that asshole who donated the sperm for us are off on a rant about what "ungodly" things I've been doing with it, how I'm the Whore of Babylon, etc. We've both heard it all before. The look on their faces when I told them I use it to talk to you was priceless.

It was also the only thing that shut them up long enough for me to point out they'd ransacked my room for no good reason I could think of. I said I get top grades in school, have a job, blah blah blah. I got the usual sermon about how those are things of this world and how deeply unclean I am. I can see you rolling your eyes right now.

Were you serious about that emancipated minor thing and taking me in? Because if you are, I'm doing it. I can't take much more of this madhouse.

You know what else? I hate spending all my time talking about these people. It's like there's nothing in my life that matters and that's so not true. I never tell you about school… which subjects I like or which boys I pretend to date or things like that. So tell me something exciting about your life, something that's not my whiny-assed complaining.

Kissy-poo,

V

Stuart sighed and rested his forehead on the computer monitor for a moment. Valerie put on a brave face in her e-mails, but he knew enough about life in that house to read between the lines. His parents' screeching about religion verged on the abusive. Hell, it crossed the line. It might rarely involve corporal punishment anymore, not since he'd told his guidance counselor about it in high school and she in turn had told the Department of Human Services, but he didn't understand why psychological abuse was A-okay when his parents gussied it up as religion, because calling his sister the Whore of Babylon and all that other nasty shit? That was flat-out wrong.

Hey there, Little Sister,

Oh well, Skyping wasn't our major form of communication anyway, even though it means I won't get to see Freddie. We email or text and we can do that from anywhere. I'm so sorry you had to put up with all that religious crap. We both know it's abusive. I don't know if that makes it any easier to take or not. Validation, maybe?

Yes, I was serious. Like I said, I've got some money saved up and so do you. Between the two of us, we can get you out of there. Tell me when. Because I can tell you from personal experience that freedom is delicious and covers the taste of ramen noodles well.

Okay, my life…. There's nothing much that makes good press, I have to confess. Your older brother's boring. I still get up stupid early to cox, only now it's for the Capital City Rowing Club, instead of CalPac College. Given the number of people I know who followed our old coach to CCRC, you'd never know we've all graduated. There's been some loose talk of me being recruited by the National Team, but it's only talk and before you wet yourself with excitement, all "recruited" means is the chance to compete with other short people for a chance to cox in the big leagues.

I'm not sure how I feel about that, to be honest. Can I confess to you that I'm tired of it? I'm extremely good at what I do, but that doesn't mean the passion's there anymore. Then, too, med school starts this fall, and I'm committed to that. The National Team would mean deferring that, and the thought of deferring real life for crew isn't sitting so well right now.

I might've met someone. He shops where I work. He's a few years older, I think, but not too old. I think he's got some money, or at least he drives a Merc. That said, just because he drives it, doesn't mean it's paid for. Besides his obvious physical attractions—seriously, this guy's hot and if anything comes of it I'll send you a pic— he seems like a gentleman. Some college kids, young ones, were using the store as a playground and knocked over a display. This guy chewed them out because I couldn't and then helped me restack the display. Then I took his groceries to his car and… I don't know how to put it into words. We talked, and it was easy. He felt right. Since then, and I might be imagining this, but it seems like he always tries to get into my checkout line.

I'll keep you posted. You keep me posted.

You know I love you,

Stuart

CHAPTER
Six

IF THERE'D been a specific time when the sight of Stuart started to soothe him, Philip couldn't put his finger on it, but after that day at SunHo and then Suburban Graveyard—Brad's name for it was perfection itself—he only knew seeing the fiery ginger felt like balm, and that was before Philip had put a single thing in his grocery cart. Some people got massages; he went to the grocery store.

Then Stuart looked over and caught Philip's eye and smiled at him. Philip smiled in return, a big goofy smile. As he floated through his shopping, it occurred to him he was probably crushing on Stuart, but that was cool. Crushes made life worth living, right? It meant he was alive and kicking and finally recovered from his breakup with Angie. Crushes—not just for schoolgirls anymore, Philip thought.

Sure, Philip drove out to Food Faire to make eyes at Stuart and would have even if the canned goods bloated on the shelves and flies buzzed through the produce department, but fortunately, Food Faire's standards were sky high. Canned goods were pretty much the same from store to store, but the fresh produce really was that much fresher. It allowed him to feel like he bought the best he could for another dinner for Brad and Drew. That mattered to him for some reason, maybe because he felt like he was meeting his brother all over again as an adult and he wanted to make a good impression. Or maybe because he didn't know how else to tell Brad, "I love you."

Philip pushed his cart to the checkout lines, trying to find one that had both few people in line and Stuart bagging groceries, but struck out. So he pretended that he forgot something and turned around and then kicked himself mentally for the pantomime because really, who cared? He acted as if he found the fizzy water entrancing until circumstances at the front looked more auspicious, but finally the time was right and he made his move.

"Did you find everything you were looking for, sir?" Stuart asked him. Philip couldn't tell if he was imagining the extra hint of challenge in his voice or not.

"I have now," Philip replied.

Stuart smirked. "I'm very glad to hear that. Can I help you out with your bags?"

"Definitely." As soon as they cleared the doors to the warm June night, Philip laughed. "I think we confused that poor cashier back there. Somehow I doubt most people are that into who bags their groceries."

"I hope not," Stuart growled. "I missed—it's good to see you."

Philip blushed in the darkness. "That's okay, I like seeing you, too."

He flipped the trunk up as they approached his car. Unlike the other times, Stuart didn't give him any guff about helping. As the door came down, they faced each other in the semidarkness of the parking lot.

Stuart frowned. "Can I ask you something?"

"Sure." Philip wasn't sure he liked the sound of that.

"Please don't take this the wrong way, but is it a coincidence you always seem to end up in whatever line I'm working in?" Stuart said, looking at the ground.

Philip felt his face heat up. He almost dodged the question, but Stuart wasn't stupid and Philip's gut told him his answer mattered. "I hope this doesn't make me sound like a creepy stalker dude, but no, it's not a coincidence. Tonight in particular I was dawdling until I could find you."

"Good, because I was really hoping it wasn't," Stuart said. He looked up into Philip's eyes. "I've been thinking about you since you helped me clean up the cereal."

"Yeah?" Philip quirked a smile.

"Yeah. Is that okay? Some guys would get freaked out, you know, hearing another guy's thinking about them," Stuart said, his voice barely above a whisper.

"It's okay, Stuart, it really is. I've been thinking about you, too."

They looked at each other awkwardly for a few moments, the silence growing thicker and thicker.

"Okay, now I get to ask you a question that puts you on the spot," Philip said, unable to take it even a second longer.

"Oh yeah?" Stuart responded. "What would that be?"

"Can we get together sometime when you're not at work, so I don't feel like I'm keeping you from something?" Philip said, scratching the back of his head.

Stuart smiled shyly. "I thought you said that it'd be a hard one. I'd love to, but I have to warn you, I mostly work evening shifts, but I can meet for lunch, or even breakfast, since I'm off the water by seven thirty or so."

Philip looked at him blankly. "Off the water?"

"Crew."

"Oh, are you a rower?"

Stuart shook his head. "No way, not at my height. I'm the cox'n." He grinned evilly. "I get to tell the big oafs what to do. Frequently, and at high volume."

Philip laughed. "Yes, I've actually heard about cox'ns. So, which do you prefer, lunch or breakfast? Either's fine with me."

"Let's go with lunch. I have to confess I go home and sleep after practice," Stuart said.

Philip pulled a business card out of his pocket. He usually carried a few, just in case. Then he patted himself down for a pen, or even a pencil. Then he tried his back pockets, turning in circles trying to reach them. Hell, at this point, he'd even open a vein to write his number down for Stuart.

Stuart laughed. "Oh my God, you look like a dog trying to bed down."

"Do you have a pen?" Philip asked plaintively.

Stuart pulled one out of his apron. "All you had to do was ask."

Philip bopped him on the nose with it. "Mean!"

Stuart caught his hand and held it for a second, staring into Philip's eyes briefly before releasing it.

Philip fought the almost overpowering urge to kiss Stuart. This time, he felt reasonably sure Stuart would welcome it. He coughed and instead jotted his cellphone and personal e-mail address on the back of his card. "Catching me at home is iffy, but the iPhone's glued to my thigh, and even when I'm at work I have my personal laptop open. Besides, I do as I please at work."

"Must be nice," Stuart said with a laugh. He pulled his wallet out and put Philip's card away.

"Use one or both of those. I'm serious. Let's set up lunch so I can ogle you in natural lighting," Philip said.

Stuart laughed. "That works both ways, you know."

Philip was nonplussed. "Why would you want to ogle me?"

"That hair, for one thing." Stuart reached up and touched his bangs.

Philip caught his hand. "Now I've got you," he said softly.

"You do," Stuart said, his voice husky. "What're you going to do with me?"

"This." Philip turned Stuart's hand over and kissed his wrist. "Call me."

Philip climbed in his car, a spellbound Stuart still standing behind him. Fortunately no one blocked him, so he could pull forward to leave. He looked in the rearview mirror, and Stuart still stood there, waving good-bye.

"Good-bye, Stuart, please please please call me, if only so I can apologize for that," Philip whispered. "I don't know what I was thinking."

STUART TRUDGED in the door that late-June Saturday morning, back from practice, not sure why he bothered. Another early morning spent carefully assessing his rowers' strengths and weaknesses, trying to find the one correction that would prove key and then coaching them through it, at least in theory. He'd had a mixed boat that morning. Half his rowers were recent college grads, some from CalPac, some from other local schools, but the rest were from the masters learn-to-row program. He was all for people picking up the sport, and word around the Capital City boathouse was that they had some real talent. Maybe,

maybe not, but Stuart had seen none of it in his boat that morning. He felt like he spent the entire practice ignoring the men who knew how to row to focus on people who should never have been in an advanced boat, making the same corrections over and over. He only hoped he kept his frustration out of his voice as their boat flopped around on the river, not coincidentally splashing him frequently. Not only had he recorded the row—audio and video—that morning, but he suspected one of the rowers had been asked to record the audio, as well.

He shed wet clothing as he headed for his bedroom. Uncivilized? Sure. But Jonathan was in England committing assault and battery on his liver, so who cared. By the time he crawled into bed, he wore only a slightly damp pair of briefs.

He had just pulled the covers over his head when his phone rang. He debated ignoring it, but curiosity and a need for validation got the better of him. Valerie! He flipped the phone open and pulled it under the covers.

"Hey, Little Sister! This is a surprise."

"Hey yourself. I'm on break at work. I needed to hear your voice. Whatcha up to?" Valerie said.

Stuart smiled. "I got back from practice a few minutes ago and am now hiding under the covers sucking my thumb."

"That bad?" she said with a laugh.

"No, not really," he said, sighing. "It could've been far worse, especially with the crew I had today. I mean, we only came close to rolling the boat once."

"At least you recognize that," Valerie said. "Some never realize there's a capital 'I' in the middle of 'unhappy'."

Stuart smiled in spite of himself. "Very profound. Didja read that in a fortune cookie?"

"Ass."

"Jeez, I wish. Do you know how long it's been since I got laid?"

"We'll get to that subject in a minute," Valerie said. "We're not done with rowing."

"Oooh, a woman with an agenda. I like that," he said. Seriously, did she have a checklist?

"I've been giving some thought to your last e-mail," she said, confirming Stuart's suspicions. "In particular, what you said about crew and the National Team. Being tired of the entire sport is one thing, but I wonder if you're cutting and running too soon."

"Oh? How so?" He was intrigued in spite of himself.

"It's like this. You're thinking of med school as 'real life' and the National Team as putting it off, but what if both are real life for you? From what you've said and I've read, you're really good at this. I mean, *really* good," Valerie said. "Like, have a shot at it good. You might be one of the lucky ones who has two choices for real life, and choosing crew for now doesn't preclude med school in a couple of years. You might be a little older when you finish, but so what?"

Stuart didn't have anything to say to that. His first reaction was to reject it, but that would be wrong.

"Say something, Stuie."

"Something, and don't call me Stuie."

"Something else," Valerie said with a sigh. "Just give it some thought, okay? The sun used to rise and set by crew for you. Don't throw it away because you're cranky."

"Cranky?"

"You know what I mean. Now, let's talk about this man you've met."

"Yes, let's, because there have been," he said, pausing dramatically, "developments."

"Ooh, I love developments!" she squealed.

Stuart filled his sister in on Philip's last trip to Food Faire. "…and then he gave me his card with his personal, not work, cell phone number and e-mail addy."

"Sweet! So you've called him, right?" Valerie said.

Stuart didn't say anything.

"Right, Stuart?"

"Um, no? Because if I call him, he might've changed his mind?" Stuart said. It even sounded lame to his ears.

Valerie sighed. "Stuart, he kissed your wrist. He's not going to change his mind."

"But what if he…."

"I know. I'm that way, too. They've done a real number on us," she said softly. "At least take the card out. I'll be your immoral support."

Stuart snorted at the thought. He reached for his wallet. "Okay, are you ready?"

"Yes, hurry up, my break's almost over and I really have to pee."

"Okay, here it is. There're his digits, as the kids're saying."

"The kids aren't saying that anymore," Valerie said.

"Shut up. Turning it over." Stuart sucked in his breath. Oh no, this had to be some kind of joke.

"What? What is it?" Valerie yelped in his ear.

Deep calming breaths, he told himself, *lots of deep calming breaths*. "Remember me bitching about that big, irritating Neanderthal?"

"Yeah...."

"Philip appears to be his brother." Unless there was more than one developer named Sundstrom in Sacramento....

"Really?" Valerie said. She started laughing. "That's hysterical. His brother? Classic."

"I couldn't make this up if I tried. The man I've been boning for is Brad Sundstrom's brother."

"That's awesome. Good going. Speaking of, I have to. Chat with you soon, Big Brother."

"Bye, Little Sister. Try not to laugh too much."

"Are you kidding me? This will last me for days. Weeks!"

With that Valerie ended the call. Stuart snapped his phone shut and dropped it on his battered nightstand. He rolled over, pulling the blankets tight, staring at the card. Philip was a Sundstrom, huh? Wow, that was... wow.

"DAMN, YOU'RE a big one," Philip said, looking up at Brad after releasing him from a hug that was only a little awkward.

Drew hugged Philip. "Try keeping him fed. He likes steak, but only the good cuts."

"What's wrong with that?" Brad looked perplexed.

"It's expensive," Drew said patiently, like this was a discussion held at least weekly.

Philip smiled. They were so married. "That shouldn't be a problem," he said. "Or did you do something stupid like not tell him how much the buyout was?"

"Oh, he showed me, and we've invested a lot of it in our business," Drew said.

"But c'mon, it's steak. You gotta buy the good stuff. Tell him, Philip," Brad said.

"I almost never eat meat, and when I do it's not dead cows," Philip said.

Brad looked like he'd been hit on the back of the head with a plank. "You…."

"Ha!" Drew crowed.

"Come on in," Philip said. "It's a bit rude to shock people in the entrance hall."

He and Drew walked ahead, but Philip noticed Brad hanging back, looking around. "You okay, Brad?"

Brad smiled. "It's a bit weird, you know?"

"Coming back to your childhood home?"

"Only it's not anymore," Brad said, nodding.

Philip could easily imagine what Brad felt because he'd felt it himself the first time he'd walked in after the decorators had finished going over the house. "I've gotten rid of every trace of *him* I possibly could."

"Thank God," Brad muttered.

They headed into the family room, which is what Philip had made of Randall's television room.

"Philip?" Brad said.

Philip turned to look at his brother, a question on his face. "Yes?"

"I really like what you've done with the house. For what it's worth, it almost looks like something Mom would've done, don't you think?" Brad said as Drew worked his way under the larger man's arm.

"You really think so?" Philip said. That one went right to his heart. He remembered their mother better, of course. Brad had only been in middle school when she'd died in that accident, but he'd been in his senior year of high school, an adult for all intents and purposes. But for Brad to say that…. "Thanks, Brad."

"Come on, you two," Drew said. "Let's sit down. You can be sentimental on the davenports."

"I think we're done, at least for now," Brad said.

Philip nodded. "I'd rather talk about Suburban Graveyard. It shouldn't take long, and then we can get down to catching up."

"So what do you want to know? It's been a while since I was out there," Brad said.

Philip nodded. "I get that, but unlike my senior veep of tract homes or his hand-picked lackey, I trust you. Frankly that wreck of a subdivision is ruining SunHo, or our reputation, at least, and that means a lot in this business."

Drew snickered. "SunHo?"

"I slipped and referred to it that way in front of Randall, and he said it sounded like a sunburnt whore. Once I saw how much it pissed him off, I made it official. It's on a lot of our promotional literature now, including all our business cards."

"That's all I needed to know," Brad said, grinning broadly.

Drew rolled his eyes and opened his mouth to say something, but Philip got there first. "You know about Brad's issues with Randall, I presume?" When Drew nodded, he continued, "I have my own reasons to hate him, I assure you, and the fact that he played me off against my brother isn't even the least of it, if only because Brad and I can fix that."

"I can't believe I ever thought you were his lackey," Brad said.

"I was playing the long game," Philip said. "I've always had more patience than you."

Brad nodded. "Now that's the honest truth. Anyway, my own impression of Suburban Graveyard was that whoever designed the houses had a lot of anger issues to work through, because the interiors couldn't be comfortable to live in, and the less said about the landscaping the better. It really seemed like Randall and Sund—SunHo were only phoning this one in."

"There are other factors, too," Drew said. "There was an open-house for real estate agents when the original developer—Sunset

Homes?—first opened it. The flowers were fresher, but the fact is, it's just too remote. I got lost trying to find it—"

"So did I and technically, I own it," Philip said as Brad and Drew howled with laughter.

"Anyway, it's out in the boonies. The closest grocery store is almost a half hour away, and there's only one road into it. It's too far to commute into Sacramento, maybe if there were another road on the other side or something."

"That's good to know," Philip said. He made more notes on the audit folder. "It's also something said veep should've been hounding Sacramento County about before this."

"And if that feeder road or any future roads led to any of the major highways, or even larger county roads, not only could people find it, it could actually be the bedroom community it was designed to be," Brad added.

"And then maybe the amenities residents need would start filling in," Drew said. "Any idea who owns the property around the subdivision?"

Philip shook his head. "My people should, but probably don't. I'm being stymied every step of the way on this. I'm not kidding when I said I'm a week away from lopping off heads. I'll fire people down to the clerical staff if that's what it takes."

"Damn, Randall really didn't know what you'd become, did he?" Brad said.

"No, probably not, but that's because he was playing his own games in the CEO's suite," Philip said, sighing. "Frankly, it's very tiresome, but it's all I know how to do at this point, and there's a certain satisfaction in it."

"You need another girlfriend," Drew said.

Philip thought of Stuart and smiled despite his earlier worries. "There are plans afoot."

"Oh ho!" Brad cried. "The truth comes out!"

"If you behave yourself at dinner, he might tell us," Drew stage-whispered to his partner.

"We shall see, won't we?" Philip's smile looked just like the Mona Lisa's. He was saved from further interrogation by the buzzing of his iPhone. "That's the timer for dinner. I'll be right back."

When Philip got to the kitchen, he pulled his phone from his pocket to find a waiting voice mail. As he listened to it, his smile grew. He hit "play" again.

"Uh, hi Philip, it's me. Stuart. If you're still interested, give me a call. Hopefully your phone captured my number. I'll send you an e-mail, too, but in case it didn't, it's…."

Still interested? Philip snorted. He was going to have to dawdle in the kitchen to give the chubby time to go down, since his pants left little to the imagination. *How's that for interested, Stuart?*

He checked the coq au vin he'd prepared for dinner. Meat wasn't his favorite, but for his brother and Drew? He made an exception. Then he switched on the oven to preheat it for the rolls. "I'll be right out, guys," he called.

"Can we help?" Brad called.

"You can come keep me company."

So Brad and Drew came into the kitchen with the hors d'oeuvres while Philip puttered around assembling the salad and making the salad dressing. He paused to pull down some tumblers and set out bottles of lemon- and lime-flavored fizzy water.

"Did you blow out a wall or something?" Brad said, looking around. "The kitchen looks bigger. Doesn't it look bigger, babe?"

"How would I know?" Drew said with a shrug. "I certainly never set foot in this place when your father lived here, but if you did it without calling Renochuck, we're going to be hurt and pissed."

Philip rolled his eyes. "As much as it would serve you right for not telling me about your opening your own real estate brokerage, no, I've moved no walls or anything else. I hired professional decorators and they rearranged things, got rid of some of those useless cabinets, that sort of thing."

"Well, it looks great," Brad said. "Too bad Randall never renovated this place. It actually looks like someplace I'd want to spend time."

"Thanks," Philip said.

The oven pinged when it reached the preset temperature, and Philip pulled a cookie sheet out of the glass-fronted refrigerator.

Brad looked over with more than casual interest. "Yeast or buttermilk?"

"Buttermilk." Philip put them in the oven.

"Lots of butter or are you part of some low-fat fad?" Brad said.

Philip laughed. "You don't want to know how much butter's in there, but let's just say we all need to work out tomorrow."

"What difference does the amount of butter make?" Drew asked.

While Brad answered his partner's question, Philip checked the chicken. Yep, finally done. He killed the flame and set the lid beside the Dutch oven containing the chicken on another burner.

"You guys okay with eating in the kitchen?" Philip asked. When Brad and Drew nodded, he carried the salad and dressing in there. After the rolls finished and he'd put the coq au vin and its sauce on a platter, they went on the table, too, along with the bottle of wine that had been chilling.

"Damn, this is good," Drew said. "How'd you both learn to cook so well?"

Brad and Philip looked at each other and shrugged. "It was that or starve," Philip said.

"And why should we eat slop if we don't have to?" Brad added.

"Whatever, I'd almost consider throwing you over for Philip, except that he doesn't bat for our team," Drew said, winking at Brad.

Philip picked up his glass, smiling coyly as he took a sip. "Who says I don't bat for your team?"

Then he sat back and watched the show. Drew choked on his roll, but Brad? He actually spat out the wine in his mouth.

Once he and Drew had recovered, Brad said, "Who says? Uh… three years with Angie?"

"Maybe I'm a switch hitter," Philip said.

Brad stood up abruptly. "I so did not hear that."

"But Braaad, you're the one who told me ass is so much tighter than pussy," Philip said, all wide-eyed innocence. "I've been dying to try it ever since."

"La la la la, I can't hear you!" Brad yelled as he strode from the kitchen, leaving crashing silence in his wake.

"He's taking it well," Drew said.

"He hasn't punched any holes in the wall, if that's what you mean," Philip said, not quite believing this was how it was going.

Drew sighed. "Try to look at it from his point of view, Philip. He thought you were straight and then you spring this on him. On us."

"Yeah? I thought he was straight until he told me he'd screwed up and you'd dumped him for it," Philip said sharply. "That's how I found out my little brother, who'd been pretty moody and furtive for a while—not to mention the drinking problem he was developing because he thought you hated him—was gay, so you'll forgive me if I'm not all that sympathetic to Brad finding out I'm bi over dinner."

Drew stood up.

Philip threw his napkin down. "Great, so I've run you off, too?"

"You Sundstroms are such drama queens," Drew said with a sigh, putting his hand on Philip's shoulder to take the edge off his words. "I'm going to find Brad, because as melodramatic as you are, you're basically right."

While Drew left to find his partner, Philip sat at the table, leaning his head on one hand, using his fork to toy with his dinner with the other. His appetite had deserted him along with Brad. Drew was right about one thing. Why did everything between him and Brad have to be a production? Couldn't they try to relate to each other like adults, instead of weighting everything down with their unspoken pasts? Or were they doomed to keep reenacting this same farce over and over again?

Christ, Drew was right, Philip thought, dropping his fork. They were drama queens, and any minute Drew would drag Brad out here, and he'd look contrite and apologize and they'd sweep it all under the rug and move on to dessert. Well, screw that.

Philip got up and, moving silently, went out to the backyard to think. Drew and Brad could clean up the dishes, if Drew ever pulled Brad out of whatever room he was hiding in. Philip decided to go ahead and have a moment. He'd just come out as bi, and his brother the cocksucker had flipped out. Maybe that would make sense someday.

He thought about hiding in the small hedge maze, but that felt petty. Besides which, it wasn't that big, and as soon as one of them got the idea of looking out one of the upstairs windows they'd find him, since there'd be no way he could stay off his iPhone. The glow would give him away. On the other hand, the maze's gates could be shifted….

He went for it. It was his party, he could sulk if he wanted to.

He moved on cat-like feet through his backyard, avoiding the pool area with its motion-activated lights and fountains. If he really wanted to be an ass, he could roll a large inflatable ball through there, but Brad had been assy enough for both of them.

He made it to the maze quickly enough and arranged the gates so that they enclosed him within the maze's center. Brad and Drew could wander around the maze's heart in the dark to their hearts' content and they still wouldn't find him. He planned to stay in the small folly until he was good and ready to emerge. Yes, he was being a princess, and he didn't care right then, because he realized that Brad's reaction had hurt him like a son of a bitch.

He pulled out his iPhone and checked his mail. Sure enough, there was one from Stuart. He wrote back to assure him that he most definitely was still interested. Since he had a flexible schedule, he suggested Stuart set the date and time based on his work schedule and other commitments. Philip would be there and could even give him a ride if he needed one.

Philip thought about calling, but didn't when he realized what he really wanted to do was cry, and it was a bit soon to dump that on Stuart.

CHAPTER
Seven

PHILIP WOKE up in the folly. The clock on his iPhone told him it was 2:38. Great. Not only had he been a total princess, he fallen asleep out there, so he'd ignored his guests. Way to go, dumbass.

He let himself out of his hedge maze and shuffled back to the house. At least they'd cleaned up. That was nice of them. It was also the least they could've done, considering how dinner ended. To say nothing of the fact that they'd made no effort to find him. Not that he necessarily wanted to be found, but the effort might have been nice. Hi, I'm Philip Sundstrom and I've turned into an adolescent girl.

He started closing windows. He knew his hurt fee-fees were getting in the way of his relationship with his brother and Drew, but still. He'd come out to them, and Brad, at least, had flipped the fuck out. Not cool, Brad, not cool. He really thought Brad would've handled it with aplomb, but no. At least Drew had kept a level head—once he'd finished choking on his roll, at any rate.

On his way out of the kitchen, Philip saw a note on the edge of the counter.

> You two….
>
> Since we can't find you, I'll assume you don't want to be found, not that I can blame you.
>
> Brad's being Brad, and you're being you. I'll let him know that he's got his head up his ass tomorrow and he'll come around. I'm not sure why he freaked, to be honest, but at this point he doesn't know how to walk it back.

> But you? I'm not sure what to do with you, and you
> don't even have a boyfriend—or girlfriend—I can appeal
> to for help.
> I'll call you tomorrow.
> Love,
> Drew

Huh. That was interesting. The closest the Sundstrom boys came to an outside opinion thought they were both melodramatic. Drew might've had a point, but that didn't mean that he was ready to admit it.

Instead, he switched off the lights and went upstairs and got into bed. Wanting to see if Stuart had written back, he checked his e-mail and indeed found one from Stuart.

> Hey there, Philip,
> How about Tuesday at Sandwich A Go-Go? 11:30
> to beat the executive set?
> Stuart

"Ha!" Philip cackled. He hit reply and proceeded to fat-finger his response.

> Hey, I resemble that remark! But I'll see you there
> and then.

And with that, he put his phone in the charger next to his lamp and tried to get back to sleep.

STUART WIPED his hands on his shorts for what felt like the millionth time. He'd dated before. He'd hooked up before. This wasn't either one, so why was he so freaked out by meeting Philip Sundstrom—and was it *really* the same family—for lunch? Wait, was it a date? Suddenly it felt like a date. But if it *was* a date…

Then he saw Philip walk up, and the man took his breath away. Turned out, that wasn't a figure of speech. He understood now why his best friend Morgan had turned goofy when he and Nick Bedford had been courting, or why that alarmingly tall vet Adam Lennox always settled down when Owen Douglas walked into the boathouse. Sure, Stuart still wanted to hurl somewhere, but the sight of the man who'd held his wrist and kissed it made him feel better. Stuart admitted that if they'd been somewhere private, or hell, if they went somewhere private right now, Philip could hold both wrists down and do just about anything to him.

Dressed in a suit, Philip strolled up the block toward Stuart, pulling off his tie as he walked, which made Stuart feel better about his board shorts and a shirt from some forgotten regatta. Then Philip swung his blazer over his shoulder. Stuart's mouth hung open. Philip looked like a model, especially with those fantastic bangs of his and a pair of mirrored shades, the sunlight glinting off both, one gold, the other silver.

Damn. All that was here to have lunch with him.

Stuart was still staring when Philip walked up.

"Hi, Stuart," Philip said. "Thanks for meeting me."

Stuart forced himself to snap out of it. "Thanks for being free during the day. I really appreciate it."

"Not a problem. Like I said, I think it's easier for me to get away than you to get time off," Philip said. He smiled and Stuart felt the bottom drop out of his stomach again. Is this what he'd missed by only seeing Philip at night? The fluorescent light at Food Faire did him no justice, not like sunlight. It brought the gold out of his hair, and from there, it seemed to bathe him in its light.

"Definitely," Stuart said, "but that doesn't mean I don't appreciate it."

They stared at each other for a few moments, and Stuart really didn't know what to do. He tended to defer to older men, but Philip looked like he was content to stand out on the sidewalk indefinitely.

Then his stomach growled. Loudly. And he blushed. Noticeably. He really hated looking like a leprechaun sometimes.

"Sounds like we'd better get in there," Philip said.

If possible, Stuart turned even redder. "Sorry, we had a land workout today and I shared it with the crew. Gotta keep up my boyish figure, right?"

"You do not," Philip said, "have a *boyish* anything, and believe me, I've been watching."

Stuart cocked his head. "Did that come out how you meant it?"

"That sounded creepy, didn't it?" Philip turned bright red.

"A little, yeah." Stuart was grateful, actually. For some reason, Philip's gaffe made him feel like he was back in control of himself instead of freefalling into… what?

Philip held the door open for him. "Thank you," Stuart said.

Stuart liked Sandwich A Go-Go not only because of its wild array of choices, but also because people ordered at the register before finding a table or taking their food to go. It also allowed a certain cox'n meeting someone for the first time outside of work and its predefined roles to avoid the question of an older, obviously better-off man paying for his lunch. By the look on his face Philip knew exactly what Stuart had done and why, but Stuart didn't care. He might be one of the poors, but that didn't mean one of the riches could trample his dignity.

Stuart found a table in a quiet corner and waited for Philip. "Is this all right?"

"It's fine," Philip said.

They sat quietly for a few minutes while Stuart felt the tension grow. Damn, this is why he hated dating. Wait, was this a date? He still had no idea. Why couldn't relationships start in the middle after all the awkward garbage was over?

Stuart couldn't stand it anymore. "So… uh, what do you do?"

"You didn't read the front of the card?" Philip said, surprised.

"Actually, I did."

Philip cocked his head. "Is that why you're so nervous?"

"One of the reasons, yes," Stuart said.

"Can I tell you something?" Philip said, smiling a little.

Stuart nodded. "Go for it."

"I'm nervous, too," Philip said softly.

"No way. You don't look it."

"Practice," Philip said with a snort. "Lots of practice. But no joke, I'm shaking inside."

When their food arrived, they murmured their thanks and waited until they were alone again before resuming their conversation.

That was the last thing Stuart had expected to hear from Philip, the very last. The man always looked like he was in control of every situation. Okay, he only ever saw Philip at Food Faire, but he walked through it like a master, dammit. "You? What do you have to be nervous about? You're the owner and CEO of a huge company."

"I'm having lunch with you," Philip replied softly, hardly daring to meet Stuart's eyes.

Stuart had no idea what to say to that. He wasn't anyone special. Years of lusting after rowers who didn't pay him the slightest attention had taught him that. Flummoxed, he said, "I'm sorry the restaurant's probably not up to your usual standards."

"Usual standards?" Philip said. He looked perplexed, as if he had no idea what Stuart meant.

"You know, fancy business lunches, dinners at white-tablecloth restaurants, that kind of thing," Stuart said. He felt like an idiot for even bringing it up, still unsure why a man like Philip would even be interested in him.

Stuart almost saw the light bulb go on over Philip's head. "I think I understand."

"Understand what?" Stuart said.

Philip looked a little sad. "This talk of standards and restaurants. Oh, and for the record, I almost never eat out. That's for people who have to wine-and-dine clients, and that's usually done below my level. I'm only involved when it's company to company. You know where I eat most of the time?"

Stuart shook his head. He really couldn't imagine.

"My kitchen table."

Stuart wanted to smack himself. Jeez, he was an idiot. "Hence the frequent trips to Food Faire. You like ultra-fresh ingredients."

Philip nodded. "I don't have a domestic staff, other than a cleaning service that comes in twice a week." He sighed. "Stuart, I'm older than you are. I'm at a different place in my life than you are in yours."

"You're not that much older, less than ten years I bet," Stuart said. Why did he suddenly sense he'd assumed exactly the wrong thing about Philip?

Philip shrugged. "Probably not, no." He was silent for a moment, thinking. "Then is it perceptions about money?"

"Perceptions? Don't play me," Stuart said. He laughed, but it was devoid of humor. He closed his eyes. He didn't want to go there.

"Money, class, just… you're so far out of my league, I don't know why you'd want to be with me."

Philip's jaw twitched. "Okay, let's get this out of the way right now. I wasn't born rich. I worked for my father's company right out of college and before that, I interned every summer during high school, and believe me, while I was paid well and saved every penny, I was also tied to my father with a very tight rope. Randall did some shitty things, including hire goons to bash Drew St. Charles. Did you hear about that? You're part of the CalPac circle, and as I understand it, Drew's best friend was the CalPac crew coach."

Stuart nodded. It had been a horrible time and it had pushed Nick Bedford out of coaching and into physical therapy. Yeah, he'd heard all about it from his own best friend, Nick's partner. "Your dad did that?"

"Yes," Philip said. Philip's sunny, handsome face looked so grim, Stuart wanted to make it better, but he didn't know how. All he knew is that he'd started this, but Philip plowed relentlessly on. "Randall's doing hard time now for that and a whole lot more. So yeah, I got rich the old-fashioned way. I played the loyal lieutenant, hating my father's guts the entire time, and then," Philip said, smiling like a predator, "when the time was right, I tricked him into signing away the entire kit and caboodle to me."

"Shit," Stuart said, sitting back in his chair. Talk about Machiavellian. Talk about patience. He could never have done that. He was too prone to outbursts. Damn Celtic temperament.

Philip smiled sadly. "I really am a nice guy, Stuart. Don't arrange to have anyone gay bashed, and we'll get along fine."

"I think I can manage that," Stuart said, nodding. "So then what happened?"

Philip shrugged. "I bought my brother out, figuring that if Randall knew a boatload of his money was going to make a nice life for Brad and his boyfriend it might drive him crazy—truly crazy—and you have no idea how worth it that would be. Ever since, I've run the family business and tried not to be a jerk about making money."

Stuart still felt perplexed. Philip was hot and loaded. He, Stuart, was dirt poor, butt white, and covered with freckles. Oh yeah, and there was that burning red hair to contend with. He'd always hated his hair. "I still don't understand what you see in me."

"Are you serious?" Philip looked at him as if he were nuts. "You're a nice person, for one thing."

"And nice guys always finish last," Stuart muttered.

Philip shook his head. "Not with me, they don't. And I don't meet many nice people, so when one comes along? I pay extra attention, especially when he's incredibly attractive. And hot. Damn, Stuart. You have no idea what you do to me. But mostly? You seem like someone I need to know. I hope you'll give me a chance. So yes, I'm what they call 'loaded.' It doesn't make me a better person, but it doesn't make me a bad one, either. I hope you won't hold it against me. We can talk about what money can and can't do some time, but until then, I'd like to pay because I remember what student budgets are like, and lunch or dinner or a movie cost you proportionately far more than they do me. If that bothers you, then I'd love to cook for you, my place or yours."

Stuart sat back. "Okay, Philip. Point made, mind blown. I have to admit, you're not what I expected for a…." He was about to say "rich asshole," but Philip wasn't an asshole and Philip had just dressed him down—gently, of course—about the whole money thing, "…Sundstrom."

"So what did you expect?" Philip said, toying with his soda can.

"Brad. Assuming you're *that* Sundstrom family."

Philip laughed, and Stuart was so glad. He thought maybe he'd killed the mood and maybe his chances, and that was the last thing he wanted to do. He'd realized that maybe Philip was someone he needed in his life, too.

"Yes, I'm part of *that* Sundstrom family, no matter how much I might wish otherwise, sometimes." Philip sighed. "But to set your mind at ease, I'm nothing like my younger brother."

"Thank God," Stuart said. It just slipped out. His mouth needed a filter in the worst way. Maybe insulting his brother wasn't the best way to endear himself to Philip. He was blushing from his hair all the way down his chest, he could feel it. "I'm sorry—"

"Don't be. Brad's a force of nature. That can be both good and bad, and these days, he's not my favorite person."

Stuart let that one go. He'd already committed more than enough blunders for a first date. If this were a date. Suddenly he wanted it to be. "So can I ask you something?"

"Of course," Philip said, smiling once again.

He looked up at Philip from under his bangs. "So… is this a date?"

Philip smiled his usual enigmatic smile. "Do you want it to be a date?"

"I want—no, I need to know what you're feeling. I've been putting myself out there—okay, sticking my foot in my mouth—and you seem to be very good at dodging things," Stuart said.

"I'd like it to be a date. I'd like to see where things go," Philip said.

Stuart smiled. "Good. Me, too."

Stuart had his concerns, unvoiced at this point. It was early July. He started medical school in August, a serious commitment of his time and energy for the next seven years at a minimum. Then, too, the National Team kept pestering him. So *of course* he met someone with the most potential for a long-term relationship of anyone he'd dated in years.

"There's one more thing," Philip said. "I'm bi. Is that going to be a problem for you?"

"No, why would it?" Stuart said, even though yeah, he didn't know quite what to make of it. He'd never hooked up with a bi guy before, only guys who'd said they were bi because they were too chickenshit to come out all the way.

Philip shrugged. "Beats me, but Brad freaked out when I told him."

"Brad and I aren't exactly the best of friends," Stuart said, grimacing. "His bull-in-a-china-shop routine drives me insane. I'm sorry, I know he's your brother, but… I mean, hell. He calls me Cockring. That's a little hard to love, you know?"

"A lot of that's an act. That's what our father expected of him, so that's what he delivered," Philip replied. "Our father was a grade-A fucking son of a bitch, by the way. If you get the chance, watch Brad with his partner or that adaptive rowing program. I bet he's a totally different person."

Stuart frowned. That beer-soaked jackass had a gentle, even sensitive side? Unlikely. "If you say so."

"Anyway, to avoid the charge of dodging—and yes, I'm very good at it—I'm bi and my last serious relationship was with a woman," Philip said. Stuart thought he looked sad.

He took a breath to calm his nerves. It didn't work. Did it ever? "Can I ask what happened?"

"Three years into it I discovered I was the only one who thought we were exclusive," Philip said, his lips pressed into a thin line.

"Ouch."

"You've got that right. So obviously if we get serious, I'm kind of hung up on monogamy," Philip said.

"I can see why," Stuart replied. Damn, talk about a kick in the teeth.

"Anyway, this is waaay too heavy for a first date," Philip said.

Stuart smiled. "You're right. It's third date or later material, definitely."

Philip laughed. "I'll be sure to remember that."

They chatted for a little while longer, but then Philip looked at his watch. "As great a time as I'm having, I should probably get back to work."

Stuart understood, but that was the last thing he wanted. "I know a great coffee shop that's not too far away. We could move our conversation there. Are you sure you can't play hooky?"

Philip looked at him with wry amusement. "You're a bad man. I'll call my assistant. If you'll excuse me for a moment?"

This was so cool. Concerns about the future aside, Stuart finally had a date with someone who interested him and yeah, who turned him on, and he never wanted it to end. He rested his chin in his hand and watched Philip out the restaurant window.

When Philip returned, he was all smiles. "Apparently it's dead quiet in the office, which now that I think about it is itself cause for worry, but let's get out of here. Coffee sounds great and if we stay here much longer, we'll never get the smell out of our skin. But let's drive. I have to move my car or the meter maids will put one of those clamps on the tire."

CHAPTER
Eight

PHILIP SPUN around in his desk chair when Jyoti came in. Since his personal assistant rarely came to see him without cause, and he hadn't summoned Jyoti, perforce he had something to say.

"What can I do for you?" Philip said.

"Something's going on, boss." Jyoti closed the door to Philip's office behind him. "Talk stops when I enter the copy room."

"Does it, now?" Philip sat up straighter. One of the first things he'd learned when he'd started interning at SunHo even before he graduated from high school was that the personal assistants and people in the clerical pool knew almost everything that was going on. Whether they told their bosses or not was another issue.

"The first time talk stopped when I walked in, I assumed it was because it was 'girl talk,' you know? I get that I'm one of the few male PAs. But it's happening more and more often, and I don't think it's a good sign."

"No, it's not," Philip said, his eyes narrowing. "Whose PAs are involved?"

Jyoti frowned. "It varies, but Billie, Winch's PA, is almost always part of the group. She's not very subtle."

"Winch. Isn't that interesting?" Philip mused. "Feel like doing some snooping?"

"Isn't that what I've been doing?" Jyoti said.

"I was thinking something a bit more focused than that, a bit more active." Philip smiled but it never touched his eyes. "Perhaps see if you can find others who agree with Billie, or better yet, people who disagree."

"I think I can do that," Jyoti said, nodding slowly. "It'll give me a chance to practice my broken English. I spend most of my time up here, so no one down there in Purgatory really knows what I sound like."

Philip arched one eyebrow. "Purgatory?"

"Sure. The building's got eight stories, right?" When Philip nodded, Jyoti continued, "So the ground floor, where the clerical pool is, is Purgatory."

"Of course. So what's our little aerie up here called?" Philip said.

"The Elysian Fields, of course."

Philip shook his head. "This was your idea, wasn't it?"

Jyoti shrugged modestly. "I might've made a few suggestions, yes."

"It's going to suck around here if you ever decide to go back to school," Philip said. He really didn't want to think about that.

"Do keep that in mind when it's time to negotiate salaries," Jyoti said, winking.

Philip laughed. He couldn't help it. "Get out of here."

Lovely. Winch was stirring the pot against him. As much as it infuriated him, it shouldn't have surprised him. He'd ousted Randall for personal reasons, and while Randall's conduct would sooner or later have had serious implications for SunHo, he'd been naïve to think that Randall wasn't without his supporters. In fact, the C-level and the people immediately below were almost entirely his hand-picked cronies, and Philip now recognized that he'd slit his own throat by allowing the fantasy and sentiment of institutional memory blind him to practical necessity. Sure, some had been appalled by Randall's criminal activities, but others had secretly condoned them. Somehow he had to figure out which of those who'd been appalled might be in his camp.

Or maybe he should shitcan the lot of them. It was his company, after all. But he prided himself on being fair, and some of those people were—relatively—blameless. He doubted anyone made it to the C-level under Randall with entirely clean hands.

He looked at the clock on his desk. The morning was already a perfect shitshow and it wasn't even noon yet. He made sure the link to his home computer was active and then locked the desktop of his work computer. Should the password fail, custom security software would destroy the computer through a complicated cascade that disabled the cooling fan, maxed out the processors with busy work, and cooked the hard drive with the resulting excess heat. He didn't pretend to understand, but the IT department seemed to be impressed with it.

He fired off a text to Stuart:

Coffee? Food? Company? I really need not to be at SunHo right now.

PHILIP MADE himself back off the gas pedal many times as he drove away from SunHo. The Merc was limited electronically to 120 mph or so, but that still put it well into the ticket-bait zone on the freeway. That was the last thing he needed. Well, maybe not the last, but it wasn't high on the list, and definitely not in his present frame of mind. He should've anticipated something like this. His ability to think several moves ahead of his opponents had been the key to his success at SunHo, but maybe he shouldn't have used the fact that he'd outfoxed Randall as the measure of his abilities. Randall had been one person, a man he'd studied at close range for years. Philip knew his every strength and weakness. He'd only known his board well for a year, and he certainly didn't live with them and thank God for that. He'd studied them, of course, but not like he'd studied Randall.

Philip parsed it every way he knew, but nothing changed the fact that he'd made a major miscalculation in assuming his board—or members thereof—weren't every bit as scheming as… as he was. He hated thinking of it that way, but it was true. The only difference between him and them was their greater experience. Angie had always warned him not to try to beat people like that at their own game, that they'd only drag him down to their level and then beat him through their superior experience. Turned out, she was right.

Nothing changed the fact that he was young, possibly too young, and while he'd always been nervy, this time he just might've bitten off more than he could chew. For the first time in a long time, he didn't know quite how he was going to find his way out of this thicket.

He glanced at his iPhone where it lay hooked into the Merc's sound system. Stuart had texted him back. He was free. Finally, a bit of good news! Merely knowing he could see Stuart made him feel better. He couldn't text him back. Besides being illegal in California, texting at 70 mph was mind-bogglingly stupid. Fortunately, the car was a giant

Bluetooth device, and he spared enough attention to find Stuart's number in the car's memory and call it.

"Hello?" Stuart said.

"Hey you!" Philip said, relieved at hearing his voice. "I can't text you back while I'm fleeing my place of employment—"

"That bad?"

Philip shuddered. "Yes. I need food and you."

"As it happens, I'm good for both of those," Stuart replied. Philip smiled. He had to. "Where do you want to eat?"

Philip suggested the first thing that popped into his head. "Bijou?"

"Okaaay, that's fine, if you want me squirming the entire time."

Philip exited the highway for downtown. Shit. He'd forgotten Stuart's allergy to money. "Then you suggest something. Or I can pick you up and you can choose someplace. You know I'm easy."

Philip realized what he'd said at the same moment Stuart did. "Oh *really*?"

"Just give me your address," Philip said, sighing.

"Where are you?"

"I'm about to exit the Cap City Freeway at N Street."

"Turn left on Capitol and then…."

Philip jotted notes on a pad of paper while he waited for the light at the bottom of the off-ramp. No need for the navigation system, he could find it, and a good thing, too, since the light had changed.

When Philip pulled up, he found Stuart waiting at the top of the steps that presumably led to his apartment. Even in shorts and—was that another regatta T-shirt? how many did he have, anyway?—a comfortably worn shirt, he looked amazing. He imagined him in a suit as they attended a play. He imagined him naked in his bed afterward. Philip almost got out to open his door, but Stuart was already letting himself in, and thank goodness for that, because Philip would've embarrassed them both with his massive hard-on. Maybe those absurd baggy jeans that were inexplicably still in style weren't so silly after all….

Stuart slid into the passenger seat. He'd ridden in the car before, so they'd gotten the "I'm not going to get it dirty, am I?" nonsense out of the way. "I still can't get over how nice this is. Hi, by the way," Stuart said brightly.

Philip longed to lean over and kiss Stuart on the cheek, but they weren't there yet. They'd only seen each other on a casual basis since that first coffee, but Philip knew what he wanted. He settled for saying, "Hey, Stuart. Thanks for meeting me."

When Stuart smiled at him, Philip felt like he was the only thing that mattered right then. "No problem. If it weren't for our lunches or coffee dates, I'd either be in bed asleep or studying in my underwear until it was time for work."

"Where're we eating today?" Philip asked. He knew if he said anything else, it would be about Stuart in his underwear, and there be dragons. Dragons with milky skin and red hair. Dragons with perfectly proportioned asses. He shook his head. "I'm sorry, what'd you say?"

"Are you okay?" Stuart looked at him closely.

Philip shrugged apologetically. "My mind wandered a bit. Can I have the address again?"

Stuart repeated it, even as he gave Philip some side-eye action. Philip pretended he couldn't see it, just as he'd pretended that lunch, once they got there, was tasty. He ate mechanically, hardly noticing what he put in his mouth. He chatted with Stuart throughout lunch, but couldn't have told him what they'd discussed even five minutes later, which was why he missed Stuart's narrowing gaze and went along quietly when Stuart insisted they get iced coffee and go sit in the shade at McKinley Park to enjoy it. Only temporarily distracted by Stuart, Philip was caught in a loop of worry about the situation at SunHo, and he knew it. That didn't mean he could shut it down.

Stuart made himself comfortable on a park bench, one knee drawn up in front of him. He sat closer to Philip than usual, but Philip found he liked that very much indeed. "All right, Philip. Spill it. You've been distracted ever since you picked me up."

Philip opened his mouth to deny it, but wasn't that why he'd called Stuart in the first place? His company was nice, and being around him had made Philip feel better, at least for a little while, but Stuart was right. His mind had been elsewhere for most of their time together.

"It's business garbage," Philip said, groaning. "Are you sure you want to hear it?"

"If you talk it out, will I get your attention back?" Stuart asked.

Philip snorted. "I've been that bad?"

"A little, maybe," Stuart said, the color rising in his cheeks. "Yes."

"I've had some trouble with the C-level and those immediately under it at SunHo, but this morning my personal assistant brought me his suspicions that some members of my board may be actively working to oust me," Philip said.

"C-level?" Stuart said.

"I'm sorry. Corporate shorthand for the titles that start with a C, like chairman of the board, chief executive officer, chief operating officer, chief financial officer, that sort of thing," Philip said. "Jeez, just thinking about those assholes makes me sick to my stomach."

Stuart looked thoughtful. "If they bother you that much, can't you get rid of them?"

"I can, and I probably should've, but when I first took over the company, they were the institutional stability. Now? I don't know who I can trust and who I need to fire."

"What, exactly, did your personal assistant tell you?" Stuart asked. He stared at Philip intently, moving closer.

Philip ended up relating the entire story to him, although he hadn't intended to bore Stuart with all the details, but something about the younger man's intense interest made him want to open up.

"Okay, that sounds pretty bad," Stuart said, nodding, "but it doesn't sound totally hopeless, either. So let's talk this through, because you're the man who pulled that power move and took control of the company, remember? You can't let those assholes beat you. So talk to me. I'm short, but I'm sneaky!"

"You don't say?" Philip said, smiling for the first time since he'd picked Stuart up.

"You have no idea," Stuart said with a grin that made Philip's stomach flutter. He really was just that charming when he smiled.

"So. What's the absolute worst that could happen?" Stuart asked.

Philip blinked. "Well, they could force me out as chairman of the board and chief executive officer. It'd be hard, but there are ways it could happen."

"So what would that leave you?" Stuart pressed.

"Owner of a company that I no longer control. I would no longer have any say over any aspect of the governance of SunHo, which I have to say, freaks me out, because if the company did something wrong, I'd be left holding the bag," Philip said. The thought made him shiver.

"Really? The owner has no say or influence? I find that hard to believe," Stuart said.

"Well, I could think of two things I could do," Philip said, "but I'd hate to do them. I could sell the company to another construction company, or I could sell off the company's assets and end the company."

"Hmm, let's call those the nuclear options." Stuart frowned. "I wonder what the threat of those would do to encourage a change of attitude? You wouldn't even have to pursue them seriously, only plant the rumors. Or even have your PA 'accidentally' leave incriminating documents in the photocopier. That copy room sounds like a hotbed of activity, by the way. Have you considered copiers for each floor or department?"

Philip looked at Stuart with admiration. "You're good at this."

"I told you. Sneaky!" Stuart winked at Philip, whose stomach did another flip-flop. "So, we've established worst-case scenarios, both of which would still leave you stinking rich, by the way."

Philip rolled his eyes. "Not the hot issue."

"Look me in the eyes and tell me you don't like it."

"Okay, guilty as charged," Philip said, laughing.

"All right then," Stuart said. "Now keep in mind I didn't take that many business classes, but a number of the men on the crew did, and I overheard things. Even if they forced you out, what would happen if you took the company public?"

Philip opened his mouth to protest, but then snapped it shut. Damn. Stuart had a point. So long as he retained even a slim majority of the stock, he would effectively be back in control. He smiled. "Usually you need to have a reason to raise that kind of money, but yes, it'd work. And Stuart?"

"Yeah?"

"It would infuriate them." Philip had to admit, hashing it out with someone who didn't have a stake in it helped. He already felt better. "I need to find out who my allies are, because I don't think the entire board is against me. Also, some of the people on the level right beneath them would have every reason to support me."

"How come?" Stuart said.

"Because if I start lopping off heads, there will suddenly be room for advancement," Philip said, grinning. "Since my father stocked the board with his cronies, there wasn't much turnover, but now? There may be quite a bit."

Stuart grinned wickedly. "You're getting into the spirit of things, I can tell." He thought for a moment. "Speaking of promotions, once you find your supporters, promote them. Water down the C-level. The second President Roosevelt threatened to do that to the Supreme Court when the sitting justices looked like they were going to strike down the New Deal. It's your company, so pack the board with your supporters."

"I should be talking to my IT department," Philip said, shaking his head at his own blindness. "If these people are using company e-mail, there'll be a record. Even if they're not, it's still going through SunHo's servers."

"That's the spirit," Stuart said, sipping the last of his coffee. Then he reached for Philip's untouched one. "May I?"

"Yes, I hate iced coffee," Philip said. He felt nothing but relief. When he left his office that morning, everything had looked hopeless, but Stuart had solved his problems as he sat there sucking on his iced coffee. Philip doubted Stuart realized just how much he'd helped him. Without stopping to think, Philip grabbed Stuart in a one-armed hug and kissed his cheek. "Thank you so much, Stuart. You've no idea what this means to me."

Then they both froze.

Philip dropped his arm. "Oh jeez, Stuart. I'm so sorry! I didn't mean to presume on our friendship. I didn't—"

"It's okay, Philip," Stuart said, a big, silly grin on his face. "No, wait...."

Philip's heart sank. "Wait?"

Stuart reached for him. "I think we need to do it again, just to be sure."

CHAPTER
Nine

STUART DIDN'T know how much longer they'd spent kissing. Sure, he could look at the clock or his cell phone and figured it out, but that wasn't the point. He'd lost himself in Philip's kisses, and Philip was an excellent kisser. Philip had definitely seemed to enjoy Stuart's stubble, too. He tucked that away for future reference. He could only hope Philip didn't get off on chest hair, because he barely had any.

"Here we are," Philip said as they parked near Stuart's apartment.

Stuart made a face. "I don't want to go home. Do I have to go home?"

"You can come home with me," Philip said. "Go pack an overnight bag. I'll wait."

Stuart knew he was joking, but he suddenly found it very hard to breathe. Philip, in Philip's house? All he'd need was a toothbrush, because he'd have his clothes off soooo fast…. "What kind of man do you take me for?" he said in mock outrage.

Philip chuckled. The fact that Stuart was busy climbing over the center armrest onto Philip's lap took the bite out of his words. It was times like this when Stuart truly enjoyed being a pocket gay. He wasn't straddling Philip's crotch, but he was close enough.

"A damn hot one," Philip said, tipping his head up to kiss Stuart some more.

"Good answer," Stuart breathed as he leaned down to capture Philip's willing mouth. He moaned as Philip's tongue probed gently at his kiss-swollen lips. Philip ran his hands up Stuart's chest and he arched into the touch. When Philip gently fanned his hands over Stuart's now-pebbled nipples, Stuart shivered.

"Somebody likes that," Philip said, catching his breath.

Stuart broke free, breathing heavily. "We either need to stop this, or you need to come upstairs."

Philip stared into Stuart's eyes. In its way, Stuart found that even more intimate than what he had suggested they do. "Is that what you want?"

Stuart nodded slowly. "I hope you do, too."

Without breaking eye contact, Philip took one of Stuart's hands and kissed the palm before placing it on his crotch. "That answer your question?"

Stuart kissed him gently. "How do I get out of this car of yours?"

"Delicately, so you don't step on my groin," Philip said. He kissed the tip of Stuart's nose. It was a strangely familiar gesture, as if they'd been lovers for months instead of hours. Or weeks, because if Stuart were honest with himself, he'd been increasingly entranced by the older man ever since he took on those college brats who knocked the cereal over.

Philip opened the door for him and Stuart climbed out, careful not to damage the goods. Now that he had Philip in his clutches... wow. Great time to get nervous, Cochrane. But he *was* nervous. They hadn't planned this. He didn't know where he stood with Philip, only where he wished he did. But damn, he really wanted into Philip's pants right then. He'd worry about the details later.

Stuart admired that Philip didn't even bother to adjust himself as he got out of the car. That more than anything else told him Philip had his confidence back. What did they call that in business? Oh yes, BSD. Big Swinging Dicks. *Please, God....* Stuart thought.

Maybe that's why Philip stopped to kiss him right there in the middle of the stairs. He only cared what Stuart thought. He hoped.

What if he's staring at my ass? Stuart thought, suddenly hyperaware as he climbed the stairs, Philip hard on his heels. *He's said he's hot for it before.* "Are you staring at my butt?"

Philip laughed. "Uh, yeah. It's amazing. It demands to be stared at."

"Great, now I'm self-conscious."

Philip reached up and cupped his hands around Stuart's ass. "I've been dying to do that since the moment we met. Now let's get inside so I can try that without anything in the way."

Stuart blamed his red face on the summer heat. Fumbling with his keys, he opened the door to his apartment and pulled Philip in after him.

"Any roommates we have to worry about?" Philip asked.

Stuart grinned. "Nope. He won't be back until right before CalPac starts back up in the middle of August."

Philip looked around. "I never would've seen you living in a place decorated quite like this. Don't get me wrong, it looks like it's very high quality, it's just...."

"Exactly," Stuart said, shuddering. "Don't blame me for any this. My roommate's mother took one look at the place and decided it was unfit for her son. Mommy Dearest was only one of many things that came between us."

"Came between you?"

Stuart sighed. "We were boyfriends for a while, until I realized what an idiot he was about money, among other things."

"Spent it all?" Philip said.

"No," Stuart said, "Okay, yes, he spent it like it grew on trees, but there was always more. No, the problem was he never understood that not all of us are rich and some of us are quite poor."

Philip looked horrified, and Stuart had to laugh. "You don't do that, if that's what you're wondering. You've been a perfect gentleman about it. Jonathan? He wanted me to fly back to England to spend the summer drinking. He tried to get me to quit my job, rationalizing that I'd be taking on debt with med school, so what's a little more?"

"That's classy," Philip said. He pulled Stuart over to the sofa and brought him down onto his lap. For his part, Stuart let himself be led and held. He found he liked it a lot—even more when Philip started nibbling.

Stuart lifted his neck to give Philip better access to the delicate skin behind his jaw. "You? You've eaten at every dive I could think of without complaining once."

"Some of those places have been very good, and all of them have been acceptable," Philip murmured. Stuart gasped as Philip found a new spot that made him quiver, right behind his left ear.

"That's one of the things I like about you," Stuart said. "You're not hung up on appearances, and you're open to quality wherever it might be."

Philip looked up from his exploration of the back of Stuart's neck and whispered directly into Stuart's ear, "That's because I know quality when I see it, regardless of how it presents itself."

Stuart swallowed. He had the feeling that Philip wasn't talking about sandwich shops and taco wagons anymore. He started to pull Philip's arms tighter around himself, but Philip took the hint and finished the job. "You say the sweetest things."

"They're sweet because I mean them," Philip said, resting his head on Stuart's shoulder. "And for the record? I'd never have put you in the position of having to choose between your job and a vacation. I'd have found some place local to go on your days off."

Stuart pulled back a little, turning to look at Philip. "I know, and that's another thing I like about you. But right now? There's something else I want you to do."

"And what's that?"

Stuart got off Philip's lap and held out his hand. Philip stood and took the hand and the promise that went along with it.

Stuart was afraid of what Philip might say. Rooms could reveal a lot about their occupants, but all his room seemed to say was "Just passing through." Maybe not the impression he wanted to make on Philip. Sure, he had a few pictures of his years on the CalPac crew scattered among all the books, but overall his room was Spartan. His parents had taught him not to express himself too fully and that no place was permanent.

But Philip said nothing, focused only on Stuart, and didn't that make him feel like a prince? He couldn't think of the last time a partner made him feel like that, and then he realized none of his partners ever had. They had always focused more on the act, and to be fair, so had he. But Philip? Philip had eyes only for him, rarely letting his glance leave Stuart's face, and even then, it was only to look him up and down in a way that made him feel desired.

"Can I undress you?" Philip said.

"Only if I can undress you," Stuart said.

"It's a deal," Philip said.

Stuart smiled. "One I think I got the better end of. I'm only wearing a T-shirt and shorts."

"But that only means I get you naked faster," Philip said.

                      CHRISTOPHER KOEHLER

Stuart blushed again.

"You're beautiful when you blush," Philip said. He toed off his shoes. "Why don't you go first?"

Philip had removed his tie before lunch, so Stuart started with his shirt, enjoying the smoothness of the high-end fabric beneath his fingers. He gently pulled it free of Philip's pants. Then, starting at the top, he unbuttoned it, one button at a time, enjoying the production of it. He pulled it down Philip's shoulders and struggled only briefly when pulling the rolled-up cuffs off his hands.

He took the opportunity to run his hands over Philip's chest atop the undershirt. He wanted Philip to feel the friction from the soft cotton. He wanted to feel the mystery of Philip's chest and abs before revealing them when he pulled the shirt off.

Based on the changes in Philip's breathing, Philip enjoyed it too. When Stuart's fingers danced around his nipples, there was a definite hitch in Philip's breath. "Looks like I'm not the only one who likes that," Stuart said.

"You're killing me," Philip said hoarsely.

Stuart grasped the hem of the undershirt and lifted, working it up Philip's chest. He put his face against the hard-soft surface, feeling the warmth, inhaling deeply of Philip's smell: faint traces of his cologne and something underneath it that could only be Philip himself, something that went right to his cock. He loved the feeling of a man's chest beneath him, the light dusting of Philip's blond chest hairs mingling with the red hairs of his stubble. The living, breathing man beneath his face brought him comfort, yet jacked him higher.

He pulled Philip's undershirt off, and yeah, Philip bent a little to help, but no one ever accused cox'ns of being tall. Then Stuart sank slowly to his knees, running his face down that wonderful chest again, stopping to flick his tongue over a nipple on the way by, smiling at Philip's gasp.

When he knelt before Philip, Stuart fanned his hands across his belly, then kissed his way down the treasure trail. "These pants are in the way. I'm going to have to do something about that."

He smiled when he thought he heard Philip mutter, "Finally."

Stuart took care of the belt and the fastening and then looked up to meet and hold Philip's brown eyes as he pulled the zipper down one tooth at a time, running his tongue over his lips the entire time.

"You're killing me, Stuart," Philip said again, his voice unsteady this time, and needier.

"Isn't that the point?" Stuart said as he pulled Philip's pants down. He could've drawn it out, but he wanted the main event beneath them, so he let them pool around Philip's ankles.

Philip's light gray boxer briefs fitted him like a second skin, covering his slender but muscular legs. Yet their tightness left nowhere for his erection to hide, and no way to disguise the wet spot left by his leaking cock.

Stuart grinned. "This is what I love to see."

This time, he licked his way down the treasure trail, pulling the waistband of the boxer briefs down to just above the pale, nearly colorless curls around Philip's cock as he shook beneath him.

Using hands and mouth, Stuart kneaded Philip through his underwear. "Stuart…," Philip whined above him, and Stuart took pity on him and pulled his cock free before tugging his underwear the rest of the way down.

Stuart stroked Philip's dick lazily, not really hard enough to give him the friction he wanted, but just enough to let Philip know he was there. Then he darted in and licked the mushroom tip. He definitely wanted to admire it for a while, but Philip had reached his limit.

"I want you naked *now*," Philip growled, kicking off his pants and underwear.

Philip pulled Stuart upright, keeping eye contact. His pupils were blown wide with lust, and his cock was pressed up between them. Philip ground into him. "Feels good, doesn't it?"

Stuart nodded. He couldn't say anything, because Philip was working his hands under his shirt, seeking out his nipples and—damn!—finding them.

"It's going to feel a whole lot better when I get your clothes off and get you on the bed and under me. I'll cover you with my body and make us both feel good. Have I read you right, Stuart? Do you like giving up control sometimes? Loud and dominant in the boat, but a very different man when the door's locked and the blinds are down?"

Stuart nodded. He tried to say something, anything, but only managed to whimper.

Philip smiled down at him. "I thought so. You want me to take control, don't you?"

Stuart nodded again, because he couldn't do anything else.

Philip scooped him up, putting him over his shoulder in a fireman's carry. The bed wasn't that far away, but it felt like it took forever to reach as Philip blinded him with desire.

Philip bit him through the fabric of his shorts. It didn't hurt, but it was hot. Philip worked his hand up one leg of the shorts to caress his ass. "You've got a great ass up there," Philip said. "I can't wait to see it."

Then Stuart was flipped off Philip's shoulders and set gently on the bed. He hadn't expected that, but as he was learning, Philip could be very tender.

Philip pulled his shirt the rest of the way off, trapping his arms, but before Stuart knew it, Philip had straddled him. Leaning in close, Philip whispered, "This is exactly where I want you. Under me, your arms helpless over your head. Is this okay?"

Stuart looked up hungrily and nodded.

"If it becomes not okay, tell me."

"Yes," Stuart rasped. He could barely speak, and if Philip didn't stop grinding against him this would be over far too quickly.

Still pinning Stuart's arms with one hand, Philip kissed him on the lips, gently at first, but Stuart would have none of that. He pulled Philip's lower lip, sucking hard. Philip rewarded him with a loud groan.

Philip pulled free and moved lower, kissing his way under Stuart's neck and down to his chest. "You are so hot," Philip breathed.

"I wish I could touch you," Stuart whispered.

Philip circled one of his nipples with his fingers, tracing a spiral path but never quite touching. Then Philip licked the nipple, drawing a low moan from Stuart. Philip bit it lightly, and he arched. Philip was killing him, but damn, what a way to go.

"If I let go of your hands, can I trust you to behave?" Philip asked.

Stuart nodded. This was what he needed and he hadn't even known how much. But he needed to touch, to explore, too.

Philip pulled Stuart's T-shirt off the rest of the way, and Stuart pushed up, reaching for Philip, running his hands down the older man's chest. "I love that you're fit but not over-built."

Philip took one of Stuart's hands and pulled it to his cheek for a caress, something he seemed to need a lot of. Stuart loved that sensuality, that physicality. He himself had always been so self-contained, but maybe he could open up a bit more with Philip.

Philip climbed off him, kneeling to one side. "You're still half dressed. What a horrible oversight."

Philip pulled Stuart's underwear off. "Next time, I promise to admire you in your briefs, because believe me, I've been thinking about them a lot, but for now? I need you naked."

Philip traced Stuart's treasure trail with his fingers, a thin line of red hairs extending from his navel before flaring right above the goods.

Suddenly, Stuart felt nervous. He was falling out of the mood, his throat dry. When he wore his shorts, they were just making out, but without them, they were going to do it, they were going to have the sex. He hoped his body measured up. He hoped he didn't disappoint. He laughed nervously. "I hope you don't have a thing for bears."

Philip smiled at him. "I've got a thing for you." Then he whistled. "Sweet Jesus, you're hung like a tiger, and next time, maybe you'll show me how you fuck like one, yeah?"

"I don't know how you keep doing it," Stuart whispered. His emotions ran so high at that moment, he needed to block something—anything—out, so he closed his eyes, because he wasn't about to end the touching.

"Do what?" Philip said, cupping Stuart's sac, gently playing with his balls.

"You make me feel like I'm the only person in the world who matters."

Philip leaned forward and kissed each eyelid so softly it felt like butterfly wings brushing him. "Maybe that's how I see you."

Stuart opened his eyes. "You're unreal, you know that?"

"Does this feel unreal?" Philip said, stroking Stuart's cock.

Stuart grinned. "Yeah, because life never feels this good." He took Philip's cock in hand, returning the favor. "See?"

"Hey, you told me you'd behave if I freed your hands," Philip said, closing his eyes.

"And you believed me? I told you, short and sneaky." This easy familiarity and the lightness of mood? Stuart knew he could get used to it if he weren't careful. Keeping it casual, because that's all he had time for this summer, right? But damn. This is what he'd been looking for all along.

Philip kissed Stuart again, and when he was done, Philip looked deep into his eyes. Stuart wanted to look away, but couldn't. Combined with Philip's exploring fingers, it was the most intense foreplay he'd ever experienced.

"I hope to hell you've got condoms and lube," Philip breathed.

Stuart nodded. "Nightstand, bottom drawer."

Philip leaned over and retrieve the supplies, and Stuart watched Philip glove up, mesmerized by the sight of the condom rolling down over that hunk of meat, knowing it was for him, knowing it was going in him.

"Lie back," Philip said, and Stuart did. Philip's lubed finger pushed slowly in and all Stuart could do was rise to meet it, curling his lower body up. Then one became two, and his breathing came quicker as Philip scissored back and forth.

Then Stuart's world lit up.

"I knew it was there somewhere."

Stuart gasped, and then there was lube and yet more lube and Philip whispering in his ear. "Are you ready?"

"Please." He closed his eyes and just felt.

Stuart put his legs on Philip's shoulders. There was some fumbling, but then Stuart felt the breach as Philip's cock nudged into him. He gasped at the stretch and burn.

"Are you okay?" Philip said.

"You're bigger than I thought."

"I'll pull out."

Stuart's eyes flew open. "Don't you dare. Just take it slowly."

Stuart willed himself to relax as Philip eased his way in. By the time Philip rested against him, Stuart was enjoying the slide and the feeling of fullness.

"Is this okay?" Philip whispered.

"Stop asking me that, and fuck me already," Stuart growled.

Philip grinned. "Remember, you asked for it."

Philip started out slowly, his thrusts shallow as Stuart ran his hands up and down Philip's chest, enjoying, encouraging, playing. Stuart teased Philip's nips, earning a smile as his own enjoyment built with each sweep over his prostate. He floated on a cloud of pleasure centered on his groin and the base of his spine, a feeling that grew more powerful as Philip went faster and faster, pistoning in and out. He'd certainly topped, but this was why Stuart loved bottoming. It was so much more intense for him.

His cock jumped each time Philip pushed into him, painting his belly with precum. He stroked himself lazily, keeping the fire burning at a certain level, pacing himself off Philip. When Philip's breathing grew jagged and his rhythm faltered, Stuart picked up his own pace and felt his climax brewing behind his eyes and down his spine as light and heat.

And then he was there, crying out as he exploded in pleasure, body and mind. Philip's own cries were on the distant edge of his consciousness, as everything receded into the red-hot life of the receding wave of his orgasm, and even that grew fuzzy as his awareness diminished, tunneling down to a circle of being centering on his eyes.

Stuart came back to himself to find Philip resting next to him on his side, stroking Stuart's hair off his forehead. Stuart felt amazingly relaxed and he leaned into Philip's touch.

"Do that often?" Philip asked.

Stuart looked up at him with a smile. "Do what?"

"Gray out like that."

"Is that what that was?" Stuart stretched. He tugged on Philip's arm until he lay down next to him and then burrowed under that arm until he was cozy. "No, I don't think I've done it before. Did it scare you?"

"It was mildly disconcerting, but I wasn't that frightened," Philip replied. He kissed Stuart's forehead. "You were still breathing, after all."

Stuart enjoyed cuddling. He just didn't get to do it much. He felt secure under Philip's arm like that, which he knew he'd have to think about later, because he hadn't been aware of feeling insecure. "I thought it was amazing."

"I thought I was going to lose it the minute I was in you."

"Yeah?" Stuart said. That was hot. He liked hearing that.

"Because it was you," Philip said. "Also, you seem to push a lot of my buttons."

"Me?" Stuart said. Usually when he pushed someone's buttons it was to irritate him….

Philip pulled Stuart on top of him and looked up into his face. "Oh yeah," Philip said reverently. "Turns out I've got a thing for hot little redheaded men." He paused, smiling wickedly. "Well, maybe I should say on the shorter side, because believe me, some things are definitely not little."

"I'm glad you qualified that, because for a moment, I thought you had a thing for leprechauns," Stuart said.

"You are most certainly not a leprechaun," Philip said testily. Stuart was actually taken aback. He almost sounded pissed. "Do people actually call you that?"

"Starting with your brother, yes. St. Patrick's Day is not one of my favorite holidays."

"I can see that," Philip said. He brushed his lips across Stuart's forehead again. Stuart decided that he couldn't get enough of that kind of casual affection. He certainly hadn't seen much growing up. Wait… older man? Affection? Did this mean he had daddy issues? If the sex was that mind-blowing, he realized he didn't care.

Then Stuart glanced up at Philip. "Philip… your hair. Despite hot, sweaty monkey sex, it's unscathed. Not a strand's out of place."

Philip waggled his eyebrows. "But of course."

"What do you put in it?" Stuart reached up to touch it, but Philip caught his hand. "What? I can't touch it?"

Philip only smiled and pulled Stuart closer. "Playtime's over. Now it's time for a nap."

"You know I'll figure it out eventually," Stuart said.

"But not today. Now hush. Some of us are trying to sleep."

CHAPTER
Ten

IT WAS early evening, an hour or two after Stuart had seen Philip off. He stretched and scratched his belly. He couldn't remember enjoying an afternoon like that in... huh. Forever? He found that sad, if not downright pathetic. His grades and study habits had gotten him a full ride to California Pacific, and they'd carried him into medical school, where he had every expectation they'd continue to serve him well. But at what cost? What had he closed himself off from? He knew part of the answer. Part of it was heartbreak from seeing all those hunky rowers look everywhere for love but the cox'n's seat. Watching his former roommate Morgan Estrada fall in love with their then-coach Nick Bedford had only been the latest link in a long chain of being ignored by guys he could easily fall for. But did that also mean he hadn't opened himself to something like that afternoon?

And what had the afternoon meant? It had started with a simple kiss, unthinking on Philip's part, although he had his doubts on that score. But that simple kiss had turned into a lot more kisses and then the hottest fucking he could remember. That plus long weeks of growing mutual interest suggested that the next logical step would be some sort of official declaration of purpose, but as Stuart was starting to realize, life didn't always follow the formulae and logic of science and math. And his heart? That could be an even bigger cipher.

No, he found the sciences much more familiar, if less urgent, territory. The irony of it all was that his plan for the evening had included studying for the medical school that hadn't even started yet. That was starting to feel kind of pitiful, but if he didn't study, what else was there? Sure, he'd e-mail Valerie, but he would've done that anyway. He decided to put off such annoying questions and their implications or thinking about what the afternoon might've meant by getting the mail now that the breezes were cooling the evening sky off.

He tossed things for Jonathan into a bin on the counter. Jonathan could separate what was important from the junk mail when he returned from England. Besides, his parents paid all his bills so Stuart doubted any of it mattered, but then, it was no longer his problem. No, what mattered to Stuart right then was the letter from the National Team, because damn, his life just got more complicated.

Then he checked the messages on his cell phone. Ugh. No fewer than three messages from various coaches for the National Team. In the blink of an eye he went from a well-fucked mellow to a nervous bundle of anxiety. At every step along the way, he'd never really considered the ultimate end—that it might work, that all the recordings and recommendations would get someone's attention at US Rowing. Now he faced a hell of a dilemma—crew or medical school—and all he could do was spin his wheels.

Morgan. He needed to talk to Morgan. Between his job and Morgan's graduate work, he rarely saw his bestie these days, but he was still Stuart's closest friend. When he got Morgan's voice mail, he all but growled his message. "Damn, Morgan. You study more than I do. Call me, I need to talk. This is your chance to prove it's not all about you."

He flipped through his address book for Morgan's landline, but when someone picked up, it wasn't Morgan.

"Oh hey, Nick, is Morgan around?" He still felt weird calling his former coach Nick. Despite the fact that CalPac was in their rearview mirror, he'd always be Coach Bedford to Stuart.

"Hi, Stuart," Nick said. "No, actually he's not. He's at the library. I'll tell him you called."

"That'd be great, thanks."

Stuart felt as much as heard Nick pause. "Are you okay, Stuart? You sound kind of freaked out."

"I heard from US Rowing, so… uh, yeah. Definitely freaked out."

Nick gasped. "And?"

"They want me to come down in August for seat racing for the Senior National Team." Thinking about that was making him sick to his stomach.

"Stuart, that's fantastic! Congratulations! Do you know what this means?" Nick all but yelled. Stuart held the phone away from his ear. "I knew you were under consideration, but they didn't tell me they'd invited you to compete. A crack at the Olympics, Stuart. I'm so proud of you."

"Thanks, Nick." If it was so fantastic, why did he feel like puking?

Nick chortled. "I always knew you were one of the best cox'ns I've ever seen, and it's not just me, you know. I've heard it from a lot of coaches, too."

"Yeah? Good to know," Stuart said, his mouth on autopilot. "Anyway, if you could have Morgan call me? I want to tell him myself."

"Sure, Stuart. I won't spoil your surprise."

Only after Stuart hung up did it occur to him that Nick was supposed to be in the Bay Area doing a clinical rotation for his degree in physical therapy. Maybe it was his "weekend" or something.

He knew a lot of men and women who'd jump at this opportunity. Some of them even deserved it. But really? This? He intended to start med school in two months. This was...ugh. Too much. He really needed to talk.

He'd never felt quite this alone before. Sure, he'd always been kind of a lone wolf with very few close friends and even fewer confidants. Now he was paying for it.

Stuart pulled up another name in his contacts and hit the call button. "Hi, it's me. Are you busy?"

STUART THREW his overnight bag in the back of Philip's Merc. "Thanks for coming to get me. I hope I'm not derailing your evening."

"You sounded like you were having a major meltdown," Philip said, "so of course I came to get you."

The truth was that right then, Philip knew he would've have done nearly anything for Stuart. He wasn't sure when he'd crossed that particular line. He realized he had absolutely no interest in seeing anyone else. He didn't know what his future held, but he refused to rule anything out. He glanced at Stuart, who sat with his arms crossed over his chest and radiated… what? Not anger, exactly, but something close enough. Confusion, perhaps, or profound irritation.

"Have you eaten?" he asked after a few minutes of letting Stuart simmer.

"What? Oh, no," Stuart said. "But you don't need to feed me, really."

Philip rolled his eyes. He should've known his beau would say something like that, if beaux they were. "Well, I haven't eaten yet, and it'd be kind of rude to eat in front of you."

That pulled a ghost of a smile from Stuart. "Oh, well then, yeah, I am kind of hungry."

"Why didn't you say so?" Philip said.

"I didn't want to impose any more than I already was," Stuart replied in a voice barely above a whisper.

That poor man…. Philip reached out and smoothed his thumb across Stuart's cheek, then rested his hand on his neck. In front of everyone else, Stuart acted so strong and forceful, but Philip was learning that was just a pose. "Stuart, spending time with you is not, nor do I ever see it being, an imposition. Got that?"

Stuart leaned into Philip's hand. "Okay."

They drove in silence the rest of the way home, although Philip had to pull his hand back. He could feel Stuart's tension coming back or getting worse as he pulled into his neighborhood. They weren't— quite—mansions, but the houses affected a certain grandeur that more than anything highlighted the differences between their respective material resources. He hoped this wasn't a mistake, and not for the first time, he wondered if he should sell and move somewhere less pretentious than his childhood home.

"Nice place," Stuart said once they were inside.

Philip shrugged. "It's where Brad and I grew up. Rather, what our father did to our childhood home over the years. I've had the worst of his excesses removed or softened, but the reality is this is way too much house for one person."

If Stuart had muttered, "Or ten" once they were inside, Philip pretended not to hear it. He riffled through the fridge and pantry to see what he could put together in a hurry. "Is a stir-fry all right? And do you eat tofu? I'm mostly an herbivore."

At Stuart's questioning look, he said, "I don't eat meat."

"You don't eat any meat at all?" Stuart said.

Philip grinned. "Just yours."

"You did not go there."

"I'm pretty sure I did."

Stuart looked like he was trying not to laugh, even biting his lip to keep it all in, but it was useless. He had to laugh, and Philip thought *Mission accomplished.* "I'll get to cooking. It won't take long. Feel free to wander around or stay right here and keep me company."

"I'm not sure I could find my way back to here," Stuart said.

"It's not that big," Philip said.

"My ass says differently, Philip."

Philip shook his head slowly. "I walked right into that one, didn't I?"

"Not yet, but maybe later," Stuart said.

Philip stared at Stuart through narrowed eyes, but he only pretended to be mildly annoyed at being outdone at double-entendres. In reality the return of Stuart's sparkle relieved him. "You're a bad man."

"And you like it like that," Stuart said.

"All too true, Stuart. There's some fizzy water in the fridge. Will you pick out a flavor?"

Philip finished slicing and dicing while Stuart poured them something to drink. They made chitchat while dinner cooked. It was moderately late by the time they finished eating, and that gave Philip an idea.

After cleaning up, he pulled some milk out of the fridge and, screwing up his courage, sniffed it. It passed. He put it to steaming in his espresso maker while he got two large mugs and some pulverized chocolate he kept for this very reason.

"What are you making?" Stuart said.

Philip smiled. "Hot cocoa the old-fashioned way."

"They made it with steamed milk back in the good old days?" Stuart said.

"Okay, maybe not," Philip said, "but this way's more fun and I don't risk burning milk down on the bottom of my pots."

When he'd made the hot chocolate, complete with handmade marshmallows, he grabbed both mugs. "Why don't you get your bag and follow me?"

"What're we doing?" Stuart asked.

"Since you seemed like you needed to talk earlier, we're going to go upstairs and drink hot chocolate and have a pajama party in my bed," Philip said, smiling tenderly at Stuart. "And if you feel like telling me what's bothering you, you can."

Philip knew the look Stuart gave him. It was the one that said "You're absurd."

"A pajama party? The two of us? In your bed?" Stuart said.

"I certainly wouldn't have any more people in my bed. What kind of man do you take me for?" Philip said loftily.

And then Stuart smiled, looking very vulnerable to Philip. "A very special one."

IF STUART had any preconceptions about Philip's bedroom, they failed to match the reality. "A canopy bed."

"Yep," Philip replied as he undressed in a closet bigger than Stuart's entire bedroom.

"Doesn't it get hot in the summer?"

"That, my friend, is why the curtains are silk sheers. When the weather cools off, I'll add heavier drapes," Philip said.

Stuart felt a twinge when Philip said "friend." He hoped he was more than that, but then, who had pajama parties with "friends" in his bed? Of course, there'd been plenty of indications that as conventional as the owner of Sundstrom Homes might appear in some ways, he definitely marched to the beat of his own, very different drummer. Given him another decade or two and Philip would be a rich eccentric, Stuart thought as he stripped down to his underwear. Philip, he noticed, slept only in a T-shirt and his own underwear. He'd been hoping for a harem costume or maybe silk pajamas.

"Can't argue with that. I guess," Stuart said. Eccentric he might be, but Philip was also charming, and Stuart realized how much he already liked the charming part. "So tell me how this pajama party of yours works?"

"We get ready for bed, make ourselves comfortable, and I make you feel as safe as I can. Then you tell me what's bothering you," Philip said. "If you want to. If not, we cuddle up and sleep."

"You did this a lot growing up?" Stuart asked.

"Only when I was younger and only when my mother was alive," Philip said, "and even then, it was groups of friends and piles of blankets and pillows and sleeping bags downstairs. This here? This is just for you."

"Oh." Stuart smiled.

Philip held one of the curtains back for him. "A word of advice. Put the hot chocolate on one of the nightstands, and then climb in. Otherwise we'll have wet sheets."

"Gotcha."

After they both climbed in, Philip closed the drapes. He pushed several pillows and bolsters to Stuart. "Feel free to arrange these as you want."

Stuart watched Philip make a sort of nest with them and then did the same. They were close enough to each other that he could reach out to Philip if he wanted, as well as reach his hot chocolate. He could see how this would make a very alluring retreat come winter.

Philip smoothed Stuart's bangs off his forehead. "So."

Stuart exhaled, trying to gather his scattered thoughts about crew and the National Team. "It's about crew."

Philip nodded. "Go on."

"It's always about crew, and that's a big part of the problem," Stuart said, sighing. "In a way, I guess, I've been trying to put the sport behind me, since surprisingly, some of the more painful moments of my life have come from crew." He thought for a moment. "But so have some of the best. Odd. Anyway, this sport has dominated my life since I was thirteen. I'm twenty-four."

"That's a long time," Philip said.

Stuart snorted. "No shit. I start med school at UC Davis in less than two months. I figured that was the end of it, even for Capital City Rowing Club. Then I got the mail today. Well, mail and voice mail."

"If this were a TV show, is that where the ominous music would play?" Philip asked, holding out his arms. Stuart didn't even think about it. He crawled over the pillows and curled into Philip's side, resting his head on his chest.

"Yes. The calls and letter were from US Rowing, specifically the National Team. They were sufficiently impressed with my recorded workouts and recommendations from coaches that they've invited me to a selection camp to compete against other cox'ns for a spot on the Senior National Team."

The Senior National Team. The big time for crew. The thought of that alone made him shiver.

"That sounds pretty important," Philip said, but Stuart could tell he didn't really get it. Of course, he hadn't explained it, either.

He looked up at Philip. "The Senior National Team is where the Olympic athletes are chosen from."

This time, Philip's mouth made an O-shape, but no sound came out. Stuart snorted. Yeah, now he understood it.

"It's not all the Olympics. Along the way it's other races like the world championships, but this is the pinnacle of the sport, the best of the best," Stuart continued.

Philip kissed the top of his head. More of that casual affection. He liked that. "That sounds like quite an honor," Philip said. "So what form does this competition with other cox'ns consist of?"

"Seat racing. They put us in boats and race us down a set course. Then they swap the cox'ns out and do it again, and again, as many times as necessary to see who can coax the best row out of the athletes," Stuart explained.

"That sounds intense."

"You have no idea. Cox'ns don't expend much in the way of physical energy. The more still we sit the better, and it really doesn't take much physical effort to keep a boat on course. But mental and emotional energy? Oh yeah."

Philip started stroking his hair, not quite petting him like a cat, but close. "So what do *you* get out of it?"

"That's an interesting question, isn't it?" Stuart replied. "There are two to three training sessions a day for the athletes and someone needs to drive the boat. So of those who pass muster at the selection camp, the coaches are going to pick the cox'ns who're there all the time. Go big, or go home, right?"

"Where is 'there,' exactly?"

"There're three selection camps. One's in Southern California, one's in Oklahoma, and one's at Princeton."

"And none of them is anywhere near the UC Davis Medical School," Philip said.

"Bingo," Stuart said. He shivered. Philip pulled the blankets up. It wasn't that kind of cold, but Stuart appreciated the gesture.

"So what do you want out of this?" Philip said.

"This is an amazing, probably once in a lifetime, opportunity. I mean, how often do you get a chance to reach for those rings? To get a chance to try to be the next Yaz Farooq? Or better yet, to train under her? She was an amazing Olympic cox'n, and she's now that voice you hear commenting on Olympic rowing."

Philip tipped Stuart's chin up to look in his eyes. "I didn't ask for the guidance counselor answer. I asked what *you* wanted."

Stuart sighed. "I thought I knew. I thought I wanted out of crew. I started coxing in middle school, and it's been a long slog since then. I've met some of the best people I've ever known through crew—and some of the worst. College rowing is over, I moved on to coxing the men's masters at Cap City Rowing. I'm starting med school. End of discussion. Only it's not."

"When do you have to give the National Team a decision?"

"A couple of weeks, I guess. I didn't pay it that much attention," Stuart said.

"Then try not to worry about it right now," Philip said, holding him closer. "For tonight, give yourself permission to set it aside."

"Easy for you to say," Stuart said, his voice muffled by Philip's chest. On the whole, he liked it there. He'd said his piece, and since Philip hadn't showered after picking him up, Stuart thought he smelled terrific, with hints of his doubtlessly high-end body wash and matching cologne, as well as sweat and man and *yum*.

Right about the time Stuart was debating with himself whether or not he should start something, Philip made the decision for him.

"You're kind of quiet. You doing all right?" Philip said.

Stuart thought for a moment. Philip held him closely and neither wore very much, and much to Stuart's surprise, he actually *could* put the decisions aside, thanks to the very distracting man holding him. "Yeah, I think so."

"Good." Philip scooted down until they were face to face. "Because I've been dying to do this."

Philip's kisses started out gentle and stayed that way for a whole twenty or thirty seconds before Stuart rolled on top of him. "Oh yeah?" Philip said.

Stuart smiled. "Yeah."

CHAPTER
Eleven

"SO ARE we good?" Brad asked hesitantly.

"We're good," Philip said. He resisted the urge to roll his eyes. They were good, but only because Drew was a busybody, and thank goodness for that. There'd been no end of "he said, he said" by Brad and Philip for Drew to wade through, and it had still taken a week or two of back and forth by the long-suffering Drew, who, being married to one stubborn Sundstrom, had some idea how to manage the other one.

So Philip and Brad met after work one afternoon on neutral ground, a neighborhood Starbucks. Drew had bowed out, saying, "I've done all I can. It's up to you two drama queens."

"I'm still sorry," Brad said.

Philip sighed. "Me, too."

"I don't know what you're sorry about. I'm the one who had a massive freak-out."

"I'm the one who ran and hid in the backyard and cried myself to sleep," Philip said. He still couldn't believe he'd had a total princess moment like that.

"Yeah, about that," Brad said. "Where'd you go? We couldn't find you anywhere."

Philip turned red. "I hid in the maze and then moved the gates so you couldn't get in."

Brad started laughing, loud enough that the people around them stared. "Seriously? That's awesome. If I had any doubts about your sexuality before, hearing that's taken care of them."

"Brad!"

Brad shrugged. "What? You're the one in corporate America who has to watch his tongue. I'm self-employed. I can be as offensive as I want."

"But do you have to prove it to me?" Philip said. He took a long pull on his blended coffee drink.

Brad made a face. "I thought you were a vegetarian."

"I am," Philip said, "but I'm not a vegan, so the whipped cream's all right."

"But aren't you supposed to be all into healthy eating and whatnot?" Brad said. "Because that stuff? It's a chemical shitstorm in a twenty-ounce cup."

"I have to have some fun. I don't drink, smoke, take drugs, or chase young men." Philip watched Brad closely. "Oh. Wait. Scratch that last one."

Brad's eyes bugged as he spat out his iced tea. "You did that on purpose!"

"Would I do that to my baby brother?" Philip said, a picture of perfect innocence.

Brad grabbed a bunch of napkins and started mopping up. "Yes."

"Then I guess I must've." Philip picked up a napkin and dabbed at Brad's face.

"Would you stop that?" Brad said, batting at Philip's hand. "You're a very bad man, you know that?"

"Well, I do try to set an example for you, after all," Philip said.

"Some example," Brad muttered. "So are you seeing anyone these days?"

Philip smiled at the thought of Stuart. He couldn't help it. He loved every moment he spent with Stuart, even if it was just holding him while Stuart tried to figure out what to do about the National Team versus med school.

Brad laughed. "Never mind. That answers the question. Have you done it yet?"

"A gentleman doesn't kiss and tell, you know," Philip said primly. He knew he was going to string Brad along for a while and then spring the identity of his new interest on him. Because he could.

"Which means yes," Brad said, cackling obscenely.

Philip sighed again. He did that around Brad a lot, he noticed, although four times out of five it was for effect only. "It means yes."

Brad looked like he was warming to the subject. "So. Man or woman."

"Does it matter?" Philip asked, sitting back in his chair. This was almost too easy. All he needed to do was wave the bait in front of Brad's face just a little longer....

"Aww, come on."

"All right. Man."

A crafty look stole over Brad's face. "See what I mean? Ass really is better than pussy."

"Oddly enough, that's exactly what Stuart Cochrane asked after we were done."

This time Brad sprayed his iced tea from his nose. "You bastard."

"That's what you get for saying things like that," Philip said. "Also, it's kind of an obnoxious thing to say, and that goes for both of you. Neither one's better. Men and women both have their different charms, that's all, and right now, I'm charmed by Stuart."

Brad started to chuckle, and before long, he progressed to a full-on belly laugh, holding his sides and biting his lip, Philip assumed to keep from screaming out loud. When the tears ran down Brad's cheeks, Philip knew he'd struck pay dirt.

When Brad finally calmed, he said, "I'm sorry, for a minute there, I thought you said Stuart Cochrane."

Philip smiled. "I did."

"Huh." Brad sat back. "I can't wait to hear this story."

So Philip obliged. He owed his brother that much, considering how much he'd teased him. "So one lunch led to a bunch of meals out, then me calling him when I needed to talk, and then him calling me when he needed someone to listen."

Brad smiled at him, a sweet, soft smile that Philip couldn't remember seeing before his brother had met Drew. "That's great, Philip." Then his smile gave way to a furrowed brow. "I'm probably out of line, and please don't stomp off, but I feel like I have to say this because I don't want you to get hurt or anything. Do you maybe need to give it some time? I mean, you just dumped the bitch. You don't have to make the switch right away, you know."

Philip was rocked back by that, both the language and the caution itself. "That's a rather crude way of putting it, Bradley."

Brad stared at him for a moment, his jaw hanging open. Then he started chuckling. "Crap, Philip. Don't do that. You sounded so much like Randall it's scary."

Philip tried to look contrite. "I'm sorry."

"No, you're not."

"Maybe a little," Philip said. "But I get your point. It's not something I was necessarily looking for, but it happened, and I want to see where it ends up." Then, softly, "I'm ready to settle down, Brad."

"I can see that, be careful is all I'm saying," Brad said. "I don't want to see you hurt. I also know Stuart seems tough as nails, but I've gotten the impression the last few years that maybe that's not the case."

Philip nodded. "No, you're right. He's already shown me that vulnerable side."

"I think he just got out of a relationship, too," Brad said. "Rowers gossip like you wouldn't believe. The texts started flying within hours, I'm sure. I've been out of school for a couple of years, and I still found out right away."

"He said something about ending a relationship recently, but then, I did, too," Philip said. "Do you think it means he's not ready for another one?"

"I wouldn't have thought you were, either," Brad pointed out.

Philip shrugged. "I only know one thing for sure, and that's I'd very much like Stuart around more."

"Friends with benefits?"

Philip felt Brad watching him closely. He knew people thought Brad could be nothing more than a loose cannon who shot first and aimed later, but that wasn't—or at least wasn't always—the case. His little brother didn't miss much. "No. That seems too disrespectful, and my feelings for him are already stronger than just friends."

"Aww, my big brother's in looooove," Brad sang.

Philip smiled around the straw as he finished his drink. "Maybe not yet, but probably soon."

"Just be careful, okay? Stuart's pretty intense, but he's not as strong as he seems. You, you're pretty chill, but underneath the surface you're probably one of the most cunning, even manipulative, people I know," Brad said. He held up his hand when Philip started to object. "Yes, you use your powers for good and not evil, but that doesn't change the fact that you've got them. Exhibit A? You now own SunHo. The point is, not only are you older, but you could go for what you want and easily make Stuart think it's the best possible thing ever."

Philip nodded. He hated when Brad was right, but what he said made sense, and even more, it resonated. "I hear you, and more to the point, I've listened."

Brad glanced at his watch. "Damn. Is it really that late?"

Philip looked at his iPhone. "It appears to be, yes."

"I have to get home. Drew's probably got dinner ready by now," Brad said.

Philip stood and hugged Brad. "Thanks for meeting me and for the pep talk."

"Any time," Brad said. "Oh, and a word of warning… Drew's been playing with a vegetarian cookbook, with mixed results. But he's probably going to invite you over for dinner soon."

"Can I bring Stuart?" Philips said, mostly to bust Brad's chops.

Brad grinned as he turned to leave. "I'll make sure your boyfriend's included."

"He's not my boyfriend!" Philip called to Brad's retreating back.

"Suuuuure he's not."

Philip sat at the table, watching Brad leave. Damn, his little brother was a strapping fellow, but being an outstanding physical specimen wasn't why people stared. Men and women looked at him as he passed because Brad radiated a certain something. Brad had found his groove, and it showed. That made Philip smile.

Just be careful, Brad said, meaning he should be careful not to take advantage of Stuart. But what about him? He hoped he wouldn't be taken advantage of, either. Chill and cunning or not, he had feelings too.

Philip sighed as he headed out. That was the trick, wasn't it? Putting yourself out there without being handed your still-beating heart in return.

PHILIP SAT before an array of file cartons. He'd found them in a small air-conditioned room in an attic above the garage, a room he hadn't known about until the last week or so. He owed its discovery to Stuart, who'd asked him what all the apparently not as faux as he'd thought windows above the garage were for.

"Are you sure those dormer windows are just for show?" Stuart had asked. "I'm pretty sure I see boxes or something in there."

They'd spent the next two hours trying to verify there was indeed a hidden room and then trying to get into it. They'd been successful, obviously, and now Philip tried to decide whether or not to use the results.

"You know what these are?" Philip had said to Stuart. "These are Randall's dirty files, or some of them."

"Dirty files?"

"Secret files on his high-level employees. Anything that could be used against anyone who might be in a position to threaten him," Philip had explained. "I had no idea he was this paranoid, but he's got all kinds of shit on them. Who's got debt, having affairs, children out of wedlock, you name it. I can't imagine how much he spent on private investigators."

Stuart had looked troubled. "I wonder if those PIs are still toiling away, waiting to report in."

Philip had tucked that notion away. He had no idea how he'd track those people down, unless he found some indication in the files.

Philip left many of the files undisturbed because they related to people who no longer worked for SunHo for one reason or another. Once he sorted things out with the board, he'd look into shredding the old files. There was no reason to keep them.

For that matter, he needed to decide whether or not he'd even read, let alone use, Randall's files on the current board both Sundstrom men had to contend with. His few cursory glances that let him know he had the current board's dossiers made him feel like he was swimming in a septic tank. Actually using the information? That would make him no better than Randall, and in both his personal and professional lives, Philip used Randall as an example of what *not* to do. Part of him thought that it would be better to lose it all than keep it by dirty means. He'd always seen himself as a pragmatist, maybe even something of a realpolitiker, and not at all an idealist, but face to face with some potentially quite damning information, he wasn't so sure.

Philip stood up. He told himself he wanted a glass of fizzy water, that his back and forth wasn't really pacing. Okay, not using Randall's dirty files was one option, but what happened if he fell? He and Stuart had worked out some worst-case scenarios and how Philip might respond. He supposed there were worse things than living the life of the idle rich, but probably not for him, an avowed workaholic. He ruefully admitted that without SunHo, he'd lose his grip within weeks.

None of that acknowledged the large number of good people who worked for Sundstrom Homes. Sure, there were some complete jackholes on the higher levels, but Philip also knew there were many, many people who didn't deserve to have their lives and livelihoods disrupted by the antics of ambitious C-level officers and those immediately below them. Those people, middle managers and extending all the way down to people who built the homes, stood to suffer if Winch succeeded in ousting him. Randall had perforce protected them because he knew they were cogs in the SunHo money-making machine. Philip knew he was no knight in shining armor, but he and they both stood to suffer if he didn't clean house.

With that in mind, he dove into the files, starting with Winch's. "You've been a very naughty boy, haven't you? Very naughty indeed."

CHAPTER
Twelve

"IT'S GREAT that you're around more evenings and weekends," Philip said, one hand on Stuart's knee as they drove.

Stuart shrugged. "Changes in the schedule. It happens. Since I'm not in school, it doesn't matter. Why not leave the afternoons and evenings for those who're taking classes? Honestly, they should've done it a while ago."

As the summer headed from warm to blistering—as summers in Sacramento were wont to do—Philip and Stuart spent more and more time together. Philip seemed to think it the most natural thing in the world, but in reality, Stuart had changed his hours at Food Faire, even though he had only another six weeks before he started medical school, give or take a few days. Not that he was nervous about that or anything. But he wanted to work more or less the same schedule as Philip.

"So what's this surprise you've got planned for us?" Stuart asked. "We're in the car. I think you can let the cat out of the bag now."

Philip smiled. "I guess so. I saw a flier for an open-air production of *A Midsummer Night's Dream* and thought, why not? We're both sick of reruns, and the movies this summer suck."

"Yeah, but outside? How's that going to work outside?" Personally, Stuart didn't see that working too well. At the very least, wouldn't the great outdoors swallow the actors' voices?

"Very well, I should think, given all the faeries and whatnot. It's been a while since I've seen the play," Philip said.

Stuart frowned. "Won't we get cold?"

"That's what the windbreakers are for." Philip gestured behind him with his chin. "Them, and the blankets in the trunk."

Stuart's phone chirped, cutting off any more objections. "It's my sister. I need to answer this text."

"Sure," Philip said, even as Stuart did so.

V: Hey Big Brother! How R U?

S: Not bad. On a date with Philip.

V: Oooh, the boyfriend. Must B serious.

*S: Not actually sure. It *feels* committed.*

V: What does that mean?

S: It means I'm not looking for a long-term commitment, but last weekend when we were out dancing and some guy was checking me out? I swear 2 God, Philip growled at him.

V: LOL! You've got 2 be kidding.

S: And he's completely missed guys flirting with him.

V: How'd he miss that?

*S: *blushing!* He was talking 2 me.*

V: Aww, my big brother's in lurv :-)

S: Maybe.

Philip looked over at him and smiled. "You two are busy."

"Yeah, Valerie has to sneak around to communicate with me."

Philip made a face. "Do I want to know why?"

"Because our parents have forbidden her to talk with the sodomite son they pretend doesn't exist." Stuart's phone chirped again.

"That's grotesque," Philip said.

V: Still there?

S: Yep, explaining to the BF why you have 2 sneak 2 talk 2 me.

V: What'd he say?

S: He called it grotesque.

V: Tru fact. H8ers.

S: R parents R white trash aren't they?

V: This isn't news.

S: They exposed us 2 nothing U could call culture, right?

V: No way in hell.

S: Literally.

V: What's brought this up?

S: We're going 2 The Theater and feel like I should dress up. 2 bad I really have no good clothes. Philip says shorts R fine. He's wearing them 2. I bet it's just 2 make me feel better.

V: Even if true, he's sweet 2 do it.

S: Yeah, I guess. Ever feel like R parents have crippled us?

V: You mean like the theater's sinful unless it's a morality play? Hate to break it to them, but a lot of Shakespeare is morality plays.

S: How'd you know?

V: My friend Cynthia's parents R trying 2 civilize me and thank God for them. So what R you seeing/doing?

Stuart knew it was a legacy from their lowbrow parents, who really didn't have much culture at all and so tended to think any expression of it was "high fallutin'," as opposed to Philip who was clearly conversant with it and moved with ease among its many expressions. It still made him feel like the prole he was, a prole dating a slumming prince.

How to answer Valerie's questions about what they were doing? "Valerie wants to know what we're doing tonight."

"So tell her," Philip said.

Stuart sighed. He didn't want to admit to Philip that he hadn't understood what they were doing, but it looked like he might have to.

"Something about theater outside…," Stuart said apologetically.

S: Hang on, Philip's being complicated.

"Call her. I've programmed the car to recognize your phone," Philip said.

"Huh?"

Philip smiled. "Trust me. Call her."

Stuart had no idea what to expect, which was why he almost jumped out of his skin when he start calling Valerie and the touch tones from his phone came over the car's sound system. "The fuck?"

"I told you," Philip said, laughing. "The car recognizes your phone. Think of it as a huge Bluetooth device. Enter the phone number and press dial. Then speak normally."

Stuart shook his head. Rich people and their toys. He did as Philip told him to do, and sure enough, he heard Valerie's phone ring through the fancy sound system.

"Hello?" Valerie said.

"Hi, Little Sister. Philip didn't feel like explaining what we were doing to me again, so here he is."

"What?" she laughed.

"Hi, Valerie, I'm Philip Sundstrom," Philip said. "It's a pleasure to meet you. Stuart talks about you a lot."

"It's all lies, I swear," Valerie said. "Wait… how can you both be talking?"

"My car's got built-in Bluetooth," Philip said.

"Cool!" Valerie said.

Stuart couldn't believe it. His sister and his… whatever they were, chattering away like old friends.

"We're going to a play. It's performed outside," Philip said.

"Oh, like Shakespeare in the park?" Valerie said.

"Exactly!" Philip said. "And it's even a Shakespeare play. I can't think why Stuart keeps forgetting that."

Stuart gave him the stink eye. "Because I'm a science geek. I only took the humanities classes I needed to in order to graduate."

"And because our parents tried their best to raise us as ignorant freaks," Valerie muttered.

Philip glanced over at Stuart. "He seems to have done all right for himself."

"It's an act. You should've seen me when I first arrived at CalPac. I stuck out like you wouldn't believe." Stuart sighed. "I didn't get most pop culture references, I hadn't seen most of the movies or TV shows people talked about, things like that. I had no idea what to wear, and I still don't. Shorts? For the theater?"

"Shakespeare outside?" Valerie said. "You're fine, Big Brother, you really are."

Philip looked at him, and Stuart thought his eyes were bright, like he was trying not to tear up. "It's a college town in the summer. For that matter, people wear Birkenstocks to the symphony during the season in Sacramento. Trust me, I wouldn't let you go someplace if I thought you'd be underdressed," Philip said, "especially now."

"Thanks," Stuart said, his voice thick.

"Awww, that's so sweet," Valerie said. "You two are so into each other. But seriously, if I don't get off the phone right now, I'll end up in a diabetic coma. Philip, nice to meet you, and Stuart? If you let him get away, you're a moron."

The call ended, and Stuart looked at Philip. "So that was Valerie."

"She seems like a good kid," Philip said as they exited the freeway at Davis.

Stuart smiled, but it faded quickly. "She is. I've about got her convinced to move out here and then work on declaring herself an emancipated minor. All that religious garbage our parents heap on her has to count as emotional abuse."

"I… uh, don't know anything about emancipated minors, but if it would help, I've got an attorney. He's the one I use when I don't want the corporate sharks SunHo employs to know what I'm up to…," Philip said.

Stuart looked at him, suddenly so grateful this man was in his life. He couldn't remotely imagine affording a lawyer that Philip would keep on retainer, but the thought that Philip wanted to help meant the world to him right then. And the way Philip had started speaking to Valerie like he'd known her for years? That was the awesome. That was the closest he'd ever come to his boyfriend meeting his family, until or unless Valerie fled like he had.

The whole conversation gave him a warm fuzzy if Stuart thought about it. He and Philip did so many things as a couple and he loved every minute of it, even if they weren't necessarily a "couple." He knew if he asked Philip, he'd say they were, but in his own mind, he couldn't yet answer that question. Neither of them ever said anything to make it official, and Stuart had only clues to go on, like that time when they were dancing and Philip growled. Stuart liked the growling. That went right to his heart. It said, "Look all you want boys, but my buttoned-down preppie boyfriend will literally bite your head off if you get too close." The only problem was, he didn't know if he was ready for the "boyfriend" part. What did being a couple mean, anyway, and why did the idea freak him out sometimes?

STUART WOKE up alone the next morning, but he knew exactly where he was. He snuggled deeper under Philip's down comforter. It was thick and warm and perfect for going back to sleep. After all those years in crew, plus working on top of that, sleeping in was a novel treat. Since he'd changed his schedule to free up the oddball hours for other people, he was coming to love sleeping in and intended to take full advantage of it. Maybe he'd never drag his sorry ass back to Cap City Rowing again....

Happily drowsing in a pleasant state somewhere between full sleep and full consciousness, he drifted in that timeless place until something roused him. A smell. He pulled the duvet back only as far as necessary to reveal his nose. He smelled... breakfasty smells. Something involving flour, as well as bacon, and was that maple syrup? He ducked back under the covers, torn by a newfound awareness of hunger and the stubborn desire not to budge from his warm sanctuary until he absolutely had to.

His stomach won.

"Damn you for being so considerate," Stuart grumbled, throwing back the covers. He blinked several times and pulled on a pair of sweatpants and a T-shirt before allowing the heady aromas to coax him downstairs.

Philip looked up and smiled when Stuart walked into the kitchen. "Morning, sleepyhead."

"Morning." Stuart made no attempt to stifle another yawn. "What's all this?"

"Breakfast." Philip smiled. "I didn't know what you liked, so I made blueberry and regular pancakes. I even made you bacon, but don't get used to it. Cooking it was almost more than I could handle." He shuddered. "Seriously, how can people eat that?"

Stuart grinned. "Like this."

He grabbed a piece off the plate and munched happily away. "Hmmm, crispy meat, tender fat."

Philip looked at him, lips pressed into a thin line. "I'm not kissing you until you brush your teeth, just so you know that."

"Awww, I'm sorry," Stuart said, but he only pretended to pout. Philip had always been so easygoing, so subdued about not eating meat, he sometimes forgot that left to his own devices, Philip only occasionally used animal products. The eggs, the butter, and especially the bacon? That was for him. Maybe he should act grateful instead of trying to gross Philip out. "Seriously, Philip, this is amazing. Thank you."

"You're welcome," Philip said. "There's orange juice and maple syrup, too."

Philip pushed a plate at him, followed by the butter and syrup. Stuart took it all in, and all he could think was that Philip was going to make someone an amazing husband someday. Would he be the one? Unused to emotions that raw, that naked, he tried to cover them by smothering his pancakes. "Real maple syrup? I'm not sure I've ever had it."

"You're gay, Stuart. The real deal is your birthright," Philip said.

"Gay people only eat pure maple syrup?"

Philip rolled his eyes. "Accept no substitutes, that's all I'm saying. There are quality things at all price points, and a budget is no excuse for tolerating crap."

"What brought that on?" Stuart said around a mouth full of light and fluffy pancakes dripping butter and the best syrup he'd ever tasted.

Philip shrugged. "The people I saw at the store at six this morning when I went to buy the ingredients I needed for breakfast. What a freak show."

"But wouldn't that include you? I mean, you were there, too."

"Yeah, probably," Philip said, "but at least I bothered to throw on some jeans and a sweatshirt. Some of those people? No. Just… no."

Philip shuddered, and Stuart had the feeling it wasn't for effect. He didn't know Philip could be this much of a queen, but he realized he liked it. It made him a little more human. Philip could come across as a bit too buttoned-down and perfect, always there when Stuart needed him, always cool and collected and perfectly matched. The fact that he was freaking out about people wearing ratty pajamas to the grocery store early in the morning brought him back down to earth. "Don't worry, I'll protect you from the poors."

"But who's going to protect me from you? That's what I want to know," Philip said.

"Me? I'm harmless," Stuart said. He made his eyes as big as he could.

"Awww, jeez, don't do that," Philip said. "That's so creepy. Besides, short and sneaky, remember?"

"Fine, throw my words back in my face, just keep feeding me like this," Stuart said. "These are really good."

Philip blushed. "Thanks. I like cooking for people."

"And I like to eat, so it's perfect," Stuart said. "Not only that, now I can."

He sighed in contentment and took another bite of Philip's heavenly pancakes after he made sure they were dripping syrup.

"Am I to assume that you didn't eat before, despite evidence to the contrary every time we had lunch or dinner together?" Philip said.

Stuart made a face. "When I coxed for CalPac I had to watch my weight. By the end, Coach Bedford made me weigh in weekly during racing season."

"You're kidding," Philip said flatly. He made a show of checking Stuart out. "You're quite slender and very well proportioned, if I may say so."

"It's possible that you're biased, but there's a push throughout crew to keep cox'ns as light as possible. Despite our contributions—hello? we're the only ones who can see where we're going—we don't actually provide any force to move the boat. We're dead weight. So coaches and rowers want us to weigh as little as possible," Stuart said. He ate more pancake. Because he could.

"So during the season you...."

"Lived on moss, twigs, and steam," Stuart said. "It sucked, and if I were to compete for a spot on the National Team, let alone earn one, I'd be looking at more pressure to be skinnier than I've ever been as an adult."

"So you'd be signing up for an eating disorder? That's horrible." Philip pushed his plate away. "Look, I realize I don't get a vote here, but if you want my opinion—and since you brought it up, I'm going to pretend you do—that can't possibly be healthy and I really don't think you should try out, if only for that reason alone."

When Stuart felt only gratitude at Philip's words, he knew he had his answer to the question about whether or not he should try out. It was such a relief to hear someone else vocalize what he'd been thinking, even if Philip's reasons were different than his. Truth be told, he'd never considered the eating disorder angle. He had no idea how other cox'ns handled that aspect of making weight, but now that he thought about it, it only stood to reason that some developed problems. Food was a complicated subject.

"Do you mind talking it out?" Stuart asked hesitantly. "I feel like I keep hijacking our time together with the same tired subject."

"No worse than me and the nonsense at SunHo. If it's weighing on your mind, go ahead and get it out."

Stuart made a face. "I'm so sick of thinking about this subject. I want it behind me, but I'm getting a lot of pressure from my old coach—"

"This is the Nick Bedford I keep hearing about?" Philip said.

"Yeah, but it's not just him. It's his partner Morgan, who's one of my closest friends. I really thought Morgan knew me better than that, but I guess he's blinded by the possibilities of the National Team." Stuart sighed. "Or maybe he never realized how much crew weighed me down. Our deep heart-to-heart conversations were usually about him and his crush on Nick, and we haven't lived together for a while."

"Okay, so your old coach wants this for you. That makes sense, if only because from what you told me, he's done a fair amount of work to get you this chance," Philip said, "but what do *you* want?"

"It's a great opportunity to do something most people only dream of—"

Philip shook his head. "That's not what I asked you. What do *you* want to do? Where do *you* want to be this fall?"

Stuart didn't say anything for a few moments, only swirling a piece of bacon through a puddle of cooling maple syrup. "I want to be in school. I'm not sure what that means for us, though."

"We'll sort that out later," Philip said, sighing. "But it sounds to me like you've got your answer. It may not be your coach's answer, and it may not be your best friend's answer, but it's *your* answer, and if they're really your friends, they need to respect that. Any disappointment they might feel is their own problem and for them to process without bothering you."

"But—"

"No buts. Well, maybe one butt," Philip said. "There's one butt I can't get enough of."

"What about your butt? Maybe I want to explore it this morning," Stuart asked.

Philip leaned back and stretched, and sure enough, it pulled his T-shirt up over his abs, enough to tease Stuart, and oh yeah he looked. How could he not, with that treasure trail leading to parts he knew very well? "Well, now. That's an interesting proposition. Maybe we should discuss it further."

Stuart couldn't believe he was about to reward Philip for that bad joke with sex, but he was horny, dammit. Or grateful that Philip, at least, took his concerns about the situation with crew seriously enough to listen. None of his other friends had heard what he wanted, they only heard some fantasy of the sport. Except Philip. Of everyone he'd talked to, only Philip hadn't responded with some bullshit about how good he was and how it'd be a shame to waste that talent. Instead, Philip responded with a question that got to the heart of the matter—where did he, Stuart, see himself that fall? The sad fact of the matter was that he'd come to resent crew, at least on the competitive level, so taking it to the highest levels of competition? That'd just be stupid. Only Philip understood that. *That* was why he was about to reward Philip with sex.

Stuart slid off the barstool. "So I haven't brushed my teeth yet. Think you can bring yourself to kiss me?"

Philip got up close and personal, wrapping his arms around Stuart's waist. "I think I can manage that, Bacon Breath," he said right before he captured Stuart's lips.

Stuart enjoyed the kissing. They weren't in a hurry. Sure, sex was in the offing, but they'd get there. Right then, Stuart reveled in the feel of Philip's full lips sliding over his own. He pulled Philip's lower lip in, biting and sucking. Philip's moans made it all the hotter.

Philip snaked a hand down Stuart's front. "Mmmm, I think I like you in sleep pants. You should wear those all the time."

They certainly left little to the imagination, especially Stuart's erection. "I thought you didn't like people wearing their sleep clothes out of the house?"

"You I'd make an exception for," Philip said, palming Stuart's cock through the thin fabric. "On second thought, maybe you shouldn't. People would see what you're packing, and we can't have that."

"We can't, huh?" Stuart said. He took the opportunity to unzip Philip's usual skinny jeans. "Philip, you've got to quit wearing these things. You're going to injure yourself one of these days. Or worse, people will see what *you're* packing."

"You don't share well, do you?" Philip said.

"What do you think?" Stuart kissed Philip again, this time hard and wanting.

Philip reached into Stuart's sleep pants and liberated his cock. "Hmmm, loves me some ginger cock."

Yeah, it was cheesy, but teased relentlessly well into adulthood for his fiery red hair, Stuart couldn't hear it enough from a man who thought it was a bonus feature. "Yeah? Well, it's gonna be in you soon."

Philip whimpered at that.

"Oh, you like that? It'll be in you, stretching that hole of yours."

"Yes," Philip breathed as Stuart jacked him. "You'll be the first."

Then Stuart realized something. "You've never been fucked by a guy?"

"No, toys only," Philip said.

"Not the same." Stuart left off stroking Philip's cock for a moment and reached around him to run his hands down Philip's ass. The thought of being Philip's first turned him on like crazy.

"I'm glad it'll be you," Philip whispered. He started thrusting against Stuart.

Stuart slid his fingers down Philip's cleft, avoiding the puckered opening. "That what you want?"

"You know I do," Philip said hoarsely. He reached for Stuart's cock, but Stuart danced out of reach.

"Nuh-uh, I'm going to make this about you," Stuart said. "Upstairs?"

Philip shook his head. "There're supplies in the side table in the family room, and the sofa's plenty wide for what we've got in mind."

"But the leather—"

"Is surprisingly easy to clean up," Philip said.

"Then what're we waiting for?" Stuart grabbed a couple of kitchen towels from the counter.

Philip led the way, taking short steps because he hadn't bothered to pull his jeans up.

Confronted with that shapely ass, Stuart smacked it, not hard enough to hurt, but hard enough to get Philip's attention. Philip gasped. "Oh God."

"I think someone likes that," Stuart would never have guessed that about his buttoned-down preppie, but weren't they always the ones?

Stuart tugged Philip's pants down while Philip pulled his hoodie and T-shirt off. Philip stepped out of his jeans and briefs to stand naked before him. He marveled at Philip's ease in his own skin. He knew he wasn't half so comfortable undressed in front of people, even people he was supposedly intimate with.

"You like what you see?" Philip's eyes held a hint of challenge. Stuart was sure it wasn't a coincidence that one of Philip's hands strayed to a nipple.

Stuart growled and grabbed Philip, who laughed and went willingly. Stuart circled the nipple slowly with his tongue, eliciting a low moan from Philip. Then he nipped it and Philip yelped, but Philip scarcely had time to react before Stuart smoothed the sting away with his tongue. "That answer your question?" Stuart said.

"I don't know," Philip said, breathing in shallow gasps. "I think you might need to do that again. I'm still a little un—aaaaah!"

Stuart knew what he had to do. He needed to reduce Philip to a moaning puddle of man, and Philip had just told him how. He'd play along for a while, but he had plans of his own for Philip.

Stuart slowly jacked Philip's cock as he worked the taller man's nips, not too hard, not too firmly, barely enough sensation to let him know someone was touching him. When he felt Philip swaying, he figured it was time to move on to what he wanted. Besides, Philip was leaking fairly heavily. Stuart had a lot more planned, and he didn't want Philip going off too soon.

He guided Philip the rest of the way to the broad leather sofa and then pushed him down. Philip took the hint and assumed the position, kneeling on the sofa's cushions with his hands gripping the back of the sofa. Yeah, Philip looked a little nervous, but the way his ass was jutted out and waiting for Stuart's ministrations? Philip was into it, and Stuart intended to give that ass his undivided attention.

Stuart leaned over Philip, rubbing his back. "You ready, babe?" he whispered in Philip's ear. He nibbled on the earlobe, probing with his tongue, sending a ripple down Philip's spine.

"Yes." It sounded like a whine.

Stuart got right behind Philip, his own cock, hard and leaking, lined up perfectly with Philip's hole. It rushed right to his head, leaving him dizzy. He had to lean against Philip for a few moments to catch his breath. "Damn, you make me crazy."

"Yeah?" Philip said over his shoulder.

Stuart shook his head to clear it. "You have no idea."

He thrust against Philip a few times. He couldn't help it. Then he had to pull away, reminding himself this was for Philip, and Philip seemed to like Stuart's hand on his ass.

He caressed Philip's firm and frankly gorgeous ass. It was beautiful, and exploring it with his hands and eyes was treat enough, but he knew Philip wanted more.

Stuart gave it a light slap, more sound than sensation, but Philip moaned anyway. Stuart pulled him up, holding Philip's back to his front. "This what you want? How you want it?"

"Uh-huh," Philip breathed. He guided one of Stuart's hands down to his cock. "Feel that?"

"Damn. I had no idea this would turn your crank so hard," Stuart said.

"I… I'm not sure I did, either," Philip whispered.

Stuart held Philip tightly, resting his head on Philip's muscular shoulder as if to say: *You're safe with me. Thank you for trusting me, and I will never violate that trust.* Still holding tightly to him, Stuart kissed Philip and then guided him back down.

Stuart smacked that beautiful ass, nothing too heavy, only light slaps at first until he saw how Philip reacted. Stuart himself talked a good line, and he wanted to make his man fly, but he was as new to this as Philip and didn't want to hurt him. He only hoped Philip could sit down later.

"Shit!" Philip swore. "I know you can go harder than that."

So Stuart spanked him again, hard enough to make Philip's cheeks go from pink to bright red.

"Oh yeah," Philip gasped as he reached down to stroke himself.

The spanking itself did nothing for Stuart, but Philip's reaction to it was hot. He had no idea how far to take it, however, and his hands were beginning to hurt. "Where's the lube?"

"Chest of drawers on this end of the sofa, bottom drawer," Philip said. He rose up on his knees and reached one hand back to maintain contact with Stuart.

Stuart's hand slid down Philip's leg while he reached for the rubbers and lube in the end table. He didn't know why it was important not to lose contact with Philip, but suddenly it was.

Then he was back, supplies in hand. He set them beside Philip on the sofa and then pulled Philip to him again. He loved the closeness he felt this way as he let one hand range across Philip's chest from cock to pecs and back again. He loved feeling his own cock sliding down Philip's ass. "You ready?" he murmured.

"Yes," Philip replied. "But go easy on my cock when you're fucking me. I'm pretty close."

"Noted," Stuart said as he squirted lube in his hand, warming it for a few moments. Then he put one slick finger against Philip's red pucker, slowly circling it as Philip's breathing changed.

As Stuart loaded up his finger again, he realized that while it might be Philip's first time with a cock in his ass, he had said something about toys. Right. He didn't need to go super slow. This time he eased one finger inside. "This okay?"

Philip nodded. "Uh-huh. I'm hoping there'll be more soon."

"Topping from below, are we?" Stuart rewarded him with another smack to his ass, a light one.

"Aww, jeez." Philip gasped as his head fell forward between his arms on the sofa's back.

Stuart quirked a smile and filed that one away. More lube and more fingers, this time he sought and found Philip's prostate, gently stroking it.

Philip groaned. "What're you doing?"

"Playing with your prostate." Stuart smirked even though Philip couldn't see it. "This here joy buzzer is the goal of those toys you or someone else put up here."

"No shit. Wow," Philip said.

"You like that?"

"You know it."

Stuart grinned an evil little grin and then spanked Philip again, setting up a rhythm of moderate blows that, combined with the prostate play, ought to send his man over the moon. "Still like that?"

Philip didn't say anything. He couldn't. He seemed to be too blissed out, and Stuart recognized that as his cue.

A little drop of lube in the condom to increase the feeling, a whole lot of lube in Philip and on the condom, and Stuart positioned himself right at Philip's entrance. He pushed in a little way, then paused, giving Philip a chance to adjust. "Breathe," he said softly. "Exhale and push against me. Sometimes that helps."

Stuart waited until he felt Philip relax around him and then pushed in a little more, stopping when Philip tightened again. "Breathe, baby."

Philip relaxed again, but this time as Stuart started pushing in Philip started pushing back, slowly fucking himself on Stuart. They met somewhere in the middle, and Stuart found himself balls deep in Philip's body, and it was all he could do not to cry out.

Stuart found the sofa to be at an almost ideal level, one that evened out the differences between their heights. "Spread your knees a little."

Philip complied and then Stuart was home free. He moved slowly at first, even though his body howled at him to move like a piston, in and out and in and out and slam slam slam, over and over again into Philip.

He forced himself to take it easy, to take long, gentle strokes that were slowly driving him crazy. *Philip*, he reminded himself. It's about Philip, but damn that man was tight, and the temptation, no, the need to let himself go and ride Philip like a pony until they were both sated and exhausted threatened to take over with each stroke.

"This... jeez, you're amazing," Philip breathed. "You're killing me, though."

"Not really... not yet," Stuart said.

"Then what're you waiting for?"

Stuart didn't need to be told twice. His hips snapped and Philip grunted. "Too much?"

"Do it."

Stuart let go. There was no technique, only pounding, and both men worked it. Stuart held Philip's hips so tightly he knew he'd leave bruises, but he didn't want to let up. Maybe he couldn't. Philip braced himself on the back of the sofa with a white-knuckle grip, the better to push back against Stuart's thrusts.

"C'mon, harder!" Philip cried.

Stuart grabbed Philip's shoulders and pulled him up. Yeah, he was pounding Philip's ass, but Philip had to hold him, too. Thrusting was awkward, but so worth it to hold Philip across the chest, jacking him with one hand and tweaking a nipple with the other.

"Stuart! I'm gonna—" Philip cried.

Stuart felt Philip's ass contract around him as Philip's cock, as hard as it had ever been, jumped in Stuart's hand and shot creamy ropes of jism onto the back of the sofa.

As Philip shuddered out the last of his climax and fell forward onto his forearms, Stuart neared the edge. Seeing Philip get off was amazing, the sight of his cum hitting the leather, the pungent smell reaching his nose. Mansex, his man and their sex, and he was there. "Philip!"

Stuart collapsed onto Philip's back. As lightning ripped up his spine to explode in his brain, he couldn't have remembered his own name, but he knew Philip's. Stuart rested one cheek against his back, coming down as intense waves of pleasure that bordered on pain diminished into something bearable. "Philip… that was…."

"Yeah," Philip said.

Stuart held onto Philip; his emotions were too raw to speak, his feelings too vast for him to contain. He knew he'd burst if he let anything escape.

Then he was rolling and falling, but still on Philip as the taller man fell to one side, pulling Stuart on top of him. Philip grabbed a fleece throw from the floor and covered Stuart before holding him.

"Hmmm, this is nice," Stuart mumbled.

"I just realized I didn't do a damn thing for you," Philip said. "I'm sorry I was so selfish."

"Oh yes you did. Each and every reaction made me quiver. You were so genuine, so open, so hot to see when you lost it," Stuart said. "Besides, I said this was for you."

"Then I want to keep holding you," Philip said.

"Works for me," Stuart said, content to drift in his post-orgasm haze.

Stuart returned to awareness with Philip's fingers in his hair. "Did I fall asleep?"

"You might've dozed off," Philip said. "I think I did, too."

"You wore me out," Stuart said. He pulled himself up Philip's chest so his face was even with Philip's. Stuart needed to kiss him. They kissed lazily for a few moments. Then he was struck by a thought.

"You know, it seems kind of funny to be fucking around in what was once Brad's family room, doesn't it?"

Philip laughed weakly. "Can we please leave my brother out of this?"

"Really? That thought doesn't titillate you?"

"No."

"Okay, I'll behave."

Philip kissed him again. "I didn't say you had to behave, only that we not talk about my immediate family while my cum's drying on the sofa."

"Picky picky," Stuart said. He rested his head on Philip's chest again, thinking. He'd had more fun that summer with Philip than he could remember having in a long time. More fun, more heart to heart conversations, more everything. He felt like he'd experienced life—plain ol' ordinary life—more vividly with Philip than he ever had before. He knew he'd never felt about any of his boyfriends the way he felt about Philip. He knew what he was heading for, too, but he also realized a commitment was the last thing he should make. Why did being honest with himself make him feel like a grade-A shit?

But maybe… maybe there was a way to express what he felt without leading Philip on too badly. Stuart pushed himself up a little way. "You know," he said, looking into Philip's eyes. "You're my best friend. I can tell you anything and you never judge. You're fun to be around. We never run out of things to talk about. When I'm with you, I never want to go home."

Philip looked at him with such tenderness and care, it made Stuart cringe inside. "Best friends," he said softly. "I never really had one of those, so I guess you're my first in two ways today. Best friends," he repeated. "I like the sound of that. A lot."

CHAPTER
Thirteen

THE HOUSE was once again pristine, the kitchen clean, the family room and particularly the sofa were spotless, and still Philip felt restless. He finally gave up and sat down in the living room. He never went in there much. Of all the rooms in the house, this one bore the least evidence of his determination to erase all traces of Randall from the house, but then, maybe that was because of all rooms save for that absurd shrine upstairs, this room bore the most traces of his mother. People said he resembled her when he was a teenager and Helena Sundstrom still lived. Personally he didn't see it. Then again, his mother had died half his lifetime ago, and even the best-intentioned memory dimmed after enough time had passed.

His mother had always called the living room décor "classic," which at the time he didn't understand. As an adult, Philip took it to mean that while the furniture was marked by a certain oldness of fashion, it nonetheless also possessed a certain timelessness, from the davenports to the deep chairs that looked as if they ought to be stiff and uncomfortable but had lulled Philip to sleep on many occasions, both as a child and as an adult. He sank into one. Yep, still the best chairs around.

His mother had come from money, and the formal living room/library most closely duplicated the rooms she remembered from her own childhood on the East Coast. Instead of lamps, there were prism chandeliers hanging from the ceiling, the only truly elaborate things in the room with their cascades of cut glass that scattered and amplified the lights. They made reading easier and the dimmer switches allowed for atmosphere.

Philip found the room to be quiet and serene, but that Sunday not even the living room calmed him. He lived in a huge, empty house, and it felt even more cavernous without his best friend in it. In the space of a few short months, Stuart's presence had filled the house and made it a place Philip wanted to be. In those months, he'd managed to put his workaholic tendencies on hold—it would take more than that to cure him—and enjoy spending time with someone he thought was very special. And as long as he was brooding, what was up with that, anyway? Best friend? He loved that he and Stuart were so close as friends, and if he were honest with himself, he knew they were more than that. He hadn't pushed it yet, for a variety of reasons, but best friends?

"Best friend," he said aloud. "Yeah, right. How many people get drilled into their sofas by their best friends? He's my boyfriend even if he doesn't know it yet."

He was up and pacing without being aware of it.

Then Philip stopped, struck by a nasty realization. It was mid-July. He'd better take what he could get. Stuart started med school in less than a month.

What was he going to do? His best friend was about to marry med school and eventually residency, so what right did he have to ask for a commitment? He knew he was ready to commit and settle down with one special someone. He also knew bone deep that of all the people he'd dated, man or woman, Stuart had some indefinable something that he wanted to wake up next to every morning and see each night before he turned the light off.

Or maybe, Philip thought, suddenly excited, maybe the "best friends" talk was Stuart's attempt to speak his feelings while still leaving his future open, of keeping a fig leaf for himself since he knew he couldn't offer Philip all he wanted. If so, ten points to Ravenclaw for smarts and self-knowledge.

If only Stuart would give him a chance. He could be patient. Hell, his entire history at SunHo was marked by patience and playing the long game. Stuart should know that since he'd listened to Philip talk enough. Sure, Stuart might have to relocate in four years for his residency, but he hadn't even asked if Philip were willing. Stuart and his stubbornness…. Philip kicked an ottoman. Damn, that man was proud. Philip smiled. Proud or strong-willed, it didn't matter. That's what gave Stuart his fire. That's what drew Philip to him. Stuart wouldn't be Stuart without that essential fire burning at his core.

Philip found himself back in the family room and on *that* sofa, still restless. The house felt empty without Stuart, but he was at work. The more he thought about it, the more Philip realized he needed to get out of the house. Maybe Brad and Drew were at home and felt like playing.

He pulled out his phone and called his brother.

"Brad Sundstrom."

"Hi, Brad, it's Philip. Are you busy?"

"Kind of, yeah."

"Oh. Well, I'm sorry to bother you. I'll talk to you later."

But before Philip hung up, he heard Brad yell, "Wait! Philip, wait!"

"Yes?"

"You sound like you're not," Brad said. "What's up?"

Philip thought about parsing, but this was Brad. "Stuart had to go to work and I'm not handling being alone very well."

"I remember that feeling." Brad laughed. "I have to warn you, I'm working. You can come find me, but prepare to get your hands dirty."

Philip copied the address down. "I'll see you soon, Brad. And thanks."

"WOW," SAID Philip when he finally tracked his brother down in the bowels of the most horrendous suburban tract home he'd ever seen. "I thought Renochuck specialized in bringing the quaint and charming houses of Midtown and East Sac back from the dead?"

"We do," Brad replied. "Are you going to have a queen-out about this place? Because I'm not sure I can handle another one."

"Another one?" Philip said.

Brad sighed. "Drew had a hissy fit when he saw this place. He said there's nothing we can do with ugly that goes this deep, and he's right, but even people who live in homes like these deserve nice bathrooms. At least, that's what I told him."

"Yeah?" Philip said with a laugh. "How'd he take that?"

"He put me in charge of the entire thing, no help from him at all, even when he's free," Brad said. He looked a little glum to Philip's eyes. "The thing he doesn't understand is that the economy isn't bouncing back, at least not very fast. He should, since his own business isn't doing as well as we'd like. But he doesn't, so maybe we can't be so picky right now. If people in cookie-cutter houses want to put nice bathrooms in now that maybe they've paid some bills, I'm not going to say no."

Philip nodded. "Pride has a price."

"Exactly. Then there's the fact—hello?—this may not be the cutesy bungalows of Midtown and jaw-dropping mansions of the Fab Forties, but it's a market that we haven't penetrated. If people in the burbs start calling us, we need to take their work. I can't speak for Drew, but I'm not too proud to bid on their jobs," Brad said, "and I'll take pride in everything I'll do for them, too."

"That's my brother," Philip said, suddenly proud of the man Brad had turned into. "Speaking of work, didn't you want some from me?

Brad eyed his clothes. "I bet that's the closest you come to grubby, isn't it?"

"Pretty much," Philip said.

"Oh well, not my problem. I need you to grout the tile in the shower. Remember how to do that?"

"I think so, and besides, you'll be right here to point out where I'm screwing up, right?"

Brad grinned. "I'm counting on it."

Philip didn't have the heart to tell Brad that at least as far as the family business went, things were humming along just fine. Maybe it was time for Brad to come back? "You know, if it ever comes down to it, SunHo is the *family* firm and you can always come back whenever—"

"Oh, fuck no!" Brad all but yelled. Then, more quietly, "That means a lot, but no."

"You know he's gone, and even if he gets out, he won't be back at SunHo. I'll drive the company off a cliff before I allow that."

Brad took a deep breath and let it out. "That helps, but… right now, I can't think about that or him."

"Hell, I'll be begging at Renochuck's door before I allow Randall to do anything associated with SunHo, and that includes cut the grass," Philip said.

"Dude, don't take this the wrong way, but you don't know shit about this," Brad said.

"Too true," Philip said, sighing.

Brad set Philip to work mixing the grout, some new kind of urethane mixture Philip had never heard of. At first, Philip thought the mindless task of grouting would take his mind off Stuart, but it didn't take long for him to get the hang of it. That meant plenty of time to ponder.

Philip sighed.

Brad turned to look at him. "Something wrong?"

"Kind of." Instead of telling Brad what he was thinking, Philip came at it from a different angle. "How'd you know Drew was the one you wanted to settle down with?"

"He had a cock."

Philip rolled his eyes. "Seriously, Brad."

"It's a really nice cock, Philip."

Philip made a face. Brad was in one of *those* moods again. "Brad…."

"I'm serious," Brad said, setting down the wrench he'd been using to tighten the bolts holding the toilet to the floor. "I finally figured out my true nature and cock was what I needed, but also because Drew had been there for me even before I realized I was gay. He listened to me while I worked through it all, and he was patient with me when I screwed things up. I waited for him while he screwed things up, too, and I showed him I was worth the time and the trouble… just like he'd already showed me the same thing."

"That makes sense."

Brad nodded curtly. "I'm so glad you approve. You want to tell me what this is about?"

"You know Stuart and I have been spending a lot of time together, right?" Philip said.

"You've mentioned that, yes. Please tell me there's not already trouble in paradise," Brad said.

"No, quite the opposite." Philip smiled at the recollection of their time together. Simply being around Stuart made his day better. "Honestly, he's become my best friend, that and more."

Brad grinned at him. "Then what's the problem?"

"I've lately been wondering about more, that's all." Philip sighed. He kept going around and around with this one, and every time he thought he was close to an answer, it eluded his grasp yet again. "I think I'm falling in love," he blurted.

Brad put his tools down. He smiled at his brother. "That's great, but I still don't see the problem."

"I'm not sure Stuart feels the same way." Philip sighed and tried to wallow in melancholy.

"Oh?" Brad said, crossing his arms across his chest.

Philip nodded, suddenly nervous. "I think he's the one. I know he's younger than I am, to say nothing of starting med school… I… It seems like such a huge step. Honestly, it scares me."

"It is scary," Brad said, nodding his understanding. "Love's big. It consumes you, it changes you. You don't think *I* as much and start thinking *we*."

"I get that," Philip said softly. "Honestly, I already do that."

"Have you told him that yet?" Brad said.

Philip shook his head. "I've been too afraid to."

"It's a big risk, and as I said, it's scary as hell. You put yourself out there and there are all those terrible moments that you're hanging there, waiting to hear if he's going to say anything back."

"You sound like you know this firsthand," Philip said. He shivered at Brad's description, imagining himself hanging there, waiting for Stuart to say something, anything, back to him.

"I do. Who do you think made the first move? It wasn't Drew. He was too worried about taking advantage of me or some such noise." Brad snorted. "He let me make the decision about gay or straight on my own. I get why now, but at the time I was terrified."

"I can see that. Even articulating it makes me anxious." Philip frowned at the grout and attacked it with renewed vigor.

"Easy there, tiger, you've got a few minutes yet before it sets," Brad said. "There's something else you need to know about love."

"And what would that be?"

"It also makes you more yourself, your better self," Brad said. "In some ways, it's the final step to maturation, and I'm willing to bet that even if the love goes away, you don't lose what you've gained."

Philip stared at Brad. *This* was his younger brother, the one their father thought was little better than a half-wit? "How'd you get so smart?

Brad shrugged, his cheeks pinking. "I've got a lot of time to think on the job."

Philip mulled his brother's words while he grouted more of the shower tiles. The loss of freedom didn't seem like such a big deal, not when he and Stuart spent almost every available moment together. Damn, he'd ask Stuart to move in that very instant if he didn't think the younger man would freak. Most of their outside interests didn't overlap if only because of the age difference, so it's not like they were joined at the hip. No, he felt surprisingly comfortable with Stuart being out of his sight. Either he had Stuart or he didn't, so abandoning *I* for *we* would happen or it wouldn't. Beside, Philip thought smugly, Valerie liked him.

"What's in here? This stuff stinks."

"That's the urethane. It's expensive up front, but makes a non-porous grout when it dries," Brad replied.

"That's handy."

"You have no idea."

"I wonder if my contractors know about this?"

"Philip, if they don't, you need to fire every single one of them and hire some random vagrants from Alkali Flats street corners. Seriously, there's no reason on earth not to use this stuff."

"Stuart said we were best friends," Philip said. "That has to count for something, right?"

Brad laughed. "The person you need to ask about that is Stuart, but in my book? It's worth about as much as a bucket of warm spit."

"Brad!"

"Seriously, what's he offering you with that?"

Philip didn't say anything. What was there to say?

"I'll tell you what. He's giving you nothing, and not only that, he's keeping you from finding someone who will commit to you."

"Ouch." That hurt. Philip didn't want to hear the truth in Brad's words, he really didn't, even though it was hard to ignore.

"What do you want me to say? You asked what I thought. If you want someone to lie to you or blow smoke up your ass, you'll have to look somewhere else."

They worked in silence for a while. Philip tried to make sense of Brad's words, even though there was an incredible amount of light between what Brad said and what Philip longed to hear. Find someone who would commit to him? He didn't want *someone* who'd commit, he wanted Stuart, which was why he didn't intend to give up. Stuart might not be ready to hear the L-word, but Philip intended to show him in every way he could think of.

Philip thought about that for a while, but when the silence grew too thick for him to stand, Philip said, "I'm thinking of moving."

"Good. You've done what you can with that house, but it's still ugly and way too big for one person."

Philip blinked. "You approve? I was afraid you'd object. Childhood home and all that."

"I hate that place." Brad shuddered. "Get rid of it whenever you want and spare me the details."

Brad missed the look of sympathy Philip gave him. They each dealt with Randall's legacy in their own way, and he couldn't blame Brad for refusing to have anything to do with things he saw as tainted by Randall's touch. In that light, he was lucky Brad had even consented to come to dinner there.

"So anyway, I was thinking maybe a condo, or even a bungalow near the Med Center."

Brad groaned. "Philip…."

"Look, I know money's tight for him and he's going to have to stop working when med school starts. So a place near the Med Center…."

Brad sighed. "Are you at least going to ask Stuart to move in with you or just spring this one on him like it's some huge coincidence?"

"Yes, I'm going to ask. His pride's kind of touchy but his sister likes me, and let's be honest, it's not like I need the rent money," Philip said. He thought for a moment. "Think Drew will take me as a client?"

"Yeah, he'll take you, although—and not to harp on the obvious—you own a building company—you could buy something and tear it down and build anything you want," Brad pointed out.

"And infuriate the entire neighborhood in the process," Philip said, "and that's assuming the neighborhood doesn't have some kind of historic status or an aggressive neighborhood association. I also know that SunHo's looking into turning the old Coca-Cola bottling plant on Stockton Boulevard into condos, but that would take too long, even if the deal had already been inked."

Brad whistled. "Seriously? If that goes through, that'll hit the local real-estate market like an atomic bomb."

"Probably," Philip said. He hated having to do what he was about to do, but he could already see Brad's excitement. He knew as soon as Brad could, he'd be calling Drew. "And Brad?"

"Yeah?"

"I won't ask you to keep that from Drew, but anything else is inside information and is probably illegal," Philip said.

Philip watched Brad deflate. It was like watching a beach ball with a leak as his brother's excitement slowly collapsed in on itself. "I'm sorry."

"I guess you can't show favoritism," Brad said, "but damn, Philip. The bottling company conversion...."

"You're wrong, Brad, I can't show *open* favoritism. SunHo's still a privately owned company," Philip said. "We're builders, not real estate agents. You know that. We typically partner with real estate agencies, especially on things like condo conversions."

"Yeah, but the bottling plant?" Brad said. Philip could see the hesitation on Brad's face.

"I'm pretty sure Drew felt like that before he took on the Bayard House, and look how that turned out," Philip said.

Brad opened his mouth but no sound came out. At last he forced out, "That's not fair!"

Philip shrugged. "The fair happens every year at Cal Expo, and features deep-fried Oh My God I Ate *What* on a stick, horse-riding exhibitions, and unicorns crapping glitter. I'm not interested in fair, and I'm not interested in helping you cut yourselves off at the knees. Didn't Drew say the same thing about the competition to give young designers a chance to restore the Bayard House? Look how well that turned out." He pulled out his iPhone and started typing. "I sent a note to my assistant. He'll be expecting Drew to e-mail him, and Jyoti will give Drew information on applying to partner with SunHo. Give me some credit for being your brother."

"I'm sorry, Philip." Philip was pretty sure Brad's eyes were a little brighter than usual.

"This isn't charity for Drew or anything. I plan to make him work, both when it comes to showing me homes to move my 'best friend' into and in applying to work with SunHo, assuming *we* get the bid on the bottling plant."

"Of that I have no doubt," Brad said, shaking his head.

CHAPTER
Fourteen

"SO DO I really have to indulge your *My Fair Lady* fixation?" Stuart said as they crossed the Bay Bridge into San Francisco. "And why're we going into the city? They have decent suits at the department stores in Sacramento, don't they?"

Philip looked at him as they came to an inevitable stop in traffic. Most of Philip's looks made him hot, but this one made him squirm. His eyes held something Stuart couldn't interpret. "Starting medical school is a pretty big deal in my book. I thought you deserved something better than off the rack."

"You know, I don't really need a suit right now," Stuart said. They'd gone around and around on this, Philip in all his evasive glory and he at his stubborn best. "I've already had my med school interviews and I won't interview for residency positions for three years."

"Everyone needs a suit," Philip replied. Stuart rolled his eyes. A little harder and he'd be able to see his brain. "Besides," Philip continued, "this is something I want to do for you, and we're going into the city because—and don't take this the wrong way—you'll get a better fit at Brooks Brothers here instead of a department store."

"Are you saying I'm short?" Stuart said, one eyebrow arched.

Philip grinned. "No, I'm saying you're fun-sized."

"Fun-sized? I'll show you fun-sized," Stuart said.

"You showed me last night and I'm still feeling it," Philip replied. "So no, not all of you is fun-sized. But for the fit of a suit? I think we'll have better luck with a bespoke suit."

"Bewhat?"

"Custom tailored."

Stuart shot Philip a look of purest consternation. "Why didn't you say so?"

"I did. There's a word for it, so I used it," Philip said, shrugging while he drove.

"You're a very complicated man, sometimes." But then, Stuart knew he'd have been bored by now if Philip were anything less.

"Oh, and you're not?" Philip grinned ear to ear, and that warmed Stuart right down to his toes.

"We're not talking about me, we're talking about you," Stuart said loftily. "You and your need to make me over and spend way too much money on some contrived starting-med-school-present."

Philip put his right hand on Stuart's leg, the smile sliding from his face. "Call it whatever you want, but everyone working on a professional education should have a suit. You never know what you'll need it for, and if not me, then who? This is something I want to do for you."

"You could've bought me a new computer, instead. Might've been more useful," Stuart mumbled. Then he mentally kicked himself. The last, the very last, thing he wanted to do is suggest more ways for Philip to spend money on him.

Philip didn't look at him. He couldn't. He was busy shoehorning his car into a parking place on some side street near Brooks Brothers. But he could still talk. "What makes you think I haven't?"

"Me and my big mouth," Stuart muttered, sliding down in his seat.

"Stop that, you'll hurt your back. Besides, we're here." Stuart watched as Philip got out of the car and jogged around to open his door. He had to admit he'd grown used to that. At first it rubbed him the wrong way. He could open his own door, thank you very much. Damn rich people and their stupid rituals. But slowly he'd come to recognize it for the respectful, not to mention loving, gesture that it was. Stuart wasn't ready for the L-word, but Philip showed that he cared in a hundred ways great and small, like today. Stuart knew he'd already grown accustomed to those from his best friend.

"Thanks," Stuart said as he exited the car, kissing Philip lightly on the cheek.

"So the way this works is that you'll be measured and then you'll try on cheaper suits to get a sense of your personal style. I'll proffer my opinions, of course, but you're the one who'll need to be comfortable in it. Once we narrow down what you like, they'll bring out the fabric swatches. If you can't visualize from those, you can always look at suits in those fabrics."

Stuart frowned. "This sounds complicated."

Philip shrugged. "The pastimes of the rich usually are."

"Great. So how long will all this take?"

"Depends on the backlog," Philip said. "The fitting is usually in about three weeks, with the suit ready in six. Bespoke almost always involves a lot of hand tailoring."

"I guess there's a reason it costs so much," Stuart said. "But how will I get in here for that? School starts soon."

"I should've gotten the ball rolling sooner, to be honest." Philip held the door open. "Ready?"

"Sure, why not?"

"Oh, a word of warning," Philip said. "Some of the measurements will be pretty close to your crotch. The tailor will not, in fact, be groping you."

"Good to know," Stuart said as they walked in.

Several people with measuring tapes draped around their necks looked up when they walked in. Stuart couldn't actually hear anyone say, "Fresh meat," but he was willing to bet at least one of them thought it.

One separated himself from the pack. "Can I help you gentlemen?"

Philip stepped forward like he owned the place, and for all Stuart knew he did. "Yes, my friend here needs a suit."

"Then you've come to the right place," the tailor said. "I'm Jaime and I'll be happy to help your friend.

"What kind of suit are you looking for?" Jaime's tone gave away nothing, but the look in his eyes as he shook Stuart's hand told him what he thought about this "friend" business.

Stuart shrugged. He was so out of his element here. "Well, I'm starting med school in a few weeks, and Philip here thinks I need a suit."

"Everyone needs a suit," Jaime said, nodding. "We'll start with measurements. If you'll step over here...."

Stuart and Philip followed Jaime deeper into the store to the made-to-measure department. There were fitting rooms, fortunately quite spacious.

"Will your... friend be joining us?" Jaime asked Stuart.

Stuart nodded. "Yeah, I've got no idea what I'm doing and he's paying for it."

"Gotcha," Jaime said, exchanging a knowing look with Philip. Stuart pretended he didn't see Philip shrug.

Philip sat down on a spare chair and started typing away on his iPhone while Jaime got to work with his measuring tape, jotting the results down on a small notepad.

"Anything interesting going on back at the office?" Stuart asked Philip.

"Probably," Philip replied. "I haven't checked that account. Right now I'm looking at how many messages Brad and Drew have left me."

"His brother and brother-in-law," Stuart explained.

"Ah," Jaime said, not looking up from his measuring.

"Why're they e-mailing you so much?" Stuart asked.

Philip looked up and smiled at Stuart. "Drew's helping me look for someplace smaller to live. I'm also trying to talk him into applying to work with SunHo if we get the bid to redevelop that old bottling plant across from the Med Center—"

"You mean where I'll be starting med school very shortly?" Stuart said. He couldn't believe it, and yet he knew he should. It was so typically Philip, and what was this about someplace else to live? Should that set off alarms?

"Why yes, I think it might be," Philip said, a portrait of innocence.

"And I'm sure you're going to tell me that's a coincidence," Stuart said.

"Of course I am, because it is." Philip grinned. "Honestly, Stuart, it really is a coincidence. I didn't have anything to do with it, but as long as my company's bidding on the job, I might as well throw some work to my brother's partner, right? He's still trying to get his own real estate company off the ground, and this could make him."

"Yeah, I guess," Stuart said. Everything Philip said made sense, but he nonetheless smelled a rat. Coincidence and Philip Sundstrom weren't well acquainted, if only because Philip possessed the knack for arranging things to suit his whims. But Stuart made a mental note, just in case Philip ended up in a penthouse in the converted bottling plant.

"I think that does it," Jaime said. "Now I'd like to show you some ready-to-wear suits to get an idea of what you like."

Stuart nodded. It was as Philip had told him it would be.

Jaime looked at Stuart's feet and hesitated. "I can't help but noticing the sandals. To ensure a proper fit, it really is best if you wear dress shoes. We have a fine selection of shoes here, so if you'd first like to follow me to the shoe department...."

Stuart looked up at Philip in a panic. They'd brought shoes, but what had happened to them?

Philip frowned. "I think I left them in the car. I'll meet you both in the cheap section. Be right back!"

Jaime flinched. "Cheap section?"

"To him, they are," Stuart said.

"No doubt," Jaime said. "If you'll come with me, we'll get started. Something tells me your 'friend' is used to getting his way."

Stuart smiled. "Oh yes, he is. When I let him."

"So tell me before I drag out every suit we carry, is there any particular style of suit you love or refuse to see on your body?" Jaime said.

"Jeez, I don't know," Stuart felt like the rug had been yanked out from under him, and where the hell was Philip? He hadn't parked that far away. "My only suit before this was something I bought at a thrift store before my med school interviews. It's blue. I think the color looks good on me."

"Navy will, yes." Jaime started pulling out suits and holding them up to Stuart for a moment. Some he put back with a frown, some he held up for a moment longer before shaking his head, and some he set aside.

Then Philip returned with the canvas satchel holding Stuart's one good pair of shoes, and Stuart relaxed. "Double-breasted. You're kidding, right? This is something you've dragged out for comic relief? Are you going to put a jaunty little sailor's cap on him, too?"

"It was just a suggestion," Jaime said stiffly.

"A very bad one," Philip said. "Single-breasted, obviously, and two-button. Stuart, how do you feel about a waistcoat?"

"Is that the vest people wear under the jacket?" Stuart asked, secretly proud he actually knew something about this.

Philip's answering smile made it all worthwhile. "Exactly. I think the look could be very charming on you."

"Then yes, let's look at suits with waistcoats," Stuart told Jaime.

"How do you feel about a subtle pinstripe?" Jaime asked Stuart.

Stuart thought about it. "That could look good."

He met Philip's eye. Philip looked up from his iPhone, but he didn't fool Stuart, who knew Philip watched the goings-on closely. Philip winked at him.

Jaime and Stuart went back and forth on various shades of navy and various widths of pinstripes. When Jaime pulled out a suit with too-bright pinstriping, even Stuart thought it made him look like a gangster and he rejected it before Philip even had a chance to clear his throat.

Stuart had no idea buying a bespoke suit would be so arduous, which was why his class prejudices didn't rear up on their hind legs when Philip sent one of the employees out with fifty dollars and an order for sandwiches and Starbucks. Then Stuart glanced at his watch and was appalled to discover that they'd only been at this for two hours.

Fortified with food, Stuart made progress and at last came up with what he thought was a good-looking suit. "What do you think?" he asked Philip.

"What do I think?" Philip repeated as he circled around Stuart to get a good look. "I think if you look this good in a cheap, ill-fitting suit, you'll look positively edible when you get the fitted one." Then he leaned in close. "I want nothing more than to drag you back to the fitting room, rip this off you, and have my way with you."

Stuart gulped and turned bright red. Somehow Philip always did it to him.

"I'm guessing he approves," Jaime said dryly. "Now, let's talk about fabrics…."

Fortunately, from Stuart's perspective, Philip exerted himself, insisting on something called "tropical weight."

"Trust me," Philip said. "You'll thank me the first time you have to wear a suit in the summer."

Stuart still wasn't sure. "What about winter?"

"We live in California. It really doesn't get that cold here," Jaime said. "Go with the tropical weight."

"What about this fabric? It's so soft and snuggly," Stuart said, looking at Philip coyly.

"Snuggly?" Philip said, amused.

"Well, it is."

Philip laughed. "Get the cashmere, then."

Stuart sat up. "Is that what this is? Forget it. That's too expensive. I'll—"

"Don't worry about it." Philip waved a dismissive hand. "It's not like 'economize' is a particularly pretty word to begin with."

And so it went. If forced, Stuart would've had to admit that he'd found the process not as miserable as he'd initially feared. It still struck him as a waste of money and he still wasn't convinced he needed this new suit, but then, Philip liked projects and maybe this one was his way of dealing with Stuart's starting med school. Stuart knew the thought made *him* nervous.

He also found it odd that of everything he tried on and Philip paid for, the only things they took home from there that day were the ties they'd selected.

"Do you really think I needed custom shirts too?" Stuart said as they left Brooks Brothers an exhausting five hours later.

"I suppose I could say something about the bulk from ill-fitting off-the-rack shirts bunching up under your handmade suit and spoiling the lines," Philip said, "but the real answer is why not?"

"Oh, very nice," Stuart said. "There's nothing I can say to argue with that."

"I know." Philip giggled. "That's why I said it."

Stuart shook his head. Then he looked at his watch. Great. Rush hour. "So what do you want to do? If we leave now we'll spend most of our time sitting on the 80."

"Hmm, anything you want to see? We could check out the de Young or MoMA," Philip said.

"Or Fishermen's Wharf," Stuart said. If he'd grown up in Northern California, he'd probably have done it as a kid, but he'd only moved out there to go to school.

"Have you ever been there?" Philip gave him the side eye.

Stuart shook his head. He actually had once on a crew road trip while he was an undergrad at CalPac, but he wanted to see where this landed.

"It's noisy and it stinks, and that's before we mention the sea lions," Philip said, wrinkling his nose.

"Snob. That's where we're going." For some perverse reason that he chose not to investigate too closely, Stuart longed to drag his "best friend" headlong through the muck of lowbrow tourist culture, especially after that business with the suit.

Philip put up a token fuss, but Stuart knew he'd won when Philip said, "My car better not get scratched in whatever passes for a parking garage down there."

So Stuart spent the rest of the afternoon happily dragging his "best friend" up one end and down the other of the admittedly somewhat odoriferous tourist trap. Philip took pictures of him in front of the sea lion haul out, and Stuart had to admit it reeked to high heaven. So he held his breath and smiled for the camera, and he didn't even fake the smile, because he couldn't remember the last time he'd let go and enjoyed himself without worrying about studying or rowing and making the grade in both.

After a dinner of clam chowder served in hollowed-out miniature loaves of sourdough bread, Stuart dragged Philip to an "Old West" photo shop where they were dressed up in western duds and posed in the rigid and smileless poses from an era of long exposure times and sepia-tone prints. Stuart smiled anyway, because he'd enjoyed a day away with his "best friend."

"Will that be one print or two?" the knowing photographer asked.

"Two," Philip said, reaching for his wallet, but Stuart beat him to it.

"Thank you," Philip said as they walked back to the car. "But you didn't have to."

"I know." Stuart nudged Philip. "But I wanted to."

Philip yawned. "Damn. I must be more tired than I thought." He held out his car keys. "Will you drive home?"

Stuart eyed the key to the Mercedes. "You're letting me drive your baby?"

"It's not my baby, it's a car. An expensive car, yes, and one I wouldn't want to replace frequently, but still, it's only a car. You're my best friend, right?" Philip said, smiling at Stuart in a way he knew Philip never looked at anyone else.

"Yeah, but—"

"No buts," Philip said, shaking the key at Stuart. "Well, if we're talking butts, we could find some a shadowed corner and do something trashy, I guess."

Stuart had to laugh when Philip waggled his eyebrows at him. "Wasn't you being too tired to drive back to Sacramento what started this conversation?"

"True." Philip unlocked the doors and slid into the passenger seat... which he could barely squeeze into. "Damn, you don't seem this short."

"Well, that's settled that," Stuart muttered to himself as he settled into the driver's seat... and found himself nowhere near the pedals or steering wheel. He kicked his feet until he caught Philip's attention. "Dude. Seriously."

Philip leaned over him to point out the three-way seat adjustment. Before he leaned back in his seat, Philip took advantage of his proximity to kiss Stuart on the lips. "Subtle," Stuart said when he came up for breath.

"I didn't hear you complaining." Philip buckled his seatbelt. "Once you've got yourself comfortable, hit the button marked '2' and hold it until it beeps. That'll set the car's memory so the next time you drive, all you need to do is hit the button and everything will readjust itself to you."

"Slick," Stuart said as he adjusted things on the Mercedes. Sure, these were mere "creature comforts," but what a difference they made. Who knew what other wonders the car held?

"Okay, all set, but you're going to have to give me directions out of San Francisco, or at least to the highway," Stuart said. "I've never actually made the drive myself."

"Not a problem," Philip said. "Turn the key until the dashboard lights up."

After Stuart did so, Philip started fiddling with yet another feature of the car. "Where to, sir?"

"And that is…?"

"The navigation system."

"Of course," Stuart said. "Your house? My roommate's back from his summer of debauchery back home and obviously didn't get enough, because he's continuing the festivities. I don't get much sleep there."

Philip leered at him. "What makes you think you'll get much at my place?"

"The difference is I have fun when you keep me up past my bedtime." Stuart stuck his tongue out. "Now make with the navigator."

Philip complied, and Stuart realized he could get used to that as the navigator and Philip both steered him toward 80 East and the Bay Bridge. Or had he, already? But settling down scared him, or was it settling down with Philip?

Philip was loaded, but lately Stuart had realized he might not necessarily hold that against him. It wasn't as if Philip were some birthright jackass, unlike certain previous boyfriends Stuart could name. Philip *knew* he'd been born on first base and then stolen second and third through connivance and hard work. Sure, Philip insisted on buying him things, but he had to admit Philip always put thought into his gifts and they made Stuart's life easier. Still, gifts were also burdens, tying him down at a time he couldn't make that kind of commitment. Each one was another rope binding him to Philip, and sometimes he resented them.

Philip was older and seemed ready to settle down, and he definitely knew where he was going with his life. Despite the skullduggery at SunHo, Philip still helmed a lucrative company that allowed him to live in relatively high style. Stuart was just starting his professional education and frankly had no idea what his future held. Who knew, in five years, maybe he'd be ready to settle down, too, but right now Stuart couldn't imagine it. Philip had never applied so much as an ounce of pressure—except for those gifts—but sometimes total silence on a subject constituted screaming, didn't it? He felt like Philip screamed his patient affection in his ears.

Then, too, was the matter of his bisexuality. Stuart knew he was being biphobic, but he found it hard to shake the fear that Philip could dump him for the next set of big tits to catch his fancy. After all, his last serious relationship, a relationship that as far as Stuart knew had been heading for the altar, ended not because of something Philip did but because the woman had cheated. What if the spell cast by his cock and his tight little ass wore off and Philip went looking for poon? Didn't bisexuality mean twice as many opportunities for dates? Dropping him for another man he could handle. It'd upset him, but he could deal. But dropping him for a woman? There'd be nothing he could do with that.

Stuart glanced over at Philip, sleeping as the miles flew by. He knew he felt more for Philip than mere friendship. That one wasn't even a hard call, so why did he struggle with accepting more from Philip? As his "best friend" snored gently beside him, Stuart reminded himself to be grateful for what he had rather than what he didn't. Glass half full, right?

CHAPTER
Fifteen

MEDICAL SCHOOL started off with a bang. Stuart would've thought orientation would be dry and boring, and while picking up his schedule and buying textbooks hadn't exactly enthralled him, Dr. Hormel of the Student Health Service more than made up for it. Stuart had naively assumed that being students at a highly ranked medical school would've meant that they would be treated by these world-famous specialists, but no. It was the same kind of university student health service he'd dealt with as an undergrad.

Dr. Hormel shuffled on stage, an assistant of some kind—young enough to be his granddaughter—following along behind him. Dr. Hormel looked like he'd been practicing since before penicillin had been discovered, possibly since before the development of anesthetic and sterile surgical techniques.

Stuart watched with some trepidation as the geriatric physician fiddled with the microphone at the podium for a few moments, staring out at the freshman class through glasses that covered his rheumy eyes. He eyed them a little longer while the students in the packed auditorium grew restless. "You're having too much sex! Stop it!"

His shocked assistant whispered in his ear, but he waved her away angrily. "Leave me alone. I know what I'm doing. I'm not senile." He turned his attention back to the medical students. Stuart wasn't sure he'd heard Dr. Hormel right the first time. "You know you are. Enough of you young ladies keep coming into my consultation hours for prophylactics. I know what's going on. So unless you're married, you shouldn't be having sexual intercourse."

Then the mic started shrieking and Dr. Hormel's assistant lunged for it while people near the speakers covered their ears.

The man sitting next to Stuart leaned over and whispered, "I don't know about you, but I'm not having nearly enough sex, and it's looking like the next four years aren't going to help."

Stuart, who had slowly come to realize that in nailing Philip's ass that first time he had created a monster, nodded sympathetically. "I've got all the ass I can handle, but good luck with that."

"Damn, buddy, what's your secret?" Stuart's neighbor asked, his voice quiet. He looked like a man who smiled a lot, and that set Stuart at ease. "I'm Eddie San Filipo, by the way."

"Stuart Cochrane, and I'm not sure, to be honest," Stuart whispered back. "A friend of mine's older brother was looking to jump the fence and I was there when he landed?"

Eddie looked at him with a mixture of surprise and delight. "You're gay? Awesome, man, third day and I've got my first gay homey."

"Oh you do, do you?" Stuart gave him the ol' beady eye.

"Sure, man." Eddie grinned. "I'll be your wingman. You're adorable. Women will fall at your feet and I'll be there to pick them up."

Stuart laughed. He couldn't help it. "I guess you've got your first gay, then."

"Damn straight," Eddie said, winking.

They both knew, however, that time to shake their asses on a dance floor would be virtually nonexistent for years to come. Although come to think of it, Aspects might well be quieter than his apartment now that Jonathan was back and making as much noise as inhumanly possible. He was such a loser. Stuart had no idea what he'd even seen in Jonathan, especially now that he had someone to compare him to. He sighed. Maybe Philip wouldn't mind a live-in best friend or boyfriend or whatever they were to each other. He couldn't imagine why in this one area of his life he settled for wallowing in ambivalence. Morgan would never believe it, if they could only find the time to do more than e-mail. Usually he was hard-charging and took no prisoners. It made him an effective cox'n and carried him to med school. But maybe he needed a soft place to land, too. It was something he'd never considered about himself, and it required some reflection, maybe some…. Valerie. He'd have to run this by her, and he owed her an e-mail or a text conversation anyway.

Stuart pulled his attention back to the stage below. He realized he'd missed one entire introduction. He hoped it was no one he needed to care about, like his professor of gross anatomy or something. Maybe Eddie had paid attention....

"Thank you, Dr. Ellison," said a woman of middle years with longish hair, wisps of which escaped the practical braid meant to contain it. Stuart and the rest of them recognized her. She was Dr. Eleanor Cobb, the director of first-year education, and she had been the first one to welcome them to the next four years of their lives.

Dr. Cobb smiled at them. "We've thrown a lot at you, I know. It'll make sense soon, I promise. You'll learn where the classrooms and labs are. You'll get over your squeamishness where your corpse in gross anatomy is concerned, if only because you'll quickly come to see him or her in terms of component systems. In some ways, that's what medical training is all about. You start off by reducing everything into manageable chunks in the classes in blocks one and two, because that's the only way you can make sense of the vast amount of information that will shortly be coming your way, while your doctoring curriculum, which brings you into patient exams, cross-cultural medicine, and medical ethics, strives to remind you that those manageable chunks belong to human beings."

Dr. Cobb sighed and took off her glasses before she stepped out from behind the podium. The first-years assembled before her watched in silence as she seated herself on the edge of the dais. Unlike Dr. Hormel, she had a wireless mic.

"Here's the blunt reality of medical education and practice. Get used to exhaustion. Even if you could somehow do nothing but study twenty-four hours a day without interruption for sleep, food, or anything else for the next four years, you would still be unable to learn everything we have to teach you. There's just too much information."

"So why's med school only four years?" someone asked.

"Because the line has to be drawn somewhere," Dr. Cobb replied. "Get used to studying, too. It'll be a lifelong habit for you, because your board certification will only be good for a decade. Even for those of you who already know that family practice or internal medicine is the way you want to go, those board questions are written by specialists so don't be complacent.

"And if none of this has served to put the reality of what you've signed yourself up for into perspective, there's this—roughly a quarter of what you will learn in the next four years will be flat-out wrong." She waited for that to sink in. "There's one little problem. We don't know which quarter that will be. If we did, we wouldn't teach it to you. Medicine and surgery are a lifelong learning process, and if you think it's only the four years in this school plus your residency you should probably leave now. Even if you never plan to set foot in a laboratory, you'll be keeping up with the research because as a clinician it will be your job to figure out which quarter of your education was wrong so you can take the best care of your patients. Similarly, if you're a surgeon, techniques change all the time."

Stuart shared a worried look with Eddie as they both slid down in their seats. Intellectually, Stuart knew that med school promised to be the hardest thing he'd done with his life thus far, but hearing it spelled out so starkly…. From glancing around, he could see he wasn't the only one feeling a little panicky at the moment.

Dr. Cobb allowed the worried whispers to carry on for a few minutes before she awkwardly climbed up and returned to the podium. She smiled slightly. "Don't let your panic run away with you. Countless people have successfully completed medical school since the modern medical curriculum was established in the early twentieth century, and trained practitioners are more in demand than ever. Remember, break it into manageable pieces and never forget that those pieces form a whole greater than the sum of its parts.

"Tomorrow's the big day, so go home, have a little fun, and come back tomorrow prepared to learn. I look forward to working with you. I'll linger up here if any of you have any questions that haven't been covered, but if the Q&A turns into hand-holding, it's over. You're adults and you're here voluntarily," Dr. Cobb said, smiling.

"Wow," Eddie said as they gathered their notebooks and shoved them into their backpacks.

Stuart nodded. "No kidding."

"You doing anything tonight? Want to grab something for dinner and try not to think too hard about what we're in for?" Eddie said.

"That sounds great, but I've got plans," Stuart said. "I think."

"Your boyfriend?"

"That's the big question, isn't it?" Stuart said.

STUART HAD only just parked his rolling slag heap of a car and he could already hear the music—if that's what it was called—thumping away from the apartment he shared with Jonathan. Fuckshitdamn. Jonathan knew perfectly well Stuart started med school bright and early the next day, but Stuart could already tell the party machine was cranking up for the evening. Not only did he feel the music where he sat in his car, but red cups already littered the ground in front of their second-story "flat," as Jonathan called it in his now-grating accent.

Jonathan had returned a mere week before, but already he'd escalated—or maybe plunged—their alleged friendship to something like World War Three. Stuart's preference to disengage and act as if they were cordial strangers infuriated Jonathan. Stuart couldn't imagine what Lady Macbeth had told Jonathan this summer, but while they'd parted amicably at the beginning of the summer, Jonathan returned gunning for bear. Didn't the UK have stringent gun laws? So even though Stuart had tried to keep things cordial and ask politely for things to be quiet, Jonathan appeared to have taken that as permission to screw him over. Sure, one of them was supposed to have found new digs, but since Stuart had seniority in the apartment, why should he vacate?

Stuart left his backpack in the car. There was no point in bringing it in. He wouldn't be spending the night there. In fact, he planned to pick up his other books and take them to Philip's too, along with a few days' worth of clothes. It didn't look like he'd be home any time soon. He really didn't need this right now.

Ordinarily, he wouldn't mind coxing up and cowing one of his rowers, or former rowers as the case was. The old mindset to jump when a short person yelled never really left rowers, according to Adam Lennox, who'd been away from rowing for years before returning over a year ago. Brad had once said more or less the same thing. It occurred to him that he now knew a number of reasonably large adult men who'd be more than happy to set things straight with Jonathan, men like Owen Douglas, who seemed to be perpetually irritable, or Brad, who just liked a good fight. But dammit, it shouldn't come to that. He and Jonathan were both adults, allegedly.

Given the noise and the accumulation of non-recyclable plastic trash, Stuart would've thought a party was in full swing, but no, it was only Jonathan and a few people Stuart thought he recognized from the novice team his last year at CalPac. Somehow that only made it worse because now it was pathetic, as well as infuriating. So while on one level he was pissed as hell, on another he looked at them and thought, "Thank God."

As soon as Stuart opened the door, all eyes were on him. He refused to let it bother him, if only because he was apparently the only adult in the room. When two of the rowers snickered, he gave them his best stink eye and said, "So much for your training. I'm sure your coach will be very impressed. But then, you were never A-boat material anyway."

As he continued to his room, he heard voices but couldn't understand the words. Except Jonathan's. He heard his ex-boyfriend's voice quite clearly. "Oh that is it."

Jonathan thundered down the short hall to their bedrooms. Stuart expected it. Jonathan never had been able to bluff. But when Jonathan spun him around, he snapped. Enough was enough. Stuart shoved his knee into Jonathan's groin hard and fast. "Don't you fucking touch me. You lost that right months ago."

Jonathan leaned against the wall, legs crossed at the knees, moaning. "Duuuude…."

"Don't 'dude' me," Stuart called over his shoulder as he continued into his room, locking the door behind him. He pulled a suitcase out from under his bed and stared at his closet. He knew he shouldn't give that much of a damn about what he wore, but he did.

Stuart heard Jonathan fumbling with the lock and sighed. The locks weren't that profound, and as big as his ex's hands were, Jonathan could probably overcome the lock with brute strength alone.

A crunching noise from the door confirmed Stuart's hunch a few moments later. Stuart ignored Jonathan when he entered.

"What was that about?" Jonathan whined.

Stuart waved his hand in the direction of the living room. "What's all that about out there? You know I start school tomorrow. We talked about this."

"It's just some friends over." Jonathan sounded petulant, even spoiled. Stuart wondered why he hadn't seen that sooner.

"Yes, the night before I start medical school." Stuart decided he didn't care what he looked like. He started throwing clothes in his suitcase, figuring that between what he brought over and what was already at Philip's, he'd be fine.

"Look, UCD's med school may start in August, but classes won't resume at California Pacific for another week or so," Jonathan said. "I don't see why I have to suffer for your choices."

"Because I pay half the rent? Because a little courtesy between roommates goes a long way?" Stuart said. "Because if you respect my needs I won't fuck you over when the time is right?"

"Fuck you. If courtesy between roommates were so important, we'd still be together. Hell, you'd have gone to England with me," Jonathan said, glowering at him.

"That had nothing to do with courtesy and everything to do with incompatibility, to say nothing of a lack of money," Stuart said, sighing. Suddenly the small number of years between them seemed so glaring. Stuart didn't feel any more mature than he had at the beginning of the summer, so that left only the possibility of Jonathan's regression.

"Where're you going?" Jonathan said, noticing the suitcase for the first time.

"Somewhere I can sleep undisturbed." Even though Stuart knew the chance of him and Philip keeping their hands—and other things—to themselves was so vanishingly small as to be microscopic. "Somewhere," he said, and he knew it to be absolutely true, "I'm respected enough to be taken seriously when I make a request."

"Jesus, Stuart, it's only a party," Jonathan said.

Stuart nodded. "Yes, the night before I start the hardest phase of my schooling. You know, I shouldn't even have to justify it to you. It's like asking for peace and quiet the night before a huge exam, but then, you don't study for those much, do you?"

"You're such an asshole," Jonathan said.

"Really? Name calling?" Stuart zipped his suitcase closed and swung it off the bed. "That's all you've got?

"You're seeing someone, aren't you?"

Since Stuart didn't owe Jonathan anything like an explanation, he merely said, "I've met someone, yes."

"Who is he?" Jonathan demanded.

"No one you'd know. He's older than I am by a few years," Stuart said. "Actually, he's the older brother of someone I coxed at CalPac and Capital City Rowing."

Jonathan crossed his arms over his chest, which made Stuart think of someone trying to ward off the inevitable. "What can he give you that I can't?"

"Respect." Stuart saw the rest of his medical books and crammed them into his suitcase. "I'm leaving now."

Stuart heaved his suitcase with both hands. Damn, those books were heavy. He'd have to read the syllabi again. He was pretty sure he'd seen something about electronic options, but without a tablet computer it was useless information. That said, at the cost of these books, he might be able to pick up a refurbished iPad....

Jonathan stood in the doorway. "When're you coming back?"

"Why do you care?" Stuart said. So much for civility.

SURPRISINGLY, IT wasn't that late when he arrived at Philip's house, not even 6:00 p.m. No wonder Philip wasn't there. Stuart let himself in and disarmed the alarm system. He texted Philip to let him know he was there and then got to unpacking. The textbooks he left in an untidy heap in the family room, but the clothing he took upstairs to Philip's bedroom and put them away on the shelves set aside for his use in that cavernous closet.

Back downstairs, Stuart found himself at loose ends. He knew he should probably work on something for dinner, but he also knew this was his last free evening for the foreseeable future. He poked around in Philip's refrigerator, but there wasn't much that inspired him, and he'd never really learned to cook. His parents had never encouraged that, saying it wasn't for boys, and once school had started, he'd simply never had the time.

He ended up on the large leather sofa in the family room. He loved that sofa, and not only for the obvious reasons, although yes, it was still one of their favorite places to have sex. For that reason alone, Stuart got a semi every time he sat down on it. Good times.

He pulled out his phone and texted *Valerie: Is this a good time 2 call?*

When his sister didn't reply right away, Stuart settled back and pulled a small throw over him. Sure, he could've turned the air conditioner down, but that necessitated moving and the blanket was right there at his feet.

Right as he started to doze off, his phone buzzed.

V: There's no such thing as a good time 2 call anymore. Hours cut back at work mean less time 2 talk, less time 2 escape my jailors, etc.

S: More time w/Freddie?

V: Yeah, but more time for bible studies. That's where I am now.

S: Hiding in the bathroom?

V: How'd U know?

S: That's what I did. Only w/o a cellphone.

V: So what, U just hid?

S: Yes.

V: Weak, man. Weak. So whatdja want to talk about?

S: Nothing you've got time to go into unless you fake a butt explosion.

V: Gross.

S: Med student now. Wait until classes start officially. Then it'll be gross.

V: Awesome man.

....

S: U still there, sistwerp?

V: Yeah, someone checked on me. Gotta go, big bro.

S: Love U, Valerie.

V: Love U 2.

Well, so much for that, and so much for running by her why he couldn't seem to commit to the perfect man. Oh well, there was always napping to be done. Better rest up now, since sleep would shortly be the stuff of fantasies. Speaking of fantasies, he had a good man ready to hurl himself at his feet. Stuart also knew med school was one of his worries about a relationship. Maybe there were peer counselors, older med students, who might have useful information about the longevity of relationships started during medical school....

With that on his mind, Stuart drifted into a pleasant drowse, not quite asleep but not entirely awake. He was cozy and in the one place in Sacramento that he truly relaxed. Sure, the start of academic instruction tomorrow made him nervous, but classes were still classes, and that was familiar territory. He knew he could do this. He knew he had at least one person in his corner, and he'd already made one friend in his year in the person of Eddie. Things would be okay. He would be okay.

The next thing Stuart knew, someone was kissing his forehead. His eyes fluttered open and there was Philip, seated next to him on the sofa, smiling tenderly. "I was hoping that was you," Stuart said.

Philip laughed. "Were you expecting someone else?"

"Nope." Stuart wrapped his arms around Philip's neck, pulling him down for a kiss.

"Hmmm, my favorite flavor," Philip said eventually. "So what's up?"

"What do you mean, what's up?"

Philip pointed back the way he'd come with his chin. "Well, I almost tripped over the largest pile of books I've ever seen, or maybe I should say a pile of the largest books I've ever seen...."

"Jonathan's home." Stuart sighed. Funny how suddenly that caused much more anxiety than starting classes tomorrow.

"This I knew." Philip started rubbing Stuart's back, and he arched into it. Stuart marveled how Philip always seemed to know exactly where to rub.

"He's having a party tonight."

"Aww, jeez. That's the last thing you need." The back rub stopped, much to Stuart's perturbation, but then Philip lay down next to him, partially covering his body with Philip's bigger one. A human blanket. There were worse things.

"You got that immediately, but even after I explained that to Jonathan, he still pissed and moaned," Stuart said, his voice muffled by Philip's body.

"You need out of there."

"I know, but part of me hates being chased out of my own home by that silly child." Stuart didn't say anything for a moment. He'd never confided this to Philip, but if he couldn't tell Philip, he had no business underneath him. "Besides, I'd always hoped that I could bring Valerie out here. We have this plan to declare her emancipated from my parents. She'd live with me, and then she'd work on her GED and eventually go to community college while I'm in med school."

When Philip didn't reply, Stuart start squirming, figuratively and literally. "You probably think that sounds stupid."

"No, I think it sounds complicated," Philip said, sitting up, "but then, most things are, if people and emotions are involved."

Stuart sat up. "I'm serious about this, Philip. I have to get her out of there."

"I never said you weren't serious. I said it sounded complicated, and yes, from what you've told me about your parents, quite necessary." Philip lifted Stuart's chin up, which made Stuart feel like a child, at least a little bit, and pissed him off. "But do you have to do it the night before classes start?"

He wanted to be angry and slap Philip's hand away, but damn it if Philip didn't know how to cut right to the heart of the matter. Yes, Valerie needed rescuing, but not that exact moment.

Philip stood up, holding out his hand. "Let's go see about that heap of books. It's only a matter of time until one of us breaks something by tripping over it in the middle of the night. You wear me out and I might need to rehydrate."

"*I* wear *you* out? The other way around more like it," Stuart said. He looked at the stack of books he needed and made a face. "And this is only for the first semester or block or whatever they're calling it. Block 2 will have another set of books."

"You'll need someplace to put all those, won't you? Not to mention a quiet room to study." Philip looked around, his face scrunched up in thought. "I have an idea. Come with me."

"You mean there are parts of this house I *still* haven't seen?" Stuart said as Philip pulled him along. "What is this, the Winchester Mystery House?"

Philip's answering grin made Stuart's knees wobbly. He loved that. Maybe he could tempt Philip after dinner….

"What about the library?" Philip asked, ushering Stuart inside.

Stuart looked around, and yes, it certainly looked what he'd always thought a rich family's library would look like, but good God, talk about overdone. Wood paneling? Chandeliers? On the other hand, it was quiet and the reading table or desk was huge…. "Are you sure you want to give this up to my medical books when I need to study over here?"

Philip put his hand on Stuart's shoulder and pulled him gently into a one-armed hug, his back to Philip's front, making Stuart feel like he rode a rollercoaster. "Much of this was my mother's. Randall never touched it because it was hers. Brad and I never went in here because… well, for a variety of reasons. But it's specially insulated for sound and there's not even a phone in here."

Stuart found himself nodding. "This is great, Philip, thank you. It's the next best thing to having a second set of books to keep here all the time."

"Come with me," Philip said.

"Oh no you don't, you're not writing me a check," Stuart said sharply.

Philip laughed. "Evidence to the contrary, my first resort isn't always to throw money at things. No, I have another idea."

Stuart followed Philip up the stairs to a small room down the hall from his bedroom. All their time together, and he had no idea Philip even had a home office. Philip pulled an iPad off its cradle.

"Here," Philip said. "It was my first foray into truly lightweight computing, but it doesn't do what I needed it to and it's impossible to type on for more than casual e-mails. I replaced it with a MacBook Air. If there're electronic editions of your books, you might be able buy them more cheaply or even rent them. You can borrow the iPad for as long as you want. As you can tell from the dust on it, it doesn't get much use."

"Seriously? That'd be fantastic!" Stuart's face lit up with a smile. "I could have all my books on this, maybe for all four years."

Philip fiddled with it for a moment and handed it over to Stuart. Stuart saw in the dust SC+PS surrounded by a heart.

Philip was blushing, but Stuart didn't say anything. He stood on his toes and kissed Philip's forehead. "Thanks. I'll see what I can find tonight. Maybe I can even return some of my books. Those things are heavy and spendy. Oh, what's the password?"

Philip turned even redder. "Shortandsneaky, same as all the rest of my passwords at home."

Then Stuart had to laugh. "You're too funny. Loveable, but funny."

Philip looked up. "You think I'm loveable?"

"And funny," Stuart said.

"Then that's all that matters." Philip looked at his watch. "I'll leave you to get acquainted with your new toy while I make dinner."

Stuart snapped the cover closed. "I'll keep you company."

Philip held out his hand. Stuart smiled and took it, and together they headed for the kitchen. Stuart set the iPad on the island and then fetched all his syllabi from his backpack. With pen in hand, he merrily went through each syllabus to check for electronic copies of books while Philip fixed dinner. He felt vaguely guilty about not helping, but they both knew he couldn't cook and there was no use pretending otherwise.

Stuart set everything aside when Philip brought dinner to him, because duh, he had manners. So he concentrated on dinner and the man who'd fixed it for him.

Later, after cleaning up, he joined Philip on the leather couch in the family room, he on one end, Philip on the other. Their feet touched in the middle, with the occasional foray up one another's calves. Philip's legs were longer, so he had the advantage. Stuart found this distinctly unfair, but given where Philip's foot ended up and what it did when it got there, he didn't complain like he might have.

"What're you reading?" he asked Philip.

Philip put down a yellowed file folder. "My dad kept dirt on virtually everyone who worked for him above a certain level. I'm trying to see who I might be able to trust."

"Yeah? Did he keep one on you?"

Philip was thoroughly taken aback. "I… don't know."

"We should look." Stuart grinned, his eyes alight.

"You'll have to satisfy your unwholesome curiosity later. This batch of files is too old."

"Sure they are," Stuart said.

Philip pushed the filed box on the floor closer to him. "Look for yourself. How's the textbook search going?"

"It's going awesomely," Stuart proclaimed. "I've already ordered—and downloaded—full electronic copies of two of my most expensive books, which I'll return first thing in the morning. You've already saved me almost five hundred dollars. You have no idea how grateful I am."

"I can think of a way you can show it."

"Oh, and what would that be?"

Philip ran his foot all the way up Stuart's leg, this time working his bare foot under Stuart's shorts. Stuart snickered as Philip slid down until he was halfway lying down to complete the task, but his laughter cut off suddenly.

"Ooooh."

"Yeah, I thought you'd like that." Philip continued to massage Stuart's growing erection.

"Wanna go upstairs?" Stuart rasped.

"In the worst way."

CHAPTER
Sixteen

THAT SUMMER, the employees of Sundstrom Homes had grown accustomed to the increased absence of the company's owner. Jyoti had become the face of the CEO's suite. Anything that required Philip's attention went through his gatekeeper first, and since Philip was rarely around and with Jyoti apparently at loose ends, Philip's PA could be found anywhere in the SunHo corporate headquarters. Jyoti knew how to reach Philip, and all seemed right in the universe.

Then, late in the summer, Philip returned, and instead of a vague and shadowy presence lurking high in the executive suite, he was everywhere in the SunHo corporate offices. "Like God and cockroaches," muttered one harried midlevel manager. "I can't figure out what his problem is, but suddenly he has to know *everything* about what goes on around here. As if my own boss weren't bad enough, now the big boss is underfoot, too."

Philip smiled when Jyoti reported this back to him, after Jyoti himself heard it from that woman's secretary.

"I know this wasn't your plan, boss," Jyoti said, "but we're now at the pinnacle of a reasonably efficient information-gathering system. You see, first you disappeared for virtually the entire summer, and—"

"I didn't 'disappear'," Philip said, making air-quotes with his fingers. "I was—"

"Dipping your wick, yes." Jyoti coughed. "Now that you're back, you're sticking your nose into everything, and it's making everyone—"

"Squawk like spooked chickens?" Philip grinned like the proverbial fox in the henhouse.

Jyoti smiled in return. "And their admins run right to me with everything. We couldn't have planned it better."

"Who says I didn't?"

Jyoti didn't say anything. He crossed his arms and gave his boss "the look."

Philip pouted. "What? I could've."

"While you're more than capable, we both know how distracted you were this summer," Jyoti said, patting him on the cheek in the most condescending manner possible.

Philip batted at his hand. "Stop that. It's not as if I've been completely AWOL. In point of fact, I've found all kinds of interesting and disgusting things my father has left hidden in the house, and I plan to use some of them to bring certain members of the board to heel."

"Oh? Do tell."

Philip shut and locked the outer door to his suite and pulled Jyoti into his office before locking that door, too. "My father kept dirt on anyone who ever worked for him, anyone who might rival him. I found it this summer while I was, as you put it, dipping my wick."

"I'm sorry about that, Philip, it was out of order." Jyoti turned red beneath his dark skin.

Philip waved it away. "Don't be. It was true. Stuart has the most amazing ass."

"So why're you back?"

"Because he started medical school and I'm bored," Philip said, pushing a few file folders to his assistant.

"Or," Jyoti breathed, "because you've found a way to muzzle some of your harshest critics. These files are current almost through your father's incarceration."

"That's right," Philip said. He spun idly in his chair. "Winch's goose is cooked as soon as I get around to warming up the oven."

Jyoti nodded. "Not quite, but close."

"It's the 'not quite' part that keeps me up at night, and why I'm off to see Candice Kane in her labyrinth in the basement." Philip stood up and unhooked his MacBook, his personal one, not one of SunHo's.

"Candy Kane? She's hard to track down."

"Which is why you shouldn't call her that. She's hard enough to find as it is without thinking you're laughing at her name. Can you imagine doing that to your daughters?" Philip shook his head.

"I assume it must've been a long labor. Amrit thinks the nurses gave her mother too many sedatives." Jyoti shook his head in sympathy for the unfortunately named head of IT.

Philip paused on his way out the door. "You two talk about that?"

"Only when we run out of things to say about you."

WHY, PHILIP wondered as he rode the elevator down to the bowels of his building, were information technology departments always underground? It wasn't as if this were a server farm and cooling was of critical importance. Sure, Candy Kane—damn, she must hate Christmas—controlled any number of servers, but their own coolers plus the augmented air conditioning was enough to preserve them. So why live like a mole? He shrugged. He planned to move her somewhere with more light in the very near future.

IT's locked doors presented no obstacle, although Philip doubted anyone behind them knew it. Oh well, that cat would shortly leave the bag. He held his corporate ID to the magnetic sensor and heard a soft *snick* as the doors unlocked. His ID looked like everyone else's, but all kinds of goodies were encoded in it.

Philip sighed when he encountered the thumbprint reader at the next door. Someone staffed this door at least. He signed in and then pressed his thumb to the reader, pulling the door open as soon as he heard the lock click.

The person behind the desk finally pulled his eyes off the computer to notice that someone had opened the door he was supposed to be guarding. "Hey, you can't go in there."

"Two things," Philip called over his shoulder. "One, read the sign-in log, and two, the fact that my thumbprint unlocked the door should tell you that I have access."

He pulled the door shut behind him to the sounds of protests. "Stout lad. He'll go far… at a fast-food franchise."

Philip made his way through a maze of softly humming machines and his own increasing perturbation. He knew SunHo leased space to other companies that presumably had their own IT departments and security concerns, and while it made sense to consolidate them in a central location, the fact that security doors with the SunHo logo on them and attendants whose faces were bathed in the glow of computer monitors kept stopping him was beginning to make him stabby.

The area behind the thumbprint scanner was a cube farm where the grunts of SunHo's IT department labored away to keep SunHo's IT functioning smoothly. Occasionally a head popped up, giving Philip the oddest sensation, as if he were in a life-sized game of Whac-a-Mole. Only if he bopped anyone, his lawyers and insurers would skin him.

"Sir? Sir! You can't come in here," Philip heard someone call from behind him, but he ignored her, at least until he came up to another door.

"A retinal scanner? This is too much," he said, turning around. "Open this door. Now."

"I'm not authorized to do that," the woman said stiffly. "And how did you make it this far?"

Philip gritted his teeth and shoved his SunHo ID card in her face. "I just authorized you. Open it."

The cube dweller went pale. "I—"

"If the next word out of your mouth is 'can't,' clear your desk. I've had it with this. Either open this door, or get Kane out here. This is an order from the man who signs your paychecks." Philip stood there, arms crossed and a benign expression pasted on his face.

Cube Dweller pushed the talk button on an intercom with a shaking hand. "Philip Sundstrom to see you, Candy."

The intercom crackled, and if electronics could express surprise, Philip swore this one did. "Send him in, please."

Philip ignored the cube dweller as the retinal scanner fried her eye, and as soon as the door unlocked, he pulled it open and tried not to stomp as he entered what he presumed was the inner sanctum of his IT chief. Hopefully she hadn't gone completely insane yet.

Philip forced himself to calm down. He wanted her cooperation, after all, and while he had ultimate control over the computer systems at SunHo, it was a Pyrrhic sort of thing. He would ultimately win a confrontation with his IT chief, but he would do so only by destroying the entire IT system, at least back to the last off-site backup. He needed to be sure the cost was worth it before he brought all work to a halt.

"Mr. Sundstrom! This is certainly a surprise," Candy Kane said as she emerged from her office.

I don't doubt it, he thought. "I need to talk to you, and I thought it better to do it in person," Philip said, smiling.

"Hmmm," Candy said, appearing to think. She shook her head. "Come into my office."

Candy Kane was rail thin, and she held lank blonde hair back in a no-nonsense bun, although in Philip's opinion it only accentuated her blade-like cheekbones. He could only describe her outfit as "business severe," and her assertive red lipstick made him shudder. Not with her coloring, she shouldn't. Oh well, if he spoke up, it was grounds for a sexual harassment suit.

But when Philip saw her office, he realized Candy probably didn't care. It reflected her severity, and both it and her dress probably suited some part of her personality he hadn't met yet.

They eyed each other over her antiseptic desk. "So what can I do for you, Mr. Sundstrom? I'm still not sure how you got in here, by the way."

"Call me Philip." He smiled. He intended to enjoy this. He held up his corporate badge. "It's like a pass at a rock concert. All-access, at least until the retinal scanner. That will be disabled by the end of business today, and that is a direct order."

She shook her head. "Uh-uh. I control who gets in and out of here."

"Not anymore." Philip looked her straight in the eye. She would acknowledge his primacy and that's all there was to it. "Besides, I control the master system."

"You most certainly do not!" Candy gasped, rising from her chair.

"Have you ever noticed that deep, deep within the very root of the most fundamental system there is what appears to be nothing but a legacy system?" When she didn't say anything, he continued, "That's a hatch door, and only I can use it. Any attempt to get around or modify that apparently useless legacy system will freeze the entire shebang. Not my access, of course, but everyone else's, including yours."

"The outside 'contractors' who come in to service the custom system when we're quite capable ourselves," Candy said, nodding her head. She watched Philip idly swing his badge by his index finger.

There were things he still hadn't told her. "Among other things."

"Well done, Philip, well done." Candy nodded her appreciation. "So what may I do for you?"

"How much do you pay attention to what goes on outside this spider web of yours?" Philip said.

"In all honesty, I try to avoid the machinations, if only because minding my own business down here is a full-time job." She steepled her fingers. "Have I missed anything I should've been paying attention to?"

Philip made a face. "That depends on how you feel about Winch and his opinion that he should occupy the CEO's suite."

"Winch?" Candy cocked her head.

"Winchester Chapman."

"Oh good grief. Doesn't he have enough to do as it is?" Candy drummed her fingers on the desktop. Her nails, Philip noticed, were the same too-bright red as her lips.

"That's more or less how I feel about it." Philip replied. He said nothing more. He wanted her to speak next. It was an elementary, even childish, bit of manipulation, but that didn't make it any less effective.

After the seconds dragged by with agonizing slowness, Candy broke. "So how does that relate to me? To your presence down here?"

A slow and lazy smile spread across Philip's face. He loved it when people did what he wanted. "I want access to the e-mail of everyone on the C-level, as well as that of their personal assistants and immediate reports. I also want to know what calls they made and received from SunHo phones."

"Absolutely not," Candy snapped. "It's a breach of confidence and against privacy laws for you to demand those records without a court order."

"Nice try," Philip scoffed, his grin going from genial to predatory. "Any communication on company computers or phones isn't protected by privacy laws, not according to the Supreme Court. You're welcome to take it up with the justices. Not only that, every terms of service they agreed to with each software upgrade included clauses notifying them that communications are property of SunHo."

Candy shook her head. "You're not SunHo."

Philip stared at her until she squirmed. *"L'état c'est moi,* sweetheart."

"You're a fucker," she said with a certain admiration.

"You have no idea, but I'm also a fucker with a proposition."

"Why do I suddenly feel I need a lawyer with me?" Candy said, laughing.

Philip knew she meant it as a joke, but he detected a waiver in her voice, a slight one, but it was there. "Now, now, none of that. This will be entirely to your benefit. In return for your cooperation—because we both know you could stymy me for months, months I may not have—I propose to make IT a C-level position itself, in charge of integrating all of SunHo's IT departments across the country. The head of this new position, the Chief Information Technology Officer, would then be in charge of all of SunHo's IT, not just the IT here in Sacramento."

Then Philip sat back and let human nature finish the job for him. He had suggested nothing illegal to her. In fact, the promotion of IT to a C-level position was long overdue. Of course, given Randall's distrust of innovation, it didn't surprise Philip that it hadn't happened. Sure, he might've opened the search to all the heads of the local IT departments, but when it came down to it, the decision whether or not to do so was his prerogative. Suddenly he felt like Britney Spears before she went insane.

Candy looked at him speculatively. "So if I help you access what's yours anyway—"

"And continue to help me—"

"And spy for you, you'll give me a ginormous promotion, one I've never even imagined?" Candy looked him straight in the eyes. He liked that.

Philip nodded. "Essentially. Instead of being a spider in a small web down here, you'll be a spider in a much bigger web and have an office with a halfway decent view of the outside and a salary to match."

"You'd raise my pay?" Candy's eyes all but bugged.

Philip raised his eyebrows, feigning shock. He tried not to laugh at her surprise. "You think I'd ask you to perform vastly increased duties for free? Even with newly hired assistants, you're going to be busy."

"You think I wouldn't jump at the chance to get my hands on all those other systems? Mr. Sundstrom, I'd pay for the privilege."

Philip laughed. "Fortunately for you, that's not how we do things in business. You'll be paid for your skills and increased responsibilities."

He told himself repeatedly the gleam in her eye wasn't evil, but the fact that it was there said he'd chosen the right person for the job, a capable technical expert with a streak of low cunning akin to his own.

"Now I know where college is going to come from. I have twins, you see. Juniors in high school, with one more two years behind." Candy sat back in her chair, both relieved and overjoyed.

"Well, I've now screwed your kids out of financial aid, but hopefully the increase will be enough to cover it. My assistant will contact you later this afternoon with the new contract and salary proposal, if that's convenient for you?"

"I'll wait for his word, and in the meantime, I'll set up a secure line between your computers and mine, a private mail client, if you will. There'll be a new icon on your desktop. Given your little quote from Louis XIV, I think it'll be the Sun-King emblem from Versailles." Candy pulled out a yellow pad of paper and started jotting notes.

Philip cocked an eyebrow. "And working to find that hatch?"

"You're not paying me to be stupid, are you, Philip?" Candy didn't even look up. "I think we should be able to communicate even after hours, if it comes down to it. Is that yours or a company laptop?"

"It's mine." He held it to his chest.

Candy laughed. "None of that, now. Hand it over. I've seen everything, so a few dirty pictures aren't going to shock me, and in any event, I don't plan on snooping."

"I...." Philip turned lobster red. "I don't have any pics like that on here!"

"Of course you don't." Candy held out her hand.

Philip handed over his MacBook Air. Why did he suddenly feel like Candy had gotten the better of him?

"Great, Philip. Like I said, I'll get right on this. I'll have someone run this back up to you after lunch. If you decide to leave early, give me thirty minutes' notice and I'll finish it up," Candy said without looking up. She had already turned to her monitor, her hands flying over the keyboard.

Philip sighed on his way back up to his office. He figured he'd feel a greater sense of victory. At that very moment, his tame IT boffin was working on a secure pipeline from her computer to his private ones, and before long he expected a flow of information along it that would send some to the figurative guillotine and help him figure out which others of his board he could trust to help him out of this mess. But none of this distracted Philip from the fact that he missed Stuart terribly. When he did see his fiery boyfriend, the poor guy had his nose in an electronic text. Philip took what he could get and was grateful, but he still missed the easier times of earlier in the summer.

CHAPTER
Seventeen

"So Brad tells me you have some fairly specific parameters in mind," Drew said.

"I take it Brad didn't tell you the specifics?" Philip used his straw to push the whipped cream down into his blended coffee drink.

Drew made some notes in Philip's file. "No, he seemed to think it'd be more fun if you told me."

"More fun? Your home life must be one adventure after another," Philip said.

"Sometimes, yeah." Drew smiled. "So. Parameters."

"To begin with, I'd like it somewhere around the Med Center but without it being in a ghetto, obviously."

Drew looked up from his note-taking, his pen poised over the paper. "The Med Center? Really, Philip?"

"Yes, Drew." Philip smiled at him, a business-bland smile.

"Something you want to tell me?"

Philip could tell how hard Drew worked to suppress his smirk. "Yes, I'm thinking a condo, unless you find something in the neighborhood of bungalows right around the Med Center. I don't want anything I have to do too much to, because I don't want to alienate the neighborhood before I move in."

"Uh… yeah, that makes good sense," Drew said, looking to Philip like he was struggling manfully to squash any number of comments.

Philip laughed. "You should see the look on your face right now."

"Well, what did you expect?" Drew said, tossing his pen down. "You can't tell me something like that and then expect me not to react."

"I bet you know what your husband meant by 'fun' though, don't you?"

Drew rolled his eyes. "Sometimes I think Brad's unclear on the meaning of the word. Come to think of it, despite your differences, the two of you have fairly similar senses of humor."

"Do you think we should come with warning labels?" Philip said.

"No. The only people who need to know are me and Stuart," Drew replied. "I'm assuming that's what this is all about."

Philip sighed. "Yes and no. Yes, he's the reason I'm looking around the Med Center. I mean, duh. On the other hand, there are too many ghosts in the old house, if that makes sense."

"I think it does." Drew picked up his pen again. "So… other than neighborhood, what do you want?"

"At least two bedrooms and bathrooms," Philip said. "Four bedrooms would have to take my breath away."

Drew nodded. "Right. You're trying to get away from a huge house. For what it's worth, the neighborhood we'll be talking about doesn't have many large houses, so two to three bedrooms is the norm, and four bedrooms in condo infill projects is rare, too."

Philip took a draw on his coffee milkshake. "Right. Two to three bedrooms, two bathrooms, established neighborhood or infill, fixer-upper is fine. Oh—square footage. I'm thinking fifteen hundred square feet, plus or minus. That's enough for one—"

"Or more—"

"I can't imagine what you're talking about," Philip said with a perfectly straight face. "Anyway, I have an enormous house. I don't need another."

"Yeah, about that…." Drew rummaged around in his battered leather messenger bag until he found a map. He spread it out on the table between them. "Here's your house," he said, circling the approximate place on the map. "Here are the neighborhoods you're targeting—Med Center, Elmhurst, Tahoe Park, and possibly West Tahoe Park, although it's too close to Oak Park for my tastes."

"I've heard it's cleaning up and gentrification is right around the corner," Philip said, frowning at the map.

Drew laughed, a short, derisive bark. "They've been saying that for more than a decade, and in my estimation it'll never happen. Unless you like drive-by shootings and people shooting up on the sidewalk in front of your house, you're not moving there. The point I'm trying to make here, Philip, is that at most you'll be moving five miles. Is all this really worth your time and money?"

Philip knew what Drew didn't say—was it worth Drew's time and commission. "In terms of mileage, no. You're right. It's not that different from moving across the street for a better view, but in terms of conceptual worlds? Whole different universes."

Drew nodded. "Okay, then. One more blunt question. You own a construction company that has some infill projects, so why're you working with me?"

"Because I'm not interested in new construction," Philip said. He treaded very carefully. The last thing he wanted was Drew to get the idea that this was some kind of charity project on his part. Sure, that thought lurked at the back of his mind, if only because the economy still sucked and he knew Brad and Drew had sunk a fair amount of Brad's SunHo buyout into their businesses. But Philip would be damned before he told them that. "And because other builders do things differently, and it never hurts to check out the competition."

"All righty, then," Drew said. He gathered up the map and his file on Philip's likes and dislikes. "It's a buyer's market, so I ought to be able to find something for you. I'll give you a call in the next day or two when I've set up some appointments."

Philip stood and shook Drew's hand.

"Ooooh, so businessy," Drew quipped.

"Sorry, force of habit," Philip said.

"No worries," Drew said, "and speaking of not worrying, might you be interested in not worrying about dinner on Sunday? I've got some more veg-head recipes I want to dump on you."

"I'd love that, thank you." Philip smiled. He definitely appreciated having family nearby, and that disastrous dinner aside, they'd made a semiregular thing of it over the summer. Now that summer was winding down, they'd established the pattern.

"Great! Brad or I will text you the time." Drew gave him a quick hug.

"And what I can bring."

Philip sat back down. Why did a solution to one problem raise a host of new ones? When the idea had first occurred to him, he'd honestly thought that moving was the solution to a number of problems that stood between him and Stuart. He lived in his childhood home, and despite working it over with designers, the ghosts of his childhood still haunted him and the house. Then, too, he knew that despite all the good times they had in his house, Stuart would never truly be comfortable in a house so large it was just shy of a mansion. But with ghosts of his own past and the ghosts of Stuart's present, either way Philip sliced it, his childhood home was haunted, and try as he might, he couldn't exorcise them.

So move, right? Relocate close to the Med Center and blink innocently when Stuart gave him the side eye about living within walking distance of his new school. Solves the old problems, plus the new one, namely that they never saw each other. Philip wasn't just falling for Stuart like the proverbial ton of bricks, he *had* fallen for Stuart. Past tense, done deal, get married since the Supreme Court had ruled the right way in June, the majority opinion stating that the Prop h8's supporters had no standing to appeal at any level whatsoever. He never saw Stuart anymore because of school, and it was killing him. But the last thing Philip wanted to do was pressure him either by telling him that or by whimpering about never seeing him anymore. Stuart was already under enough pressure. When he'd first thought of it a place nearby seemed ideal. Stuart could crash there after a late night of studying or maybe—this was his secret fantasy—move in when he finally ditched his place with Jonathan.

Then reality intruded and his name was Drew. Philip didn't blame his brother-in-law, far from it. Someone had to bring him back down to earth, apparently. In all his grand planning, he'd never really considered the fact that he was spending a few hundred thousand dollars to move a handful of miles. It sounded silly if he said it aloud, even though people had done weirder things for love. As far as he was concerned, it would only build his reputation for eccentricity that much faster. But Drew was right. All Philip was really doing was switching which side of Highway 50 he lived on.

Maybe to throw Stuart off the scent, at least for a while, he'd tell him he planned to look at some of the high-rise condo towers downtown. Then he'd rave about this fab place Drew found somewhere else and—what a coincidence—it was near the Med Center. That might fool Stuart for five whole minutes, Philip thought. He never had been able to hide much from Stuart, it might be worth a try.

But first he had to tell Stuart he was moving.

"SO HOW'D Stuart take the news you were moving?" Brad asked. He tossed another crouton up into the air and caught it in his open mouth.

Philip looked at Drew askance, but Drew only shrugged. "I can't really say anything. I'm the one who taught him to do that, although I do wish he'd stop picking them out of the salad."

Philip liked Brad and Drew's house. It had always struck him as warm and cozy, although he supposed it wasn't actually that small. It must've been something they themselves added to it. He sighed quietly.

"Philip?" Drew, the more emotionally attuned of the two, said.

Philip knew Drew probably meant the sigh, but he ignored it. "Basically? He told me that if it's what I want, then he's happy for me. He never really did understand why one person would keep so large a house, and he kept saying that it must cost a mint to heat and cool."

"He's a practical one," Drew said.

Brad snorted. "One of you two has to be."

"I don't have to be practical." Philip sniffed, making a face at his brother. He pretended to pat a stray hair back into place. Feeling subdued that evening, he'd styled his hair with minimal embellishment, no *up up and away*, no wall of bangs, only enough product to keep his hair swept to one side and out of his eyes. Between that, glasses in fashionably nerdy frames instead of contacts, and clothes suited for early fall—deck shoes, chinos in khaki, a plaid shirt—he barely recognized himself. "I'm sitting atop a money-making machine."

Brad threw a crouton at him.

"Eww! That one was wet." Philip deposited the remains of the soggy wad of bread on his plate and then wiped his forehead.

"I know." Brad gloated for a moment, but he enjoyed his triumph only for a few seconds. "Ow! What the hell was that for?"

Drew gave him a bland look. "What was that, dear?"

"I'll get you for that," Brad muttered darkly.

Philip snorted. "No, you won't."

Brad and Drew looked at him. "You won't, Brad, and you know it. One word from Drew and you come right to heel." Philip sighed, surprised at how melancholy he felt. He missed Stuart. He smiled. "You'll blow and bluster, but you don't mean anything by it, and Drew'll pretend to be shocked and shudder theatrically, but you're both only acting, and I really need to stop talking now."

Philip's face heated up. He hated that. His fair coloring served only to make his freckles jump out. Philip pushed back from the table. "I'll be right back."

Unlike the last time a hissy fit boiled up when the three of them ate together, no one ran out to the backyard. Philip locked the bathroom door behind him. He looked in the mirror and shook his head. He needed to talk to Stuart, because this was already out of hand and he wasn't sure how long he could keep being the supportive boyfriend in the background.

He washed his face in cold water, anything to banish his blush. There was something about Stuart… even thinking about him made Philip all the more prone to flushing. It had better be good for the skin, dammit, he thought as he patted his face dry.

When Philip rejoined Brad and Drew, he found they'd finished their dinner, but it didn't bother him. He'd lost his appetite. "I'm sorry, guys. I seem to be a bag of emotional slop these days."

"Are you all right?" Drew asked, concern etched on his handsome features.

Brad looked at Philip calmly. "I think," he said, "that my big brother suffers from nothing more and nothing less than lovesickness."

"You know?" Philip looked at him sharply.

"You've been a little obvious." Brad shrugged his apology.

Philip slumped in his chair. Because he didn't feel foolish enough. "I'm not always a head case, I promise."

Drew reached over to cover Philip's hand with his. "I had no idea that Sundstroms were two for the price of one when I acquired Brad."

Philip blanched. "I didn't mean to overstay my welcome, I'm so sorry—"

"Hush, I didn't mean it that way. I meant, I got a brother-in-law I happen to like very much, alike to my beloved and yet so very different. We're happy to have you over as often as you want to be here, and I for one appreciate the chance to help you," Drew said.

Brad nodded. "It humanizes you."

"What?" Philip lifted his gaze from his intense study of the grain of the wooden dining table.

"You come across as this unstoppable machine, going after and getting what you want. Sure, you've got a sense of humor—kind of—but try and look at it from an outsider's point of view," Brad said. "You get what you want, whether it's Sundstrom Homes or Drew's attackers. Don't get me wrong, we're super grateful for that and your heart's obviously in the right place, but you always look like you stepped out of *GQ*, and if your blood's up to room temperature, it's news to me. It's reassuring to know that when RoboPhil takes a break from kicking corporate ass love makes as big a fool of you as it does the rest of us."

Philip grunted. "Thanks. I think."

"So are you?" Brad grinned. "Lovesick, I mean."

"Brad!" Drew hissed.

"It's okay, Drew. If I can't tell my family, who can I tell?" Philip said.

Brad nudged Drew. "See? I told you."

"So yeah, I'm in love with Stuart. We're basically boyfriends, even if we haven't had 'the talk'...." Philip shrugged. Surprisingly, after everything else, it didn't even make him flinch.

"Have you told Stuart?" Brad asked.

Philip shook his head. "No. That would make him bolt, and then there's med school. He has too much going on right now for me to dump that on him. When he's not asleep, he's got his nose in a book."

"Don't you think you should let him make that decision, Philip? I've noticed you've got this big-brother tendency to want to protect people, but doesn't that rob people—Stuart—of their decision-making abilities?" Brad said.

Philip smiled. He wasn't the only Sundstrom boy with big-brother tendencies, he'd noticed. "I appreciate the advice, Brad, truly. It's helped in the past, but in this instance I know Stuart better than you do."

"You do not!" Brad snorted. "I rowed with him for I don't know how many years. Five? Six?"

"We've been much more open and intimate, and I don't mean sex, Brad. How well did you know him while you rowed? How much did he open up to you?" Philip said. "Given that Stuart was shocked that I was your brother but gave me a chance anyway, I'm going to guess you two weren't that close and were even antagonistic."

Brad ran his hand over his shaven scalp. "Yeah, probably...."

"There's no 'probably' about it," Drew said. "I've seen you both at regattas."

Brad started to speak, but then stopped. "You know, you're right. I called him Cockring, after all. That wasn't exactly an endearment. I'm sure you know him much better than I do by now, and if you love him, then I'm happy for you, Philip."

Conversation moved on after that, because really, what more could Philip say? He'd hardly expected his brother and brother-in-law to solve his problem, but the fact that they'd listened helped him feel better. Not every problem came with a solution wrapped in a pretty ribbon.

No, Philip knew he needed to solve this problem on his own. What he didn't know was how to do that.

SOMETIMES, STUART thought, gross anatomy was aptly named, even if he'd grown used to the smell of formaldehyde. At times like that, he focused as narrowly as he could on the organ or system or tissue that he and Eddie were dissecting at the time until the feeling passed. He knew he needed to understand how the parts of the body fit together, but he also already knew that he would not be focusing on any of the surgical specialties for his residency. He supposed surgery was for those who'd loved spatial geometry. He preferred a more intellectual approach over cutting people open and wading in to see what was wrong.

That said, every so often it struck him that he was slowly disassembling a body, a human body, a person who had once walked the earth just like he did, who lived and loved and laughed and cried, just like he did. It cemented in his mind exactly why he'd chosen to go to medical school and made the sacrifices worth it. It helped if he reminded himself of that when he missed Philip.

"That's so cool that your boyfriend's letting you use his library for our study group," Eddie said, looking around. "Must be nice. Dude, you need to get a ring on his finger immediately, if not sooner."

Stuart gave him a pained look. "It's complicated."

"How complicated can it be? He's head over heels for you. You're gone on him. Why is this so difficult?"

"It just is," Stuart said. Thinking about it made him feel like shit. He knew Eddie spoke the truth. He and Philip fit together like lock and key. More and more, Stuart thought *we* and not *I*, and he suspected Philip had beaten him to that by a month or more. He sighed. "It just is."

Eddie shook his head. "Whatever, man. You white people sure make things complicated."

"Anyway, don't get too comfortable. Philip's looking for someplace smaller. I think he's tired of rattling around here by himself," Stuart said, bracing himself for another onslaught from Eddie.

"I can think of an easy solution to that problem, as well as your problems with your asshole roommate," Eddie said.

Stuart wasn't sure whether he should smack himself on the forehead or Eddie for not leaving well enough alone. Either way, he'd walked right into that one. "Why is everyone trying to push us toward the altar?"

"I'm going to throw this out there, but maybe it's because you two are perfect for each other and everyone but you can see it?" This time Eddie didn't even bother pretending to be stupid or clueless.

Stuart sighed. He saw it, but he couldn't deal with it. But he knew Eddie was right about one thing. Both he and Philip deserved more than they had at the moment. Nonetheless life continued as it had with little change on the personal front, Philip distracted by work and Stuart by school. They took what time they could, even though it was never enough. Philip did what he could to make Stuart's life easier, and Stuart loved him for it. On most nights, Stuart and his study group could look forward to homemade snacks, including handmade pizzas the night before an exam. After that, Stuart was pretty sure even Eddie was ready to marry Philip.

The food lasted right up until Philip's movers packed up his kitchen. "Don't worry," Philip said to Stuart and his fellow semipanicked med students. "Once the new place is set up, you take over the dining room or my office there. Both have doors that shut."

"Thanks, Philip." Stuart gave him a big hug.

"Oh come on, Stuart. After everything Philip's done for us, the least you could do is kiss him," Eddie said. "I'm disappointed in you, man."

"Kiss him, kiss him," chanted the other two members of their study group.

Stuart knew he'd turned the same color as a stop sign. He felt it. But egged on by his friends, he knew what he had to do. He wrapped his arms around Philip's neck and laid one on his boyfriend. He'd intended to make it a quick buss on the lips, but Philip had other ideas, wrapping his own arms around Stuart and deepening the kiss. Stuart flailed helplessly for a moment, but soon realized Philip had no intention of releasing him.

Then Philip took pity on him and turned them around, shielding Stuart with his body. "There," Philip said. "Think that about evens us up?"

"Yeah, but now I've got a huge boner," Stuart whispered.

Philip shrugged. "So get rid of them and I'll help you out with that."

Stuart checked his watch. "We're about done…."

"Then I'll see you upstairs in fifteen minutes."

Then Philip groped him. "So you don't forget," he said, barely more than a whisper that sent shivers up and down Stuart's spine. Or maybe it was the nibble on his earlobe. Whichever.

Either way, Stuart cleared the study group out by pretending to be dog-tired. Actually it took very little pretending; they were all dog-tired all the time. Eddie gave him a look that said he knew exactly what was going on, but so what? Stuart was getting some on a Saturday night.

ONE THING Stuart and Philip had instituted almost as soon as Stuart had started med school was that Sunday mornings were reserved for them. Sometimes that meant waking up early to spend time together before Stuart hit the books or left for the library or the lab, but they reserved some portion of the traditional day of rest for the two of them alone. Philip cooked and Stuart kept him company, because if there was one thing he'd learned, it was that cooks were frequently happier if they didn't cook alone, and his Philip was no exception.

His. Stuart knew it was true. It was… yeah. That last step, that plunge off the cliff, that same feeling of the bottom dropping out of his stomach, that making the final commitment entailed…. He made a face. "Remember that conversation a week or so ago when Eddie said I should move in and solve two problems, you rattling around here by yourself and me living with a jackass?"

"Vividly."

"Well, he must've jinxed me or something, because I can't live there anymore." Stuart shook his head slowly. "Jonathan's drinking most days now, and he starts as soon as he gets home from practices. Between the noise and the… uh, overtures—"

Philip stilled. "Overtures?"

"He tries to get into my room, sometimes," Stuart said, pinching the bridge of his nose and wishing to hell he didn't have to tell Philip this part. "For sex. To get back together."

"That's not an overture, Stuart. It's attempted rape."

"Not yet, and I can't believe I'm about to say this, but I'm reasonably certain it's only a matter of time."

Stuart thought Philip looked like a storm cloud. He'd seen Brad look like that, but had no idea it was a family trait.

"You're not going to get all macho alpha-male, are you? Because I don't think that would help," Stuart said, even if a small, atavistic part of him was secretly thrilled—even turned on—that his boyfriend was all riled up.

"I don't have to get all macho. I have other ways to destroy people," Philip said, his voice low and menacing. "Let's start with CalPac's crew. It's a club sport thanks to Title IX, is it not? That means they're self-funding, correct? A large enough check and a few words in the right ears will take care of Jonathan's rowing career. CalPac itself is a private school. More money and a 'Do you know what one of your students is doing to one of your alumni, who, by the way, is being courted by the US National Rowing Team?' and Poisonwood will be suspended. For that matter, I can look up his father and have a few words, businessman to businessman. Then that brat will be on the next flight back to England."

Stuart stared, his jaw hanging open. "You could do all that?"

"To someone threatening your physical safety, to say nothing of your sexual health? In a short second, Stuart. You mean everything to me, but I'd do the same for Brad or Drew, or even Valerie because she means the world to you." Philip sighed. "It's one of the advantages of money and it's perfectly legal."

"Wow. I… I didn't know you felt that way," Stuart said.

Philip laughed. "Don't let the suit and hair fool you. I may lack my brother's barbarian physique, but I'm every bit the savage he can be. I go about it differently, that's all. Either way, we look out for our own."

"Huh. I could get to like this fierceness. No one's ever been fierce for me before," Stuart said, "even if you kind of shocked me with it."

Philip pushed his chair back from the table and held his arms open. Stuart felt pulled right to him and sat on his lap. Philip pulled him close, kissing the top of his head. "Don't worry about it, okay? But I bet there've been other guys who'd have done it if you'd let them."

Maybe so, Stuart thought, but there'd never been guys he'd felt that strongly about before. He thought he'd felt that way about Jonathan, at least for a time, but events since Jonathan's return had shown him how wrong he'd been.

"But now that your living situation's gotten worse, you could crash here," Philip said.

"You mean move in?" Stuart said, his eyes widening. He took deep, centering breaths so he wouldn't hyperventilate.

"Yeah," Philip said, smiling. "That."

"I'm stuck on the lease."

Philip waved that off. "Those things aren't worth the paper they're written on. If it comes to that, my lawyer will get you out of it."

"Thanks, Philip. I really appreciate it. Hopefully Jonathan will come to his senses, but if not…." He was glad to know he had options, but moving in? His heart started drumming a tattoo.

Philip twisted around to look him in the eye. "But what? You're waiting for him to break into your room? You're going to use a sexual assault as an excuse to break the lease?"

"No!"

Philip's expression went flat. "But you won't move in with me, either, because that's what it sounds like."

Stuart slid off Philip's lap. "That's not it at all. I—"

"What, Stuart? What about me can't you accept? What can't you stand about me? Why does the thought of living with me cause a panic attack?"

"Why can't you accept that this isn't about you, Philip?" Stuart ran a hand through his hair. He tried to stay calm, but this was exactly why he'd dreaded bringing this up, and he'd rather install extra locks on his bedroom door than say hurtful, stupid things.

Or hear them.

"Why can't you accept that we mean something to each other?" Philip said, a world of hurt in his soft brown eyes.

"I can. I do, Philip. We're exclusive and we've slouched into being boyfriends without having a real conversation about it. But more? I don't think I can give you more than that right now. You know what my life's like. You know there's no one else. I'm married to med school, but—"

Philip drew Stuart back to him. "That's an excuse, Stuart, an excuse and a copout. Many people start or maintain relationships in med school. What're you afraid of?"

"I don't know."

"Not being the best?"

"Maybe." Stuart shrugged. This was moving into uncomfortable territory, but it beat sexual assault.

"I hope you know your worth to me doesn't depend on your grades. God, I hope you know that." Philip pulled Stuart's head down, kissing his forehead.

"It's always nice to hear." Growing up, he'd never had any worth to anyone. The fact that Philip found worth in him for his sake alone… even at CalPac his worth had been measured by his grades and his skill in coxing a boat. But Philip? He was the real deal, and he'd never be able to put into words what that meant to him.

"Are you worried I'll leave you for the first woman to catch my eye?"

Stuart tried to laugh at Philip's comment, even though that was exactly what he feared, or one of the things. "Really, Philip? Biphobia?"

"I'm throwing words out, hoping some of them will stick." Philip leaned into him in a way he found wholly satisfying, ghosting butterfly kisses down his neck. "Letting yourself down? Letting me down? Not giving me the best you have to give?"

"What if I'm afraid, Philip? What if I can't put my finger on exactly why? I didn't exactly have the best home life, and growing up, I learned fast that I'm the only one I can depend on. You? You've been amazing. You've been there for me every time something's blown up since we've met—"

"Likewise," Philip said softly.

Stuart nodded his head to concede the point. "We've been there for each other, but don't you see, Philip? It's September. It's been four months. You're sure, but I'm having to learn that I can depend on someone else. It's been a struggle."

Philip rested his head on Stuart's shoulder. He rubbed Stuart's back, trying to relax him, but Stuart could've told him that was a lost cause. "I'm sorry I can't be what you want right now."

"Shhh, none of that, now," Philip whispered. He pressed his face against Stuart's neck, holding the smaller man tightly. "Who said anything about that? You're exactly who I want and need."

Stuart looked up at him. "Are you for real? You're too good to be true."

"No, I happen to lo—be very fond of you. I assure you, at work I'm a different person, and my board is coming to view me as an unholy terror. We haven't had as much time to talk lately, so I haven't told you the latest, but I'm reading all their e-mails. Because I like them to be uneasy, I let the occasional tidbit drop so they suspect something."

"You're terrible, Muriel."

"I know." Philip grinned. "That's the point. Some of those assholes assumed I was nothing but a wet-behind-the-ears child that they could easily shove aside. I'm reminding them whose surname matches the company letterhead before I shitcan the guilty. If they give me too much crap, I'll publicize their extramarital affairs and other misdeeds."

"Damn, remind me not to piss you off," Stuart said.

Philip kissed him. "You have nothing to worry about."

"Hold me?"

"I thought that's what I was doing." Philip tightened his hold around Stuart anyway.

"Full-body contact." Stuart hoped Philip understood him, even though he'd buried his face in Philip's neck.

"Ah." Philip changed his hold on Stuart and carried him to their familiar leather davenport in the family room. Then he snuggled down next to Stuart, pulling a cozy throw over them both.

"This is nice," Stuart said. Somehow all the pressures he faced felt a little farther away when Philip held him close, at least for a little while. "There's only one problem."

Philip turned his head to look at him. "And what would that be?"

"I need some kisses."

"I can't have you unkissed. Where do you need these kisses?"

Stuart pointed to his cheek. "Here."

And Philip obligingly kissed it.

"And here." Stuart pointed to his lips.

Philip lavished special attention on those, and Stuart didn't mind one bit. He certainly didn't object to the way in which Philip worked his hands up under his T-shirt, touching and caressing.

"What about here?" Philip said, breaking the kiss. He bent his head and flicked his tongue over one of Stuart's nipples.

"Do that again. I'm not sure." Stuart shuddered.

Smirking, Philip went to work, laving with his tongue and scraping with his teeth. "You seem kind of hot and bothered," he said once Stuart had lost the power of speech. "Where else needs a kiss?"

"That's not kissing," Stuart said, groaning. For someone who hadn't had any significant relationships with guys, Philip had sure learned fast, and was Stuart ever grateful.

"You arguing?"

"Not on your life. But there's something else that needs kissing."

"Yeah?"

Stuart pointed south, hoping Philip would figure it out.

Philip grinned and then kissed his way south. When he encountered Stuart's treasure trail, he abandoned kisses for licks. Then he made short work of Stuart's pajama bottoms. "See? I told you those were the best thing ever."

Stuart lifted his head off the cushion he used as a pillow. "No, the best thing ever is that is that I'm going commando this morning."

"Makes this easier."

And before Stuart knew it, Philip had swallowed his cock to the root. The muscles of his boyfriend's throat fluttered around his rock-hard dick, and he was helpless. He tossed his head and moaned, swearing and yelling and speaking in tongues. When Philip came up for air, he met Stuart's eyes. Stuart's were dark with lust; Philip's too, but his held something more, but right then Stuart couldn't decipher what.

"Those… those aren't kisses."

"Are you really arguing?" Then Philip engulfed him again. This time, Philip encouraged him to throw his legs over Philip's shoulders. Philip used hand, tongue, and throat to bring Stuart to his climax. It was different from the times they'd fucked, Stuart thought, subtler, gentler, but all the more intense for it.

Sometimes when they fucked, he felt like he'd taken a bit of a battering, but not that morning. He knew he'd be able to go again in an hour or two. Philip milked him dry, then released his softening cock before it grew too sensitive or painful. He was really getting to like having a sensitive lover.

But speaking of sensitive…. "What about you?"

"I can take care of myself later, if only because," Philip kissed his nose, "I sense someone's antsy to get to work today."

Stuart made a face. "That hardly seems fair. You gave me an awesome blowjob but I didn't do a thing for you."

"I think you underestimate the pleasure I take in making you feel good, and how much mileage I'll get out of this when it's added to my wank bank."

Philip pulled himself up the davenport, up Stuart's body, and kissed him. He tasted himself on Philip's lips, a turn-on all its own.

"Well, as long as you're sure."

Philip looked him in the eyes, deeply, a smile playing about the edges of his mouth. "I've never been more sure of anything."

He had the sense Philip meant more than he said, but perforce had to content himself with words spoken. "Can we cuddle for a bit longer?"

Philip burrowed into Stuart's side. "Hmmm, I like cuddling."

After that, they went about their Sunday like they always did, he with his studying at school, Philip with his work. Stuart found he really didn't want to know the details, if only because if or when it blew up, he would be able to say in all honesty under oath he knew nothing about those details. Plausible deniability and all that, your honor. I'm only a medical student and although Mr. Sundstrom is my boyfriend, he never confided the details of his business dealings to me, just like I didn't introduce him to my cadaver from gross anatomy.

When Stuart woke up Monday morning, Philip was spooned behind him. He liked waking up that way, with one of Philip's arms across his chest possessively. He felt loved. It would be so easy to give in and move in, but still….

In the shower, the solution came to him.

"I thought of a solution to my problem."

Philip looked up from his oatmeal. "Oh?"

"I'll pay you what I was paying in rent at the other place," Stuart said, "and I'll have my own room if I need some space."

"You don't have to—" Then Philip shut up. "If that's what you have to do, Stuart."

"It is."

Philip smiled at him. "You're going to love the new place, especially your commute. I hope you'll sleep in my bed at least some of the time."

"I think you can count on that."

CHAPTER
Eighteen

"HELLO?" PHILIP sat at his desk, reading through his father's files and idly glancing at his favorite pop culture watering holes on the Internet, particularly some covering the music industry. When his iPhone went off—his personal phone, not the electronic leash with which SunHo tried to tether him to the office on occasion—he frowned.

"Philip? It's Valerie."

"Valerie! What's up?"

She cut right to the chase. "Do you know where Stuart is? I keep calling and leaving messages, but I can never catch him."

"I know where he is, all right. Med school." Philip laughed, but there wasn't much humor in it. "Knowing him, the messages are piling up and he feels like crap."

"Yeah, that and five bucks will get you a Frappuccino."

"Someone's awfully young to be so cynical, but then, Stuart's the same way."

"Yeah, it's a family trait. Can you give him a message?"

"Sure." He flipped to a clean page in the notepad he'd been using to jot notes about the concert.

"Our parents dragged me to one of those stupid tent revivals and he—"

"Those still exist?"

Valerie let out a bark of bitter laughter. "They most certainly do, at least in the most backward and superstitious parts of the country, which are unfortunately only a long drive from here. Do you know what my brother told me the last time?"

"I'm almost afraid to ask."

"Stay away from the snakes."

Philip laughed. "Sounds like good advice, particularly if your definition of 'snake' is a broad one."

"He's an asshole," Valerie said cheerfully.

"He certainly can be." Philip smiled. He couldn't help himself.

"Anyway, could let him know that his advice of going along to get along has backfired? Since I seemed to take the last one so well, our parents think I've had some kind of 'spiritual awakening' and are taking me on a tent-revival tour over Christmas break. Thank him for me, will you?"

"We've got to get you out here, don't we?"

Then something occurred to Philip. He jotted a note to remind himself to use Stuart's rent check to set up a custodial account for Valerie. They could use the money for her GED or community college tuition or even legal fees for her emancipation when she moved west.

"I need to, but I'm… scared. It's a big step, you know?"

"Say the word, and I'll have a ticket waiting for you at the nearest airport, and never mind what Stuart says. But the thing is, you have to be ready to take that step and no one can take it for you," Philip said gently.

"I know," she said with a sigh, "and thanks."

"But when you're ready, go. Take what you can carry in your backpack. We'll take care of everything else when you're in Sacramento."

"Why're you being so nice?" Valerie asked.

Philip sighed. "Because I love your brother and he won't let me help him, but maybe I can help you. I know he worries about you."

"For what it's worth, I tell him he's an idiot for not taking what you're offering." Valerie sniffled, and Philip wished he could do more than offer reassurance over the phone. "Jeez, if he ever finds out we're scheming behind his back…."

"Then we'll have to make sure he doesn't find out, won't we?" Philip said. "Question for you… do you like 'Kill the Wendybird'?"

"Like them? They're only the biggest act on the alt scene these days. Why?"

Philip spun his desk chair around to look out the window behind his desk. "I'm thinking about taking Stuart to see them when they play at the Warfield in San Francisco. I found all their CDs in his backpack so I figure he likes them."

"I'm turning green with jealousy. I hope you know that."

"Don't turn too green. I thought I'd see if I could score you a T-shirt, maybe an autographed CD or anything else I can get them to sign with a Sharpie."

Philip had to hold the phone away from his ear as Valerie squealed. He was certain men's voices couldn't reach those registers. He knew his couldn't.

Then Valerie came back down to earth. "Aww, shit. There's no way I can have those. My parents will find them."

Philip sighed. "Let me guess. They're satanic or something?"

"Got it in one. But could you get them for my BFF Cynthia? She loves Wendybird maybe more than I do, and she's been great about receiving all my mail from Stuart."

"Yeah, sure. I'd be happy to." Philip decided he'd slip something for Valerie into the Wendybird care package, too. The poor kid deserved to have some fun, regardless of what her Holy Roller parents thought.

"Thank you soooo much. I'll text you her address. I'll warn her who you are, too. Wait… how're you going to get an autographed CD?"

"Oops, my bad. Did I forget to mention my all-access pass, including a meet and greet with the band?"

He could practically hear her stewing on the other end of the connection. "Admit it. You made a deal with the devil, didn't you?"

"Only if you count putting up with my father long enough to take over the family company," Philip said.

"Stuart told me about that," Valerie said quietly. "Guess we're not the only ones with shitty parents."

Philip sighed. "My mother was a wonderful person, at least. The concert's in a week, right before Halloween. So if you could let your friend know to expect the goodies right after that? And I'll let Stuart know you called and are worried."

"Thanks, Philip, and…."

"Yeah?"

"Stuart's really lucky to have you," Valerie blurted out.

"Thanks, Valerie. That's so sweet," Philip said, touched in a way he hadn't been in a long time. "Remember, just say the word. As long as there's an airport of any size, I can get you out of there."

"SO HOW'RE things?" Morgan said as he pulled away from the Med Center where he'd picked Stuart up after classes.

Stuart looked over at his best friend. Former best friend? It felt weird to think that, but he realized in many ways that Philip was his best friend now, and not as a dodge to avoid saying boyfriend. Morgan was now only a very close friend. "Only." Ha!

"Med school things or Philip things?"

Morgan threw his head back and laughed. "I still can't believe Brad's older brother is gay, too."

"He's bi."

"Whatever. He's currently putting a smile on your face, that's for sure."

Stuart smirked. "Oh yeah."

"That's really funny, given how much you hate Brad." Morgan fiddled with the controls on the car's stereo.

"Hate's too strong a word. Brad can be year 'round, bone-deep annoying when he wants to be, but Philip's told me a lot about what it was like living with their father. It's hard to hold that against him, and besides, Philip's nothing like his younger brother." For some reason, Stuart felt compelled to defend both of the Sundstrom boys, and not only the one he loved.

"…. Next up, 'The Burning Nerve Ending Magic Trick,' the latest from Kill the Wendybird. They'll be in concert at the Warfield in San Francisco for their Halloween show on the thirtieth, but don't bother trying to get tickets. Tickets sold out within fifteen minutes of being released."

"Assholes. What's the point of announcing something if it's already sold out?" Morgan said, consternation plain on his face. "Nick will be home that weekend and I wanted to surprise him."

Stuart slid down in his seat. "Don't hate me for what I'm about to say, but Philip's taking me. He's forcing me to put the books down for a night and have some fun."

"Yeah?" Morgan smiled. "I'm liking him more and more. But seriously, how on earth did he get tickets?"

Stuart shrugged. "Beats me. Want me to see if he can score any more?"

"No, that's all right. You two have your fun. Besides," Morgan said, a wicked glint in his eyes, "I can think of other ways to make Nick's weekend memorable."

"Of that, I have no doubt. But you know what really surprises me?"

"No idea."

"All those years we lived together and I had no idea what a pervert you are."

Morgan laughed long and loudly, the kind of laugh that would draw attention if they were in public. In his own car, Morgan laughed unselfconsciously. "Maybe I was just waiting for the right man to draw it out of me."

There'd been a time when Stuart had longed to be that man, but now he found those memories relegated to the past where they belonged. Funny, he hadn't even thought of that for a while, not since Philip had entered his life.

"What're you smiling about?"

Stuart didn't know he'd been smiling. "I'm really happy for you. You and Nick are amazing together."

"Yeah?" Stuart could tell Morgan was pleased.

"Definitely." Stuart reclined his seat a bit. "So how're your parents? I miss them."

"They're well. Mom has a question for you, but before you reply, you need to realize that if you answer it the wrong way, you'll be inundated with food."

Food and Mrs. Estrada. Stuart couldn't imagine. "Okay… go for it."

"Mom wants to know if you're eating well enough with the ridiculous hours med students keep."

"How'd she know?" Stuart's suspicions kicked into overdrive. He first suspected Philip, but couldn't fathom how he'd know Morgan's mother. "If you're related to Eddie San Filipo...."

"Never heard of him. One of my cousins is a doctor, and she ratted you out to Mom," Morgan said cheerfully. "I held her off by telling her you'd moved, but you'd better prepare yourself. I think she's signing you up for the Everything of the Month Club."

Stuart shook his head. "When will she see that I can take care of myself? Seriously, Morgan. When?"

"Probably once she's got you married off. You know how she works. She took one look at you, parentless and alone, at freshmen orientation and that was that. You were Mother Estrada's ginger baby and nothing you or anyone else said could change that." Morgan shot him a sly glance. "Think of it as incentive to make sure things work with Philip."

"So what you're telling me is that she's in on the conspiracy?"

"What conspiracy? There's a conspiracy? I wanna play, too." Morgan pouted.

"*Et tu, Brute*? Besides the fact that Philip's the perfect boyfriend, my sister and my study partner—"

"Would this be the aforementioned Eddie?"

"Yeah. Anyway, Valerie and Eddie think I need to get a ring on Philip's finger yesterday. Meanwhile, Philip's as patient as a rock, but it's pretty clear he'd fly us to Boston or New York tonight if I said the word, probably on his corporate jet. Never mind that we can marry in California again."

"Corporate jet?"

Stuart nodded. "Apparently Sundstrom Homes is a much bigger deal than Brad ever let on, and Philip ousted his dad at the helm. Actually, thanks to Philip, their dad's doing hard time for that attack on Drew."

Morgan gasped. "Damn, I'd forgotten that."

"I presume Nick told you?"

"Yep, and I hope that son of a bitch rots in hell." Morgan spat out the window.

"That's the prevailing sentiment, yes. Where Brad thought Philip was kind of milquetoast, it turned out he was quietly Machiavellian. When the time was right, Philip struck hard and fast. Anyway, the point is Philip now controls the family company, so not only is my boyfriend all kinds of good things, he's richer than God."

"Interesting that you list that differently from 'all kinds of good things'. Is that a problem?"

"You know my hang-ups where rich people are concerned," Stuart said, hunching his shoulders.

Morgan put his hand on Stuart's knee. "Yes, but I'd hoped you might've outgrown them after living with me for four years."

"They're better. I mean, Philip's my boyfriend, isn't he? I'm willing to be seen in his car."

"Dare I ask?"

"Some kind of Mercedes two-seater, the speed of which is electronically controlled to keep it from lifting off."

Morgan laughed softly.

"What's so funny?"

"Don't ever change, Stuart."

Stuart shook his head. "So what're you going to tell your mother?"

"What, have the fumes from the corpse you're dissecting made you stupid? You don't think I could get away with lying to her, do you?" Morgan looked at Stuart as if he'd taken complete leave of his senses.

"Noooo, but maybe you could get her to believe I'd lied to you."

"You keep living in that dream world, sweetie. So… where do you want to eat?"

"What is it with you people and food?"

THE NEXT time Stuart caught a ride, it was to the airport. He left his last class to find a liveried chauffeur holding a sign waiting for him. "Stuart Cochrane," the sign read.

Eddie elbowed him. "I think that's you, dude."

"I'm doing my best to ignore it." Seriously, was Philip trying to kill him by embarrassing him publicly? If so, this might do it.

"I don't get you. What's Philip doing this time, and if you don't want it can I have it?"

Stuart chuckled. "He's taking me to see Kill the Wendybird in San Francisco tonight. I thought he was picking me up himself, not sending a car for me."

"Put your angst on hold. I just got a text." Eddie pulled out his phone. Then he laughed, no mere chuckle but the kind of laugh that made Stuart worry his friend was getting enough oxygen. "It's... it's for you."

Stuart took Eddie's phone. *Tell Stuart to get in the damn car.*

"Oh for crying out loud. How the hell did he get your mobile number?"

Eddie was laughing so hard tears streamed down his cheeks. "I gave it... to him." He gasped for air. "You should see your face."

Their classmates streamed around them, along with a few residents and more senior physicians and surgeons in their blue scrubs. A few smiled at Stuart when they saw the driver and sign, but most of them ignored it all.

"I guess I'd better do as Philip says. Then perhaps he'll call and tell me what's going on." Stuart hoisted his backpack. "I'll see you tomorrow for our usual study session."

Stuart made it halfway to the waiting town car before Eddie heard what he'd said. "Wait!" he called. "Did you say the Wendybirds?"

Stuart turned around, walking backward with a shit-eating grin. "Did I?"

"Asshole!"

The driver opened the back door for Stuart. "Mr. Sundstrom requests that you activate FaceTime on your iPad once you're settled. The car has onboard Wi-Fi. I'm to take you directly to the airport."

"Oh. All right, thank you." The airport, huh? That was new. Stuart couldn't wait to see what had led to this development.

He settled back against the black leather upholstery as the driver pulled smoothly away from the curb, and then did as Philip had apparently instructed. After fiddling with his borrowed iPad for a few moments to hook into the car's Wi-Fi, he activated FaceTime.

Philip appeared almost immediately. "Hey, Stuart. I'm sorry about sending a car. I'd planned to meet you myself, but something came up at work I had to deal with. At this point, I'll be flirting with the ragged edge of disaster to get to the airport on time."

"The airport?"

"Yeah," Philip said, sighing. "We're not going to have time to drive, so I've chartered a helicopter—"

"How's that?" Jyoti yelled in the background.

Philip rolled his eyes. "Excuse me, *Jyoti* chartered a helicopter, as well as a car once we reach the city. I'll have a change of clothing for both of us. I hope you don't mind a sudden change of plans."

"No, of course not."

"Thanks, Stuart. If I could've warned you ahead of time, I would've. I sent you an e-mail, but I know you don't have time to check that sort of thing when you're in class."

Philip looked like he was nothing but relieved, and that made Stuart wonder—was he really so high maintenance or so prickly that his boyfriend was afraid that a change of plans would cause a volcanic eruption? Notice might've been nice, but like Philip said, he was all but impossible to reach when he was in class. Maybe he'd better start leaving his phone on but silenced. At least that way there'd be texts waiting for him. Maybe he should look into a smart phone, too. Of course if he so much as breathed a word of it to Philip there'd be one waiting for him on Christmas morning at the latest.

"No worries. How long until you're at the airport?"

"No more than an hour," Philip said. "That'll give you some time to study, if nothing else. I'll text you when I'm in my car and about to leave the garage, how's that?"

"Sounds like a plan. I'll see you soon, Philip." He leaned forward and made a kiss at the screen. He caught Philip off guard, he could tell that much.

"See you soon, Stuart."

When he arrived at the Sacramento International Airport, Stuart discovered another advantage to flying on a private chartered flight. He didn't have to bother with any of the TSA's security theater foolishness. He walked up to the counter, identified himself and Philip, and then sat down to wait. Philip texted him sooner than expected, but Stuart managed to fit in some quality study time nonetheless.

When the parking shuttle dropped Philip off, Stuart saw that he indeed carried a small suitcase. He waited for Philip right inside the small charter terminal's doors.

"Hey you," Stuart said, kissing Philip before the doors closed behind him.

Philip gave him a one-armed hug, kissing him back. "Hey yourself. You ready? We're cutting it close."

"Yep. Where're we going to change?" Stuart pointed at the overnight bag in Philip's hand.

"Is here okay? I'm honestly not sure what we'll find when we land in the city."

Stuart took the bag from Philip. "You coming?"

Based on the look on Philip's face, one of them might be very soon. No sooner had the bathroom door shut behind Philip then Stuart pulled him into the handicapped stall.

"What's this?" Philip asked as Stuart started pulling his clothes off.

"You said we had to hurry, so I'm helping you undress." Stuart left all of Philip's work clothes in a heap on the floor, save for his pants and shoes.

He sank to his knees and freed Philip's cock from his boxer briefs.

"Stuart!" Philip hissed. "What're you doing?"

Stuart looked up at his boyfriend. "If you can't tell, it's been way too long."

Philip may have asked silly questions, but his body knew, and in short order, Philip's length filled Stuart's mouth.

"Close, Stuart…."

Stuart looked up at Philip, working his fingers around to Philip's ass. He raked his fingernails across Philip's most sensitive skin, applying subtle pressure. Philip's hips bucked and just like that, he shot down Stuart's throat. Stuart pulled back so he didn't choke and then milked Philip dry.

Philip hauled Stuart up and kissed him deeply. "You sure do spoil me."

Stuart winked at him. "Didn't you say something about hurrying?"

"I did indeed, to say nothing of avoiding arrest on a morals charge." Philip unzipped the overnight bag. "I'm glad you picked out what you wanted to wear last night. I'd have been so wrong if I'd had to guess."

Stuart dressed in the clothes he'd selected while Philip pulled on a pair of black leather pants that looked like an extension of his own skin along with a black T-shirt so tight it showed every single muscle.

It was only once they were in the helicopter catching up on their week did Stuart realize that the clothes he wore weren't actually the ones he'd selected. They were close. They looked a lot like them. But they weren't his. The tells were little things, like missing wear patterns or the lack of familiar rips. The shoes were his, but that was it. Philip, or more likely some personal shopper at a high-end department store, had done a cunning job of duplicating his concertwear, he'd give him that much.

"I've got a surprise for you," Philip said into the headsets that connected them to talk over the noise of the chartered helicopter. They were set to a private channel for conversation.

Another one? He felt like he'd been kicked in the stomach, like all of a sudden he wasn't good enough for Philip or that his admittedly somewhat tatty clothes embarrassed Philip. He tried not to cry. "Oh?"

Philip handed him a box. He smiled. "Open it."

Stuart took it reluctantly. He was sure he looked at it as if it was a box full of scorpions, which was how he felt. He lifted the lid. It was a leather jacket that, unless he missed his guess, was identical to Philip's. "I can't accept this."

Philip looked crushed, but all Stuart could think was, *Join the club*. "How... why not?"

"Because I'm already wearing a new outfit." He lifted his eyes to look into Philip's. This was why he distrusted the rich.

Philip sighed. "They told me you'd never be able to tell."

"It was an excellent job. I'm pretty sure whoever did this for you even switched the labels, but there were a few things off," Stuart said. He surprised himself at how calm he kept his voice.

"I wanted to do something nice for you." Philip stared out the window as they flew in low over San Francisco. The sun was setting over the Golden Gate Bridge in the distance, and both it and the Bay Bridge were lit up beneath them. Ahead, the buildings that gave the city its distinctive skyline already lit up the night.

Stuart said nothing. There really wasn't anything to say, not to something this ham-handed. If Philip had truly wanted to buy him a new outfit, it should've come in shopping bags, not disguised as his own clothing.

"Where are we landing?"

"On top of a building. A friend of mine owns it. There'll be a car waiting for us on the street level. We're actually a bit ahead of schedule, so we can take some time and enjoy the scenery," Philip said. He glanced at the leather jacket still in its box between them. He replaced the box's lid and put it back in the bag it had come from without further comment.

"Prepare for landing," came the pilot's voice over the headsets. "Remember, when you exit, stay down until you're outside of the circles painted on the landing pad, sirs. I hate cleaning brains off the bird."

"Thanks for the warning," Philip said dryly. "As it happens, we both have a thing about keeping our brains inside our skulls. We'll see you later this evening."

The pilot gave Philip a thumbs-up as Philip and Stuart left the helicopter, making a crouched dash for the small terminal on the roof, which was little more than a shack with an elevator.

"Are you going to be warm enough in your windbreaker?" Philip asked Stuart. "It won't be as cold once we're off the top of this building."

Stuart nodded and hurried inside as Philip held the door for him. "I knew it'd be cooler in the city, but somehow I didn't expect the wind up here."

Philip pulled him close as the elevator made its descent, rubbing Stuart's arms to help warm him. It helped, but the incongruity of it all struck Stuart. They *flew* into San Francisco and landed not at the airport like normal people, but on top of a *building* owned by one of Philip's friends. Philip had friends who owned buildings in one of the most expensive real estate markets in California, if not the United States. Sure, Philip owned a building, but it was his corporate headquarters and for some reason it didn't seem like the same thing to Stuart.

Stuart wondered why on Earth he'd ever thought something long-term could work with Philip. Despite all the things they had in common and despite all the things that made Philip a wonderful boyfriend, the strike in the "negative" column was a huge one, and that strike was Philip's money. It changed everything, setting them on either side of a chasm too wide to bridge.

This evening made Stuart feel helpless and more alone than ever. Their date was supposed to be fun, even unforgettable. He knew that. Philip had clearly gone to a lot of trouble to make this night happen, and the all-but-impossible to obtain concert tickets were the least of it. Instead, Stuart felt like it was the death-knell of their romance. He cared for Philip something fierce, slowly coming to learn that he could trust someone else, and that was the most messed-up part of this bedroom farce. Even as he knew the money was the death of "them," he finally knew that Philip was someone—maybe even the one—he could trust with his feelings, his secrets, hell, even his life. So why couldn't he overcome his poor but proud attitude? Why did the money have to be a deal breaker? Why the fuck did his American male ego have to get in the way of not only a good thing, but—and he was honest enough to admit it—the one good thing in his personal life in maybe forever? Most guys would know they'd fallen into the clover with a rich boyfriend who wanted nothing more than to make their lives easy, but all he was doing was rooting around for the cow shit. Seriously, what the hell was wrong with him?

Stuart's mouth was on autopilot over dinner at a fancy schmancy restaurant, the kind with prices only on the host's menu. He should be screaming and climbing the walls. Instead, he felt alone in a crowded room, alone across a table from his perfect man. At some point in the near future, he knew he'd kick his own ass for this, but right then he only wanted out.

SOMETHING WAS stealing Stuart's attention, and Philip knew it. Sure, Stuart went through all the motions, but this wasn't Philip's first trip around the block and if he went through life that blind, he'd deserve to be the mincemeat his board planned to make of him. If he had to guess, it'd be Stuart's tiresome reaction to money. When would the younger man stop crucifying him because he had some? Okay, that bit with trying to replace Stuart's clothes had been moronic, and Stuart had every right to skullfry him for it, he admitted that, but the leather jacket was a gift and would actually have helped Stuart. San Francisco could be unpredictably cold any time of the year.

Oh well. Stuart was going through the motions and Philip decided to take them at face value. That Philip could guess what was going on beneath the surface didn't mean he should have to. Or was going to. No, the night was going more or less as planned with the car and restaurant being in place and on time, and Philip planned to sit back and enjoy the rest of it.

He looked over at Stuart. "Ever been to the Warfield?"

"No. Concerts in San Francisco weren't really a part of my budget when I was in school." Stuart said it in an even tone of voice, so Philip ignored the subtext.

"In some ways it reminds me of the Crest Theater in Sacramento. It's part of a dying breed, one of the old baroque movie palaces that people have saved. Beats the hell out of other venues in the city," Philip said. "I can't take the Cow Palace. They play hockey there. Need I say more?"

Stuart chuckled. "No, not really."

"Where do you want to be dropped off, Mr. Sundstrom?"

"Around back, please," Philip replied.

"Yes, sir."

"The back?" Stuart said.

"Yep. I've got another surprise for you, but I don't want to spoil it too soon," Philip said. He tried not to smirk. It was unbecoming and he knew wherever his mother was she'd hate it, but it was hard not to.

He'd set out to make this a night to remember for his boyfriend, and he did what he set his mind to.

"What are we doing back here?" Stuart demanded after the car had let them off behind the theater.

Philip grinned. "You'll see."

With Stuart in tow, Philip strode up to a woman with a clipboard. "Philip Sundstrom and Stuart Cochrane. We're on your list."

She cracked her gum. "Sure you are, sweetie. Stagehands were supposed to be here hours ago."

"You're cute." Philip pointed out their names. "You've got sixty seconds to check our IDs before I start making calls, the first of which will be to Another Planet Entertainment's CEO. Did I mention I sit on the board of directors?"

The woman's eyes had grown progressively wider as she checked Philip's ID against her list and read exactly how important a person he was, at least on that evening and at that concert.

"I'm sorry, Mr. Sundstrom. I didn't recognize you."

Philip rolled his eyes. "The light's a bit dim back here."

"If you'll come with me, please?"

Stuart held out his driver's license. "Don't you need to check my ID?"

"That won't be necessary, Mr. Cochrane. If you're with Mr. Sundstrom, you're fine."

Philip and Stuart followed the door's guardian into the backside of the theater.

"Do you really sit on the board of directors?" Stuart whispered.

Philip nodded. "It's customary to have people from outside the company on the board to make sure everything's on the level. Randall conspicuously didn't and I've been busy enough that I haven't been able to find people I like."

"So how'd you get onto this one?"

"I went to college with the CEO's son," Philip replied as they walked up to a man just into middle age.

"This is Jack Fenster, the stage manager," Clipboard told them. "He'll get you set up with everything you need. Enjoy the show."

Jack was a handsome man, built like the storied brick edifice, who dealt with his thinning hair in the only sensible manner: he shaved it off. When Philip and Stuart walked up, he was speaking into a headset. "No. The lighting plan. Look at the lighting plan… that's why we have a plan. So you can look at it and know how the stage is supposed to look…. You're a moron, that's why. Look, Wendybird has a pretty simple show. It's them and they sing. There are no dancers, there are no fires, lasers, or anything else that detracts from the music. Look at the fucking plan and make sure the audience can see the musicians. If you can't do that, then you don't have a job, got it?"

Jack turned to them. "Sorry about that. We're not using our usual crew. Instead I've been saddled with stand-ins from Planet Fucktard. You are?"

"Philip Sundstrom and Stuart Cochrane," Philip said, extending his hand.

"Mr. Sundstrom, yes! Welcome to chaos." Jack shook their hands. "I'm glad you could make it. I've got the passes ready for you, and I've got one of the sound hounds who'll show you around until I need him right before the show starts. I wish I could show you personally what goes on getting ready for a Wendybirds show, but as you may have heard, the crew I'm working with here isn't exactly firing on all cylinders. If I get the chance, I'll catch up to you before the show starts."

Philip and Stuart exchanged a look. It sounded great to Philip. When he'd arranged this, he'd had no idea there'd be so much to it. All he'd really wanted was a pair of tickets to a sold-out show. "It sounds great, and thank you."

Jack handed them two laminated passes with the words ALL ACCESS written boldly across the top, along with the details of the concert.

Stuart flicked it with his finger, grinning. "Suitable for framing."

"You probably could, yes." Jack snorted. "I've seen people do weirder things with them, but you two look pretty clean cut. For that matter, so's Kill the Wendybird. It's refreshing."

Philip wanted to ask for details, but figured he wouldn't get far, if only because Jack wouldn't get far with a promotions company by telling tales out of school.

"Anyway, if you'll follow me to the green room, you can meet the Wendybirds and pick up the swag bags that were put together for you. Your tour guide will meet you there and show you around. Then you'll be shown to your seats and then all you have to do is enjoy the concert with the other VIPs."

Philip and Stuart fell in behind Jack as he took off at a brisk pace, leading them deeper into the bowels of the Warfield.

"What're we getting into?" Stuart hissed.

"No idea, but I'm so turned around I'm not sure I could find an exit." Philip glanced back over his shoulders at the way they'd come. "Never mind finding the way we got in."

When they reached the green room, Jack showed them in and introduced them to the members of Kill the Wendybird, fronted by one Wendy Stockman. A guitarist, a bassist, a drummer, and a keyboardist, all of whom loved *Peter Pan* as much as Wendy, supported her onstage. Philip and Stuart found them to be very friendly and down to earth, not at all spoiled by their sudden rise to fame, but also distracted not only by their preshow rituals but by preparation for the show itself.

"I'm sorry we're so distracted right now," Wendy said by way of apology. She paced back and forth, leaving a frustrated makeup artist in her wake.

She took several deep breaths and then released her voice, starting at the lower end of her vocal register and working her way up, only to sing her way down again. "Warm-up exercises. I have to stretch and warm-up my vocal cords just like an athlete warms up her muscles."

"No worries, we get it. If you think about it, you're getting ready for work," Stuart said.

Wendy looked at him strangely. "Thank you for understanding that."

"You! Sit!" the makeup artist barked, pointing to a backless chair in front of a mirror with bright lights on either side.

Wendy sat, the backless chair forcing her to sit up straight. It also allowed her to continue her vocal warm-ups. For their part, Philip and Stuart watched the makeup artist transform her from Wendy Stockman into the Wendybird.

"So what do you think?" Wendy said when the makeup artist was done with her, twirling around like a little girl in her first princess dress.

"It's very… bloodthirsty," Philip said. He'd listened to Kill the Wendybird's music, of course, but hadn't paid much attention to their visual representations. Stuart looked similarly nonplussed. Philip guessed that seeing airbrushed pictures of the band members in CD inserts was quite a bit different from seeing them in the flesh. Used to the Disneyfied version of J. M. Barrie's story, they were unprepared for this modern update of the beloved children's tale, because what emerged under the makeup artist's skilled hands owed more to a homoerotic St. Sebastian or a witch from a Goth interpretation of Macbeth than to Disney's animators. The rhinestones were a nice touch.

Stuart looked at Wendy, frowning. "I'm guessing you're Wendy after Tinker Bell's gotten done with her?"

"Basically, yes." Wendy smiled at him. "Have you read the original story?"

"It's been a while," Stuart said.

"Why don't you refresh our memories?" Philip said. He'd look it up on his iPhone, but he couldn't get much of a signal down there.

"Tinker Bell's usually presented as this kindly fairy who helps out Peter and the Lost Boys, right? In the book she's so jealous of Wendy she tries to trick the Lost Boys into shooting down the terrible Wendybird. Even in the Disney movie, Tinker Bell's jealousy almost destroys them all, and only Peter's cunning saves the day," Wendy explained.

"That's right." Stuart snapped his fingers. "Peter's so self-absorbed that he doesn't even notice that one of the only two women in Neverland is about to destroy it through her jealousy."

Philip nodded slowly. "I remember now. Tinker Bell's an unpleasant creature of low intelligence, and Peter? Makes you wonder why they fought over him."

"Kind of, yeah." Wendy glanced at the big clock on the wall. "We have to head upstairs to be waiting in the wings for the opening band to finish. It's been great to meet you guys. Thanks in advance for coming to the show. I hope you like it."

One of the Lost Boys pointed to something on a side table, talking quietly to Wendy. "I almost forgot," she said. "Swag bags! That's part of the fun, right? I don't really know what all's in them beyond the usual free CDs and autographed posters, but enjoy!"

Then the promised sound hound showed up to escort them to their seats so they couldn't riffle through the bags. "I don't need all this stuff," Stuart said, hefting his swag bag.

Philip forced out a laugh, but really, why was that his response to everything? It's not like it was being offered for sale. They were gifts from the band. Shut up and take it already. "Good, because a bunch of it's going to Valerie's friend Cynthia to thank her for being the go-between for you and Valerie."

"You and Valerie talk a lot, do you?" Stuart gave Philip his best stink eye, but Philip laughed it off.

Philip smiled. "Only when she can't reach you."

When they reached their seats, both men were taken aback. Stuart stood looking at the small stand of stadium seating that sat on the stage itself, even if off to one side. "The stage, Philip? We're going to go deaf."

"I have to admit it's not what I was expecting, but it can't be that bad," Philip replied.

"'Can't be that bad'? Did you get a look at those speakers? They're taller than I am."

Philip frowned. He saw what Stuart meant. They were huge, but they were also— "Wait. They're pointed out toward the main seating area. Of course! Think about it. If the sound were too loud on stage, there'd be all kinds of feedback from both the musicians' microphones and the ambient mics. I bet it won't be that terrible."

"Care to make a wager about that?" Stuart said, some of the gleam returning to his eyes. That heartened Philip. It had been missing since the flight into the city.

"Yes. If I'm right, you have to tell me what's been eating at you all night," Philip said. That rocked Stuart back and Philip was pleased to see it. Yep, he'd struck pay dirt with that stake.

"So what do I get if I'm right?" Stuart said, trying to recover.

Philip lifted one eyebrow. "What do you want?"

Stuart inhaled to speak, but the roar of the crowd when Kill the Wendybird took the stage cut him off. As it happened, Philip's hypothesis about the speakers was the right one. Jack Fenster's sound engineers had done a magnificent job, and the people in the VIP seating enjoyed the concert at just the right level of noise without compromising their hearing. In any event earplugs were available from the complimentary concessionaire who catered to their every whim during the show.

"SO WHAT'S been eating at you all evening?" Philip asked Stuart the moment the car door shut behind them. Philip reminded the driver—the same one who had dropped them off—where to take them, and then raised the privacy window.

Stuart crossed his arms. "Nothing. What're you talking about?"

Fine, be that way. Philip switched the heat on and then cranked it all the way up. The car would quickly become unbearable, but if nothing else it might teach Stuart not to shut him out like that.

"Stuart, after our handful of months together, you choose now of all times to play me? Really? You were fine up until we landed in San Francisco."

Stuart stared out the car's window for a moment. Then he turned to face Philip. "It felt like you were trying to buy me or influence me by showing me what money would be like, everything from the clothes to the helicopter ride to the VIP access to a sold-out concert. I mean, my friends couldn't even get tickets in the nosebleed seats and then with a flick of your manicured finger all this stuff just… happens."

"I wanted to show you a good time. Of course this wasn't an effort to bowl you over with money. I'd hope you'd know me better than that by now. Okay, trying to replace your clothes without you noticing was downright stupid, and I really am sorry about that, but the concert?" Philip couldn't believe they were still having this same damn conversation. "An opportunity presented itself and I took it, and who else would I take to a concert?"

"Yeah, but it was an opportunity most people don't get," Stuart said. "You only got it through clubby, old-boy connections."

Frowning, Philip spent a moment choosing his words. "You know, if I'd done nothing to earn this money, if I'd gone to prep schools in New England instead of a public high school in Sacramento, if I'd gone to an Ivy League college where making contacts mattered more than learning something instead of attending the University of California, I might—only might—deserve that."

"We're here, sir," the driver interrupted.

Stuart waited while Philip squared things away with the driver. Neither said much as they took the private elevator up to the landing pad on the roof of Philip's friend's building, and conversation was all but impossible until they'd tucked themselves into their seats behind the helicopter pilot and donned the headsets that allowed them to converse.

"I recall telling you once that having money didn't make me a bad person and that money itself was neither good nor bad," Philip said. "Beyond that, I don't think it's fair to expect me to be something I'm not. I don't flaunt my... resources... fuck." Philip turned away, staring out the helicopter's window, biting down on his tongue to keep from saying something silly and hateful. "You've got me so afraid of my own money that I can't even say I'm rich." He turned back to Stuart. "Face it, Stuart. I'm more than comfortably well-off. I'm loaded. I've got money in numbered offshore accounts. I'm filthy, stinking rich, and I'm going to get richer, assuming I'm not forced out of my own company."

"Damn," the pilot breathed. "I'd marry you myself and I'm straight."

Never mind the thumpa-thumpa-thumpa of the rotors, they could've heard the proverbial pin drop.

"I... uh, wanted to tell you that you forgot to switch your headsets to the private channel," the pilot added lamely.

Philip and Stuart swore and switched their headsets over. "I know," Stuart said. "I remember that conversation...."

"And?"

Stuart looked at the floor. "Nothing you've done since then has made you a liar."

Philip sighed, more weary than angry. "Then why do I feel like I'm always on trial? And spare me the 'learning to trust' business.

We've already been there. Sooner or later you'll need to see a therapist."

"Are you telling me I'm crazy?"

Philip shook his head. "No, I'm telling you a lot of people have crappy childhoods and they don't get to punish those around them indefinitely. For that matter, my own childhood with Randall wasn't exactly a romp through the rose petals, but I'm not dumping it on you."

"No, you took it all out on Randall," Stuart said, snorting.

Philip nodded. "Exactly the one who deserved it."

"Intellectually, I know you're right, Philip. I really do, but emotionally…. It's hard to let go."

Philip reached out and took Stuart's hand. "I know, but you've got to." He thought for a while. "The mistake I think you're making is in assuming that you have to go it alone. I hope you know that I'm first in line to help, although I suspect Valerie would be jabbing me with her elbows to push me back to second place. But Morgan? Your old coach? For that matter, Brad's turned into a real sweetheart. He'd help you if you needed it. He's not who he was in college. Trust me on that one. What about your friend Eddie?"

Stuart kissed Philip's hand, their fingers still interlaced. "Philip, the night's been magical, even enchanting… but also utterly depressing—"

"What? How?" That was the last thing Philip expected to hear.

"Because this is what I'm giving up for the next seven to ten years while I pursue my medical education."

"Oh" was all Philip could say.

Stuart nodded. "I find myself asking, 'Is it worth it?' Then there's the fact that I'm depriving myself of your company. I'm greedy, Philip. I want you all to myself. I may look like the perfect med school grind, but I know perfectly well that if I shifted my priorities you and I could be the perfect gay power couple. On nights like this, after a fun evening like tonight, I'd be warm and secure in your arms, only I'm not, am I? I'm at the library or the lab. I know this wasn't your intention, but tonight showed me everything I've been missing and it pisses me off."

"Oh, Stuart… I hope you know that was never my intention," Philip said.

Stuart nodded. "I know. You don't work that way, not where the two of us are concerned, but that doesn't change the fact that I look at all this and realize that if I bailed on med school we could be at City Hall first thing in the morning to get married and then live like this much of the time."

"We could do that anyway, you know, and you wouldn't have to quit school," Philip said.

Stuart had thought about marriage? Wow. Perhaps he'd lose his money hang-ups if he had more of it to call his own. Quitting med school… maybe Stuart was starting to doubt his calling, and that troubled Philip. But would he eventually blame Philip for turning him away from what he'd worked so hard to achieve?

They passed the rest of the flight in silence, each man lost in his own thoughts. Philip's were a whirlwind of all the things Stuart had told him, particularly that Stuart resented the demands that med school made on his time, that he missed being around Philip as much as Philip missed being with Stuart. Philip had also been soft-pedaling his money in part because that's what his mother said you did if you had any—you never called attention to it. But mostly he'd been low-key about it because of Stuart. Maybe money wasn't the issue per se. As usual, Philip realized, his boyfriend only managed to reveal himself as more complicated than Philip had thought.

He noticed, however, that Stuart conspicuously left the leather jacket behind in the helicopter.

CHAPTER
Nineteen

A FEW days after the concert Philip sat at his desk at SunHo, all signs set to "Do Not Disturb." He and Stuart tiptoed carefully around each other, which gave him the perfect excuse to throw himself into the worsening situation at work. His e-mail mining was producing tantalizing leads, but no smoking gun, and his temper grew worse each day. He'd already instructed SunHo's outside counsel to draw up papers sacking the entire board, just in case. He preferred finesse, but it was looking more and more likely that a cudgel would have to suffice.

He pored over yet another set of files written in his father's dreadful handwriting, as crabbed as Randall himself. He still couldn't believe how much Randall must have spent on private investigators so he could to have something to hold over his board, although given what he, Philip, faced from that same board it made a certain sick sense. Almost to a person, they appeared to be sharks, and it dawned but slowly on Philip that he was the chum. Speaking of, he still couldn't understand how SunHo's internal auditors hadn't squealed like stuck pigs about all these expenditures. He knew SunHo had been a smaller, more casual company in the early days, but still.

He picked up another file. Estelle Candler. He chuckled as he read Randall's file on the vice-president of the custom homes division. Somehow, her record was squeaky clean, no mean feat under his father's regime. The file documented little of a personal nature beyond her husband's name and the names of her two children and the fact that she attended an Episcopalian church. The files on some of her peers detailed innumerable indiscretions. Some even had photos, which Philip found distasteful.

Bachelor's and master's in architecture, plus a variety of related certifications. Awards from a can of alphabet soup's worth of professional groups and juried competitions, all noted dispassionately. Jeez, Randall. Have a little pride in your employees' accomplishments, or even in yourself for hiring such talented people and giving them the space to keep creating. That Randall had left her alone surprised Philip. His father had the reputation for being very hands-on when it suited him. He wondered what dark sorcery Candler had worked to keep Randall off her back.

Philip jotted a note to add copies of Candler's award-winning designs to her dossier. He picked up the yearly report from her division, custom homes. There'd never been any problem from that quarter, and even in the recent downturn, it had still turned a profit. Maybe not as large a one, but it still made SunHo more money than it cost, which wasn't something tract homes could say, not with Suburban Graveyard on the books. Apparently people with enough money to build a custom home on expensive land weren't dissuaded by little things like the worst recession since the Great Depression. He realized that the profitability of SunHo Custom Homes may well be due to Estelle Candler's designs and not much else. After all, many builders put up custom homes…. Huh.

Philip depressed the button on his phone's intercom. "Jyoti, could you come in here, please?"

Before Philip had a chance to release the button, Jyoti charged through the door connecting his suite to the outer office where Jyoti held sway. "That was fast," Philip said.

Jyoti frowned. "What're you talking about?"

"I asked if you could come in here. I think I found something."

"I've not been at my desk for the last two hours. Do you not remember the DM I sent you?"

"Was that what that pinging noise was?"

"This is why you don't pay me enough." Jyoti sighed. He reached over his boss's desk and woke his computer up.

"You know my password?"

"Figuring it out gives me something to do in my off hours. You might want to think about making it more complicated next time." Jyoti stabbed a finger at the direct message icon jumping up and down on the dock along the bottom of the screen. "DM from me to you."

Philip sighed. "Sorry, Jyoti. I've been reading files all morning and I think I've found someone who might work."

"That's fortuitous, because I believe I've found out what's wrong with Suburban Symphony and why Sunset Homes was so vulnerable."

For someone who'd just found so necessary a piece to their puzzle, Philip noticed that his assistant looked remarkably unhappy. "Then why're you so grim?"

Jyoti dropped a dusty file folder in front of Philip while he pulled a chair around next to Philip's. "Because Sunset Homes built it on top of a toxic waste dump."

"I can't possibly have heard you right." Philip snatched up the folder, but it was all there. A small post-World War Two aerospace company dealt with its hazardous waste not unlike other companies in the Sacramento area—it buried it. While not as sexy as the Love Canal or Times Beach, it polluted its locality every bit as much. No clay-lined pit, no cement vault, no nothing, just fifty-gallon drums and dirt, drums which by the 1960s had inevitably leaked. The site had been cleaned up, the original company heavily fined, etc. It was allegedly—*allegedly* being the key word—perfectly safe to build on. "Fuck my life."

"In essence, yes."

Philip sat back in his chair. "No wonder Winch has been goldbricking this for so long. I bet he knows, the son of a bitch."

Jyoti nodded. "I find it curious that he simply didn't tell you."

"That's one word. I can think of a few others. Perhaps I'm paranoid, but I wonder how this fits in with some plan of his. He's the scheming sort." Philip drummed his fingers on the desktop.

"Just because one is paranoid doesn't mean people are not out to get you. In your circumstances, I think the assumption is warranted."

"All right, you and I have two priorities for the rest of the day," Philip said. "We need to make three copies of that file you found— good work on that, Jyoti—and then put that original back. With any luck, no one will know that I'm any the wiser. One of those copies will go in my office safe and I'll take the other two with me."

"What's the other item, Philip?"

Philip looked at his PA gravely. "Before close of business today, I'll hire an environmental engineering company, one far beyond our area, Seattle or maybe Portland, for an independent analysis. I need to know just how toxic that place is before I can start assessing liability, but the fact that the landscaping keeps dying isn't exactly a good sign."

PHILIP WAS convinced that like celebrity deaths, bad news came in threes. First had been Jyoti's discoveries in the company archives. Then, following that by two weeks, the environmental analysis showed what Philip had feared. Brad had been righter than he knew when he'd christened it Suburban Graveyard, because the ground underneath was still borderline poisoned, and according to the report, that didn't look to be changing any time soon. At least the worst of it was located underneath the projected community center and not under a house. Still....

And then the spider left her web and knocked on his door.

"I'm sorry," Philip heard Jyoti say, "but Mr. Sundstrom doesn't see people without an appointment."

"He'll see me."

Philip recognized Candy Kane's voice. She never left her labyrinth. Whatever rousted her must've been important. Better head this off.

He opened his office's door. "Sorry, Jyoti, but she's right. Whatever's brought her all the way up here relates to our ongoing problem. Come in, Candy."

"He's going to punish you, isn't he?" Candy said as he closed the door.

Philip made a face, as much at what she said as at what she wore, grateful he could let it out and cover it up at the same time. "Probably. He's never been that temperamental, but he's my right hand and, if you ask him, my brain, and we're under a certain amount of stress these days. Water?"

He held up a bottle.

"Yes, thank you." Candy looked around. "So this is what daylight looks like. I guess I'd better get used to it."

"You can have your office anywhere you want. If you're more comfortable down there in your maze...." Philip shrugged. His stomach handed him another shot of acid. "I'm assuming this isn't strictly a social call."

"No, it's not." Candy sighed. "My e-mail mining's paid off. Finally. I'm going to have to send out yet another reminder about people sending personal e-mails on company accounts, because the amount of crap I've had to wade through, even with search terms, has been unbelievable."

Candy handed him a file folder. "These are printouts, obviously. The senders think they've erased them, but the originals are still on the server. They're now sequestered behind both your and my passwords."

Philip scanned the e-mails. "Yep, it's Winch. I figured it'd be him."

"There are others involved, as well." Candy fidgeted with her water bottle.

Then Philip realized... she was afraid he'd blame her. Of course, she could easily disguise her involvement, at least anything that had been committed to computer, but Philip doubted she had anything to do with this. For one thing, she struck him as perfectly satisfied with her domain down in IT. He'd had to dangle the offer of control of all of SunHo's IT to buy her cooperation. Randall had viewed IT as a necessary evil, but he'd offered to make it a C-level position. She lacked the revenge motive of the others and had every reason to be grateful.

"There'd have to be," Philip said. He didn't read it all right then. He couldn't. He was too furious. He'd have to calm down before he had the patience to scan through multiple levels of replies and carbon copies, blind and otherwise. Calming down entailed an extra-long workout and possibly stomping through the corporate offices looking like murder.

"If you haven't already, start giving some thought to how you'd like to organize and integrate the various regional offices' computer systems. I'll have to sign off on it, but that'll be strictly pro forma. You're the expert, after all." Philip forced himself to smile.

"So when will all of this go into effect?"

"Typically, such organizational changes happen at the next board meeting, in this case, right after New Year's," Philip said. "We don't have shareholders to keep happy, so it'll be a much smaller, less formal affair than you may be anticipating. Plan on calling in all your new subordinates—i.e., all the regional heads of IT—within the first few weeks to show them how you want things done."

Candy looked terrified. "I have no idea how to organize anything like that."

"That's why we have personal assistants. If I have my way, there'll be several looking for employment, assuming they're not involved in their bosses' disloyalty. Jyoti also knows everything about how to run SunHo, and he'll lend a hand here and there. Trust me, I'm not promoting you to watch you fail."

Philip chatted with Candy for a little while longer, mostly to set her at ease regarding her forthcoming promotion. He was certain once she put her mind to it, the internal logic of re-organizing and integrating SunHo's computer and information technology would present itself and then Candy would be fine. Now if he could only wean her off that horrible lipstick.

No sooner had she left then Jyoti entered. "I'm sorry, I hope you know I try never to undercut you in front of anyone—" Philip started to stand.

"Yes, yes, please hand the folder over."

"With pleasure. I assume you'll be making copies?"

"Do not insult my intelligence, Philip. Of course, I'll be making copies."

"Of course. I assume you've already burrowed your way past the Sun-King icon on my desktop?" When Jyoti stalled, Philip wagged his finger at his assistant. "Don't insult *my* intelligence, Jyoti. I know what you do out there."

Jyoti didn't even blush. Philip knew he'd lost the ability. "It makes for some unpleasant reading, does it not?"

Philip shrugged. "I read enough to realize Winch was the ringleader and no more. I may look calm, but I'm about five seconds away from picking up my chair and breaking every window in my office."

"Then perhaps you should leave. Those windows are not cheap to replace. The original of these e-mails and the copies will be in the office vault when you arrive tomorrow," Jyoti said.

"Right. I'll see you in the morning, then."

THE MONDAY after Thanksgiving, Philip sat across a table from Estelle Candler for what was ostensibly a working breakfast for two highly placed executives from one of the several homebuilders in the greater Sacramento area. In reality, Philip hoped to put his best, last gambit into play to save his place at the helm of his family's company at a small restaurant off the radar of his board of directors. While by no means was his every executive corrupt or on the make, Estelle had a reputation within in the company of being a stickler for rules and her record was spotless, even to the point of earning Randall's grudging admiration. That reputation meant Randall had excluded her from his less-than-legal shenanigans. Whether or not she'd been aware of them was another matter....

"So what brings us out here, Mr. Sundstrom? I'm certain it's not to sample the breakfast offerings at a small restaurant in a small town on the far side of Yolo County." Estelle was a striking African-American woman who wore middle age well, her silver dreads piled high like a crown from under which her light green eyes read everything they saw. "Although admittedly they're quite good."

Philip thought of every possible approach and decided that the direct approach was the only one that might win her to his side. "How much are you aware of what's going on at SunHo?"

"Well, I know that tract homes are dragging our bottom line down, but that's to be expected given the economy, although whoever authorized that expansion into South Florida needs to go back to business school because a blind woman could've seen that coming. Things seem to be astir down in IT, but I presume we'll be informed when Ms. Kane thinks it's time—"

"Cut the crap, Candler. That's not what I'm talking about and you know it."

Philip and his vice-president of the custom homes division locked eyes. Philip felt like she was measuring him, but he refused to back down. SunHo was his, dammit, founded by his father and now run by him. It was his inheritance, his birthright, and since he'd taken it over, he had led the company bearing his name to greater profits and visibility, sensible but measurable growth. He refused to let vestiges of his father's regime force him out. He knew he'd made a mistake in retaining them. It might have cost him in terms of time and organizational know-how at the beginning, but that would've been far preferable to all this subterranean scurrying now.

He knew he should've kept his face impassive, but he was beyond that. It was personal and had been for too long. He'd struck back against his father, acting out a family drama that was too Grecian for comfort, and now his father's lackeys sought to take him down. What did that make them, the Furies, those who sought vengeance against those who violated the natural order? But he wasn't Orestes and Randall certainly wasn't Agamemnon.

"I know that Winchester Chapman is making trouble for you—"

Philip snorted. "He's outright defied me when it comes to a certain subdivision his mistress is in charge of."

"Miranda Valparaiso is—" Estelle touched her napkin to her lips to cover, but Philip knew he'd shocked her.

"Yes," he said blandly. "She's falling down on the job."

Now to dangle the bait and see if she bit. "Frankly, it doesn't speak well of either of them when a subdivision that's practically under their noses is performing that poorly, and given some of my father's last acquisitions, there's some stiff competition for the 'worst performer' crown. He should've removed her for cause. Instead, they're having an affair and I'll have to remove both of them for cause, and all because of that dire little subdivision we acquired along with Sunset Homes."

"I see."

Philip watched her like a hawk spotting rabbits. She knew. She knew about Winch and she knew about Suburban Symphony, or had at least heard about it. The only question was why she hadn't said anything.

"Yes, you do. Don't try to hide it, Estelle. I can see it on your face, and not only that, thanks to some judicious snooping, I have a fairly good idea what you might know and when you knew it."

She sat back, crossing her arms. "Then why am I here, Philip?"

"Because you're one of the few honest people in that nest of vipers, and I need someone's help—your help—to extricate myself and Sundstrom Homes from the mess we're in."

"So why don't you tell me what you know."

Damn. What he'd really wanted was for Estelle to tell him what she knew or suspected, not the other way around. Instead he'd neatly fallen into her trap. Or maybe he'd grown too used to seeing traps and pitfalls everywhere he looked. Damn Winch for putting him in this position, and damn Randall for creating this kind of corporate environment in the first place.

"… So Winch is apparently a friend of Randall's and is determined to take me down for ousting my father. He's going to pin Suburban Symphony on me, since as it happens, it sits atop an old toxic waste dump."

Estelle nodded. "I know." She held up one hand to keep Philip from exploding. "Rather, let me say, I had reason to believe that was the case. Talk flies around the top floor—what do the secretaries and assistants call it, Elysium? Absurd name."

"The Elysian Fields, and you're missing the point."

"No, I'm circling around it. If this situation isn't handled properly, it'll drag the entire company down."

"But by keeping me out of the loop, I'll look so incompetent and out of touch, I'll be forced out while the board spins off the tract home division to take the fall, leaving them in charge of the far more lucrative custom division and leaving me holding the bag for Suburban Graveyard."

"They'll what, now?"

"You heard me." Maybe that would work its way under her unflappable exterior, because Philip didn't think he was reaching her.

"Aren't you being a bit paranoid?"

Philip shrugged. "It's your division. As for me, just because I'm paranoid doesn't mean they're not after me, and in this case I have their e-mails to prove it."

"You… what?"

"Oh yes, Estelle." Philip smiled, showing a lot of teeth. "I've read the e-mails of everyone at the corporate office, manager or above, at least if it's crossed the corporate servers."

"How?" she said, the full force of her attention finally focused on him.

Philip permitted himself a smug grin. "SunHo's servers. I own them and everything on them. Private company, remember? And before you say anything about privacy, I have a Supreme Court decision backing me up. If I own it, my employees have 'no reasonable expectation of privacy.' That's a direct quotation, by the way."

"You're a horrible man," she said, but Philip heard a grudging note of admiration there, too.

Philip shook his head as relief flood him. "No, Randall's a horrible man. I'm a pragmatic one. Now answer a question for me. If you knew, or even suspected any of this, how come you didn't bring any of it to me?"

The older woman, eyeing him warily, shrugged. "I wasn't sure I could trust you. You Sundstroms have been a difficult lot. Your father's record speaks for itself. Then there was your brother. He might've made a difference, but he bailed too quickly, not that I blame him for that, not the way Randall treated him. And then you. You interned with me, just like you did with everyone else."

"And that didn't teach you to trust me?" That actually hurt.

"You never said much, never revealed very much of yourself. You only watched and absorbed everything. Like a sponge. Your father didn't know what to make of you, you know."

Philip snorted. "He wasn't supposed to, but we're not talking about him."

"I'm only telling you he never trusted you."

"Brad rebelled in his way, I in mine," Philip said bitterly. "I'll leave it for you to decide which was more effective."

Neither said anything for a time.

"So are you going to help me?"

"I'll have to think about it."

Philip clenched his jaw to keep from screaming at her right there over the remains of their pancakes. "Keep in mind, I have Randall's dirty files on every single one of you bastards. He hired private investigators and left dossiers on all of you. I think it was his idea of a fail-safe, and I'm starting to understand why. You're cleaner than the rest, but that's not necessarily saying a whole lot."

"Blackmail, Philip? I thought you were better than that."

"No, nothing so crude. I… merely want to encourage you to think clearly. You're near retirement. You could decide to wait me out, but if I go down, I'll make sure the pension fund tanks. Or you can help me clean up this mess, and I'll make sure you retire at the highest possible salary level with a promotion to a C-level position, Environmental Regulations Compliance or something along those lines."

Estelle smiled. "You're handing those out like candy lately."

"They're mine to hand out." Philip couldn't even manage a twitch of his lips. The joke wasn't that funny.

"Chief of Environmental Compliance. Interesting idea."

"'Interesting'? It's brilliant. Not only will we get credit for being proactive about the shitshow that is Suburban Symphony because you will run right to the EPA—state and federal—with the news of what the outgoing board was hiding, but also because it will appear that SunHo takes environmentalism so seriously that we've made it a C-level position."

Estelle tapped her chin. "How is this any different than greenwashing?"

"At first, it won't be," Philip said, "but only at first. I actually want this implemented companywide as soon as we get our chestnuts out of the fire where Suburban Symphony is concerned. I'm thinking things like green design options and credits for recycled and renewable materials like bamboo or cork floors or tiles made from recycled glass. The full details will be your new division's responsibility, but I'm sure you see where I'm going with this."

"It's all irrelevant if we can't solve this problem," Estelle said.

Philip nodded. "True enough." He slid a bound report across the table.

"What's this?"

"The problem, as detailed by an outside firm that SunHo's never done business with before. I didn't want any of our usual vendors to feel beholden enough to pull their punches."

Estelle read for a while, frowning. "We're screwed."

"Not necessarily, but no, it's not good. I've already halted sales, which will be another mark in our favor when this blows up. We need to find a way to get people out of there ASAP."

"We're going to take a major hit on this and there's no way around it." Estelle drummed her fingers on the tabletop. "Move them to our other properties in the area. SunHo will carry their loans at below-market interest. Or at no interest. It's the only way. Or even offer them custom homes at steep discounts."

Philip nodded. "What's to stop them from turning around and suing us?"

"Contracts. We urge them to find lawyers of their own, but make sure that once they accept our offer and sign the contract they lose the right to sue, arbitration only."

Philip frowned. "More corporate evil? It pissed me off when I signed the right to sue away on my cell phone contract, and now we're doing it to our own customers?"

"It's the only way." Estelle returned the environmental report to him. "How many families are we talking here?"

"Twelve or so, I think, maybe fifteen. There were one or two in escrow, if you can believe it. We've backed out of those."

"Twelve? Fifteen?" Estelle massaged her temples. "This isn't good."

"It could be a lot worse. There are one hundred and fifty home sites there."

She shook her head. "That's still a huge hit, Philip."

"Better we start the process of relocating them ourselves than wait for the feds to figure it out. Then we'll have twelve lawsuits, or one big class action suit."

Estelle nodded slowly. "You're right. So which will it be, move them to other tract homes or put them in customs?"

"Can your division have that many custom homes ready?"

"Here's a dirty little secret about custom homes, Philip. Most people aren't all that original in what they think they want. I have a number of basic designs I use and then modify as necessary. My team can prepare the plans for a number of 'custom' houses in weeks."

Philip nodded. "I didn't think you worked that way when I interned in your department. That said, I'd prefer to put them into high-end subdivisions elsewhere in Sacramento or the Bay Area, but it'll depend on a variety of factors, including where the residents work." He thought for a moment. "I'll brief the legal department and have them draw up the necessary documents. Who would you appoint as interim head of custom homes?"

"Let me give it some thought." Then Estelle realized what he'd done. "You're bad."

Philip smirked. "Or very good. I'll have documents drawn up appointing you acting Chief of Environmental Compliance. It'll be made formal at the New Year's board meeting."

"So what will you do about Winch in the meantime?" Estelle said.

"I'm honestly not sure, probably fire most of his staff as a warning shot." Philip shook his head. "In the meantime, I'll be stripping people of their board positions, effective as soon as I notify them. There'll be a few terminations, too."

Estelle gathered her notes and placed them in a slim leather shoulder bag. "Some people will be surprised to learn it's your company, after all."

"That is entirely their problem."

Philip only wished he felt as confident as he sounded. Yes, he had a plan of sorts. Yes, he'd identified someone who would try to help him clean up the mess Randall had left him as a final fuck-you. Neither changed the reality that he was about to take on people twice his age who'd been in the building business at least as long as he'd been alive. He was drowning and he knew it, but at least he was drowning in deep water.

CHAPTER
Twenty

"WHAT'S WRONG with you? You sound like crap."

Stuart coughed. "Thanks, little sistwerp. That makes me feel all warm and fuzzy." He coughed again. "No, wait. That's my fever."

Stuart didn't actually have a fever, but that was only due to his regular intake of acetaminophen and ibuprofen. He switched back and forth for the sake of his liver. It required careful titration, but he'd excelled in chemistry.

"Seriously, are you okay?"

Valerie sounded genuinely worried and he took pity on her. "Yeah, I came down with what I thought was a low-grade flu right after Thanksgiving. It's not getting better and it's not getting worse. It's parked itself on me and I feel about like I sound."

Stuart had completely abandoned his usual discipline and studied in bed, with an array of notebooks around him, along with the trusty iPad and its charging cord. Unfortunately there was also a veritable explosion of used tissues, along with a heating pad for when the heaps of blankets weren't enough to stop his shivering.

Since he couldn't afford to be sick, he did what he always did and slogged on with the aid of caffeinated beverages. When the deep, wet cough had started, Stuart knew Diet Coke wouldn't cut it anymore and moved onto larger doses of antipyretics and energy drinks. There was a problem with caffeine, of course. He adapted to it too quickly, and so was forced by his stubborn unwillingness to rest and take care of himself to develop a regimen to keep the caffeine constantly peaking.

"Okay, I'm going to ask an obvious question. Have you seen a doctor?"

Stuart laughed, but it turned into a cough almost immediately. "Yeah, several times a day," he said when he stopped.

Valerie growled. "That's not what I meant and you know it."

"This comes with the territory. Once I've got a few years of clinical experience under my belt, I'll be immune to all this garbage." It was one of the first things they warned med students about before they started seeing patients. Unfortunately the first few years of exposure to patients meant staggering from one malady to the next. "Lucky me, my adventures in Germland have already started. Could be worse."

"I don't see how."

"I could be a pediatrician. Kids are bug farms. Trust me, people dealing with kids get it far worse." He coughed and checked the time. Nope. No cough suppressant for another hour and a half. Ugh. Why did that stuff always wear off too soon? "So what's up?"

"That's why I'm calling," Valerie said. "I talk to your boyfriend more than I talk to you."

Stuart shook his head. Why had no one believed him when he'd said med school required more time than there was in a day? He'd never been one for flights of fancy. "I'll surface again around Christmas."

She sighed. "I miss you."

"I miss you, too." He felt his energy dwindling, but he couldn't hurry her off the phone, not now. "Um… is there… I mean, are you any closer to a decision? About heading west, I mean?"

"Yeah, right after Christmas. Mom and Dad are going to drag me to another hootenanny, and I'll pretend to cooperate. You know, lull them into a false sense of security and all that. When they least expect it, I'll make a break for it. Philip said he'd help."

That got his attention. "He did?"

"When I spoke to him before the Wendybird concert he did. Cynthia *loved* all the stuff you guys sent her, by the way. She couldn't believe you gave up an iPod preloaded with their entire catalogue."

"That was Philip's. I've still got mine."

Valerie laughed. "He's a good guy."

"Yeah, he is." Stuart had to smile. He had his hang-ups about Philip's fortune, but he also had no doubts about where Philip's heart was. None at all. Maybe he needed to hear it from someone else to remind him once in a while. "He's going through a hell of a time at work these days."

"How can that be? He owns work, doesn't he?"

"Yeah," Stuart said, sighing, "but I guess some of the members of the board aren't so happy with how Philip took control from his father and are trying to kick him out of his own company. I try to follow what he's saying, but a lot of it sails into one ear and right out the other."

"Could you tell him I'm really sorry to hear that?" Valerie said. "That's got to suck."

"Yeah, I will." He lay back against his pillow, almost feeling like he would sink into it if he let go. He hated being sick.

Philip didn't return home until late that night, even by Stuart's standards, and sometimes the only way he knew Philip came home at all was by the lump on the other side of the bed. What he didn't tell Valerie is that by the time Thanksgiving came and went, he was pretty sure Philip was sleeping at his old place some nights. Some guys worried about their boyfriends cheating with other men. Lucky him, his boyfriend only cheated on him with other houses. It only served to highlight the financial differences Stuart couldn't work his way around. What normal person changes houses like underwear?

"Anyway, let's keep in better touch, and by *let's*, which is a contraction of *let us*, I mean *you*."

"I hope you're okay with texts or very short e-mails."

She made a rude noise. "Guess I'll have to be. Remember—I'll basically be running away from home after Christmas. I've got a fair amount of money saved, but Philip said to get to an airport—any airport—and he'd take care of the rest, and I'm counting on that."

Stuart made a note to talk to Philip about what he'd promised Valerie. Of course, they'd have to cross paths, first…. "I will. We both want you out here and away from them."

No need to spell out who they were.

"Thanks, Stuie. I love you."

"I love you, too, Val. I'm not even going to comment on calling me Stuie."

Philip. Stuart realized he needed to deal with his issues where Philip was concerned instead of stewing about them. Philip was nearly everything he'd ever wanted in a husband. Dan Savage claimed that no one was ever one hundred percent perfect and you had to round up. Stuart didn't think he'd had to round very much, but that little bit was proving to be difficult. He couldn't talk to anyone about it either, because none of his friends, let alone Valerie, understood breaking up with someone you loved because he was rich and understated about it.

Yes, loved. He could finally admit that to himself, if only because right then he lacked the energy to deny his feelings. He knew Philip felt the same way. That didn't obviate Stuart's problems, however. He still had trouble believing he could trust other people with his best interests. How did he know other people would look out for him? The people closest to him while he was growing up hadn't, so why should Philip? Stuart knew the answer intellectually, but emotions were another matter, and he'd never trusted those. They were big and scary and frequently escaped the limits he tried to place on them.

But he had enough on his plate. So did Philip. This would keep until after finals. It had to.

PHILIP LOOKED at the portfolio Estelle had brought him that morning, although "portfolio" was perhaps a misleading term for that thick stack of paper and files. She hadn't been kidding about keeping prefab "custom" designs in the can, because in short order, Estelle and her studio had produced a number of possible designs. They were "proof of concept" pieces for his eyes only, nothing but sketches, really, nothing too fancy. If she cornered him, Philip would admit to a certain disappointment. Oh well, one more spell broken. Somehow he'd missed all this during his internship years ago. He could learn to live with disappointment.

The legal department had sent its own contributions to the cause yesterday, so he had copies of the contracts he would shortly offer the residents of Suburban Graveyard. He persisted in calling it that to remind him why was doing this, why he risked his company and his future. He read through the contracts carefully, flagging his questions with sticky notes. He needed to be certain the all-important arbitration clause made sense to him, so he could explain it to the homeowners he needed to relocate. Wait, what was that? He hadn't discussed *that* with Legal. There was an option for SunHo to reimburse homeowners for the original purchase price of the home offset for what was owed on the mortgage. Philip thought anyone would be foolish to take it given what else SunHo would be offering, but—

The buzzing of Philip's iPhone cut off that line of thought. Eddie San Filipo. People needed to quit calling him at work, that's what they needed to do. He was about to let it go to voice mail, but took the call anyway. He was always at work these days.

"Hi, Eddie. What's up?"

"Philip?"

Why did people always sound surprised? Caller ID. Ride the wave. "The one and only. What can I do for you?"

"It's Stuart." Eddie sighed. "He's…. Where've you been, man?"

Philip bit down hard to prevent the obvious response from flying right out of his mouth. He took a deep breath and exhaled slowly. "I don't know how much Stuart might've told you, but right now I'm fighting tooth and claw to retain control of the company that has my name on it. I'm working upwards of fifteen hours a day, so drop your attitude and tell me what you want."

"Whoa, back off. I didn't mean to start a fight."

"Then maybe you should choose your words more carefully."

Neither said anything for a moment or two.

"You said something about Stuart?" Philip said at last. He could almost feel Eddie relax on the other end of the call.

"I don't know what's up with Stuart. He's always been driven, you know that, but now it's ten times worse. Did you know he's sick?"

"Uh… no. Naturally he's told me nothing about this." Philip shook his head. Typical. Stuart wouldn't speak up even if he were about to drop dead of plague and Philip were sitting atop a mountain of antibiotics.

Eddie laughed. "Philip, he had the flu, I mean true influenza. He caught it right after Thanksgiving. Then he got some kind of killer cold that settled in his lungs and wouldn't let go."

"Shit. No wonder he's refused to kiss me."

"He what?"

"He refused to kiss me for a while. I thought he was angry. We've... uh, we've been going through a rough patch." Philip sighed. "It's so hard to get him to say anything."

"Don't tell him I said this. You have to promise."

"Okay." Eddie didn't say anything for a moment, a moment when Philip began to think of horrible things.

"He's been angry, but I don't think at you. I think at the situation you two are in. Or your money. I honestly can't figure it out."

"That makes no sense." But in reality, it made too much sense. Stuart and money. Again.

"I know it doesn't, but he still cares for you. It's... complicated."

"That he is."

"Anyway, he's sick and he's getting worse and I don't know what to do, because he won't see a doctor. Can you talk some sense into him?"

"Probably not, but I'll try," Philip said, knowing Stuart would bite his head off for his troubles. "But you've also got to keep me in the loop and let me know what's going on with him, at least in terms of his health."

"I should've called sooner, but... med school. My one recreational activity for the week is going to the grocery store."

Philip rolled his eyes. At least Stuart wasn't the only one. "Take care of yourself, Eddie, and yes, call or text me sooner. Bye now."

Philip could only shake his head. He knew it had been too good to be true. He'd noticed that Stuart had throttled back on his relentless studying, at least those times he'd been around. Here he'd thought Stuart had at last achieved some balance between school and life. But no. Stuart had fallen ill, and not only ill, but perhaps critically ill. Trust Stuart to push through not one but two serious illnesses.

Leave it to Philip to have to be the one to introduce Stuart to normal human limits, he thought as he returned his focus to saving himself and his company from total ruination.

Eddie called Philip back two days later. "Philip? Stuart just collapsed. Right here in the lab. He's been taken down to the ER, but by the time you get here, he'll probably be on one of the wards."

"Damn. Okay, I'll get there as soon as I can."

Philip ended the call and looked at Estelle. "I have to go."

"An emergency?"

He nodded. "My boyfriend's been taken to the ER at the Med Center."

"Sounds like his stubborn nature and his illnesses finally caught up to him. Don't worry, Philip. I can handle this for a few days. Go take care of your young man."

"Thanks, Estelle. You know how to reach me. So does Jyoti."

Later, at the Med Center, Philip had no recollection of grabbing his keys and jacket, let alone the drive, but there he was next to Stuart's bed, his wool topcoat hanging behind the door.

Stuart looked horrible, so pale and wretched in his hospital bed. He had an oxygen feed in his nose, but Philip supposed it could've been worse. He could've been intubated. He dimly recalled Drew talking about it, and it had sounded grotesque. Stuart had only a single IV line, but two bags feeding into it, one that was fluids and one that contained antibiotics for the pneumonia, according to the nurse.

He'd never heard of IV antibiotics, but the nurse had simply said, "Mr. Sundstrom, when you ignore something as long as he has, we have to pull out the big guns. He's one very sick man." She shook her head. "Med students. They always think they're invincible."

"I suspect it's more that they think they don't have time for anything but their books. Speaking of med students, what kind of insurance do they have?"

The nurse, a short woman on the stout side, thought about it for a moment. "You know, I'm not sure, but it can't be that good. You might want to check with the financial office. It's on the first floor. Since you're listed as Mr. Cochrane's health care proxy, they should tell you what you want to know." She glanced at her watch. "They'll be open for another hour or so and he's unlikely to wake up anytime soon."

Philip stared at her. "I can't have heard you right. I'm what?"

"It says right here on his admissions form that in the absence of Valerie Cochrane, who's too young by the way, one Mr. Philip Sundstrom can make medical decisions for him. If you're unavailable, it falls to someone named Morgan Estrada."

"Oh. Okay, then." Philip stood up. "Thanks, I'd better see to that. I suspect we'll be seeing a lot of each other. Please, call me Philip."

"I'm Marge. I'm the day nurse, or one of them. The night nurses come on at four, so you may be seeing a new face when you get back up here, but I'll tell them who you are," Marge said.

"Thanks, and I guess I'll see you tomorrow."

Philip made a note to bring juice and muffins for the nurses when he came back in the morning. Stuart's comfort was in their hands, after all, and it didn't hurt to grease the gears.

Health care proxy? With all the dancing around the subject of commitment they did? Well, who knew. Morgan he could understand. They truly were best friends, Stuart and Morgan, and not just using it as a blind to sneak up on a real commitment to each other during med school without spooking anyone as he and Stuart had. But him? Stuart must feel a lot more for him than he'd ever let on. That should've made him happy, overjoyed even, but right then it only brought tears to his eyes.

Philip found the finance office well enough. "I'm here to find out what my boyfriend's bill's going to be. He was brought into the ER this afternoon after collapsing in a lab or classroom or something. He's a med student."

"Oh yes, I'd heard about that," the man at the desk said, Peter, according the sign at the window. "I'll need to see some identification." Philip handed over his driver's license for Peter to see. "Thank you, Mr. Sundstrom."

Peter spent a few minutes typing away at his computer. "Sorry for the delay. I have to verify that you're the health care proxy, or at least listed in Mr. Cochrane's files, and I see that you are. Now, for his insurance coverage." He made a face. "They really don't give medical students very good health care coverage. I'd say it's ironic, but it's just kind of mean. He's already racked up quite a bill, and unfortunately med students have a high deductible."

"Are you kidding?" The total even gave Philip pause. He knew Stuart would never be able to pay that. "If I give you a credit card, is there any way you can start a tab or something?"

Peter laughed. "Yes, of course. For the deductible?"

"For anything Stuart might possibly be responsible for." Philip handed over his black Amex. "I want him to walk out of here only having to sign his discharge papers."

Peter muttered something that might've been "Must be nice" as he processed Philip's credit card, but Philip chose not to pursue it. He wasn't worth Philip's time. The only man who was, was upstairs hooked into a ventilator and powerful antibiotics.

He realized as he took the elevator back up to the ward where Stuart slept that he had some calls to make. Valerie, of course, but also Stuart's friends in town, like Eddie. Wait… maybe Eddie would be able to check up on Stuart on his own, but still, maybe a courtesy text would be in order.

Oh, Stuart, you stubborn, beautiful, proud man. Why did you have to go and do this? You're not invincible, no matter how strong you think you are.

CHAPTER
Twenty-One

In the end, Stuart only spent a week in the hospital before the attending physician pronounced him well enough to be discharged. The powerful antibiotics pumped into his IV had worked enough of their magic that he could be sent home to finish recovering from his pneumonia, and when it came down to it, he needed rest more than anything else. Since he slept a lot, and since Philip could be very persuasive, Philip took Stuart home, along with lengthy instructions, an IV pole, and the rest of the antibiotics.

"Are you sure you'll be able to handle this, Philip?" Marge said.

Philip nodded. "I'm sure."

"And if he can't, he can always hire a home-care nurse," Stuart muttered.

"The orderly will be here momentarily, and then you can go home to sleep the rest of this off, Stuart. I expect not to see you back until you're doing rotations on this ward, young man, understand?" Marge tried to look serious, but she looked too much like everyone's favorite grandmother to pull it off.

Stuart smiled. His color was still off, his eyes still smudged with fatigue, but he smiled. "Yes, ma'am."

After the orderly helped Stuart into Philip's waiting car, Stuart said, "Thanks for looking after me. You didn't have to, you know. I could've taken care of myself."

"That didn't work so well the last time." Philip smiled to take the sting out of it, but the truth was, the entire incident scared the hell out of him. He'd never seen anyone drop from exhaustion before, and that included construction workers in the hot summer sun. Actually, they knew how to take care of themselves.

But Stuart had his eyes closed, resting on the short drive back to the condo. He didn't open his eyes until Philip had parked the car in the underground garage.

"Are you going to be okay to make it upstairs?" Philip asked him softly.

Stuart blinked a few times. "Yeah."

Philip watched Stuart open the car door and slowly swing his legs out, pausing to rest. Really, they'd discharged Stuart when he winded himself getting out of a car? In seconds, he'd bolted out of the car to extend a steadying hand to his boyfriend. "Here, grab onto my arm."

"I'm okay," Stuart snapped.

"No, you're not. You need help, so stop being an ass and accept it."

Strangely, that brought a smile to Stuart's face. "Yes, bossman."

Stuart gripped Philip's arm and as he hauled himself up and out of the car, Philip pulled up as well, to conserve Stuart's resources.

"What about the IV and the meds?" Stuart asked as they made their slow way to the elevator.

"I'll make two trips. You're pretty fatigued."

"That's not a bad idea," Stuart said. "I had this idea that I was well enough to walk, but... I'm not, am I?"

Philip shook his head. "No. An orderly rolled you out of the hospital in a wheelchair, so you didn't leave under your own power. I think all your release from the hospital means is that you're out of danger and can finish recovering at home with minimal risk to yourself and their malpractice insurance."

"Cynic."

Philip finished settling Stuart in his bed in his decoy bedroom and then brought everything else the hospital had sent home with Stuart up to the condo. After checking on the patient, who was out cold in a nest fashioned from synthetic down comforters and pillows, Philip sat down to work at the satellite office in the spare bedroom. One of Candy's helper monkeys had taken care of hooking up a T1 Internet line, and that's all there'd been to it. He'd opted for T1 instead of T3 since this wasn't a permanent thing. This way he could move large chunks of data at blinding speeds and still pretend he was economizing. Who knew, maybe it'd help Stuart catch up on his studies, at least once he felt better.

First things first… catching up on e-mails from Jyoti and Estelle. He had the first of the meetings with the residents of Suburban Graveyard the day after tomorrow and needed to have his ducks in a row before they started shooting.

He tapped the Skype icon on his computer's dock. "Estelle? It's Philip. Is this a good time to talk?"

FOUR HOURS later, right before he went to bed, Philip gently woke Stuart.

"Leave me alone." Stuart pulled the covers back over his head.

"I only need your right arm. The rest of you can go back to sleep." Philip pulled the covers back down, grabbed the arm in question, and then flopped the covers over Stuart again.

Muttered grumbles issued from under the duvet. "IV time?"

"IV time." Philip hung the bag containing the antibiotics on the IV pole as he'd been taught and inserted one end of the tubing into it. Then he poked the other end into the port on Stuart's hand.

"Fuck, that's cold! Aren't you supposed to warm that up or something?"

"No one said anything about warming it up. They only told me I had to keep the meds cold so they didn't spoil."

"You're mean."

Philip sat on the edge of the bed. "You know I'm not doing this to you to be cruel."

"I know." Stuart's hand groped for his and Philip took it in his, trying to warm the hand, since he hadn't warmed the antibiotics.

"I'll call tomorrow to ask about warming the meds before I hook them up. Is that how they did it in the hospital?"

"I don't know. I was always asleep."

Philip shook his head. "If you leave your arm accessible, I'll do my best not to wake you when I'm in here in another six hours. It'll be around four thirty tomorrow morning."

"That's mean, too." Stuart's voice grew indistinct. Philip guessed he was already falling asleep again.

"Yeah, but mean for whom? With any luck, you'll be asleep." Philip watched the fluid level in the antibiotics bag drop. Realistically, he knew Stuart hadn't been in danger of dying, but tell that to his lizard brain. Seeing Stuart hooked up to those machines in the hospital shocked and scared Philip. It reminded him that no one ever really knew how long he had.

"Oh, Stuart, what am I going to do with you?" Philip remained silent for a moment. "It sounds silly now, but for a while there, I really thought I'd lost you. You looked so frail. Hell, the sheets had more color than you did when they brought you in. And they called me because you listed me as your health care proxy. I can't tell you how that touched me. I don't know what I would've done if you'd died. I… I love you, Stuart. I have since this summer."

Philip sighed. He felt like such a coward, professing his love only to a sleeping man. He glanced at the antibiotics and noticed the bag was empty. He disconnected Stuart and the tubing, draping the latter carefully over the IV pole before tucking his arm back under the comforters.

After a quick check to ensure Stuart could reach water, acetaminophen, and tissues should he wake before the next dose, Philip headed to his own room not only so his tossing and turning didn't disturb Stuart but also for his own sake. The next few days promised to be taxing enough as it was without adding interrupted sleep due to the administration of Stuart's antibiotics.

But Philip was wrong. Under his duvet, Stuart, while drowsy, was awake and heard everything.

WHEN THE alarm on his iPhone woke him six hours later, Philip felt groggy and out of sorts. He faced the residents of Suburban Graveyard and his father's malfeasance the next day and he felt nowhere near ready. But then, how could he ever be ready to take something like this live? Estelle and the lawyers had been in quiet contact with various government agencies already, so from that standpoint SunHo was covered, but by taking it live with the residents, the company faced the real possibility of a media feeding frenzy, and that Philip was in no mood for. It was the last thing, the very last thing, Stuart needed during his recovery.

Half-asleep, Philip stumbled downstairs to the kitchen to fetch another antibiotic pouch from the fridge and went back to Stuart's room. He found Stuart's arm with a minimum of fuss and managed to get everything going without waking him. Then he sat down at Stuart's desk and rested his head on his folded arms.

When he jolted awake only to find that the IV wasn't even half done but his lower back sure was, Philip decided to ignore what he'd thought earlier. Stuart could cope with his unquiet sleep, and he could put up with Stuart's sniffling.

Carefully, Philip climbed into the part of the double bed not occupied by his deliciously diminutive boyfriend. With a gentle sigh, Stuart curled into him. Philip stiffened, fearing the IV had been torn out, but no. All was as it should've been and Philip fell into a deep and restful sleep, only rousing long enough to disconnect Stuart when the IV finished.

He woke a few hours later, an hour or so before the next juicing, later than he should've, considering how much of his subordinates' work he needed to check before tomorrow. He would've loved to curl up with his convalescing boyfriend all day, but SunHo urgently demanded his attention. So he slid out of the warm cocoon and padded off to the bathroom attached to his own bedroom. Given how much time they spent in each other's beds—even despite their hectic schedules of late—he still thought Stuart's Potemkin bedroom was the silliest thing ever, especially since Stuart was hiding the truth only from himself.

Not long after Philip sat down at his desk, Stuart wandered in. He looked better, but still not back to full strength. That would take a while, maybe months according to his doctors. Not even people in their twenties could abuse their bodies for that long without paying for it.

"I wondered where you'd gone." Stuart yawned. Then he dug at the IV port as if he'd heard there was gold under it.

"I'm pretty sure you're not supposed to do that."

Stuart stuck his tongue out. "It's driving me crazy."

"Well, in about"—Philip glanced at the time on his computer's menu bar—"twenty minutes you get to have some more ice-cold antibiotic run through it, so if nothing else, that ought to numb the itch."

"I thought you were going to call about that."

"I haven't had time this morning. I've only just sat down at my desk. No breakfast, even. I was waiting to see what you wanted. Should you be up and about?"

Stuart shrugged. "I've got a little energy. When it goes, I'll go back to bed. In the meantime, I'm taking a shower."

"Need any help?" Philip pushed back from his desk before he even heard Stuart's answer.

"Stop it, Philip. I'm not made of spun glass. So long as there's a stool to sit on and I tape over the IV port, I'll be fine."

"I'm sorry, I was only trying to help."

"I know. I didn't mean to snap. I hate being sick. Thinking about how much I'm missing makes me crazy."

"I understand. For what it's worth, the house now has a T1 connection. Even hooked into the Wi-Fi router, it'll be superfast. I don't know how your profs feel about distance learning, but it's worth a shot."

"Aww, thanks, Philip. I know I can get into at least one lecture that way." He paused on the way out of the office. "Have you heard from Eddie?"

"As a matter of fact, yes. He dropped a stack of notes off yesterday and then watched you sleep for a while in the hopes that you might wake up." Philip smiled at him. "He left disappointed."

Stuart smiled back. "He'll live. Oh, and breakfast?"

"Yeah?" Philip looked up from his computer.

"Am I pushing my luck asking for pancakes? I actually have an appetite today. I think that's a good sign, don't you?"

Philip grinned. "The best. Go clean up and I'll get to work on breakfast. You're due for more antibiotics in roughly a half hour. If your energy gives out, we can always eat up here in the office."

STUART GLARED at him in mock ferocity. "You cursed me, you know. You and your talk about my energy giving out."

Philip smiled and played along, figuring that even if Stuart had crapped out halfway through his shower, if he still had enough energy to joke he was definitely on the road to recovery. "Yep, that's me. Voodoo priest extraordinaire. Now drink your juice."

"Yes, Daddy."

"We can role-play when you're well. For now, try not to wave that arm around while you're hooked into the antibiotics, m'kay?"

The joking and bantering continued throughout breakfast downstairs and the IV drip, which was a good sign, but toward the end of breakfast Philip could tell something started eating at Stuart in return. He might not even have been aware of it, but Philip noticed that a particular, almost pensive look stole over his boyfriend's face when he was working through something.

Usually Philip could be patient, but with everything going on in his life…. "Spit it out, Stuart. What's on your mind?"

"The hospital…. What happened there, Philip?"

Philip looked puzzled. "What do you mean, what happened? You were sick, they made you better, they sent you home to complete the process."

"That's the part that's confusing me. I know what the hospital bill should've been—"

Philip laughed. He couldn't help himself. "No, you really don't, not when Tylenol, which is available at any number of drug stores at very reasonable prices, costs a buck sixty-five per pill."

"But you paid it." It wasn't a question. "The only thing I had to sign was my discharge papers. No annoying trip to the financial office to work out terms of payment."

"Yeah, so?" Philip had a hard time believing they were having this conversation at all, let alone while he was nursing Stuart through his recovery. "The financial statement is on my desk, if you're that curious. Stuart, it would've set you back years. I couldn't let that happen to you. You've worked too hard to get where you are to let a contingency take you out like that."

Stuart opened his mouth, then closed it again, exercising what Philip thought was remarkable self-control given the tiresome number of conversations they'd had on this subject.

"Philip," Stuart said, appearing to choose his words with care, "I'm grateful that you understand how important not only med school is to me, but also the striving. This is the culmination of everything I've worked for since I escaped my parents' prison when I turned eighteen."

"But…?" And Philip knew there was a *but* coming.

"Once again, Mr. Moneybags has swooped in to save the day! Knowing how I feel about it, knowing how much it bothers me, you did it anyway. Philip, your solution to every problem is to throw money at it!"

Philip stopped himself from rolling his eyes, because here they went again. "Um… yeah, because it works."

"So do brains and cleverness, but you never try those!" Stuart all but screamed.

"I don't see how either of those—and what's the difference between them, anyway—would've made much difference when confronted with a five-figure medical bill," Philip said.

"That's not the point!"

"Then what is the point, Stuart?"

"The point," Stuart yelled. He took a deep breath and tried again. "The point is that you don't respect my point of view."

Philip inclined his head. "Have you considered that perhaps it's because you've never succeeded in explaining it to me in a way that doesn't boil down to 'I grew up poor and therefore I won't let you spend your money'? Because I didn't exactly grow up with a silver spoon in mouth, you know."

"Goddamn it, Philip, you're not listening."

"Yes, I am, but so far you're not saying anything you haven't already said several times before, and it didn't make sense those times, either."

Stuart sighed, the fight leaving him. "As much as I love you, Philip, I don't think we can ever be more than friends. We're too different."

"What? Why?" Philip's breakfast turned to lead in his stomach and he struggled to keep it down.

"Because we keep having the same argument about money, and to be honest, you don't respect my position." Stuart wiped a tear away.

Philip clamped his mouth shut. The last thing he needed to say at that moment was something about Stuart not having a position so much as a prejudice or about following his stupid, stubborn pride off a cliff. It was only money. Why was it such a big deal? Yeah, he had a bunch of it and he was perfectly willing to share. What had Marx said? From each according to his ability, to each according to his needs? Philip wasn't about to follow *that* off Stuart's cliff, but he had the money and Stuart had the need. He knew he could make Stuart's life much simpler, so why wouldn't Stuart let him?

"Have you ever considered the fact that your position—to say nothing of your pride—is making your life far harder than it needs to be? That because I love you—yes, Stuart, I love you—I want to make the material part of your life as easy as I can so that you can focus solely on your studies? That I want to take care of your food, shelter, and yes, clothing to free you to learn as much about medicine as you can in these four short years? Because money's pretty useless if you don't spend it making the lives of people you love better."

Stuart's shoulders slumped. "We spend so much time arguing about it. It's always going to be a stumbling block. I think it's better this way."

"I don't agree," Philip said flatly, "but I can't make you do something you don't want to do. I've got too much to do today and tomorrow to move out, but I think it's best if I'm not around too much."

Stuart looked pained. "Philip, don't. You don't have to move out of your own home."

"Let's stop pretending—I bought this place to solve your roommate problems and so you'd have some place close to school. I'll move back into my house. It's not like it's that far away."

"If that's the way you want it," Stuart said softly.

"No, it's really not, but it's the way you want it." Philip pushed back from the table. "Just put your dishes in the sink when you're done. I'll deal with them later."

Philip couldn't decide whether he was angry or crushed as he trudged upstairs to his office, the IV pole in hand. He left it outside Stuart's bedroom.

As he sat down at his desk, he settled on heartbroken. He figured there had to be something wrong with him. Angie hadn't wanted him because he wanted to settle down. Stuart hadn't wanted him because he was rich. That crap about bisexuals having double the chances for dates? It was just that—crap. More like a pernicious lie, double the chances to be shot down in flames for things he couldn't help. Thank goodness for his workaholic tendencies or he'd be a real mess. But he knew he'd have to face this sooner or later, and when he did....

CHAPTER
Twenty-Two

DECEMBER 23, and as near as Stuart could tell, his life had hit rock bottom. He couldn't even call Valerie because their parents didn't know she had a cell phone and he would be the last person to let that particular cat out of the bag. That phone represented her only lifeline, so as much as he wanted to whine and needed to hear a sympathetic voice, he left her alone. Some people had it worse than he did.

So when his phone buzzed and Morgan's name appeared on the display, Stuart naturally assumed Christmas had arrived early. "Hey, Morgan. What's up?"

"I'm just checking in to see how you're doing before I head home for Christmas. I'm assuming now that the quarter's over, you're actually free to talk."

"Something like that, yes." Stuart tried to keep the morose tone out of his voice. The last person he wanted to be was Dr. Downer.

"Huh. What aren't you telling me?"

Stuart sighed. "That's spooky, you know that?"

"Just because we don't live together anymore doesn't mean I don't know you like the back of my hand."

"As long as it's not *that* hand."

"Really, Stuart? Masturbation jokes this close to Christmas? Someone's bucking for coal in his stocking this year."

"Given the cost of fossil fuels these days, you'd think more people would be after coal, wouldn't you?"

"Don't deflect. What's going on?"

"It's an awful lot to handle over the phone." Stuart managed not to whine. He was proud of that.

"I'll be over in an hour. You might as well pack. If it's this bad, I'm taking you home, if only because Nick and my mother both will skin me alive if I leave you in Sacramento for Christmas when you're having a crisis."

"I remember when the only crises were with you rowers." Stuart liked those days. He missed them.

Morgan laughed. "Me, too, but it's your turn now. Sucks, doesn't it?"

"Shut up." But Stuart said it to dead air, because Morgan had already hung up.

WHICH WAS how Stuart found himself in Morgan's car with Sacramento in the rearview mirror. "Nice car."

Morgan smiled. "Thanks. Since I'm the only one of the Estrada boys to go into something that doesn't make piles of money, my older brothers have decided I get their hand-me-down rides. Since they buy fancy cars, I'm perfectly fine with this arrangement. Even Nick's starting to see the benefits."

"You never were that particular about taking things secondhand from your brothers." Stuart admired that about Morgan. He wasn't too proud for leftovers even as he maintained high standards, seeing quality wherever it existed rather than being blinded by labels or price tags. Of course, it didn't hurt that his family had money.

Stuart sighed. He'd been doing that a lot lately he'd noticed, but damn it, did everything come back to money?

"So tell me," Morgan said, signaling a lane change, "why were you so willing to jump in my car when your boyfriend's back in Sacramento?"

Stuart frowned. "This isn't the way to your parents' house."

"Nope, we're meeting at the beach house for the holiday, and don't deflect. What's going on?"

"It's a long story."

"We've got time."

"You shanghaied me, admit it."

Morgan shrugged. "That might've been part of it, but I'm really worried about you. Now start talking."

"Oh, very well. I'm not sure where to start…. Did you know I've been sick? Like, really sick, in the hospital sick?"

"No. Why didn't anyone call me?"

"Probably because Philip didn't know he should've. Also because he's up to his eyebrows in trying to save his company and his place at the head of it."

"Huh. I wonder if Brad knows?" Morgan sounded like he wasn't paying attention as he navigated the twists and turns of the narrow highway through the coastal range to Highway 1, but Stuart knew better.

Stuart shrugged. "I doubt he cares. Philip bought him out. Bad memories and all that."

"What a strange family." Morgan shook his head.

"You don't know the half of it." Out of the blue, like a freak bolt of lightning, it struck Stuart then that he had almost become a part of that family, almost but no longer.

"Brad seems a lot happier the last year or so. We're actually friends, you know," Morgan said.

"Stranger things have happened. He's even stopped irritating me. I kind of like the guy, myself." Stuart turned his head and stared out the window, letting the conversation lapse.

"So," Morgan said after a time. "What's got you down? And don't bother denying it."

"Well, I told you I was sick, and part of that was I missed all my finals, which is kind of a problem in medical school."

"I can see that."

"Right? I've contacted all my professors and they've been great about it, but I can't make anything up until the next semester starts. See the problem?"

Morgan nodded. "Finishing one term while starting the next?"

"Got it in one, Estrada." Stuart started to shiver, so he pulled his jacket tighter and fiddled with the vents until Morgan noticed and notched the heater up. "The thing is, there's something called PELP— the planned educational leave program—but I don't want to take time off from school, I want to make up what I missed without losing ground and dragging myself down."

"Yikes, talk about a rock and a hard place," Morgan said. He notched his window down slightly to deal with the now uncomfortably warm car. "How's it going with Philip?"

Stuart squirmed. He didn't want to get into it, but he also knew he couldn't spend the entire holiday dodging not only Morgan but also his mother. "We broke up."

It hurt him to say, but it was true. Actually, it cut him to the quick, which surprised him. He'd initiated the breakup, so why shouldn't he be okay with it? Instead he felt hollow and empty, the thought bringing him to tears.

"What? Why?"

A tear ran down Stuart's cheek. "He didn't respect my feelings."

A quick glance to the left showed Stuart that Morgan's eyes had narrowed behind his shades. "Which ones?" Morgan said.

Stuart mumbled an answer. He didn't feel like confessing, thanks all the same, and if he spoke up right then, he'd bawl his head off.

"Stuart Cochrane, you spill and you spill now, or I'll tell my mother you haven't been eating enough."

That got his attention. Mrs. Estrada and food. The last time she thought he was malnourished, she'd sat him down with a pan of enchiladas and wouldn't let him up…. He still shook at the memory. "You wouldn't."

"Try me. Actually, she might think that anyway. You don't have to make weight anymore. It's okay to eat cheese."

"Old habits die hard, and do I really have to tell which one of my ideals a rich man might've violated?"

"Not the money again," Morgan said, groaning. He banged his head on the headrest a few times. "You've always been a head case where money's concerned."

"What!" Stuart could scarcely believe that Morgan, of all people, would say something like that. Morgan, his roommate for most of his time at California Pacific, who'd always understood and never insulted him or his dignity despite the disparities in their net worth…. "Philip knew how important it is for me to pay my own way. He was fine at the beginning, but lately—at least the last couple of months—he's just bulldozed his way over my objections. The bit with the hospital bill was the last straw."

"The hospital bill? Do tell," Morgan said.

Stuart explained, at least what he knew, although he suspected there was more to the story, but in dumping Philip, that particular source of information wouldn't be so forthcoming.

"Seriously? That's why you dumped him?" Morgan pinched the bridge of his nose. "You're going to have to walk me through this, Stuart, because what it sounds like from here is that you broke up with the man you love because he paid your hospital bill, and that's the stupidest thing I've ever heard."

Stuart hunched his shoulders, defensive and angry. "It is not."

"Yes, it is. Record it and play it back, and you'll see I'm right." Morgan shook his head. "I hope that pride of yours keeps you warm at night, maybe gives you a nice warm hug and huge kiss on New Year's Eve, because otherwise I think you'll be a little cold and lonely."

Stuart glared at Morgan. Why couldn't he make anyone understand why this mattered to him? "I'm not for sale."

"I never said you were, and you know what? I don't think Philip thought you were, either." Morgan rolled his eyes. "I think you're so hung up about money you're not rational about it anymore, if you ever were."

"Why now, Morgan? Of all the times to do this to me, why now?" Stuart was trapped and furious, and even if he ditched Morgan at a gas station or a rest stop, he'd still be stranded somewhere between Sacramento and The Sea Ranch.

"Because you've never been this psycho about it before. You've never cut your nose off to spite your face before, not like this. Did he tell you why he paid your hospital bill?"

"Why does that matter?"

Morgan snorted. "I'm suddenly curious. Humor me."

"You know what? Fuck you and your curiosity."

"That's Nick's job. Did you know he can fuck me to a hands-free orgasm now?"

"That was way more information than I needed." Stuart ignored the stab of jealousy.

"Seriously, I want to know."

"Fine. He told me he knew how hard I'd worked to get into med school and he didn't want a five-figure bill to set me back." He winced as he said it, although he'd never let Morgan see it. Thank God Morgan had to keep his eyes on the road.

"And you interpreted that as buying you? You're pathetic, Stuart. You never used to be this bad when—"

"You and your parents slipped me help?"

Morgan flinched. The only sounds in the car were the heater and the mp3 player.

Stuart grinned. "You thought I didn't know?"

"You weren't supposed to." Morgan's ivory skin blushed so prettily, Stuart thought absently.

"Morgan, please. 'Oh, I bought too much at the warehouse store. Can you use some?' only worked the first couple of times before I had to face the fact that you were either hopelessly stupid or up to something. Since you're anything but dumb, that left the other option." He was silent. "You helped me out of some tight spots, you know."

"I know," Morgan said softly.

"The thing is, you never made it feel like charity."

"That was the point, yes. Did Philip?"

Stuart thought for a moment. "No, but somehow I was always aware of it."

"I can't say anything about that since I didn't see any of it. I just hope you made the right call, because right now you really don't seem happy," Morgan said, placing his hand on Stuart's leg.

Stuart covered Morgan's hand with his. "Me, too, because otherwise feeling this crappy is kind of a waste, isn't it?"

BRAD AND Drew's door opened. "Oh… it's a dog!" Philip said, forcing as much enthusiasm into his voice as he could. "Sort of."

"Isn't he cute?" Brad cooed. He swooped down and scooped up the tiny Chihuahua that had been growling at Philip's shoe. "We don't want to get stepped on, do we?"

"Where can I put this?" Philip said, peering over the presents in his arms. He was glad his brother had removed the dog. He'd been afraid he'd step on it because he couldn't really see where he was walking and as small as the dog was, he doubted he'd feel it, either. Really? A Chihuahua puppy?

"How about under the tree?" Drew said. "Actually, everything has to go on that table. Bippy will either attack it or pee on it."

"Good thing I avoided the Pepperidge Farm display at the mall, then." Philip shuffled his feet across the floor, still worried about the dog.

"Say hewwo to Unca Phiwip." Brad waved one of the dog's paws.

Philip met Drew's eyes. Both men shook their heads. "So how long has this been going on?" Philip said. "I mean, how long have you had him?"

"It's his Christmas present." Drew laughed. "So since this morning, which explains some of your brother's eccentricities."

"The bigger the man, the smaller the dog," Brad said, joining his spouse and his brother by the tree.

"There's not really anything I can say to that, is there?" Philip said, pretending to crane his neck to see Brad's face.

"Brad," Drew said, sounding quite terse to Philip's ears. He looked at the tree and yep, Bippy had lifted his leg.

Brad groaned. "Aww jeez, not again, little dude. No one can have to go to the bathroom that much."

"I told you what would happen the next time he did that," Drew said.

"I know you did, but… the crate?"

Drew looked implacable. "Yes, Brad, the crate, which you promised you'd use to train him. I also told you what I'd do if you couldn't train him."

Philip watched the exchange with open enjoyment.

"You know, Philip, you could pretend to be busy examining the ornaments on the pretty tree," Brad said.

"I could, yes, but you two are so much better looking." Philip smiled. "Besides, I kind of want to know what Drew threatened to do."

Brad shook his head. "You really don't, not unless you're into water sports."

"Oh sure, tell him that much, you big oaf," Drew said, pushing them both toward the kitchen.

"You know I don't want to know anything at all about what goes on in your bedroom, right? Or bathroom, as the case may be," Philip said. It sounded like something he'd have said before Stuart crumpled up his heart and discarded it like a dripping fast-food wrapper. Was that bitter? He was trying not to sound bitter.

"Ugh, don't be that way. I simply told Brad that if his dog didn't knock off the marking, I'd show it who the real alpha bitch in this pack is," Drew said.

"By peeing on him, Drew. You said you'd pee on him." Brad shook his head.

Drew shrugged. "A friend of mine did it and said it was miraculous. Sure, his wife was grossed out, but it worked. Dogs are pack animals and it's one way they show dominance."

Brad cuddled Bippy protectively against his body. "But... but, my puppy."

"But... but, our wood floors and Biedermeier antiques." Drew kissed Philip's cheek. "Anyway, welcome and a merry Christmas Eve to you."

Philip felt distinctly un-merry. In fact, he was reasonably certain he could kill the holiday spirit in total strangers just by walking by them, maybe giving them a quick gimlet glance. He forced a smile. "Thanks, Drew."

"So where's Stuart?" Brad said, joining them in the kitchen after he'd crated Bippy.

"I'm not sure, to be honest."

Philip pretended not to see the look Drew and Brad exchanged. That was something lovers did, something partners exchanged, something he and Stuart had once done. While Philip was nothing but happy for the two of them, seeing Brad and Drew exchange weighted looks cut like a razor blade, a clean slice that would sting in a moment and bleed only later.

"What happened?" Drew said.

"He decided that despite the fact that we love each other, he couldn't be with me since I quote-unquote don't respect his feelings about money." Philip stifled the sob welling up from deep within in him, like a cough. Or vomit.

Brad crossed his arms. "What'd you do?"

"I paid the bill for his recent hospital stay," Philip said, explaining how his ex ended up in the hospital in the first place.

"So wait…. He worked himself until he dropped, earned himself a hospital bill in the mid five figures for his trouble, and then dropped you like a hot rock because you paid it so he wouldn't be burdened by it and med school loans." Brad ran one hand over his shaven head.

Philip nodded. "Essentially, yes."

"That's the most ridiculous thing I've ever heard." He turned to Drew. "Isn't that the most ridiculous thing you've ever heard?"

"If not, it's close to it," Drew said, sighing. "I'm sorry, Philip. Maybe he'll come to his senses?"

"No way to tell, I suppose, but given how stubborn he is, I'm not holding my breath." Philip sighed. "Don't let me kill the mood. Tell me something cheering."

So they did over dinner. Brad and Drew's various business ventures were taking off, and Philip realized that he'd actually seen more and more signs for Drew's real estate company but had been so preoccupied with his own issues he hadn't made the connection.

"Any word back on the application to work with SunHo on developing the bottling plant?" Philip said.

"Yes, as a matter of fact," Drew said. "SunHo is moving ahead on the deal and I've made the second round. I'm working on a marketing plan to show them."

"You're not real in tune with what your company's doing, are you?" Brad said, laughing.

"I've been rather preoccupied," Philip said dryly, "both saving it from something mind-bogglingly stupid—and illegal—Randall did and saving my place at the head of it."

"Jeez, now what'd he do?" Brad said.

Philip laughed, but there was little levity to it. "Remember how you called that subdivision SunHo acquired along with that smaller company Suburban Graveyard?"

Brad snorted. "Yeah." Then he looked at Drew. "Looking back, I'm sort of fond of it, because if I hadn't been stuck there, I'd never have called Drew for help with it."

"I think you'd have found another reason to call." Drew smiled back at him. "If not, then I would've called you eventually. I drove Nick insane pestering him for your number."

Philip coughed to return their attention to the here and now. He also tried not to puke up his dinner. "Anyway, your name was more apt than you knew. It's sitting atop a toxic waste dump left over from World War Two, and from what I can tell, Randall knew about it."

"Shit. What're you going to do about it?" Drew said.

Philip outlined the steps he'd taken thus far. "I had the first meeting with homeowners yesterday."

"How'd that go?" Brad said.

"About like you'd expect it to go when you tell them they're living on a chemical landfill. Three families have already lawyered up, according to my legal department. It's their right, but I thought we'd put together a more than fair compensation package." Philip sighed. "Oh well, it's not like this is going to be solved overnight."

Brad sighed. "Don't take this the wrong way, but Philip, you keep telling me all this crap like it matters. You bought me out. I have no connection to that place."

Philip shook his head. "It's still your last name. What about your renovations company?"

Brad shrugged. "We both own it, but it's still called St. Charles Renovations."

"Thank God." That removed one major item from his list of worries. At least this way if he lost everything, the shrapnel wouldn't hit Brad and Drew.

Brad looked at Drew, who nodded. "Philip, our only concern with all of this is what it's doing to you," Drew said.

"If you end up facing jail time because of crap Randall pulled, I personally will reach through the prison bars and kill the fucker," Brad said.

"That's what I'm hoping to avoid by running right to federal and state regulators with this. 'Look what we found, here's what we're doing about it, please help us.' With any luck, that'll count for something as they're fining us heavily. The banksters crashed the economy and no one's done any hard time, so cross your fingers."

"Never a dull moment, but I noticed we're back to gloom and doom," Drew said. "It's Christmas Eve. Let's go watch that cheesy eighties retread of *A Christmas Carol* I recorded on the DVR, make snotty comments, and drink hot chocolate and stuff ourselves with Christmas cookies."

"That," Philip said, "sounds like a brilliant idea. Let me help clean things up and then I will gladly make snotty comments about bad retreads."

CHAPTER
Twenty-Three

PHILIP HAD enjoyed Christmas Eve with his family and had accepted their invitation to spend Christmas Day with them. He finally left them alone after lunch, returning to the condo he had once shared with Stuart to move some of his things back to the big house, glad he'd never rented it out. Then it hit him all over again. He cried on the sofa. He didn't know how long, only that it was noticeably darker than when he'd arrived. Being alone on Christmas sucked, but not as much as being dumped right before the holiday. Part of him thought he should go out on New Year's Eve and do something really trashy, but he knew he wouldn't be able to hit the bars without sobbing at every couple he saw.

In the end, Philip never made good on his plans to move more of his clothes or other things back to the old Sundstrom house. Instead he ate a meal of cold cereal and went to bed early, the few presents for him in the condo unopened. He just couldn't be bothered.

His mood hadn't improved much the next morning, so he decided to visit Randall in prison. Brad generally opposed such visits, which is why he hadn't mentioned it, but Philip couldn't shake the feeling there was something he was missing about the whole Suburban Graveyard fiasco, something Randall knew.

Dragging himself into the shower after what meager breakfast he felt like, Philip dressed like he usually did. He couldn't help it, which irritated him. Even when he tried to dress the slob, his jeans and sweatshirts gave him away. Sighing, he threw his leather jacket over his hoodie to ward off the winter chill and aimed his car for the poky.

After having his car and then his person searched, Philip was shown to the visiting area for low-risk offenders. Too bad they didn't have one for inveterate assholes, he thought. But why waste taxpayer money on a room just for his dad?

"Huh. It's you. Where the hell's your brother?" Randall said, sitting down at the table across from Philip.

Philip shrugged. "You keep expecting him to visit. Given what you did to him and his partner, that doesn't make a whole lot of sense."

"You'd think they'd have gotten over that by now."

Philip didn't think that was worth a response, but made a mental note to ask the warden to see if Randall was using. Delusion on that scale couldn't be natural. "So tell me about Sunset Homes and Suburban Symphony."

Randall leaned on the table in a manner that Philip assumed was supposed to look authoritative and powerful. "Why? What's to tell?"

"Winch couldn't care less that none of those houses will sell and won't discipline the underling whose job it is to make sure that place is profitable," Philip said. He watched his father carefully as he spoke.

"So? You own the company now. You're the chairman of the board." Randall sat back in his chair, arms crossed over his chest. "You took it over, you deal with it."

"I know. I thought I'd see if you had any insight into why Winch, who is, after all, a friend of yours, is so curiously inert when it comes to this one development. Did you know his whore hasn't even bothered to contact the county about extending roads to it? And yes, he's screwing her. Tell me, Randall, does Winch visit you? Or was he your friend so long as you could do something for him?"

Philip sat at the table, apparently serene. He waited as time passed.

Randall blinked first, shifting in his chair. "What? Why're you staring at me like that?"

"Because you obviously know something and sooner or later you'll tell me."

"Fuck you, you ungrateful little brat. After all I did for you, the way you treated me. You should be ashamed, that's what you—"

"I'm selling the house, you know."

Randall rolled his eyes. "Why do you think I care? Thanks to you, I'll be living here for some time to come."

"That means Mom's old sitting room, too, you stupid jackass."

Philip smiled slightly as Randall, shouting truly foul words, lunged across the table at him. Philip controlled himself, every muscle tense, but Randall never reached him. The guards were on him like stink on a monkey before he ever touched Philip.

Philip wiped spit off his cheeks as they dragged Randall away. "Merry Christmas, Randall!" he called.

Philip could never figure out why they searched his car on the way out of prison. Whatever. He was impatient and he knew it. Without meaning to, Randall told him there was *something* of interest in his mother's old sitting room. Whether or not it related to Sunset Homes and Suburban Graveyard, there was only one way to find out. It was the best clue he had to go on, and when it came down to it, what else did he have to do on a holiday?

He controlled his need for speed back to the big house. A speeding ticket would only slow him down. More of that pragmatism of his that drove Randall crazy.

He arrived soon enough. After disarming the alarm system, he took the stairs two at a time, not bothering to turn the heater back on.

The door to Helena Sundstrom's private room was locked. Without considering it, Philip raised a leg and kicked the door in. It felt good to give his pent-up rage an outlet, and he enjoyed every kick it took to make a Philip-sized hole. Even a cursory glance of the room itself showed nothing out of the ordinary from when his mother still lived.

But the closet? He saw the deadbolt from the doorway. So not a problem. He jogged back down the stairs, stopping only long enough to leave his leather jacket on the back of a chair in the kitchen. When he moved out, he hadn't taken Randall's shop tools. There wasn't room in the condo, and he'd had no use for them. They were right where he'd left them, including the huge power drill that would chew right through the heart of that deadbolt.

Philip collected a sample of what he thought might be the right bits and hefted the drill, giving thanks to the good people at Husqvarna for making powerful tools that ran on batteries. Of course, he could say the same of the folks at Good Vibrations and Fort Troff....

Fitting a bit into the drill, he tightened the chuck and squeezed the trigger experimentally a few times, exhausting what he knew about power drills. Brad would be laughing himself silly right about now, and if Philip couldn't make this work, he'd have to call him or look it up on his iPhone. Given how much he owed Brad, he'd give his brother a chance to laugh in his face.

Fortunately, Philip had guessed correctly and the drill started carving out the center of the lock. It was a slow process, and a hot one. He felt the heat generated by the bit's passage as metal corkscrews fell to the floor, where they quickly cooled. He brushed them aside with his foot, noting that they left marks. Oh well. He needed to see what Randall had hidden in there, a room he'd conditioned his sons to stay out of.

At last the drill pushed through the other side, startling Philip, who'd allowed his attention to wander. He pulled the drill bit out and set the drill down on the floor before he opened the door. Eyeballing the contents of his mother's private closet, he snorted. There was nothing of Helena in here, only Randall, strongbox after strongbox, each locked, each labeled. He made a cursory scan of the contents and knew he'd hit the jackpot.

He pulled out his phone. "Estelle? It's me. I'm sorry to bother you, but I'm about to pull you away from your family."

"Why am I not surprised," she said, sighing.

"I know, I know, but you won't regret this. I found Randall's original files on Sunset Homes. We need to go through this now and then get it to my lawyer."

"Where are you?"

"My old place."

"I'll be there in a half-hour." Then she hung up.

Three hours later, they sat at the dining room table, files and papers arrayed in stacks around them.

"If there's a smoking gun, I'd say this is it." Estelle sighed. "Randall Sundstrom, you're a crook as well as an ass."

Philip shook his head. "He knew all about the little problem under Suburban Symphony, but wanted Sunset's other assets. Did I ever tell you what my brother called it?" When Estelle looked at him with her head cocked inquisitively, he continued, "Suburban Graveyard. It was funnier before it was true."

"There's that, yes. At least we have enough evidence that points to Randall that we should be able to pull our own bacon out of the fire."

"Or at least enough of it to save the company, once we run squealing to the Cal EPA with this latest information," Philip said. Despite knowing Randall, he still couldn't believe his father had done this.

Estelle frowned, thinking. "No, once SunHo's corporate lawyers run squealing to whomever or whatever they decide is the best bet. The two of us? We tell our own lawyers first."

"That's a good point. Do you have a personal attorney yet, or do you want to use mine?" Philip already had his phone out and the number pulled up from his speed-dial list.

"What about SunHo's legal department?"

"Those lawyers represent Sundstrom Homes and us in our capacities as officers of the company and its board of directors. This one represents me personally. If anyone names me in some kind of civil suit or if any regulatory agency tries to hold me personally accountable…. His primary job is to keep me out of prison and financially solvent."

Estelle nodded slowly. "I hadn't thought of that. Yes, I'd better have yours represent me unless I decide I want someone else."

Philip placed the call. "After he gets here and decides what to do with this—make copies or whatever—I'd imagine he'll contact the DA who put Randall away. I'm sure she'd be interested in more malfeasance on his part. In the meantime, you know what we need to do?"

"I'm afraid to ask, honestly," Estelle said.

"Look for any evidence that Winch and his cronies knew about this and that you didn't. Randall's secret dossiers are one thing, but these documents are the actual evidence." Philip longed to take Winch down and by this time had come to genuinely like Estelle. He didn't want to see any of the Sunset Homes blowback smeared on her.

Philip's excitement about nailing Randall for Suburban Graveyard almost made him forget his own unhappiness and his longing for Stuart. Outside, it was a beautiful winter day, crisp and cold and clear, but he was indifferent. Without Stuart he saw everything with a patina of gray.

STUART ENJOYED his time with the Estradas, but then, he had ever since they'd taken him under their collective wing. Visits to their house—houses? he didn't think they owned a beach house, so maybe it was a rental—were like going to a spa, or so he imagined, only without the apricot-seaweed scrubs. For some reason, their subtle charity had never rubbed him the wrong way. Maybe because despite his one-time crush on Morgan, he'd never planned on marrying Morgan's parents, he thought as Mrs. Estrada plied him with more leftovers. Seriously, Christmas dinner hadn't seemed that big, but the leftovers appeared to be endless.

During that liminal period between Christmas and New Year's, however, he'd compiled a list of things that depressed him: Philips-Magnavox appliances, which ruled out any number of entertainment and personal-care products like the home theater system and one of Morgan's brother's electric razor; reruns of *One Day at a Time* on TV Land (Mackenzie Phillips); and any news about the Duke of Edinburgh. He recognized that he verged on the pathetic, but if he couldn't wallow in his misery during the holidays, when could he?

"Are you sure you're eating enough? You always looked undernourished when you and Morgan were rowing," Mrs. Estrada said, jerking his attention back to the plate in front of him. "And you've been sick. How will you regain your strength if you don't eat?"

"I'm fine, honestly. If I eat any more right now, I'll burst." When she looked skeptical, he said, "Seriously, small person, small stomach."

Morgan laughed from the den. "Mom, leave him be. He's fine. If his color's bad it's because he dumped his boyfriend right before Christmas and this is the universe's way of making him suffer."

"Stuart! What a thing to do," Mrs. Estrada said, giving him a reproving eye.

"Want to go for a walk on the beach, Stuart?" Nick called from where he was entwined with Morgan.

"Yes!" Stuart said, jumping at the chance to get away from Mrs. Estrada's ministrations.

"Hey! You were keeping me warm," Morgan yelped.

"Come with," Nick said, passing through the kitchen on the way to the bedroom he shared with Morgan.

"Thank you," Stuart whispered as Nick fell in with him, as his former coach and good friend came to his rescue.

Nick nodded. "She's a good woman and they're a great family, but All Estrada All The Time is overwhelming."

Stuart laughed. "They're your in-laws, you know."

"Yes, and when all the cousins and collateral relatives are in one place I end up hiding somewhere playing with Twitter or Facebook on my phone. They can be a little overwhelming, and that's before all the abuelas and aunties decide you don't eat enough."

"Admit it. You love it." Stuart waited while Nick pulled on some trainers and a parka.

Nick smiled. "Yeah, I do. It's nice to be engulfed by a family, since my own is… yeah."

Nick waited while Stuart pulled on some shoes and a coat of his own. "Exactly. It's me and Val against the world."

In the end, it was only the two of them on the beach, since Morgan decided he'd rather hold down the sofa than brave the weather on the coast, despite the fact that it was a gorgeous day. Windy, but gorgeous. Nick held off the expected interrogation until they'd made it out of the house, which Stuart appreciated.

"You feel like talking about it?"

Stuart shook his head. "Not really."

"Okay, then."

And that was the extent of it. He'd always liked that about Nick. The man knew when not to push. Instead they caught up like the old friends that they were, friends who'd been through a lot together in crew. He even thought about coming back to cox for Capital City Rowing Club, which he knew Nick would love. Sure, it'd be lower-stress by several orders of magnitude than CalPac, but med school…. Nick would have to be content with Stuart coxing races as his schedule allowed.

When he and Nick returned to the house, Stuart was surprised to see that more than an hour had passed and he had an appetite. So when Mrs. Estrada looked like she was about to explode with wanting to feed him but was literally sitting on her hands, he went to the fridge and helped himself.

"What did you say to her, Morgan?"

Morgan blinked innocently. "Me?"

"Can I get a show of hands—anyone who believes that tone?" Stuart said loudly. No one. He thought not. He also thought the reason the Estradas—even Morgan's brothers—liked having Morgan's friends over was for the comic relief.

"Oh, Stuart? Your phone was chirping like an angry cricket while you were out," Morgan said.

"Thanks, Morgan. I'd better check it, I guess."

Getting out of the house and being around friends helped Stuart shake his earlier down mood. Yeah, life was a little sucky right then, but there were good parts, too.

He returned to the table with his phone. He really was hungry. He could listen to messages and eat, he thought as he retrieved the first of his messages.

"Hello, Mr. Cochrane. My name is Judy Antonelli, and I'm a social worker with the Department of Human Services in Philadelphia. If you could give me a call at your earliest convenience? My number is 1-215...."

That one came not too long after he and Nick had left for their walk. A couple of hang-ups followed it. Then another by Judy Antonelli.

He jotted down her number, his concerned growing by leaps and bounds. Philadelphia's Department of Human Services. The only good thing in Philly as far as he was concerned was his sister, but she and their parents were at some tent revival or something....

He punched in her number.

"Judy Antonelli."

"Yes, this is Stuart Cochrane, you've—"

"Oh, Mr. Cochrane. Thank goodness you've called back. I have some questions for you, and depending on the answers, potentially some bad news. Are you the oldest son of Daniel and Mimi Cochrane?"

Stuart's gut tightened at the mere mention of their names. "Yes, although we've been estranged for five or so years now."

"I'm afraid that won't matter now. There's been an accident—"

"What about Valerie? Shit. Is Valerie all right?"

"I'm sorry, Mr. Cochrane," Judy said quietly. "No one else survived the collision."

Older? His mind spun in circles. Valerie was dead. How could this happen? She was supposed to escape their whackjob parents and move out and now she was dead, and that wasn't supposed to happen. How could this happen?

"Mr. Cochrane?"

"Yeah? Sorry, I'm still here," he said roughly. He was barely aware of arms encircling him, of people standing quietly in the background. "You said else?"

"Yes, your brother. Frederick survived. You're his nearest living relative. We need you to come to Philadelphia as soon as possible to claim him."

Stuart nodded, his brain on autopilot. Frederick. His little brother, alone in the world. Alone in a wrecked car in the cold, everyone else dead. Jeez, poor Frederick. Valerie, his Valerie—*their* Valerie—was gone, leaving Frederick, leaving him, alone. "It will be a few days before I get out there."

"I understand. I'm so glad I was able to find you, and I know Freddie will be happy to see you," the social worker said.

Freddie? Glad to see him? "I barely know him, you know. The only way I've seen him was when Valerie would sneak him into our Skype sessions. Before our parents took her webcam."

"I understand, but you're still his closest relative."

"Okay. Do I let you know when I'm in Philadelphia? Or when I leave California? You're going to have to walk me through this." Stuart shook his head. "Wait, I'm in medical school. How am I supposed to take care of a little boy with the hours I keep?"

"You'll have to work something out, Mr. Cochrane, but right now, Freddie needs you," Judy said. "If you would notify me of your travel arrangements, I'd appreciate it. I'll be sure to meet you at the airport."

"Right, Freddie needs me. I know. Only it'll be the bus station. I don't have much money."

"Bus station, then. I'll see you soon, Mr. Cochrane."

"Right, soon."

Still dazed, Stuart ended the call. "She's dead."

"Who's dead?" Nick said gently.

Stuart stared up at him with unseeing eyes. "My sister. Valerie's dead. Car accident."

"What about your parents, Stuart?" Morgan said.

"Them, too. Only my little brother made it. I have to go to Philadelphia. To take custody of him," Stuart said, sounding hollow to his own ears.

"You'll be there tomorrow," Mrs. Estrada said firmly. "Morgan, your laptop."

"Yes, Mother." Morgan unwrapped his arms from around Stuart and jumped to it.

Stuart shook his head, bringing himself back to the here and now. "I can't take that kind of money. Bus tickets, one round trip ticket, plus a one-way from Philadelphia on the way home."

Nick shook his head. "Not the time to worry about money, Stuart."

"No, it's exactly the time. I'm broke. I need to make what I have last. For Freddie. I need to look for a new place to live since I can't keep living in Philip's place, and now I've got a child to look after on top of everything else," Stuart said, rousing from his confusion. "Jeez, poor Freddie."

Poor me, he thought. *Poor Valerie. She never escaped.*

Morgan returned with his laptop a few moments later. "Okay, I can get you on a flight out of San Francisco in four hours. If we leave in the next half hour, I think we can make it. It's a red-eye, but it's not like you'd sleep tonight anyway. Book—"

"No, no planes." Stuart shook his head.

Morgan looked shocked. "Are you insane? How're you going to get there, the train?"

"Worse, the bus," Nick said.

"Stuart…," Mrs. Estrada said, trying one more time.

Stuart set his jaw, his lips a thin, tight line. "The bus."

"All right," Morgan said with a sigh. "The bus."

CHAPTER
Twenty-Four

IF HIS head hadn't swum from the social worker's news, Stuart would've been scared shitless by the bus terminal in San Francisco. Maybe he should've taken the airplane tickets after all....

Oh well, no use second-guessing himself, at least on that score. After all, he had so many other things to chew on, like basically telling his sister to suck it up and go to that damn tent revival to avoid raising any suspicions. If she'd stayed home, she could've made a break for California while they were gone....

If she'd stayed home, she'd be alive, right now. She'd be alive and she'd make her escape.

He doubted he'd ever forgive himself for that. Stay away from snakes. He was such an asshole. And still the bus chugged on over the miles, carrying him east. He tucked his knees up and tried to sleep using his coat as a blanket. Why hadn't he noticed how threadbare it was before this? Too bad he'd been such a prig about that leather coat that Philip had tried to give him. He'd have been snug and warm under it.

Philip. It still hurt when he thought of the other man. How long had it been, a week? He didn't know. It was part of the blur of his immediate past. All that mattered right then was that he was alone except for a four-year-old. Was that how old Freddie was? He didn't even know that. Jeez, he was pathetic.

He sniffled, quashing the tears that threatened. It didn't matter. His eyes were already rimmed with red from crying for his sister. Damn. He'd have to organize funerals. Actually, his parents could burn in a crematorium and have paupers' graves if they did such things anymore. Otherwise he'd be content with using them to deice the driveway. Valerie's ashes, on the other hand, would come home with him and Freddie.

At least he and Freddie wouldn't be Valerie's only mourners. Her friend Cynthia, plus other friends from school. He'd ask Cynthia about an appropriate memorial service before he and Freddie headed west.

How did such things work? He had no idea. Maybe the funeral home would tell him? It struck him then just how much he'd come to rely on Philip, who seemed to know all about… well, everything.

Philip, who'd always made sure all the details were taken care of.

Philip, who'd always… taken care of him, not out of paternalism but because he'd loved him.

Philip, the one person he realized he could trust beyond all others, the one person Stuart knew down to the marrow of his bones he could depend on.

Philip, who'd always greased the wheels to make sure his life worked smoothly… greased the wheels with his money.

He felt like such a moron. He'd been so focused on one or two trees that he'd missed how beautiful the forest was. In so doing, he screwed up the best thing that had ever happened to him by letting fear get in the way. Athena's owl flew at dusk, and with how little money he had left, he'd better catch that owl, whether they were good eating or not. Ketchup covered a multitude of sins.

Stuart let his head fall against the window with a *thunk* as the uncounted miles of some square state rolled by, snowy and gray.

"C'MON, ANSWER answer answer…. Hi, Brad, it's Morgan." He tapped his foot on the ground under the table until he realized he'd started again.

"Hey Morgan, long time no hear. How's it going?"

Morgan gritted his teeth. Small talk. So not the time for it. "Not too bad. I wish Nick would hurry up and finish his internship."

"But you're not done with your MA and teaching credential, are you?" Brad said. "How were the holidays?"

Yes! Morgan pumped his fist in the air. "Mine were great. Nick and I dragged Stuart to my family's gathering so my mother could try to fatten him up. Yours?"

Brad laughed. "You've never told her about Stuart's metabolism, have you?"

"Well, no. Where's the fun in that? Besides, if she's after him she'll leave me alone." Okay, this is like a geometric proof, just a few more steps....

"Oh, and my holidays were fine, thanks for asking. Drew and I spent them with my brother, speaking of Stuart...."

Was that a *tone* he detected in Brad's voice? Maybe he should've invited Brad to lunch? But damn, time was a-wasting. "That's kind of why I'm calling. I need your brother's phone number. Stuart's in trouble."

"Morgan...."

"Please, Brad. I wouldn't ask if it weren't dire."

Brad sighed. "Stuart broke Philip's heart. It's a cliché, but it's true. He's got a lot going on right now, and the last thing I want is for Stuart to distract him again. Leave the man be. Let him heal."

"Brad, you don't understand. When I say trouble, I mean deep shit," Morgan said.

"What's going on, Morgan?"

"His family was killed in a car wreck a few days ago. He's on a bus to Philadelphia to take custody of his much younger little brother, since he turned down my parents' offer of plane tickets," Morgan said, outlining the rest of what had befallen Stuart.

Brad whistled. "That's horrible. Merry Christmas, Stuart."

"I know, right? I don't see Stuart ever liking the holidays again, but that's neither here nor there. Right now, I think he needs someone to lean on, someone who cares about him in a way friends like us don't," Morgan said, stilling his foot. Again.

"All right, Morgan. Just keep in mind that Philip's in the fight of his life at work and between that and their breakup may not be real happy to hear from you," Brad said. "The only reason you're getting this number is how long we've known each other. I'll text you his number and then text him to expect a call, so you're not calling out of the blue."

Thank God. "Thanks, Brad. Stuart and I owe you."

"Make sure he treats Philip right and I'll consider us even."

"I'll do my best, Brad, and thank you."

"Happy New Year, Morgan."

"You too, Brad, to you and Drew."

Morgan ended the call. Okay, next stop, Philip, a man he'd never met before. His phone pinged with a text from Brad, a phone number and nothing more. Without giving himself time to overthink it, he touched the number and his phone took care of the rest.

"Philip Sundstrom."

"Hi, Philip. My name's Morgan Estrada. Your brother gave me your number," Morgan said.

"Yes, he just texted me that you'd be calling. How can I help you?"

Philip sounded nothing like Morgan had imagined. Where Brad sounded like he might well break into raucous laughter at any moment, Philip sounded… like an adult, with adult worries, like maybe he needed lessons from his brother.

"It's Stuart. He needs your help." Morgan went on to explain what he knew of Stuart's situation. "You've got to find him. He's alone and more depressed than I've ever seen him. Or anyone. You're the only one who can make this better."

"You're his best friend, you know. Why can't you?" Philip said.

Morgan shook his head, and then realized that Philip couldn't see him since it was a phone call. "I used to be, I think. I stopped being that when you two got serious."

"He dumped me. He said we could only be good friends, but I don't think even that's going to be possible. He—" Philip stopped speaking abruptly when his voice cracked.

"Surely you've observed how cerebral he is. He wouldn't know love if it crapped in his shoes. Don't take this lying down. Be there for him. Prove he needs you, because trust me, he does."

"I'll think about it," Philip said.

"I guess that's all I can ask," Morgan said, disappointed he hadn't been able to convince Philip to do more. "Oh, and Philip?"

"Yes?"

"He still loves you, you know. He never stopped."

PHILIP ENDED the call.

He slowly turned his chair around so he faced the gardens below his windows.

All he could do was take slow, deep breaths to get his breathing back under his control. To try, rather. Estelle couldn't see the tears in his eyes, but he wouldn't let her hear him cry, either.

Valerie. He should never have listened to her or to Stuart. He should have flown her out over her own protests. Sure, if the Cochranes pushed the issue, he might've been charged with kidnapping, but he knew Valerie would've testified on his behalf. Besides, if he was going to be a rich asshole who tried to substitute his boyfriend's—ex-boyfriend's, he corrected himself bitterly—clothes for better quality rags and pay off his hospital bills since he was such a bastard, he might as well have thrown his money and weight around. Only he hadn't, and now a young woman he very much liked and respected for what she'd endured was dead. And he really didn't get to mourn, at least not publically, because after all, Valerie was "only" his ex-boyfriend's younger sister.

But Stuart had a kid brother, a brother their parents made sure Stuart didn't really know, and yeah, Philip knew he was projecting a whole lot of his feelings about Brad onto the relationship between Stuart and Frederick, but how could he not at a moment like this?

"What was that all about?" Estelle said. Philip's personal attorney had finally finished copying all the documents they'd unearthed in Helena Sundstrom's private room, and now Philip and Estelle sat in the conference room attached to his offices preparing to brief the SunHo legal department on what Randall had done. It would've gone faster if their attorney didn't keep stopping them every few minutes to tell them, "Don't say that."

Philip sighed through aching jaws, still facing the gardens, still trying to master his feelings. "A friend of my ex-boyfriend's begging me to ride to the rescue."

Estelle listened as Philip outlined Stuart's situation. Then she regarded him gravely for a few moments. "You're going to do it, aren't you?"

"Oh God, yes. His family died in a car accident, Estelle. Only his much-younger brother survived, but his sister—" A sob escaped. "His sister. She's dead. I really liked her."

"I'd think less of you if you didn't go."

He shook his head. "I should stay. We're only fighting for our *lives* here."

"I can handle this. You need to go help Stuart. It sounds like he made a mistake. He's young. We all were once," she said, waving away his objections. "Besides, he's riding a bus. With your resources, you can easily overtake him."

"I know." Philip got up to return to his desk, since he had a route to chart. "And Estelle?"

She looked up. "Yes?"

"Thank you."

"Go already."

"Yes, ma'am." Philip closed his office door behind him. Sitting at his computer, he pulled up Greyhound's webpage to check schedules and routes. Despite what Morgan thought, cross-country travel on the bus wasn't some eternal slog. Most routes took less than three to four days.

Right. Never mind commercial air travel. He'd use the corporate jet. He called Jyoti in.

"Yes, Philip?"

"I presume you've been eavesdropping so I don't have to fill you in?"

Jyoti sniffed, clearly affronted. "I'm aware of what's happening, yes."

"Good. It saves time. Please have the corporate jet fueled and ready to leave in two hours. I'm heading home to pack and then I'll meet the jet at Executive Airport."

"Very good. Destination?" Jyoti said.

Philip checked the route printout. "Pittsburgh."

"How exotic."

"Indeed. You know how to reach me while I'm gone, and for all intents and purposes, Estelle's in charge," Philip said as the doors to his private elevator closed. He hit "redial" on his phone. "Morgan? Tell me everything you know."

WHEN STUART had insisted on the bus, he'd had no idea what he was in for. The bus drove 24/7 and made frequent stops, lurching to a stop and lurching back into motion a short while later. On top of that, he had four transfers to keep track of and a bad case of nerves. No matter how tired he was and how much he tried to sleep, he never rested.

Furthermore, sponge baths in bathroom sinks really didn't cut it. His skin felt grimy, his scalp itched, and his hair hung limply from his head. So when he stumbled off the bus for his last transfer in Pittsburgh, tired and dirty and hungry, and saw Philip—a vision of edible preppie goodness—standing in front of him, he thought he was hallucinating.

"Hi, Stuart," Philip said.

Stuart said nothing. He walked up to Philip, staring in wonder. He reached up and touched Philip's face. "You're really here."

Philip smiled. "I'm really here."

"Why?"

"I heard you needed me."

Stuart thought Philip looked so serious, even grave. It was all more than he could bear. He didn't know he was crying until Philip pulled him into his arms.

"Hey now, it can't be that bad, can it? I've never made anyone cry before."

Stuart rested his forehead against Philip's chest. "It's not you." He sniffled. "I mean, it is. I'm so happy to see you. I just… how'd you get here ahead of me?"

"Corporate jet." Philip snorted. "My company's circling the drain, so I figured why not misappropriate company property, right?"

Stuart looked up, and forgetting the lessons he'd learned a day or two before, "I can't let you do that. I'll—"

Philip rolled his eyes. "If you say 'pay me back,' I'll slap you. Besides, I reimburse the company for any personal use of company resources."

"I'm supposed to get on another bus soon." Stuart didn't want to get on another bus.

"No, I'll drive you to a hotel tonight so you can get clean and catch a good night's sleep. Tomorrow we'll fly to Philadelphia, if that's all right with you." Philip hadn't stopped holding him, and that was A-OK with Stuart.

Stuart shuddered. "So do you have a rental car or something? I need to get away from these buses in the worst way."

Philip laughed. "I can imagine."

"You? Really?"

"I keep telling you, I wasn't born rich. Let's go."

Stuart hadn't realized how cold he was until he climbed into the passenger seat of Philip's rental. When Philip turned the heat on, Stuart's body, as if finally given permission, relaxed and he fell asleep.

"Stuart? We're here," Philip said, and Stuart woke up to the feeling of lips on his forehead.

"Where's here?" Stuart blinked stupidly. "Are we in Philly already?"

Philip smiled. "No, at the airport hotel."

Stuart remembered little of getting up to Philip's room, only that it had been warm in the car and that he was again warm in the room.

"So here we are." Philip looked nervous. "What's your priority? Food? Shower? A nap?"

Stuart shook his head to clear it. "Why're you here again? Why're you so forgiving?" He looked at the floor. "I didn't treat you very well."

"I'm here because I came looking for you," Philip said. Then he laughed. "And because your friend Morgan's kind of a pest, but a very persuasive one. And because I love you. So please let me help you."

"Oh, Philip, please forgive me. Please take me back," Stuart said. It started as a yawn but turned quickly into a sob, then another. Then all of Stuart's fatigue and sorrow and grief tumbled out, and all Stuart could do was hold on as great, wrenching sobs wracked his body. He sank to the floor before Philip could catch him, so that's where Philip held him until the storm passed. Philip pulled him onto his lap, holding him tight, and he didn't care about the reminder of their differences in size. It felt so good, so right to be held tight like that, to be held like a child while someone else took the burden, even if only for a little while.

Philip kissed Stuart's hair. "I've loved you from not long after we started dating. Nothing you said changed that."

"I come with strings attached now, a little boy. All kinds of strings." Stuart sniffled.

"Tie me up, Stuart."

Stuart raised his head. "Don't say that if you don't mean it."

"I've never meant anything more in my life. We'll figure it out as we go along, but I think together we can give your little brother a good life."

"I sure hope so, because I'm all he's got."

Philip shook his head. "He's got me, too."

"How should I introduce you to him? Hell, to the social worker?" Stuart said, trying to think. It wasn't working well.

"How do you want to introduce me? Don't you dare say sugardaddy."

Stuart snickered. "It might be funny to see their faces, but no. That wouldn't work, especially given my track record where not taking your money's concerned."

"I hope you're over that," Philip muttered.

"I'm working on it."

"Good."

Stuart thought for a moment. "Boyfriend or partner, I guess."

"I'm ready to marry you. Say the word and we'll fly to Massachusetts or New York on the way home. For that matter, they're marrying again in California. If you want to wait, I'll have my lawyer get all the paperwork ready and we can marry as soon as we can round up a justice of the peace."

Stuart kissed Philip's cheek. "You have no idea what that means to me, but one thing at a time. I want to get Freddie settled into life in Sacramento—"

"Since I failed to get Valerie out there in time." Philip sniffled, and Stuart could hardly believe what he heard.

"You failed? I think I screwed that one up." Stuart shook his head.

"I made arrangements with her to get her out as soon as she said the word. The rent you insisted on paying? That went into an account I set up to pay the legal fees for her emancipation," Philip said softly. "I was just waiting for her word. I'd have a plane ticket waiting for her at the nearest airport."

"You did?" That surprised Stuart. "That's right, she mentioned something about that. I guess you two talked more than either of you let on."

"I wanted to get to know the woman I'd hoped would become my sister-in-law."

Neither said anything for a time, not until the growling of Stuart's stomach broke the silence.

"Right," Stuart said, sighing. "Priorities. Food and a shower, then sleep."

"I'll order room service while you clean up," Philip said.

Then a horrible realization hit Stuart. "We left my bags on the bus. They're probably halfway between here and Philly by now."

Philip shrugged. "I packed a suitcase for you."

Stuart went to investigate. "These aren't my clothes."

"Sure they are."

"I've never seen these before in my life."

"Doesn't mean they're not yours." Philip smiled. "I had to guess on your sizes. I got some funny looks from the saleswoman when she asked for your measurements and I held up my hands like this," he said, describing Stuart's tiny, perfect ass with his hands. "Fortunately one of her coworkers was gay. He knew what I meant. It was only until later that I remembered I wrote down your sizes when we bought you that suit, which I also brought in case we have to go to court. I cut the tags off everything else so you can't make me return them."

"Damn, you're already wise to my tricks." Stuart riffled through the suitcase, which also looked new. Then he stopped cold, crushing the leather jacket from San Francisco to his chest. "You brought it."

Philip looked up from the room-service menu and smiled. "Yes. You needed something warm. There's a smaller suitcase in the closet with some things for Freddie, and yes," he sighed, "I bought one for him too. We'll be terribly matchy-matchy, but whatever. It'll show people we're a family. Or maybe it'll show a certain redhead that I want us to be a family."

That's when Stuart knew—really knew—that Philip had truly forgiven him. "You're too good to me."

"I love you."

"And I love you, too, Philip."

"I'm glad. Now go bathe while I call for dinner."

Stuart saluted smartly. "Yes, sir!"

"Save that for later."

Stuart laughed all the way to the bathroom. He had to admit that Philip had done a pretty good job with his guesswork, not that underwear and sweats required that much guessing.

After dinner, Philip told Stuart some of the arrangements he'd made to ease Stuart's way, and then they held each other until they fell asleep.

CHAPTER
Twenty-Five

STUART CALLED Judy Antonelli from the air the next day to alert her to the change in his travel plans. "Yes, that's right, I won't need to be met at my hotel. Actually, I won't be staying at that hotel."

"Oh, thank goodness. That's a horrible fleabag hotel in a hideous part of town," Judy said. Then she paused. "Are you calling me from an airplane?"

"Yes. I'll explain when I see you, but for now, let's just say my financial situation's improved." Philip stuck his tongue out at him.

Fortunately the flight from Pittsburgh to Philadelphia was a short one, and since it was a private jet, there was little of the fuss and bother associated with commercial travel. "I could get used to this," Stuart said.

Philip rolled his eyes. "That didn't take long. This is actually far more expensive than flying first class, so don't grow too accustomed to it."

"Yeah, but where are we staying again, Philip?" Stuart asked, a sparkle in his eye.

He noted that Philip at least had the decency to blush. "The Westin."

"Riiight. Better not get used to it." He'd missed bantering with Philip. Sure, they joked with each other, but they both knew why they were going to Philadelphia.

Philip had arranged for a local lawyer specializing in family law to brief Stuart on everything he needed to know about Freddie's case. It wasn't complicated since he was indeed Freddie's nearest living relative. While there were some distant relatives who might object to his sexual orientation, legally they didn't have a pot to piss in, regardless of how conservative parts of the state might be.

His local lawyer had also assembled information on estate sales for him. All Stuart and Freddie had to do was choose what Freddie wanted to keep from the house, and the estate-sale company would take care of the rest and send them the check. Same with the real estate company, at least once the house was emptied.

As Stuart had hoped, Philip had indeed taken care of funeral arrangements via the lawyer. His family's bodies only awaited his assent, which he gave upon getting up that first morning in Pennsylvania. It's not as if he would've had much appetite anyway.

So yeah, Philip or his agents greasing his wheels. Even if he weren't shocked by recent events, he doubted he'd have thought about any of that.

"I probably wouldn't have either, Stuart, but that's what we're paying the lawyer for."

"Too bad neither of us went to law school," Stuart said, picking at his scrambled eggs. They'd seemed like a good idea at the time, but meh. "We could keep it in the family."

"Are we a family?" Philip said.

"We will be. We would've been if I hadn't been such a jackass," Stuart said, staring at his feet.

"Water under the bridge. We can only deal in the—"

"We're beginning our descent, Messieurs Sundstrom and Cochrane, so if you'd make sure your seats are upright and that you've stowed anything that might break loose and hit you on the head, I'd appreciate it," the pilot interrupted over the intercom.

Stuart and Philip exchanged a look. "Better do as he says," Philip said.

"Jeez, I'm suddenly terrified." Somehow, thanks to Philip's presence, he'd been able to ignore the reality of why he was in Philadelphia, but now that they were descending through the clouds, it all came back to him.

Philip took his hand. "It'll be all right, and I'll be with you every step of the way, although if you'd prefer to meet Freddie by yourself the first time, I'll completely understand."

"Oh God, no! You can't leave me alone now."

"Well, if you feel that strongly—"

BUMP!

And with that, they landed in Philadelphia.

"Something just occurred to me. How will we get from the private flights terminal to the rental car counter?" Stuart said.

Philip shook his head. "Car service."

"We're taking a car to rent a car."

"No, we won't be renting a car. The area of downtown where the hotel is, while lovely and historical, is also riddled with one-way streets and other eccentricities. I once spent a half an hour circling a hotel I could see, but couldn't hit the right combination of one-way streets to get into it. Seriously, at one point I was fifteen or twenty feet away, but I couldn't get to the hotel unless I ditched my car. Don't think I didn't think about it."

"Lovely." Stuart exhaled noisily.

Philip shrugged. "Hence the car service. In the long run, it won't cost us that much, certainly not compared to the price of jet fuel. This trip is likely to be enough of a strain without adding city traffic. We can always rent one later."

"Good point."

A rush of cold air announced that the door was now open, so they gathered up their carry-on bags and shrugged on their coats, then walked down the stairs to pick up their bags before hurrying into the terminal. *Walk down the plank*, Stuart thought, his stomach clenching. Every step took him that much closer to the reality, and the permanence, of his sister's death.

PHILIP CHALKED up Stuart's distinct lack of comfort in the car to the reason for their visit. But when Stuart hung back while he checked into the hotel, Philip realized something. Some, perhaps even all, of Stuart's erstwhile noisy objection to money found its source in a lack of comfort around money's trappings. Stuart didn't realize that all the appurtenances around them in the lobby of this upscale hotel weren't of any better quality than what could be found in any halfway decent reproductions store. Sure, it was a damn sight better than the furniture in last night's airport hotel, but then, so were most things.

"Much of this is an illusion, you know," Philip whispered to Stuart as the elevator doors closed, startling him.

"What?"

"It's an illusion. Sure, it looks hoity-toity, but we've got better, higher-quality, furniture in our condo, you know."

Stuart laughed. To Philip, it sounded like he verged on the manic. "No, I didn't. Our stuff doesn't look like it's that expensive."

"I didn't say it was more expensive, I said it was higher quality. There's a difference."

"You rich people are crazy."

"I never claimed otherwise."

The bellhop appeared to choke, holding in his laughter until tears ran down his cheeks.

"Go ahead and laugh. I won't report you. I wasn't born rich, so I still have a sense of humor about it."

"Self-made, are you, sir?" the bellman said.

Stuart shook his head. "No, he made his fortune the old-fashioned way. He swindled his father out of it."

The bellman started laughing again. "You guys just made my day." When the elevator dinged, he showed them to their suite. "Here we are, gentlemen. Which bags go in which room?"

"The small suitcase goes in the smaller of the two rooms," Philip said. "The rest in the main bedroom, although before we're done, that room's future occupant may end up on a roll-away in our room."

The bellman nodded. "Yes, sir." Philip discretely pressed some cash into his hand when he was done. "Thank you, sir!"

"How much did you give him?" Stuart said when the doors closed behind him.

"Enough that we'll have our privacy, or," Philip said, "we'll be the talk of the bell staff." He looked at his watch. "It's barely noon. Why don't you give the social worker a call? There's no sense in putting this off."

"MR. COCHRANE, I'm Judy Antonelli," a busty woman said as soon as they'd walked in the door. "I'd recognize you anywhere. Freddie looks just like you. Is this your lawyer?"

"No, this is Philip Sundstrom, my partner," Stuart said, catching Philip off-guard. "Will that be a problem?"

"No, of course not," Judy said.

Philip extended his hand. "Pleased to meet you, Ms. Antonelli. We do have a local attorney, if you need to speak to him."

Judy shook her head. "No, there's time enough for that later if necessary. The purpose for today's visit is for Stuart—and you—to start to become acquainted with Freddie. Now, I must warn you, he's said very little since the accident. Physically, he checks out fine. Psychologically?" She shrugged. "His temporary foster parents report that he whimpers during the night, but since he won't speak we can't examine him psychologically."

"Refusing to speak can't be a good sign," Stuart said.

Judy nodded wearily. "No, you're right...."

Stuart and Judy quickly disappeared into a discussion of Freddie's retreat into silence. Philip listened with one ear, but where was Freddie? Did he really need to hear himself discussed so clinically? And if he was in earshot, what did it mean that he didn't appear at all curious about his older brother?

Philip glanced around the room and in the far corner, ignoring a tumbled mess of stuffed animals, sat a little boy with flaming red hair. That must've been what the social worker meant, and yes, he looked just like Stuart. Wow. If Stuart had a son, they couldn't look more alike. It'd be interesting to see family pictures if the resemblance was this heritable.

Philip eased out of his jacket and set his laptop in its battered leather case on top of it. He made no real effort to mask his footsteps, although the room's carpet muffled sound anyway. Glancing at Freddie, Philip sat down across the room from the boy to play with some blocks. Might as well go with the familiar.

Before too long, Philip was aware of another presence next to him. Sure enough, Freddie had taken the bait. They said nothing to each other, each doing his own thing with the blocks nearby, and there were plenty for both.

Then he stopped building things in favor of watching Freddie. The kid was good, but Philip supposed most kids were when it came to blocks. He wondered when they lost it, because SunHo certainly had a devil of a time hiring adults who understood how the pieces went together. Speaking of which—oops!

"Let's not remove that piece, okay? If you pull that block *there* out, the entire castle will come down." Philip pointed to a block near the bottom of the main tower. "If you need another of that shape, you can take one of the ones I used."

Freddie frowned. "But won't that make your building fall?"

"Yes, but yours is the better building, so I think it should have the block."

"Thank you," the little boy said. "Who are you?"

"My name's Philip. What's yours?"

"Freddie."

"Can I play blocks with you, Freddie?"

"You like to play blocks?" Freddie said, disbelief as plain as the nose on his face.

Philip nodded. "I do. I like to build things."

"What do you build?"

"I build houses."

"You don't look big enough to build houses."

"I don't, do I?" Philip said, smiling. He decided not to go into the details of how he came to control SunHo. "That's why I hire people to build them for me. That way, I can build a lot of houses at the same time."

"Oh." Freddie looked serious. "Can I tell you a secret?"

Philip nodded solemnly.

"My mommy and daddy died in a car crash."

"I've very sorry to hear that," Philip said. Then, in a whisper, he said, "Can I tell you a secret?"

Freddie nodded solemnly.

"My mom died in a car crash, too. I was older than you are, but it still made me very sad. You know what else? It still makes me sad even now."

"Really?" the sad little boy said.

"Really," Philip said.

"What about your dad?"

Philip mentally kicked himself. He should've seen that one coming. "My father did some very bad things and tried to hurt people. He's in jail, now."

Freddie's eyes grew wide. "Oh. We're not supposed to hurt people."

"No, we're not, are we?"

Philip looked up to discover two things. The first was that more than an hour had passed. The second was that Stuart and the social worker had been watching them. Stuart tapped his wrist as if to say, "Time's up."

Philip decided breaking the ice with Freddie was more important. "Do you know who that man with the red hair is?"

Freddie glanced up. "I think he's my older brother, but I've never seen him in person, only on my sister's computer. She's gone, too."

"I'm sorry."

"You already said that."

"That's because I'm extra sorry."

Freddie looked at him. "Why? It's not your fault."

"But it makes you sad, doesn't it?"

Freddie nodded but didn't say anything.

"It makes your brother sad, too, and he's very important to me, maybe even the most important person in the world to me."

"Really?" Freddie gasped.

Philip nodded. "Really."

"Then that must make me important, too, since he's my brother."

This was a four-year-old? "You're a very intelligent little boy, Freddie."

"But am I important? To you?"

Philip told himself he wouldn't cry, but it didn't seem to work. "Yes, Freddie, you are."

Then Freddie flung his arms around Philip's neck, bowling him over. "You're important, too, Phiwip."

Philip knew there would be more work to do, but he had a sneaking suspicion that at least as far as he and Freddie were concerned, he'd already accomplished the most important job.

CHAPTER
Twenty-Six

BACK IN their hotel room that evening, Stuart paced the floor. He was twitchy, ill at ease in his own skin, and determined to share it.

"Something bothering you?" Philip said without looking up from his laptop.

Stuart stopped in front of him and closed the cover. "Ya think?"

"Sure, Stuart! Go right ahead and close what I was working on. It wasn't important." Philip smiled up him. "Seriously, what's eating you?"

"Everything. Nothing. I don't know." He flopped down next to Philip, who thankfully set his laptop aside so Stuart could rest his head in Philip's lap.

Philip started playing with his hair, stroking it back off his face. "That's a lot to handle. Why don't you pick one thing to tell me?"

"I have to stay here as long as it takes for Freddie to get to know me."

"That makes a certain sense. The poor kid's life has been upended, and whisking him away with total strangers won't help."

Stuart frowned. "Makes a certain sense? Are you insane?"

"Not yet, but you're working on it," he said, sighing.

As soothing as the hair-play was, Stuart sat up. "Philip, what happens in a week or so?"

"Why don't you tell me, Stuart? I hate games and I'm under a lot of strain these days."

"I start the second term of my first year of med school, or at least I'm supposed to, and that's without a bunch of incompletes because I was too sick to take my finals." Ugh, he'd never rolled with the punches very well, and now?

"Do you want my opinion, or do you want me to listen?" Philip said.

Stuart thought about it. "Both."

Philip snorted. "Of course. Look, Freddie comes first. He has to. You're his only family, or only close family."

"He likes you better." Jeez, did that sound petulant or what?

"Really, Stuart?" Philip shot him a piercing look. "He adores you. I'm not telling you to quit medical school, but I do think you need to put it on hold temporarily 'due to a family emergency' or however the school might phrase it."

"There's a planned educational leave program. I've got the forms in my backpack." Stuart leaned against Philip, who put his arm around him. "It feels like failure to take time off."

Philip kissed the top of his head. "And leaving your little brother in the lurch doesn't? Valerie would beat the crap out of you for even having to think about this, you know."

He didn't. "How would you know what Valerie would do?"

"We talked." He noticed Philip refused to take the bait. Probably wise in his present state of mind.

"You're right, damn you." Stuart slumped against Philip. "It's just… I worked so hard to get into med school and to have it yanked away."

"Try not to think of it that way. Reframe it. It's not being taken away from you. You're voluntarily setting it aside," Philip said. "You have all the power that way. Besides, it's not forever. That's probably why the school calls it 'leave.' They want you back. People with your qualifications don't come along every day, I'm sure, and there's a nationwide shortage of doctors. It's in both of your best interests to work together to make sure you come back."

"Yeah?" Philip was so good to him.

Philip nodded. "Yeah."

"I'll call tomorrow morning, then."

"Good. Now let's talk about where we'll stay for a month. Because a suite at the Westin? That'll make even me squeal."

A DAY or two after New Year's when the city returned to normal activities, Stuart and Philip, or Phiwip as Freddie called him, took Freddie on an unsupervised visit to the zoo. Judy the social worker had been impressed with how at ease Freddie had become and how quickly, particularly with Philip. That the boy had started speaking again while playing with Stuart's partner appeared to be all the proof she needed that this would all work out.

"And you have clothing for him already! Did some shopping while you were here?" she said, grinning.

"Only because kid's sizes are pretty standard and they have these adjustable button thingies in the waistbands now," Philip said.

Stuart shook his head. "And no, Philip brought them from California."

"Now I know what you meant by an improvement in your financial situation," Judy said. "Thanks to those informational forms you filled out, plus the background checks, I'd say so."

Philip's cheeks colored. "We're comfortably well-off, yes."

Judy snorted. "If that's what you want to call it. All it really means is that we don't pick up any of the bill for the services Freddie's needed."

"That figures."

As soon as Freddie saw Philip and Stuart in their leather jackets, he refused to take his off.

"And that includes bedtime, according to his foster parents," the social worker reported dryly. "You two have definitely made a favorable impression on him."

Oddly enough, while Freddie expressed certain reservations about Stuart, he was utterly at ease with Philip, insisting Philip carry him when Freddie could get away with it, or at least hold his hand those times when Philip questioned why a boy who was perfectly able to walk didn't do more of it.

Philip worked to calm Stuart's jealousy and worries. "Once you find your deal with him, the ice will break. I was lucky there were blocks at Human Services."

On an overnight visit a week later at the residence hotel they'd decamped to, Stuart's moment arrived. He'd tickled Philip as payback for some snide comment or other, but missed his little brother's glittering eyes, and when the adults had stopped, Freddie flew out of the shadows, a diminutive carrot-haired ninja determined to take his brother down. Before long, the two Cochranes were rolling around on the floor, laughing hysterically and not doing anything but being silly.

Philip took pictures.

MEANWHILE, PHILIP managed SunHo remotely, meeting with his board through video conferences, and thanks to the deepening crisis with Suburban Symphony, the board met at least once a week while he was in Pennsylvania.

He neatly deflected calls for him to return to deal with this in person. "Ladies and gentlemen, as some of you know, I've been dealing with this in person for months. That our—that *my*—company's greatest crisis coincides with a family disaster is inconvenient, but there it is. That I'm here and not in Sacramento full-time should teach you something about priorities but probably won't. I've been present for every single interview with the appropriate authorities in person, and we've had board meetings then. Those will have to do. In my physical absence, you know Estelle's in charge because this pigfuck you've created concerns her purview. Like me, she's been working on this for some time."

There was the predictable grumbling from the predictable people, and Philip paid very close attention to it. He had a good idea by then who would be leaving the corporate office building in handcuffs, guessing that if he had to miss anything, it would spoil the fun of setting these blowhards up for a fall in person, which is what they'd intended for him.

When it finally went down, Philip indeed missed seeing Winch and a few others doing the perp walk, but Jyoti and Brad, who was there as the steward of the family honor, took videos with their phones and e-mailed them to him.

But every single time Philip was gone, he made sure he read Freddie a story through video conferencing as well.

"It's not the same, Phiwip."

"No, it's not, but it's the best we can do, isn't it? I'll be back tomorrow, and you've got your brother tonight. And your foster family. They care about you, too, you know."

"I gueff."

He could tell Freddie was exhausted since his pronunciation had gone down the tubes.

"It was very nice of Ms. Antonelli to let your brother have another overnight visit so I could read to you, but it's time to say goodnight."

"Goodnight, Phiwip." Freddie started pulling on one ear. Philip already knew what that meant, and so did Stuart.

"Sleep well, sport, and remember—I'll see you tomorrow."

Stuart took over his screen then. "Let me get him tucked in, and then I'll call you back… Phiwip."

Philip rolled his eyes. "I'll be waiting."

"YOU KNOW you need to do it," Philip said, holding Stuart tightly one night after they'd turned the lights out.

"Just man up or something?" Stuart said, his tone light. It was the only job remaining and he dreaded it: taking Freddie back to their parents' house to choose what they would take west and what they would leave for the estate sale.

Philip shook his head. "I wish you'd cut yourself some slack."

"I called Valerie's friend Cynthia today. She's still pretty broken up by it." That was an understatement. The two had been best friends for years. She'd begged his permission to hold a memorial service. Like he'd say no.

"So're you."

"Too true," he said, sighing. "According to Judy Antonelli, Freddie hasn't said a thing about it, either."

"Well, that's why Human Services insists we set him up with therapists when we get home," Philip said.

Stuart stuck his tongue out in the dark. "Don't forget the home inspection."

"How could I possibly? I asked Brad to oversee installing a fence and alarm around the pool. He said he'll ask someone named Owen Douglas, who used to be a firefighter, because he'd know all about safety," Philip said. "Is he a rower?"

"Yep, the rowing mafia comes through again."

Philip laughed softly. "I hope they don't get carried away or that we don't come home to find the pool domed over, although come to think of it, I've seen something similar in Florida. Anyway, Brad was pretty excited about being an uncle."

"He'll never grow up, will he?" Stuart found himself smiling. Where'd that come from?

"I hope not. Now go to sleep."

PHILIP, STUART, and Freddie sat in their rental car across the street from the Cochrane home for twenty minutes before anyone said anything.

"I'm bored, Phiwip."

"Is that why you're kicking my seat?"

"Uh-huh."

Quick as a striking snake, Philip reached behind the seat and grabbed Freddie's foot. "You need to stop that. Now. This is going to be hard enough for you and Stuart without irritating me."

"Freddie!" Stuart barked. This was so not the time for his brother to act up.

"Stuart, it's okay. I'm handling this."

Stuart got out of the car. "Let's get this over with. I'm suddenly homesick. I can't wait to get back to California."

"But this is where you growed up, Stuart," Freddie said, frowning.

Stuart sighed. He had to go there and with a four-year-old, no less. "The thing is, Freddie, there are places you live, and there are places that are home. This was never home for me. Our parents made sure I got out of here as soon as I could. I bet you didn't know you had an older brother until Valerie introduced us on the computer."

"No," Freddie whispered.

"When you're older I'll tell you more about it, but for now, we have to pick some things to take to our new home," Stuart said, doing his best not to take his nerves out on Freddie.

Freddie held his arms up to Philip, who picked him up without a word.

"When will Cynthia meet us here?" Philip said.

Stuart looked around the run-down working-class neighborhood, not sure what he expected. It was the middle of a workday morning. "She should already be here. Inside, maybe? I hope so. I don't have a key."

Instead they found a note on the door directing them where Cynthia had hidden the key in question. Stuart couldn't blame her. This wasn't really any easier on her than on him. Given her close involvement with helping Valerie lead a normal life despite their religious nutjob parents, she was as wrecked about Valerie's death as he was.

Stuart felt like he was breaking and entering into the home of strangers. It was at once eerily familiar and utterly alien, a piece of furniture or religious statuary jarring his memory here or there, the rest unknown to him. He wandered from room to room feeling like a time traveler or an explorer, his partner and brother forgotten. When at last he found a picture of his parents, he discovered he could look at it without being overcome by the need to slash at it with scissors or a knife. He still hated them and everything they had stood for, because they had made his childhood hell. He remembered relaxing for the first time on that first trip to California and California Pacific College, which they'd fought him tooth and claw over. Come to think of it, they'd opposed him going to any college, even the local junior college. He swore on the spot to make sure his younger brother got all the education he desired.

"Sorry, Mimi and Dan. I turned out all right in spite of you. Wherever you are, I hope you're suffering. I've got a good man I intend to marry as soon as all this settles. Freddie will make a darling honor attendant in a little suit. Yep, he'll be raised by two fags, and he'll be just fine."

It might not have been healthy, but it sure felt therapeutic. When he made it back to the entrance hall at last, he discovered that Philip—thank goodness for him—had been helping Freddie.

They'd set aside a family portrait, a more current one than the one he'd spoken to, taken at some third-tier mall, the background of which was meant to look like a blue sky but more closely resembled blue camouflage. Freddie also chose some stuffed animals, favorite clothes, and a few books.

"I'm sorry, Freddie," he heard Philip say, "we can't take all this furniture. We've got furniture at your new home in Sacramento, and I think you'll like it."

Stuart shook his head. *Yeah, this stuff's not going anywhere. Even I can tell it's cheap crap. Put this in Philip's house? Oh, hell no.*

Philip smiled at him, a knowing and sad smile, like he'd known what Stuart had done, and for all Stuart knew, Philip did. Stuart would always be grateful that Philip was with him for all of this. Dealing with Freddie's feelings as well as his own, to say nothing of all the material details? He'd been nuts to think he could handle it himself.

"What about you, Stuart? Anything you want to be sure we take? Or anything of value?"

Stuart laughed. "You're kidding, right?"

"Not really, no. I was thinking about things like wedding china or silver that Freddie might want later on." Philip gave him a pained look. "Freddie, why don't you check to see if there's anything you want in your parents' room, okay?"

"Okay, Phiwip."

Philip waited until the little boy was out of the room before speaking again. "Look, I know you'll never forgive your parents and with good reason, but try not to poison your little brother. He's going to have enough to deal with as it is without you tainting what memories he's able to preserve, especially as he gets older."

Stuart clenched his hands into fists. "I don't want to fight about this."

"So don't, but stop bad-mouthing your parents in front of Freddie."

"I found something, Phiwip," Freddie said, dragging a handmade quilt behind him.

Philip smiled. "Good, Freddie. I'm glad."

"Let's go see if Mom and Dad had any china or silver, Freddie." Stuart held out his hand. "I honestly can't remember."

Philip picked up the quilt and folded it, setting it with the rest of the things Freddie wanted to take west to his new life. Then he sat down to wait, checking his mail on his iPhone and praying there was nothing too earth-shattering. He scanned through the list, finding a lot of mail from his brother. Good, the pool was fenced in, and yes, domed over. Brad sent pictures of that and of his dog, too. Philip could only hope Brad hadn't let it run loose in his backyard, because the landscapers would have a fit if the dog peed any brown spots into the lawn.

"Good call, Philip. I'm not sure why they never used it, but Freddie found both," Stuart said, returning to the entry hall with a yellowed box in his arms.

Freddie followed behind, his little arms stretched to their limit to carry a silver chest. "Mama said they were too good to use. We had to save them for special, she said."

"There are a couple more boxes of china. There's some crystal, but it's all broken." Stuart shook his head. "I don't know why. If they never took it out, how can it break?"

"Crystal's funny that way. If you don't use it, it breaks. Something about the oils in the skin." Philip shrugged. "Or maybe they served cherries jubilee in them. Who knows?"

"Phiwip, what's cherries jub… jubbees?"

Philip laughed. "It's a dessert involving, among other things, ice cream and a cherry sauce you light on fire. The heat and the cold together really aren't good for crystal."

Freddie's eyes lit up. "Fire?"

"Now you've done it," Stuart said, groaning.

Philip smiled down at Freddie. "We'll have it when we get home to Sacramento."

"You know how to make it?" Stuart said.

"No, but if I text Brad about how much Freddie wants it as a treat, it'll be his problem, won't it?" Philip said with a smirk.

Freddie yanked on Stuart's shirt. "Who's Bwad?"

"Philip's younger brother."

Philip squared his shoulders. "I hesitate even to mention this, but there's one room left."

The smile slid from Stuart's face. "Valerie's."

Philip nodded. "Valerie's."

Stuart groped for Freddie's hand. He didn't want to do this. She was the one hole in his carefully constructed armor. If he took something to remember his sister by, he would have to acknowledge she was gone, which was stupid. He had her ashes in an ornate lacquered box back at the residence hotel.

Stuart nodded. "Then I need a break. I can't take much more of this."

"Then we're done. The rest will be left for the estate sale," Philip said.

"How will we get this home, Phiwip?" Freddie said, looking at the accumulated material in the hall.

"I think we'll have it shipped. I can take care of it tomorrow. That's an awful lot to take on the jet, even if it's boxed up," Philip said, eyeing the trove.

Together, the three of them went to Valerie's room, with Freddie in the lead since he knew the way. It was too clean—almost antiseptic—for a teenager in Stuart's opinion. Other than a little dust on the carpet, everything was in its place. He felt an immediate need to knock things off shelves and pull the blankets off the bed.

Apparently Philip felt the same way. "This is your parents' doing, I presume?"

"I guess so. It's creepy."

"No, Valerie always kept her room this way," Freddie said softly. "After they found the camera that let us talk to you she tried to get them to stop snooping in her woom by keeping it cwean."

Stuart looked at his sister's bed and it triggered something in his memory. "Help me lift up her mattress."

"Stuart, you don't need to take her bed home."

Stuart shook his head. "She kept what was important to her up inside the box springs."

Freddie sat down at her desk to stay out of the way while Stuart and Philip lifted first the mattress and then the box springs. Naturally, Valerie had left very little under her bed after the webcam incident.

"I don't understand. There's nothing in the box springs." Stuart kicked at it uselessly. "Freddie, any idea where Valerie hid things from our parents?"

Freddie pointed to Valerie's dresser.

"She kept things in her dresser?"

The boy shook his head. "Behind. She cut a hole in the wall."

"You could've told us that sooner," Stuart said, "like before we took the bed apart."

"You didn't ask me before. I want her computer."

Philip glanced at it and frowned. "We can buy you a better one when we get home."

He shook his head. "I want this one."

"Okay, but sometimes computers get dirty. You don't get to play with it until Stuart or I have had a chance to check it," Philip said. "Do you agree to that?"

"No! I want it now!"

"No deal means no computer. We're not discussing this with you, and if you argue anymore, the computer stays here when we leave this afternoon," Philip said.

Suddenly the easygoing Philip was taking a hard line? Freddie looked as if he'd been slapped. His lower lip quivered. "Stuart...."

Stuart shook his head. "Don't look at me, kiddo. He's been far nicer today than I'd have been."

"But I told you about the hole!"

"And we appreciate it, Freddie," Philip said, kneeling down to his eye level, "but that doesn't mean you get everything you want when you want it. We're not telling you no on the computer. If you'd listen, you'd realize we're telling you yes, but not right now. We might even be able to check it out tonight, but not if you're going to have a tantrum. I don't reward those, and neither does Stuart."

"So we can take it with us when we leave?"

Stuart nodded. "If you continue like you have been the rest of the day, yes."

Philip leveraged the dresser out of the way. Sure enough, there was a jagged hole cut in the wallboard. "What'd she use, a fish descaler? Whoever has to fix this will have his work cut out for him."

Sure enough, there was a locked box along with a few other things… including the iPod preloaded with the Wendybird catalogue.

"I want this," Stuart said, reaching over Philip's shoulder.

Philip nodded. "Take it."

"Anything else in there?" Stuart hovered behind Philip.

"Let's see…." Philip pulled out a package of what was obviously birth-control pills. "Oh. Well."

"What're those?" Freddie said.

Stuart turned bright red from holding in his laughter, even as he tried to figure out what his babydyke sister needed them for. "Um… vitamins."

Freddie opened his mouth, but Philip cut him off. "*Girl* vitamins. They wouldn't be good for you."

"What else can you find in there, Philip?"

"Well, I groped something furry, but it's probably just a rat."

Freddie squealed and hid behind Stuart.

"Oh. Wait. It's only insulation."

Stuart glared at him. Oh well, even his buttoned-down partner had to have some fun once in a while.

"I think that's it." Philip stood up and dusted himself off.

"Any idea how to open a combination lock when you don't know the combination?" Stuart said. "Wait, do you know it, Freddie?"

Freddie shook his head. Then he tugged at one ear before popping a thumb into his mouth.

"Right. I'll back the car up the driveway. It's time to start loading this into the trunk and then get a certain someone back to the hotel for bed."

Once they had everything loaded and Freddie belted into his booster seat, Stuart took a final look around before locking the door and returning the key to the hiding place. He'd like to be able to say that spending the day there had defanged his hard feelings, but no. They were still there and as adamantine as ever. But he'd gotten what he'd needed from the trip, his little brother and Philip, and they were all that mattered. He was ready to head home. His first-semester finals still hung over his head, but after that he had a year to get his life back on track, his and Freddie's.

Valerie's cremains were already packed for travel, along with necessary paperwork. They would bury her in California in the Sundstrom family plot, escaping in death if not in life. It felt right to both him and Philip that she be buried next to Helena Sundstrom, provided Brad approved. That Philip proposed to his brother they either buy more plots or buy a mausoleum that would have room for both of their families was sure to ease any objections Brad might have. His parents' ashes would be interred in some forgotten corner of a boneyard in Philadelphia. His instructions. He did the bare minimum required by the law and nowhere near what civility demanded. Cynthia would hold a memorial service for Valerie's friends there in Philadelphia, but Stuart found that he didn't need to be there for that. After everything, it was time for him to look forward, and he had a lot to look forward to.

"So how much longer do you want to stay?" Philip said two days later as he cooked breakfast.

Stuart looked thoughtful. "Well, we've shipped what needs to be shipped and Human Services released Freddie to my custody yesterday. I guess there's no real need to stay. The estate-sale company can mail us a check anywhere, as can the real estate agent."

"I need to get back to work," Philip said, plating three omelets, "and I can't see much reason for another cross-country trip if you're done here."

Stuart thought about it for a moment. There really wasn't anything holding him there, and to be honest, he missed the sun. It had been snowing for a week here. He'd forgotten how much he hated snow. "What about you, Freddie? Are you ready to see where we'll live in California?"

"Will Phiwip be there?"

"Yes, I'll be there," Philip said.

"Will you be there, Stuart?"

Stuart laughed. "I'll be there, too. The three of us will be there and we'll be a family."

Freddie nodded, as if that were something he'd waited to have confirmed. "Then I'm weady. Do I have to eat this?"

"Yes!" the adults said.

Freddie looked rebellious, but started to eat. "It's eggs! Mama only gave me scrambled eggs."

"But I'm not your mama," Philip said, "and this is how I make eggs, at least some of the time."

"But I want them scrambled!" Freddie wailed before breaking down in tears that came in ever greater torrents.

Philip sighed. "This was bound to happen sooner or later. Brad was the same way when our mom died, even if he was older than Freddie when it happened. The littlest things set him off."

"Great," Stuart said, muttering.

"Not helping."

Philip attempted to put his arms around Freddie, but the boy pushed him away. "No, you're not my daddy!"

"You're right, I'm not, and I'm not trying to be," Philip said.

"And I highly doubt your father ever tried to hug you." Stuart wanted to scream. Things had been going so well and then this. He took a deep breath before he spoke. "Freddie, I know this all has to be very hard for you, and you've done amazingly well, but Philip's not to blame for any of this. In fact, without his help, it would've been so much worse. No one's to blame. Sometimes bad things happen. That's the nature of life."

Actually, their parents were. Driving to some snake-fondling session on icy roads? Oh yeah. The blame rested squarely on them, but his brother was too young to hear that. Instead he held out his arms to give Freddie the option of a hug.

Freddie rushed into his arms, still crying. Stuart did his best to comfort him, but when it came down to it, he didn't know much about children. He didn't even have the benefit of a pediatrics class or clinic to fall back on. "We'll get through this, Freddie. I promise."

Stuart looked over Freddie's shoulder. "Can you call for the jet or book tickets or however that works? It's definitely time for us to get out of here. I don't think he'll move forward into his new life until he's actually living it."

"The jet's waiting at the airport. All I need to do is give the pilot notice," Philip said. He'd finished his breakfast and started cleaning the kitchen.

"You're serious."

Philip laughed. "Why wouldn't I be? I told you I needed either to make another trip back to keep an eye on SunHo or pack everything up and take you two home."

"Have I ever told you how grateful I am that you're so anal-retentive?"

"Um… no. Thanks?"

"It's a compliment, definitely. I'm suddenly antsy to show this place my backside." He cleaned Freddie up with his napkin. "Okay, sport. Blow."

Freddie made ineffectual honking noises into Stuart's napkin.

"Then I'll text the pilot. He'll need some time to have the plane deiced and whatever else it is that happens to airplanes before they take off." Philip pulled out his iPhone. "Oh, and I've had a few kid-friendly surprises installed."

Freddie lifted his head from Stuart's chest. "Supwises?"

"You'll have to wait until we're on the plane, won't you?" Philip smiled at him. "But I hope you'll like them."

"And a private jet is really cheaper than three tickets on a commercial airline?" Stuart said, shuddering at the bill for these last few weeks. He knew more or less what it cost them, too, because after he'd introduced Philip as his partner, Philip started including him in financial decisions and showing him the receipts. He still wasn't quite sure what to do with the black Amex that had shown up at the Westin via special courier, however.

"No, just more convenient, and as I told you, I need to go back regardless," Philip said, "and I reimburse the company for personal use of the jet. As for flying commercially with minimal notice... I can't say it'd be a toss-up, but three spur of the moment first-class tickets wouldn't be cheap, and flying commercially is a complete pain in the... uh, backside these days."

Stuart grinned at him. "I wouldn't know, and good catch."

"If it makes you feel any better, the bills for this make me squirm," Philip said, shuddering theatrically.

"You know, it does in a way." Stuart bussed the remaining dishes and then wormed his way into Philip's arms. "It gives me hope that we'll arrive at some middle ground on the money question."

Philip kissed the top of his head. "I think we will. You'll stop freaking out, or at least freak out less often, and you'll remind me that I don't have to throw money at everything."

"Thank you," Stuart whispered. This was why he loved Philip, or one of the reasons.

"That said, we're both going to need new cars in fairly short order."

With a sinking feeling, he realized Philip was right. His car was barely road-worthy. Philip's was a two-seater.

"I'll trade mine in the day we get back for a sedan or an SUV, since I know Mercedes-Benz's line. But I'd imagine you'll need to take some time to decide what you want."

Stuart made a face. "Ugh. That didn't take long."

"Nope, but then, no one ever said having children was cheap. I'm going from bachelor to de facto father and you've gone from grad student poverty to comfortably well-off in a short amount of time," Philip said.

"That's a charming euphemism."

Freddie wandered into the kitchen in search of his grown-ups. "What's that mean?"

Philip bent down and scooped him up. "It's a pretty way of saying something ugly. Are you feeling better?"

Freddie buried his face in Philip's neck. "Yes."

"Then we all need to pack." Philip kissed the back of his head before putting him down.

They returned the rental car and caught the courtesy shuttle to the terminal housing private and chartered flights. All three wore their matching leather coats, along with cashmere scarves in different colors Stuart had picked out at Wanamaker's.

"Look at you, riding a shuttle like a commoner," Stuart whispered as he elbowed Philip.

Philip caught Freddie's eye and made a face. "What's he mean, Phiwip?"

"He thinks he's funny. If we don't give him any attention, maybe he'll get over it."

Freddie giggled and snuggled in closer to Philip while Stuart pretended to pout, at least until they pulled up in front of the terminal.

Inside, the SunHo pilot greeted them. "If you're ready, Mr. Sundstrom, Mr. Cochrane? And—who's this? Hello, young man. What's your name?"

At the first sign of unexpected adult attention, Freddie buried his face in the nearest familiar leg, in this case, Philip's.

"Thanks for being ready on such short notice, Captain Beauvasis. This is my younger brother and ward, Freddie Cochrane. He'll be flying home with us."

"Have you ever flown before, young Mr. Cochrane?"

Without looking at Captain Beauvasis, Freddie shook his head.

"Then perhaps you'd like a tour of the cockpit as we're getting ready to take off?"

That got Freddie's attention and he quickly looked at the captain, eyes as big as saucers. "Can I, Stuart?"

"I don't see why not, so long as you're not in the way and don't touch anything," Stuart said.

"Then let's go," Captain Beauvasis said. "We don't want to miss our window with the control tower."

While their baggage was stowed, Stuart, Philip, and Freddie made themselves comfortable in the cabin.

"A big-screen television, Philip? Really?" Stuart said.

Philip looked guilty. "What? It's at the back of the cabin. We won't have to watch it."

"Stuart! Phiwip! There's a video game player!" Freddie said, squealing as he rushed forward to their seats to tell them the joyous news before running back down the wide aisle between the seats.

Stuart sighed. "You didn't."

"He only has access to age-appropriate games," Philip said, "and if he won't keep the volume down or wear the headphones, he loses it for a little while."

The intercom crackled. "Would junior copilot Freddie Cochrane report to the cockpit for preflight training?"

Freddie squealed again and dashed fore to the cockpit.

"He's going to be in a world of hurt when we start taking commercial flights," Stuart said.

Philip looked up from the papers he'd been reading. "Let the kid have his fun. He's had a lot of upsets lately."

"Okay, then you can deal with him the first time he looks at you as we're all sitting in two-thousand dollar seats and says, 'I prefer to fly in our own jet, Philip'."

"I notice in this dystopian fantasy of entitlement you've crafted that he's lost that lisp where my name's concerned."

"You're impossible, do you know that?"

Philip shook his head. "No, just highly improbable."

Stuart growled and grabbed onto Philip's hand and started biting it in mock ferocity, making his way up Philip's arm until he could bite Philip's neck. Then Philip grabbed his chin and started kissing him, which might've been Stuart's intention all along. He lost himself in the sensation of Philip plundering his mouth, realizing that what he wanted more than anything at that moment was to surrender to Philip, letting his partner take control and do what they'd not had time to do because—

"Whatcha doing, Stuart? Why is Phiwip climbing on top of you?"

Well, that was a bucket of cold water, wasn't it? "We're doing grown-up things, Freddie," Stuart said.

"And we got a little carried away," Philip said.

"Oh. The captain said to get ready for takeoff." Freddie ran back to the big-screen television and the game console.

Philip leaned back against his seat and groaned. "Now I know why my parents had a lock on their bedroom door."

"Your—our—bedroom door, it has such a lock, right?" Stuart said.

Philip laughed. "If it doesn't, it will within forty-eight hours of our return."

Once they were airborne, Philip and Stuart took turns playing the anodyne games Philip had thought appropriate for a boy of Freddie's age.

"Stuart?" Philip called after an hour and a half of such rotations. "He's asleep."

Stuart came back to see. "Thank God," he whispered. He switched off the television. "Do these seats recline?"

"Yes, but there are two staterooms. Why don't we tuck him into one of the beds instead?"

"There are bedrooms on this plane? Wow. I thought those doors back there were storage or something."

Philip shook his head. "Nope. Beds on night flights mean rested executives, who in turn perform their jobs better, at least in theory."

"These beds… how big are they?"

"Let's just say it's good you're the fun-sized kind of gay," Philip said, looking his man up and down and licking his lips.

"Good to know." Stuart picked his brother up. "Can you get the bedroom door?"

Philip was already on his way back to the staterooms. He latched the door to one open and then pulled the bed down from the bulkhead and locked it into place. After that he pulled pillows and linens from the cabinets that served as a pedestal to support the bed. Last of all, he squeezed past Stuart.

"All set."

"You're right, they're not very big."

Philip shook his head slowly. "Put the boy to bed, horndog."

"Woof!" Stuart laid Freddie down and tucked the covers over the sleeping child. "Wait… what if he wets the bed?"

"We have it cleaned. He's four. They still do that at four, right?"

Stuart shrugged. "Beats me."

They looked at each other and started snickering. "We're in so much trouble," Philip whispered.

"Nah, it'll be fine. He'll tell us when we screw up." Stuart wiggled under Philip's arm. He liked it under there. He felt warm and secure. He looked up to find Philip looking down at him, a tender expression on his face. "Thank you for all of this. A lot of guys would've turned tail and run."

"I'm not a lot of guys."

Stuart smiled. "That's for sure."

They made their way back to their seats and settled into the flight. "Beats the bus, doesn't it?" Philip said.

Stuart shuddered. "You have no idea."

The copilot/cabin attendant brought them their dinners, and then they settled in to sleep as best they could for the rest of the flight. Stuart thought the seats made that pretty easy.

Except that Philip rolled over to look at him. Then he set his seat to upright and rummaged through his messenger bag. Stuart had forgotten about that. Mr. Big Bad Corporate Overlord refused to carry a briefcase. When Philip knelt down on one knee, Stuart suspected something was up.

Philip held open a velvet ring case. "Stuart? Will you do me the supreme honor of marrying me? Will you make me the luckiest man alive and end my loneliness?"

Stuart felt like his heart rose up through his chest, blocking his throat, even as a part of his mind rattled off the correct anatomical names and then told him why that wasn't physically possible.

He nodded slowly. "Freddie will need a stable home, and this will give you a defined role."

"Stuart Cochrane," Philip said, still on one knee, "is there not one romantic bone in your body? Has it not occurred to you that I'm proposing to you because I love you and want to spend the rest of my life with you?"

"Oh." That was… wow. "Will it fit? I mean, how do you know my ring size?"

"You're missing the point, but if you must know, I measured your ring finger when you were asleep during one of the antibiotic sessions."

"Oh." Wait… did Philip just propose? Get it together. He unbuckled his seatbelt and launched himself at Philip, bowling him over. "Yes! Yes, Philip, yes!"

Philip struggled to put the ring onto a wriggling Stuart, until he finally rolled him over and sat on him. Stuart looked up at him, eyes full of trust and love. "Your left hand?"

Stuart stuck a hand out.

"No, hon. The other left."

Stuart held out a shaking hand. This was so serious. Somehow he'd always pictured the two of them living as domestic partners until California got its act back together and marriage equality was once again the law of the land, except the Supreme Court basically spiked Prop h8 and gutted DOMA seven months ago and he was babbling and really needed to stop.

"We should've done this as long as we were on the east coast," Stuart said.

"I guess we could've, but why? We can do it in California again. We'll work out the details later. I think we've got our hands full enough for right now." Philip, still pinning Stuart to the floor, leaned down and claimed a kiss. "When I picked you up in Pittsburgh, you said something about coming with strings attached. I was serious when I said I welcomed the strings, and I'm serious now. I want us to be a family and not only for Freddie's sake."

"I want that, too," Stuart whispered, realizing at last his heart had a home, a safe harbor, where he never had to worry about letting down his guard again.

Then Stuart realized what was poking at him. "But speaking of a romantic bone in my body.... Didn't you say there's another stateroom?"

Epilogue

THEY LANDED in Sacramento in the middle of the night. Given the late hour, Philip didn't expect anyone to greet them. Still, he'd sent out a group text before they'd left Philadelphia....

Philip wrapped things up with the pilot and then went to rouse Freddie while Stuart oversaw their bags. When Freddie defied rousing, Philip settled for picking him up. Freddie wrapped his arms around his neck, apparently automatically, and Philip's heart melted a little more. The little snuffling noises didn't hurt, either.

"Where're we going?" Philip said. "Condo or big house?"

Stuart considered his question. "We might as well go to the big house, don't you think? That's where we'll live anyway, right?"

"It makes the most sense to me, and Brad's already fenced the pool in for us in case the social workers make a surprise inspection. It's got the most room for a child to grow in, but the condo's much closer to the Med Center where you'll presumably resume school within the next year."

"I'm not sure the condo's all that kid friendly, and I don't want to keep uprooting Freddie," Stuart said

Philip nodded. "True enough. I'll have us dropped off at the big house."

"Another car service?" Freddie mumbled from where he rested his head on Philip's shoulder.

Philip and Stuart exchanged a pointed look and tried not to laugh. "Yes, sport, another car service," Philip said, "but after that, or at least sometime this weekend, I'll be trading my car in for something suitable for a family, so no more services or taxis."

After the driver stowed their luggage in the trunk, Philip sent Brad one more text:

Heading to our old place. Come by in the AM and meet the latest addition to our family... Unca Bwad and Unca Dwew.

After that they spent the drive trying to stay awake in the dark. Philip hated east-west night flights, but it had been past time to bring his menfolk home.

Philip sent Stuart ahead to disarm the alarm while he paid the driver, still with a somnolent little boy draped across his chest. When Stuart came back for the suitcases, Philip grabbed his and then followed his partner—no, fiancé—back into their house, locking the door behind them. The house was cold, but Philip heard the heater forcing hot air through the registers.

"Let's get everything upstairs and then the first one up can run to the store for breakfasty things," Philip said, fatigue walloping him.

"No need to worry. It's obvious I underestimated Brad when we were younger." At Philip's questioning look, Stuart continued, "I checked the fridge for some fizzy water. It's fully stocked with fresh food, which I'd imagine is his work, since I don't think too many people have a key."

"Brad's grown up nicely, and no, you didn't underestimate him. But that was then."

Stuart nodded. "I'd imagine Drew's helped."

"Love changes people."

"It does indeed," Stuart said. "It does indeed."

PHILIP AWOKE to the sounds of breakfast being made, and it reminded him of just how much he loved Stuart. He'd been carrying the can for Stuart for over a month, and Stuart knew it. This was his way of saying thank you. He burrowed under the covers and stretched, hitting... Stuart.

Huh.

Freddie ran into their bedroom from his room across the hall. "Phiwip! There're burglars downstairs!"

The boy was practically sobbing.

Yeah, burglars making breakfast. With any luck, they were making coffee, too.

Philip pulled his head out from under the duvet. "Shhh, Freddie. I can't hear anything when you scream. Climb under the covers with me and let's listen."

"You know that sounds like to me?" said Stuart, who by this time was awake. "It sounds like food being made. Let's go check."

"Right after we put Freddie in something dry."

A few minutes later, the three of them tiptoed downstairs, although Philip had a pretty good idea what was going on. Brad wouldn't have laid in that much food if he weren't planning on feeding a hoard, and a hoard was exactly what greeted them in the kitchen.

Freddie squealed and buried his face in Stuart's emerald green bathrobe, but between Stuart and Philip, they recognized everyone.

"Wow," Philip said. "I know about half the people here."

"That's Nick Bedford, my former coach, and Morgan, who you've spoken to on the phone," Stuart said, pointing them out. "The ginger with the cane is Owen Douglas, and that super tall guy hovering is Adam Lennox, his partner."

"More rowers?" Philip said. He wasn't short by any means, but he suddenly felt puny. "How do you not develop a complex about your height? These people are giants."

Stuart laughed. "It's the sport. When I coxed, I was in charge and they knew it." He looked at Philip. "You know, you'd make a pretty decent rower. You might look into the adult learn-to-row camps Capital City Rowing Club sponsors come spring."

"Spoken like a former cox'n thinking about making a comeback."

"Hi, Nick, and club-level only," Stuart said.

Nick stuck his hand out. "Nick Bedford."

"Philip Sundstrom. Pleased to meet you. Thanks for coming this morning."

Nick laughed. "Even if Morgan would've let me miss it, Drew would've given me hell."

"You know Drew?" Philip wondered just how inbred this group was, but they were off and talking. Nick appeared to know everyone, and he made sure Philip spoke to all of his guests. Of everyone in the CalPac/Cap City Rowing circle, Philip sensed Adam and Owen were, like him, relative outsiders wondering what the others were talking about.

"It was really nice of you to come," Philip said, "considering...."

Adam snickered. "Considering we don't know people that well?"

"Basically, yes." Philip smiled. "But I bet you know them better than I do."

The super tall one—Adam?—nudged Owen with his elbow. "We know Brad and Nick pretty well, although Nick's run off to do internship for his physical therapy degree."

Owen, a ginger like Stuart, pinked up. "And I've learned what happens when you ignore Brad."

"I can't wait to see where this lands," Philip said. "Do tell."

Adam laughed. "He drags you off to physical therapy whether you want to go or not."

"I sense there's more to this, but yes, that's something Brad would do." Philip loved his baby brother, he really did.

"You know him well?" Owen said.

Philip laughed. "Yes, he's my younger brother."

Owen glanced across the room from the brawny Brad, on all fours chasing the hysterically laughing Freddie, back to Philip. "Huh. I see."

"Yeah, I know, separated at birth, right?" Philip said. "As Brad says, he got the muscle, I got the hair."

They chatted for a few minutes until Stuart motioned to him. "Oops, gotta go."

"If you're going to marry Stuart, get used to him calling the shots," Adam said. "He may be retired from coxing, but it'll show back up, mark my words."

"Philip!"

"See?" Adam said, winking.

Philip joined Stuart and Freddie at the kitchen island. There was a huge cake with "Welcome Freddie, Future CalPac Cox'n" written in icing on it.

"Who's that?" Freddie whispered to Stuart.

"That's you."

Freddie thought for a moment. "So dat's my cake?"

Philip laughed. "It's in honor of you, but it's for everyone."

"Still, it's kind of for me."

Philip looked at Stuart. They'd never seen this crafty side of Freddie. Or maybe they'd brought it out, but either way....

Freddie lunged forward to grab the biggest, fattest rosette on the cake and crammed it into his mouth.

Stuart gasped. "Freddie, manners!"

"Phank you," he said around the frosting, beaming up at his older brother.

Brad laughed, long and loud. "Y'all are in trouble."

Philip had to admit that yes, they probably were. But that was something to deal with at a later date, along with preschool for Freddie, his own legal status vis-à-vis Freddie, and the future of Stuart's career in medical school. Then there was a wedding to plan. But all those details didn't matter right then. They were surrounded by friends and family, and Philip realized that love already extended to Freddie, who was a lucky little boy, indeed.

CHRISTOPHER KOEHLER learned to read late (or so his teachers thought) but never looked back. It was not, however, until he was nearly done with grad school in the history of science that he realized that he needed to spend his life writing and not on the publish-or-perish treadmill. At risk of being thought frivolous, he found that academic writing sucked all the fun out of putting pen to paper.

Christopher is also something of a hothouse flower. Inside of almost unreal conditions he thrives to set the results of his imagination free, and for most of his life he has been lucky enough to be surrounded by people who encouraged both that tendency and the writing. Chief among them is his long-suffering husband of twenty-two years and counting.

When it comes to writing, Christopher follows Anne Lamott's advice: "You own everything that happened to you. Tell your stories. If people wanted you to write warmly about them, they should have behaved better." So while he writes fiction, at times he ruthlessly mines his past for character traits and situations. Reality is far stranger than fiction.

Christopher loves many genres of fiction and nonfiction, but he's especially fond of romances, because it is in them that human emotions and relations, at least most of the ones fit to be discussed publicly, are laid bare.

Writing is his passion and his life, but when Christopher is not doing that, he's an at-home dad and oarsman with a slightly disturbing interest in manners and other ways people behave badly.

Visit him at http://christopherkoehler.net/blog or follow him on Twitter @christopherink.

Dreamspinner Press

For more of the
best M/M romance,
visit

Dreamspinner Press
www.dreamspinnerpress.com

CPSIA information can be obtained at www.ICGtesting.com
Printed in the USA
LVOW11s0826151213

365349LV00003B/51/P